A Vampire's Unlikely Alliance

by

Tena Stetler

Demon's Witch Series, Book 3

A Vampire's Unlikely Alliance

COPYRIGHT © 2017 by Tena Stetler

Cover Art by *Kristian Norris*

The Wild Rose Press, Inc.
PO Box 708
Adams Basin, NY 14410-0708
Visit us at www.thewildrosepress.com

Publishing History
First Black Rose Edition, 2017
Print ISBN 978-1-5092-1772-4
Digital ISBN 978-1-5092-1773-1

Demon's Witch Series, Book 3
Published in the United States of America

The sun slid behind the mountains,
setting the azure sky ablaze in hues of red, orange, yellow, and pink. Then red shifted to purple and dusk faded to darkness as he jogged toward the trails. She stood leaning against the rock where he had started his run last night. He'd tried to convince himself to stay away, but in the end, the urge was too strong.

In a whisper of movement, he was at her side with his hand on the rock just above her shoulder. "Waiting for someone? Brandy, is it?" The scent of warm, perfumed female skin wafted over him as he leaned into her.

"It took you long enough, Mr. Talltree." Her full lips formed a slight pout as she lifted her chin and tilted her face up to meet his. "Nice to see you again."

There was no hesitation or apprehension in her lovely features as he moved closer, placing his other hand next to her left shoulder, effectively pinning her against the rock. He wanted to wrap his arms around her lithe, warm body and brush his lips over her sexy pout. But he thought better of it, not wanting to scare her off...not yet.

"Yes, it is." He let his gaze wander leisurely up and down her luscious body. "Didn't your mother warn you about the dangers of stalking a stranger at night in the park alone?"

Praise for Tena Stetler

"It is hard because now I have fallen for these characters [in *A WARLOCK'S SECRETS*] too. I got wrapped up in the story so much that I forgot I was trying to take mental notes."

~Lisa H.

~*~

"I totally enjoyed [*A DEMON'S WITCH*]…fun paranormal romance, with enough sizzle and suspense to keep those pages turning, rooting for that Happily Ever After."

~Author Katie O'Sullivan

~*~

"What a nice surprise to discover a well-written paranormal romance with a touch of fantasy. [*A WITCH'S JOURNEY* is] a story of witchcraft, dark secrets and second chances. This author nicely blended her two main characters with magic and romance to make it a fun read!"

~Books & Benches

~*~

"I had a lot fun reading this unique paranormal story [*A WITCHES HOLIDAY WEDDING*]."

~Reviewer Ashia, Reading Alley

Dedications

To my family and friends for all their support.
~*~
To my husband
who brainstorms and proofs my books with me.
~*~
To my fantastic editor Lill
and my publishing house, The Wild Rose Press, Inc.
You're absolutely the best!
~*~
And to my fellow authors at The Wild Rose,
who are always ready to lend a hand.
What a team!
~*~
To my wonderful readers—
Thank you so much!

Chapter One
Don't Loiter on Trails After Dark

Perched on a boulder, hidden behind scraggly branches of scrub oak, Stefan sniffed the air appreciatively. In Glacier National Park, a few yards off the popular Avalanche Lake hiking trail, he watched and waited as the last stragglers made their way down the trail.

The dusky purple sky faded—his favorite time of day, when the deserted trails were his except for an occasional wolf, bear, or bat. His nightly routine of running the trails around Going-to-the-Sun Road at top speed exhausted his body and reduced his bloodlust. This enhanced his ability to work among humans with little discomfort for him or danger to them.

The blood he'd appropriated from St. Peter's Hospital in Helena sated his thirst for now. But the supply was dwindling, and finding a new source was at the top of his to-do list. *Was leaving the Vampire Council my best option? The blood supply was always fresh, but my duties sucked.* Playing politics wasn't his strong suit, but orders to terminate the loser went against even his moral compass.

Jumping down from the boulder, he landed silently on the balls of his feet and took off at a dead run, too fast for the human eye to detect. Tonight, his run covered several trails as the full moon rose over the mountain tops. Croaking frogs settled at the edge of a pristine mountain lake while an owl screeched overhead, winging its way through the night sky. This tranquil existence was very different from his previous life. Nevertheless, the premonitions that kept him alive as an assassin made him feel that things were about to change.

It was nearly midnight when he cut across the Sun Road to another trailhead, so intent on his goal that he nearly collided with an attractive young woman. He skidded to a stop, spraying gravel, rocks, and small twigs down the road in front of him. A pinecone dislodged and bounced along the road past her. Tall and slender, she had miles of fiery-red hair that hung down her back in a cascade of curls. Intense emerald eyes stared back at him as he attempted to regain his composure, not to mention balance. *What the hell was she doing here at this time of night?*

"Whoa." She stepped lightly to the side to avoid the flying debris. "You really should watch where you're going, especially at that speed." Her voice scolded, but the smile on her lips teased. "Someone could get hurt."

Pretending to pant, he shrugged, holding his palms up in surrender. "Just trying to get my run in before work. Stefan Talltree, at your service." He stepped closer, leaned over in an exaggerated bow, and caught her hand, brushing his lips over the palm and wrist, inhaling her sweet scent. *AB negative with a pulse of adrenaline. Perfect.* Her pulse beat a tattoo against his lips. He backed away.

Her heart thundered as she drew her hand from his grasp. "The name's Brandy. Pleased to meet you,

Stefan." Her smile reached up into her bright eyes as they swept over him with an appreciative glance, an experience he enjoyed.

Her voice had a hint of Irish lilt to it. He liked that too.

"Where do you work that requires you to report in at—" She glanced at her watch. "—midnight?"

Nostrils flaring, he paused. *Blood? Not hers.* The sound of Brandy's voice brought his attention back to her and the situation at hand. "Oh, shit, I've gotta go!" He sprinted off, leaving her standing alone.

As he started down the trail, the tree branches swayed in the silvery moonlight, casting eerie shadows across the trail's edge. The breeze brought with it the coppery scent of fresh blood mixed with sulfur. He turned for one last look at her as she wrinkled her nose before silently creeping into the wind, tracking the source of the stench.

****

Gravel crunched beneath Stefan's feet when he crossed the parking lot. Cody had driven his old beater of a pickup rather than his sleek black Corvette convertible. *No hot date tonight, huh, old man?*

Stefan slid the key into the lock and yanked open the radio station door. He walked by the empty reception desk; a faint scent of flowery perfume wafted past him. Turning, he rushed down the dimly lit hallway to the second door on the left. The "On Air" light glowed red above the door. Stefan waved through the glass window to the control room.

Cody flipped the mic off and motioned Stefan in. "Well, well, look what finally dragged himself to work." Cody ran his hand over the stubble on his chin.

"Come to think of it, I don't remember you ever cutting it this close. Russ's golden boy ain't perfect," Cody crowed, shaking his head in mock amazement.

"Shut up. I've ten minutes before you're off shift," Stefan said, glaring as he closed the door. He took off his leather jacket, tossing it on the back of a chair located under the tiny window to the outside. Glancing around the small room, he finally located the play and traffic (commercial) lists hanging on a hook above the computer monitor suspended from the ceiling.

He yanked the lists off the hook and reviewed all the commercials set to run during his shift. Stefan noted Cody had checked them all off and made sure they were in the correct time slots. Stefan's expression softened, the corner of his mouth lifting in a half grin as he looked down at the older DJ. "Thanks, man. I owe you."

"Gee, now there's something new. Hey, you get lost on the trails again?" Cody tugged his hand through his brown hair, which was graying at the temples. Then, turning back to the board, he checked the minutes left on the song and made sure another was in cue, though everything was computerized now. But old habits die hard, and dead air, whether from computer error or human mistake, was something to be avoided at all costs.

"Maybe." Stefan's grin faded. He snatched the playlist off the counter and quirked a dark brow, staring down at Cody. "Does it matter?"

Cody snorted and gave Stefan a sideways glance. "Or was it one of those groupies who are always hanging around at your remotes revving your engine?"

Stefan narrowed his eyes. "You know I don't mess

with that kind. Not my type."

"Hell, then send them my way. That petite brunette last week at the Flathead County Fairgrounds was HOT!" Cody wiggled his bushy salt-and-pepper eyebrows, then grinned.

"She probably has a boyfriend. You'll be hiding out like last month after you met up with...who was it?" Stefan dropped the list of songs onto the counter. An eyebrow arched. He looked at Cody.

"Sophie. How was I supposed to know she was married?" Cody's hazel eyes twinkled with feigned innocence.

"Uh, the gold band on her left hand is usually a dead giveaway." He slapped Cody on the back and gave him a shove. "Now get out of here. I'm sure you have better things to do than shoot the shit with me."

Cody raised his hand in a sloppy salute, turned, and sauntered out the control room door. The latch clicked softly behind him. Stefan checked the playlist and commercials against the computer one final time, then grabbed his headphones. It was ten minutes before his first stop set, so he swung his leg over the chair and settled in. Leaning back in the chair, he allowed his thoughts drift to the woman on the trails and the foreboding feeling that crept through him before meeting her.

Normally, the solitude of the radio station's midnight shift soothed him. But tonight he was edgy. Pacing back and forth across the control room floor like a caged animal, desire stirred inside him, and he couldn't escape the unwelcome craving for naked female flesh under him. Tired of the one-night stands, he wanted someone who mattered. He swore under his breath and muttered, "Never again."

Yet the need to find that redhead seemed all-consuming. Even though he knew instinctively it wasn't safe for either of them…unless…Ruthlessly, he shut down the emotions swirling in his gut and turned back to the control panel. *I've got a job to do.* He shoved her out of his mind, adjusted his headphones, and turned on the mic.

"Cody has left the building," Stefan said in an amused voice. "I've quite a lineup for you tonight. Kick off your boots, sit back, and relax. Need to hear something? Give me a call. I'll be here all night at Big Fish Radio." His deep, smooth voice flowed out over the airwaves to his listening audience of night owls. With a flick of his finger, the "On Air" light went off, and his mind flipped back to the mystery woman.

Avoiding the trails for a while seemed the best course of action. She'd be an unwanted complication in his world. He couldn't be trusted and certainly not with a human female. *If she was human, why didn't she shy away tonight? Normally, a warm-blood's subconscious knows I'm a danger to their very existence.* Although he had to admit, since settling down in Whitefish, not many shied away from him anymore. *The more interesting question is…what if she isn't human? She'd make an intriguing diversion.*

Knowing he shouldn't didn't keep him from wanting to return to the trails and look for her.

The blue flashing light on the wall signaled a phone call and yanked him out of his thoughts as he snatched the receiver. "The Big Fish, what's your pleasure?"

After a slight pause, a sultry female voice

whispered through the phone. "Is this the tall, muscular hunk that prowls the trails of Glacier National Park after dark?"

Waves of lust crashed through him without warning. He stood to relieve the hard, aching ridge forming under the zipper of his jeans. Staring out the tiny window into the darkness, he said, "Well, it depends on who's asking."

"I guess you'll have to come back to the trails to find out," she purred and hung up.

Standing at the counter, he stared at the receiver. "What the hell?" he said in the empty control room, slamming the receiver down onto its cradle. Rubbing the back of his neck, he rolled his shoulders to release the tension. *How in the hell did she locate me this quick? Should I risk finding her?*

Dawn brought an orange glow to the horizon as Stefan's shift ended. He walked out into the crisp morning air, unconsciously fingering the gold serpentine chain around his neck. His grandfather, a shaman, had conjured the chain to enable him to walk in sunlight unharmed. Still, he preferred the shadows and the anonymity they provided.

He strolled the few blocks to the small log cabin he'd bought from Russ, the radio station manager. Wary at first, Russ was one of those overly friendly sorts and decided Stefan needed a friend. When the previous overnight DJ moved to a bigger market for more money, Russ insisted Stefan's deep, smooth voice made him ideal for the job. It was the perfect opportunity to blend in, and Stefan grew to enjoy it.

Keys jangling from his finger, he unlocked the door to the log cabin and stepped inside. Though the sun was up, Stefan didn't feel sleepy. As a vampire, he didn't require much sleep. Usually after a shift he'd lie on the bed and relax, entering a meditative state. It rejuvenated his abilities and helped him work through problems that seemed unsolvable otherwise. That redheaded woman was going to be one of those problems. He could just tell. Still, he wanted to see her again, even knowing it could end in disaster, or worse, her death.

Still edgy, he grabbed a pint of O positive from the freezer, noting again how low his supply was, and poured it into a large mug. His mouth watered at the memory of her AB negative spiced with adrenaline. He popped the blood in the microwave and heated it to a delicious 98.6 degrees. Lifting the mug to his lips, he took a sip and closed his eyes as the rich red liquid slid down his throat, satisfying his thirst.

Mug in one hand, he picked up his guitar with the other and walked outside to sit on the shaded steps of the back porch. His fingers danced over the strings as he played the rhythm for his latest song. Music was the only thing that had comforted him while he learned to navigate the lifestyle of a newly turned, bloodthirsty vampire alone. Though it'd been years since he existed like that, the memory of his uncontrollable rage, the collage of terrified screams, gushing bright-red blood, mutilated bodies, and carnage still tormented him.

****

The sun slid behind the mountains, setting the azure sky ablaze in hues of red, orange, yellow, and pink. Then red shifted to purple and dusk faded to darkness as he jogged toward the trails. She stood leaning against the rock where he had started his run last night. He'd tried to convince himself to stay away, but in the end, the urge was too strong.

In a whisper of movement, he was at her side with his hand on the rock just above her shoulder. "Waiting for someone? Brandy, is it?" The scent of warm, perfumed female skin wafted over him as he leaned into her.

"It took you long enough, Mr. Talltree." Her full lips formed a slight pout as she lifted her chin and tilted her face up to meet his. "Nice to see you again."

There was no hesitation or apprehension in her lovely features as he moved closer, placing his other hand next to her left shoulder, effectively pinning her against the rock. He wanted to wrap his arms around her lithe, warm body and brush his lips over her sexy pout. But he thought better of it, not wanting to scare her off…not yet.

"Yes, it is." He let his gaze wander leisurely up and down her luscious body. "Didn't your mother warn you about the dangers of stalking a stranger at night in the park alone?"

The breeze caught pieces of her long curls as she threw back her head and laughed. It was a musical sound, and her eyes sparkled with pleasure. "Aye, that my mother did. Unfortunately, her advice is in direct conflict with my job description since I'm required to keep the trails safe for everyone…which hasn't been easy lately." Brandy's voice trailed off, almost as if she hadn't intended to say the last part aloud.

He looked quizzically at her. "That's kinda cryptic. What do you mean?" He leaned in a little closer.

Brandy waved her hand dismissively. "Oh, nothing. Just thinking out loud."

Sure there was more to it than that, he saw the determination in her face and decided to let it go for the moment. "Well, now that you've got me here, what do you want?"

"Join me for a run before you go to work?" Brandy braced her hands against his chest and looked up.

He could get lost in the depth of those mesmerizing emerald eyes. A little sigh escaped his lips…

The breeze teased his long black hair gently across her cheek. She brushed it aside.

He let one arm fall to his side, while a corner of his mouth curved into a quick lopsided grin. "Sure, let's go. Any particular destination?"

"No, you lead. I'll keep up." She stepped over his foot still blocking her path and moved out of reach.

We'll see. He set the pace faster than a human could manage. She stayed right beside him. As he increased the pace, Brandy struggled a bit but still managed to stay close. *What is she?* A human couldn't possibly keep up with him. Yet he didn't sense anything unusual about her. Nevertheless, he felt relief at the possibility she wasn't human. *This just might work to my advantage.*

When they reached the top of Going-to-the-Sun Road, Brandy bent over at the waist, panting and trying to catch her breath. "That was fun," she huffed out between pants. "How about tomorrow night, same time, same place?" Standing up, she moved her hands to the small of her back and stretched backward, then side to side. "You're quite the running partner. It's been a long time since I've been physically challenged."

"Thanks. I aim to please." He ran a fingertip lightly across her jaw, then let it trail down her throat, coming to rest just above the rise of her breast. "Can't make it tomorrow evening. One of the guys has laryngitis, and I have to pull a double shift." Then a grin took over his features. "It's kinda hard to be a DJ without a voice. Russ covered for him today, and it's my turn tomorrow night. How about I call you in the next couple of days, and we can get together?"

Patting his arm, she stared at his offending finger and shook her head. "No. I'll give you a call at the station. See ya."

Removing his hand, he said, "Wait," and reached for her arm, but she slid neatly out of his reach.

She ran up the trail in the opposite direction, then called over her shoulder cheerfully, "You're going to be late if you don't get moving."

Chapter Two
Be Careful What You Wish For

A week passed and then two. Brandy still hadn't called. *Perhaps it is for the best.* The last thing Stefan needed was a woman complicating his life. But, damn, he missed her.

Without Brandy to disrupt his routine of running the trails after dark, he made it to work on time or early—though he was a bit testy at times.

"Geez, that makes fourteen," Cody said, putting his paper down, looking over his half-spectacles with an irritating grin as Stefan breezed into the control room.

"Fourteen what?" No sooner were the words out of his mouth than he regretted asking.

"That's fourteen days straight you've been over an hour early for work. What's the matter? The little groupie lose interest?" Cody threw back his head and roared with laughter. Sobering, he pointed to Stefan's in-basket. "Seriously, Tracy's got a shitload of production for you. Guess word's gotten around you don't have a life."

Ignoring him, Stefan bit back a snarl, then scowled, checking the schedule and his inbox. Sure enough, there were ten commercial spots and seven public service announcements. Three of them went into rotation right after his shift. "Crap, what'd you do, piss off Tracy so I have to do all the production work?"

"Nope, I had a few of my own. Apparently, the advertisers want your smooth, seductive voice to sell their products. As I understand it, those are all requests for your voice," Cody said.

"Yeah, yeah, yeah," Stefan said.

"Talent fee, my boy. You'll be rolling in dough if this keeps up." Holding up his hand, Cody rubbed his thumb over his other three fingers. "Want me to take an hour of your shift while you produce the ones that run in the morning?"

"No, but thanks." Stefan grimaced, then sighed. "I'll get the morning ones done now and finish the rest after my shift. He turned on his heel and strode toward the production booth. Pausing in the doorway, he looked over his shoulder, about to say something. *Damn.* There she was again, dancing around the fringes of his thoughts at the most inopportune times.

Cody folded the paper he'd been reading, took his spectacles off, and laid them on the counter. "Stefan, are you sure you're okay? Seems to me you're mighty down these days even for you."

Puzzled at his concern, Stefan studied Cody for a moment. "Yeah, just got a lot on my mind."

Cody looked him straight in the eye, then glanced back at his paperwork. "Nope, I don't buy that for one minute. Something is eating at ya. Far be it for me to interfere. Better get cracking if you're gonna get all the morning spots recorded and entered in the computer before I leave. If you want, I'll upload them as you get them done."

"Yeah, that'll work. Thanks!" Stefan sprinted down the hallway to the production booth. He spent an hour recording the spots and returned to the control room. "All done. Now get your ass out of here. Thanks for the help." Recording the spots helped get his mind off the red-haired woman, though short-lived it would be, he suspected.

"You got it." Cody walked toward the door a few minutes after midnight, then turned back to Stefan. "Hey, there's a softball game at six tomorrow night." He glanced at his watch. "I guess that's tonight—with the Kalispell jocks from KBBZ. We sure could use some new blood. They got a bunch of younger guys that can really hit. It's going to be a slaughter. The game's at Memorial Park across from the high school, if you're up to it."

Stefan lifted a brow in disbelief. "Say what? If I'm up to it?"

"Well, what do you know? There's life in you after all, kid." Cody leaned against the counter and gave the thumbs up sign. "See ya there?"

"Maybe." Stefan smiled at the older man. "Yeah, I'll be there."

Cody pumped a fist in the air and closed the door behind him. The blue light flashed on the control room wall. Stefan cursed. *Telephone calls already.* Still reviewing the night's schedule, he grabbed for the receiver. It slid out of his hand, bounced on the countertop, then landed with a thud on the floor. "Shit," he muttered under his breath. It would be just his luck for the boss to be on the other end. "Big Fish. What's your pleasure?"

Her voice flowed like pure silk. "Got any tall, dark, handsome runners available?"

Without missing a beat, Stefan's voice lowered to a seductive rumble. "That depends on what you want him available for." The knot in his stomach eased a bit, and he grinned like an idiot at the sound of her voice.

"How about a rendezvous by the rock at dusk? Bet I could outrun you tonight."

At the spur of the moment, he decided to try a new tactic. "That would be great, but I can't. How about you come watch our station's softball team get stomped into a dry mud hole at six tonight?"

"Will you be playing?"

"That's the plan. Supposedly, the Kalispell team is really good and our team, not so much. Afterward, we could go for a run—" he paused for a beat "—if you're up to it, or anything else you're game for. You might even stand a chance to keep up with me since I might be worn out from the game."

"You're on. Where's the game?"

"At Memorial Field, across from the high school on Fourth Street. Can I pick you up somewhere?" he asked, hoping to get a little more information about this female who had invaded his life.

"No, I'll just meet you there around six. See ya then." She disconnected the call.

Regardless of how much he tried to convince himself she didn't matter, couldn't matter, the knot in his gut told him differently. *That woman is mine* resonated through his head.

Over the six-hour shift, he must have looked at the clock more than a dozen times. Finally, the sun peeked over the horizon and a skinny kid with freckles walked in the control room door. "Good morning."

Stefan glanced up, raising a sleek black eyebrow. "Morning. Where's Russ?"

"Had a business meeting. Asked me to cover for a

couple hours."

"Good enough. It's all yours." Stefan grabbed his coat and strode out of the control room door.

He meandered the quarter mile between the station and his log cabin. Climbing the three roughhewn stairs leading to the wrap-around porch, he stared down at the half-log steps. *I've got to replace these before someone trips on them.* After examining the steps, he sat down in one of the bright-blue Adirondack chairs to watch the sunrise. Feet propped on the railing, ankles crossed, he settled back in the chair.

The quiet life he'd created didn't take into account social events with warm-bloods. Nor courting a woman so intriguing that thoughts of her danced around the edges of his mind constantly. The frosty air of the early morning gave way to a crystal-clear view by the time the sun cleared the horizon. A pink glow spread over snow-covered mountains. He loved his little corner of the world.

After a couple hours on the porch, he pushed up from the chair and sauntered into the cabin. Tossing a load of work clothes in the washer, he spent the rest of his day in between loads of laundry and working on the problem areas in his latest song.

Late afternoon, he showered and downed a warmed pint of blood to make sure his thirst was under control before leaving for the game. His gut told him this outing could be a mistake, but like other times in his life, he'd do it anyway.

Arriving at the field half an hour early, he stepped out of his truck and scoped out the area. Russ and Cody were already there along with several other people he knew by face but not by name. Socializing had never been high on his list of priorities. Though his bloodlust was completely under control, staying to himself was a safer option for everyone. Yet here he was testing the boundaries again, and for what? He slammed the truck door and strode across the field. *I can do this.*

"Hey, you made it," Cody said, punching a fist in the air. He turned and beamed a look of triumph to the others. "See? I told you he'd come. He's not antisocial, just likes to keep to himself. Huh, kid?"

"Yeah, sure. Whatever you say." Shrugging, Stefan shoved his hands in his pockets. Being out in a crowd made him edgy. Though he couldn't remember the last time he'd fed from a human involuntarily, the bloodlust remained a strong part of him. *I've endured and inflicted enough violence to last several lifetimes.*

The wooden bleachers filled with friends and family of the Whitefish team. Across the field, sitting on blankets and folding chairs, was another group of much younger people. "Are those Kalispell players?" Stefan nodded toward the group, sizing up each person.

"Yep, you can see why I said a slaughter." Cody laughed. "Now that we've got you, they better watch out."

"Oh, I wouldn't be so sure. You haven't even seen me play."

"Son, that's a given." Cody clasped his shoulder. "Just look at you. A natural born athlete is what you are. Our team is up to bat. Let's go."

Stefan raised a dark eyebrow and stared icily at the hand on his shoulder.

Cody quickly removed his hand and tucked it into his pocket.

By the fourth inning, the score tied at two apiece,

and Whitefish players had the bases loaded.

"You're up, kid," Russ shouted to Stefan.

"Knock 'em in," Cody bellowed from somewhere behind him.

Stefan walked onto the field and watched the pitcher nod in agreement to whatever signals the catcher was sending. Feet a shoulder-width apart and bat poised in ready position, he watched the ball streak toward him. With a crack, he sent the ball out of the field, making the score six to two. *Huh, maybe a little too much effort on my part. Better dial it back next time.* Stefan jogged around the bases.

"Wow! Can you pitch as well as you hit?" Russ shouted as Stefan passed third base, headed for home. The Kalispell team was up.

Scanning the bleachers from the sideline, Stefan found Brandy sitting in the front row, clapping and cheering loudly. Something inside him churned uncertainly, a feeling long forgotten. Ignoring it, he smiled and waved to her.

She jumped to her feet, held two thumbs up, and yelled, "Way to go, Stefan!"

Kalispell held to six runs. Whitefish scored eight, winning the game for the first time in several years. Roger, the captain of the visiting team, walked over and shook hands with Russ.

"That's quite a player you got there. Is he on your staff, a relative, or a ringer?" Roger asked, grinning.

"Stefan, come over here," Russ called. Stefan strode over to where Russ was standing. He grasped Stefan's shoulder. "This is Roger, the program director for KBBZ. Stefan does overnights."

Roger clasped his hand in a friendly handshake.

"You cold, kid? I'd think you'd be burning up the way you played."

"Oh, my hands are always cold." He slid them in his pockets. "It's nice to meet you, Roger. Better luck next time."

Roger cocked his head, apparently listening to the timbre of Stefan's voice as he talked.

Checking to see if he was a ringer or actually worked at the station, Stefan surmised.

Satisfied, Roger grinned. "If you're still playing for them next year, our team will have to actually practice. It was a pleasure." Roger paused for a beat, then shrugged. "Any chance you'd consider coming to work for KBBZ?" He laughed, but the look on his face was half-serious.

Russ frowned. "What the hell are you doing, Roger?"

A flush creeped across Roger's cheeks. He cleared his throat. "Only kidding. Don't get your feathers all ruffled."

Stefan watched the uncomfortable banter. Politics no different than…"Nope, I'm happy here. Thanks for the offer." Stefan nodded to Russ and jogged off the field to the bleachers where Brandy was waiting.

As he came around the fence, she bounced on her toes, and rushed over. "You were fantastic tonight. Seems you are a man of many talents," Brandy said, batting her long red lashes at him.

"There are lots of things you don't know about me," Stefan said flatly, scenting the adrenaline in her system as her nerves ratcheted up a notch. Her excitement made her blood so much more enticing. *Adrenaline-laced blood is delicious.* His position with the Vampire Council had provided many opportunities for such blood.

"That makes you all the more intriguing, doesn't it?" She wiped her sweaty hands on her jeans and brushed a few strands of hair out of her eyes, her heart galloping inside her chest.

Her heartbeat was the last thing he needed to hear.

Russ strolled up to join them. "Wow, what a game. Great job, Stefan. You'll be a regular player on our team from now on, right?"

Cody chimed in, "Damn right, huh, Stefan?"

"Maybe." He slung his arm around Brandy's shoulders as she tightened her grip on his waist. "Brandy, this is Cody, a jock at the station, and Russ is the station manager. Gentlemen, this is Brandy."

Cody and Russ said in unison, "Nice to meet you, Brandy!" Then grinned at each other and laughed at their timing.

Giving a quick nod toward Brandy, Cody asked, "Is she the reason for your sunny disposition today?" Then he turned his attention to Brandy. "You been MIA for the last couple of weeks?"

Brandy hesitated, glancing up at Stefan. "Aye, working a lot of hours. By the time I get home, grab a bite to eat, I fall into bed. Why?"

"Stefan can be antisocial, but recently, he's been downright difficult. We didn't get too close, afraid he'd bite our heads off for no reason. His mood ranged from sullen to downright foul. Okay, not that bad, but we'd appreciate a warning next time you're going to pull a disappearing act."

"Shut up, Cody, or I'll show you foul," Stefan snarled, taking a menacing step toward Cody.

Brandy giggled, leaned over, and whispered in Cody's ear, then snuggled into Stefan's shoulder.

The last thing Stefan needed was her warm body crushed against his, heating up more than just his skin. *Oh, hell, who am I kidding? I like the feel of her warm body.* Stefan wrapped his arm around her waist and maneuvered her away from the group toward the secluded tree line.

She tilted her face up, bringing her mouth just a breath away from his. "Still wanna run?" She leaned closer and brushed her lips lightly against his throat.

Her neck was bared, blood pulsing through her veins, so close, so fragrant. His fangs started to unsheathe. His claws poked at his fingertips while thirst burned in his throat like wildfire.

Hell no, I don't want to run. I want you naked, those beautiful long legs wrapped around me, writhing under me while I taste you. He ran his free hand through his hair in frustration. He'd worked hard to make sure those feelings weren't crawling under his skin since arriving here.

But add one sexy redhead and all his efforts went straight to Hell. Giving Brandy a little squeeze, he released her. "I'll meet you at the rock in a few minutes. I need to help Cody gather up the equipment." *And get myself under control.* He looked at her one last time and began scooping up bats.

****

"See ya there," she said in a frosty tone as she turned and sprinted back to her car. *The man runs hot and cold in the blink of an eye.* She considered going home and forgetting the whole thing, but damn it, he intrigued her and not many men did. Then there was that body. *God, he is gorgeous.* As he'd swung that bat, she'd watched the muscles ripple across his back and chest beneath the tight black T-shirt he wore. She'd also noticed the snug fit of his blue jeans. That was enough to leave her aroused and cursing her heritage.

In her family, divorce wasn't an option. Once mated, only death ended the bond. Casual sex wasn't a possibility. But her attraction to Stefan was like nothing she'd ever experienced and had her rethinking the decision to pursue him.

Still fuming, Brandy sprinted to the area where they'd first met. She paced in front of the rock, staring over her shoulder. She was overreacting. He'd merely asked her to meet him while he helped his friends clean up. Finally, she leaned against the rock. *What in the hell is wrong with me? I've been on an emotional roller coaster since I met him.* She shook her head. *Something isn't right.*

****

Cody stared in disbelief as Stefan sprinted back onto the field. "Dude, what the hell are you doing? Go on. I got this," Cody said.

Stefan continued gathering up the bats and balls, then tossed them in the bed of Cody's rusty truck.

"If you don't want her, I'd be happy to take her off your…" Cody joked, then the smirk faded from his face.

With a murderous glare, Stefan growled at Cody, "She's mine." Making his intention crystal clear to everyone, he stalked away.

"She won't be yours very long if you treat her like that." The skinny kid with freckles, whose name Stefan didn't know, yelled after him. Cody gave the kid a rough shove toward his vehicle.

Stefan flicked a gaze toward them, rage flowing through him, fangs descending. He balled his fists to hide the claws piercing his fingertips. *No, not here, not now. I've worked too hard to make a place for myself.* He barreled to his truck, wrenched the door open, and jumped inside. It was unacceptable to lose control like this and hadn't happened in recent years. He couldn't risk it. No matter how badly he wanted her, he didn't see how this was going to work.

By flexing his hands over and over, he finally got them to relax. The claws withdrew. He reached down and pulled a roll of paper towels and disinfectant from under the seat, and wiped the blood off his hands and the steering wheel. Then he stuffed the bloody towel in a trash bag on the floor, making a mental note to dispose of it later. Easing his head back against the headrest, he closed his eyes and imagined he was anywhere but there. After a few minutes, the bloodlust passed just as there was a knock on his window. Stefan turned his head, slowly opening his eyes. Cody's face came into focus.

"You okay?" Cody asked, frowning as he shifted from one foot to the other beside the truck. "Rocky didn't mean anything by his stupid comment. Young and dumb, you know."

Stefan rolled the window down and gave his friend the thumbs up sign, resting his arm on the edge of the window. "Woman trouble. You understand."

Cody's bushy brows winged up in question, but he nodded and walked away. "See ya later."

When Stefan rolled the window up and got out of the truck, he'd decided that a couple of dates couldn't hurt. *I invited her here. Only a jerk would dump her tonight. I'm a lot of things, but not a jerk.* He shrugged his shoulders and gave a half laugh. *No one thought I could leave the employment of the Vampire Council, strike out on my own, and survive to tell about it. Yet here I am.*

Relieved to be under control again, he slid off the seat, locked and quietly closed the truck door, and hauled ass across the field to meet Brandy.

Brandy was waiting for him, leaning against the towering formation, knee bent with her foot braced against the rock, the other angled in front and firmly planted in the dirt. "It's about time. You really shouldn't keep a lady waiting."

Stefan bowed from the waist, straightened up, and reached for her hand. Turning it over, he brushed his cool lips across the back of her warm hand. "Sorry. I've never played on a softball team before. I didn't want to offend anyone by not helping with cleanup. You ready to run?"

"Yep."

"How about after our run, we grab a cup of coffee at the Big Sky?" Stefan asked, sure the diner would be mostly deserted at that time of night. Being attracted to a warm-blood and being with her was entirely different than working among them.

"Sounds great." She stepped away from the towering, jagged rock, bent over, touching her palms to the ground, then straightened. Putting her hands on her hips, she leaned side to side for a couple of beats. She stood up straight, her gaze catching his. "Let's go." She took off at a dead run up the trail, red hair flying as her melodic laugh echoed off the canyon walls.

Caught off guard, Stefan stood as if rooted in place, watching her cute ass sway with every step. He raced after her.

Chapter Three
Relationships—Who Needs Them?

Even after a couple of weeks, the feelings churning around inside him were still bugging the shit out of him. Not to mention they were growing stronger. Stefan knew what caring for a woman could do to a man. He'd seen the sadness in his father's face and watched him deal with the deep hurt caused when his mother left them.

The one relationship with a woman Stefan had allowed himself destroyed his life and any chance of a decent future. His grandfather, who raised him, showed no emotion as Stefan, half-crazy with bloodlust, had explained how he became a creature of the night. It tore his grandfather's heart out. The old shaman did what he could to help, but in the end, Stefan had to leave for his safety and that of his tribe.

No, I gotta cut her loose tonight. Determined to get it over with quickly, he ran toward the trailhead and their usual meeting place.

Sucking in a breath he didn't need, he paused at the vision before him.

She sat on top of the tall rock, ankles crossed and leaning back on her hands, face relaxed, looking up at the glittering stars strewn across the midnight sky.

The lump in his throat got bigger as he walked slowly toward her. *She is beautiful and...*Wishing fervently it didn't have to be this way, he glanced up to where she sat and touched her ankle. "Brandy, we need to talk."

"Oh, I don't like the way this conversation is starting," she teased, a smile playing around the corners of her mouth

He didn't return her smile. "I've enjoyed these weeks together, but I don't think this is going to work." Looking up at her, he was surprised to see her expression didn't change. "You don't know what you are getting yourself into. I'm dangerous."

She tilted her head and raised a copper eyebrow. "Don't I?"

Her calm demeanor infuriated him. "No, you don't. I'm your worst nightmare."

"Afraid, are you?" she asked quietly.

"Of course not. After giving it a lot of thought, I think this is best for both of us."

Brandy bolted straight up, staring defiantly into his dark eyes. "Who gave you the right to decide for me?" she countered, green eyes glittering.

"Brandy, you don't understand," he said gruffly.

A crimson blush crept up her neck and exploded across her cheeks. "Oh, I understand all right. You're afraid to take a chance even though your heart, mind, and body are telling you it's right."

"I'm not going to debate this with you. I came here tonight to say goodbye." He turned to walk away.

Brandy launched herself off the rock and landed smack dab in front of him. She jammed her finger into his broad chest, forcing him to take a step backward. "Look, vamp, the way I see it, you're either afraid or too boneheaded to see what's right in front of your face.

You may not deserve a chance at happiness, but I do, and that requires your participation." She paused, narrowing her eyes. She shoved him again, harder and with the palm of her hand, in the center of his chest.

Unable to keep the beast inside any longer, his fangs unsheathed and claws broke through his fingertips. Clear crimson liquid dripped from his fingers, but it didn't seem to faze her. Still grappling for control, he retracted the claws and grabbed her arm. Completely unprepared for her tirade, he couldn't think of a single thing to say or do that made any sense. In fact, at this moment, it was all he could do to maintain control over the beast.

Suddenly, a shiver shot down his spine. Panic bubbled up through his reactive haze. She'd called him a vampire. Nobody here knew his closely guarded secret. *Who was she? Better yet, what was she? Had the Vampire Council sent her?*

Stefan took a deep breath and tried to clear his head, tamp down the panic. His fangs drew back as he gained complete control. *The Vampire Council wouldn't send someone for me. Lady Rose gave me a clear release of my obligation to her.*

He'd located and helped rescue the Demon Overlord of the Western Hemisphere's mate some time ago while retrieving the stolen Vampire Council's Labrys. Lady Rose had decided his indentured servitude was at an end. He'd paid his debt. She wouldn't renege.

He closed his eyes, reducing his sensory overload, and the last bit of panic gave way to rational thought. Opening his eyes, he saw a pissed off woman standing before him, tapping her foot, staring at her arm where he still gripped her. Stefan loosened his hold.

Jaw clenched and lips tightened into a thin line, Brandy hissed through her teeth, "Take your hands off me before I do something we'll both regret." She jerked free of him, stomped a few steps, then drew in a deep breath, and let it out slowly.

He stood in the same place, waiting to see what she did next.

In a calm voice, she asked, "Did you know that you can exist on animal blood? I can teach you to hunt..." The blush that had started to recede pinked her cheeks again. "...Animals...I mean. It isn't the most pleasant experience at first," she stammered. "Not that feeding from humans is. But it'll satisfy your thirst. I know you're a troubled vampire, but it's time you take a good look at yourself, accept your fate, and make the best of it."

"And what would you know about feeding on humans, or animals for that matter?" he growled, watching Brandy intently as reddish-gold feathers erupted from beneath her curly hair, spreading across her forehead as it changed shape. Her body shimmered and the edges of her form blurred. Stefan blinked a couple times, shook his head, and opened his eyes wide. *Am I seeing things?*

"Aagggg. I can't do this right now!" She turned and ran, disappearing behind a huge stand of pine trees.

Shocked, it took a few seconds to get his feet to move. Whipping around, he felt a whoosh of air and caught a glimpse of a large form taking flight above the trees, blending into the star-strewn sky.

Searching the area where she disappeared, he found no evidence of what had taken flight. Spread across the ground were shredded pieces of clothing she had on before she escaped into the trees. Plodding back to his truck, he tried to make sense of what had just happened. *Apparently, Brandy has secrets too.* He didn't know why, but that made him feel better.

As the full moon drifted to the west beneath wispy clouds, he looked up and swore, "Shit. I'm going to be late for work." In a blur, he sped down the path, stopped at the cabin to change clothes, then bolted for the station. The tall skinny kid, whose words still echoed in Stefan's head, stood in the control room. *Where is Cody? Shit, this is the last thing I need.*

The clock on the wall struck midnight as Stefan strode in the door and said gruffly, "I'll take it from here." Without a word, the kid grabbed his coat from the chair and disappeared through the open door, slamming it behind him.

The phones were unusually busy during his shift. Each time the phone rang, Stefan hoped to hear her voice. *Pathetic.*

The days stretched into weeks, and still no Brandy. A little voice in the back of his head had grown louder and louder since the night she disappeared. *How did she know I'm a vampire? Who has she told? How did she find out, and who else knows?* He considered the questions. *Am I at risk? Probably not.* His intuition and lightning-fast reflexes were all that kept him in this world during his service to the Vampire Council. He'd given them no reason to recall his release. He shoved the pesky voice right out of his mind and immediately felt better for it.

What he wanted, needed, was her, and by God, he was going to have her. She'd hinted that fate was playing a part in their meeting. *What is fate doing now?*

Nothing. Sitting here on my dead ass isn't going to find her either.

Chapter Four
Family Emergency—Unexpected Trip with Far-Reaching Complications

For the sixth time over the past couple of weeks, the phone call to her sister went to voicemail. Brandy tapped the red icon and ended the call, tossing the phone on the couch, where it bounced once. She paced the hardwood floor of her cottage, picked up a picture of her and Hannah off the fireplace mantel, and stared at it. Shaking her head, she replaced the photo, tracing the frame with her fingertip. "What are you doing, Hannah?" Brandy said to the empty room. Scooting back to the sofa, she picked up the phone, dialed her sister's number again, and held her breath. This time Hannah answered on the first ring.

In an unusually quiet voice, Hannah said, "Brandy, how are you doing?"

"More to the point, how are you? I've tried to call you several times. Either it goes to voicemail or you put me off. Or you return my call when you know I'm on duty and leave a message. What the hell is going on? Ma and Da are worried sick."

"I've been swamped with work. Got dual citizenship now, allowing my security clearance upgrade so I can work on government ops. Had to get out from under the civilian workload so I can start working at my new position."

"What new position?" Brandy picked at the splatter of mud dried on the booted foot now resting across her knee.

"Didn't I tell you? I'm sure I did." Hannah paused. "Maybe I left you a message."

"Tell me again," Brandy insisted, getting to her feet, pacing across floor.

"I was promoted. In eighteen months or so, I'll be based out of Colorado at the Shadow Hawk Cyber facility, heading up an R&D division."

"That's wonderful. Colorado is beautiful and much closer to Montana." Brandy tapped her finger to her lips. "Oh, yeah, I remember that message. You also said you would be attending a wedding with your new man. Tell me about this new guy. Things getting serious?"

"I think so."

"I would hope so. It's the same man that took you to Hawaii on a getaway a few weeks ago, then to his sister's wedding? I'd call that serious."

"Yes. But I don't want to say too much and jinx it. You know how my relationships go."

"For God's sake, Hannah, you're nearly living with the guy and you don't want to jinx it? Come on, I'm your sister. We've always told each other everything. I know when you are lying to me." Brandy's hand flew to her mouth. *Shit, I shouldn't have said that.* She blew out a breath and tried to recoil her temper.

"I've got to go. I'll be in touch. Don't worry. I'm fine." Hannah disconnected the call.

Brandy plopped on the couch in her cozy living room, phone held to her chest. Something wasn't right. Since Hannah's recruitment right out of college by the cyber ops firm and move to Misty Harbor, they'd talked at least three times a week, sharing their lives and experiences with each other by phone. Then suddenly Hannah stopped calling or answering her phone on a regular basis. Nope, something was terribly wrong. Hannah was hiding something.

Brandy drew her bottom lip through her front teeth and hissed out a breath. She shoved up from the couch, sprinted into the bedroom, and yanked her suitcase out from underneath the bed.

I shouldn't interfere. Next she grabbed socks, jeans, shirts, and shoes and threw them in the suitcase. She bounced on the top, forcing the case closed, then she slung it onto the floor and rolled it to the front door. Pausing at the couch, she picked up her cell phone and called her boss at the ranger's station.

After a couple rings, a cheerful voice said, "Hi there, Brandy. Enjoying your day off?"

"Hey, Randy, I have a family emergency and need to take a week off, starting now."

He cleared his throat and was quiet for a beat. "Okay. I'll rework the schedule this week. Will you be back by the beginning of next week?"

"I hope so. I'll call you when I arrive at my sister's place and get things sorted out." She held the phone against her shoulder while digging her keys out of her backpack, and shoved them in her jeans pocket.

"Good enough. I hope things work out."

"Me too. Thanks." Brandy ended the call and looked up the number to the airport, then made reservations for the first flight available to Misty Harbor, Maine.

Snapping her fingers, she sprinted into the bathroom, scooped up eyeshadow, mascara, soap, toothpaste, toothbrush, and shampoo. She shoved them into a small duffle she kept in the cabinet under the sink. After running a brush through her tangled hair, she tossed the hairbrush in the bag. "That should do it." The thought of Stefan crossed her mind briefly. She slapped her hand on the counter. He'd have to wait.

Bags loaded in the SUV, she took off. Traffic was light and she arrived at the airport in record time.

Once settled in the plane, she riffled through her backpack for a book she'd stuffed inside earlier. Unable to concentrate, she pulled out her tablet and plotted directions to Hannah's house. A street address was listed beside her sister's cell number. *I hope she hasn't moved.* Hannah had taken the job with Shadow Hawk Cyber and moved to a little cottage on the outskirts of town. At least that's what Hannah had told her before she started being so secretive and hard to contact.

When Brandy arrived in Misty Harbor, it was overcast, and the rain pattered on the windows of the airport. Thankfully, her luggage arrived safely. She loaded her bags in the rental SUV, put Hannah's address in the GPS, and followed the directions to her sister's place.

The cottage was dark, though it was just as Hannah had described. A couple days' worth of newspapers were stacked on the porch. Brandy pulled out her umbrella and walked around the back of the cottage. No signs of life. No footprints or tire tracks in the gravel driveway or path to the house. If she had to guess, Hannah hadn't been here in a while. *Time to find that boyfriend of hers.*

On her way back to her vehicle, the neighbor who had been standing in the doorway of the house next door sprinted toward her. Brandy folded the umbrella as the rain had stopped.

"Hi, are you looking for Hannah?" The woman slid her sunglasses down her nose and studied Brandy. She shoved the glasses on top of her head.

"Yes. My name is Brandy Shaughnessy." She extended her hand.

The woman took her hand and shook it vigorously. "I'm Tanna Rork." She pushed her damp hair out of her face and peered at Brandy. "Are you her sister?"

"Yes. I wanted to surprise her. But I guess the surprise is on me. Any idea where she is?" Brandy shoved her hands into the front pockets of her jeans. The early spring air was crisp. The constant drizzle had her chilled to the bone even with the occasional moments of sunlight. She glanced at the sky, thankful for the sun trying to peek out again.

Taking her sunglasses off, she squinted at Brandy. "Best guess—she is at the house on the cliffs with her significant other. Doesn't spend much time here anymore. I watch the house for her. Let her know if something needs her attention."

"Oh, please don't tell her I'm here. It would spoil the surprise." Brandy glanced over at the two newspapers stacked on the porch.

Tanna made a zipping motion across her lips. "Your secret is safe with me." She giggled as the breeze tugged at her jacket. Following her gaze, Tanna grimaced. "Forgot to pick those up yesterday after I piled them on the porch. Left my key in the house, went back for it, and the rain started." She bent down and picked up the papers, shook the water droplets off, and stuck the newspapers under her arm.

"Okay, so this house on the cliffs, how do I get there? Since Hannah isn't likely to return here in the near future."

The woman ran into the house and returned with a piece of paper and a pen. She quickly drew a map with a "you are here" indicator. "It's a couple of miles away. There are only two houses up on the bluffs. Can't miss it. Just follow the main road." She tapped the pen on the paper. "Until you get here." She pointed to an intersection on her crudely drawn map. "Turn to your right, then take the first left up the winding driveway. There are gas lamps leading the way to the house. The iron gate is usually open."

"Iron gate?" Brandy asked dubiously.

Tanna waved a hand dismissively. "Gate is mostly for decoration, I believe. He keeps a low profile." She peered around, then lowered her voice. "People talk, you know. Say he's involved in some type of black ops. Gone a lot. Me, I think he's one of those that are married to their job. Until Hannah. She works government contracts too. But is always friendly enough. Works a lot of hours too."

A phone rang somewhere in the distance. Tanna jumped, glancing in the direction of her house. "Oh, that's mine. Gotta run. Nice talking to you. Hope you catch up with Hannah. She wouldn't want to miss you." She dashed up the walk, and flung open the screen door, letting it bang shut behind her.

Brandy opened the driver-side door and climbed in. She glanced at the map, started the engine, and followed the directions.

She turned left and stopped the vehicle. Tanna was right; the iron gate was open. *Holy crap. That driveway leads to a frigging castle on the cliffs.* It looked foreboding, or maybe her imagination was in overdrive. *What had Hannah gotten herself into?*

Brandy put the SUV in gear and slowly followed the winding drive, parking in the circular driveway lined by blooming flowers. Strange, the flowers in town were barely green sprouts. Glancing around, she saw two more garden plots with thriving plants. The grounds were well-kept, though only a few blades of green grass peeked through the brown.

She'd no sooner cut the engine than the massive wooden door to the house swung open. A tall, muscular man dressed in a suit stood in the doorway. He was nearly as tall as the framework; his wide shoulders almost filled the area. His movements, and the stare of his gray-blue yes, were predatory as he stepped onto the porch, watchful. The breeze tousled his blond hair, which reached over his collar.

After opening the vehicle door, she hesitated. In a blink of an eye, he was joined by several people peering out the entrance.

Wearing a light-green floor-length dress that hugged her curves, Hannah pushed her way through to stand beside the man. A halo of colorful flowers encircled her head as she covered her mouth with one hand. Recognition dawned. She squealed, sprinting down the stairs. "Brandy, what are you doing here?"

A flood of relief crashed through Brandy at seeing Hannah. She jumped out of the car and rushed toward her sister. "Can't believe…Wanted to surprise you." She engulfed Hannah in a hug. Releasing her, Brandy surveyed her sister, then glanced at the others. Everyone was all dressed up. "Am I interrupting something?"

Hannah pursed her lips and glanced from Brandy to the tall blond man and the others spilling out the door. "Sort of." Tugging her sister up the steps, Hannah paused after making it through the door and turned to face Brandy. "Today is my wedding day."

Brandy's eyes rounded and her mouth hung open for a beat. A flood of words came rushing out before she could stop them. "Oh my God, you got married without telling me, Ma, Da, or the rest of the family? Hannah, what were you thinking? Ma and Da are going to be devastated."

The teary-eyed look Hannah gave Brandy made her reconsider her words, and she clamped her mouth shut. She stared accusingly at the blond man now wrapping his arm around Hannah after following her down the stairs.

He offered a hand. "Brandy, I'm Tristian Shandie, Hannah's husband. Welcome to our home."

Brandy crossed her arms and glared at him.

Smoothly, he moved his hand to gesture her farther inside the house. "Please join our little celebration. Afterward, we'll sit down and have a long talk. I'm sure you don't want to spoil your sister's wedding day," he said in a calm, deep, soothing voice that had an edge of warning to it.

"Spoil her...Do you have any idea..." Brandy sputtered, then took a deep breath and closed her mouth again.

"Yes, I do. But we have guests and..."

Hannah put her hand on Tristian's arm and caressed it. "Let me have a few minutes alone with my sister," Hannah said firmly, her glance switching from

Tristian to Brandy, then over to her guests. "Excuse us a moment. Enjoy the food. Rena, finish cutting the cake. We'll be right back." Hannah grasped Brandy's arm and steered her to a study on the first level, closing the door behind them.

"Brandy. Please. I know you don't understand and are hurt. But I have my reasons. Tristian is the love of my life, but it's complicated. After our wedding guests leave, we'll sit down and explain everything, or as much as we can, to you. Ma and Da can't know. Not yet."

"What do you mean? You expect me to keep your marriage a secret from them? What on earth are you thinking? Unless my talents fail me, he's a warlock, not one of us."

"We both left Ireland for the same reason. Don't give me that crap. You no more wanted to marry our kind than I did, or you wouldn't have left Kevin behind."

"That's different," Brandy said vehemently, shoving her hands in her pockets.

Hannah fisted her hands on her hips, lips set in a thin line. "How?"

"For one, I didn't cut off most communication with our family, then run off and marry a man…warlock without telling anyone I was seriously involved."

"Wait a minute. I told you he took me to Hawaii, and we attended his family wedding together. Do you think I would…Oh, never mind." Hannah huffed out a breath. "It doesn't matter now. I'm married. End of story." She crossed her arms over her chest.

Brandy paced the floor, then stopped to look out the window. She closed her eyes, and temper cooled.

What in the hell am I doing? Ruining my sister's wedding day, that's what. Ma and Da would be ashamed of my behavior even given the circumstances. She sucked in a breath and rushed to Hannah, throwing her arms around her. "I'm so sorry. Didn't mean to make a scene. I was…"

"Shocked. I know. And I'm sorry about that. But we'll explain everything tonight. I promise."

"This better be good," Brandy said, trying to lighten the mood.

"Ready to go out and meet everyone?" Hannah asked.

"I'm a little underdressed." Brandy tugged at the hem of her T-shirt, staring down at her black jeans and boots.

"Doesn't matter. It's a small group of friends and family." Hannah led the way back to the intimate group. "Bruce and Angie, this is my sister, Brandy. Angie is Tristian's younger sister. Bruce is his boss. Tristian and I attended their wedding a few weeks ago. Remember, I told you."

Bruce stepped forward, his hand extended. "Nice to meet you, Brandy." He kept his arm around Angie. She glanced up at Bruce, then smiled wide at Brandy. "Welcome to the family."

Brandy's eyebrow winged up. "Nice to meet you." She offered her hand to each, then made sure her facial features didn't give away anything. The magic signatures were all over the place. Angie was a witch, but Bruce…undetermined.

Seeing her sister's confusion, Hannah's voice whispered through Brandy's mind. *Yes, I know, but it's a long story.* She motioned to a woman with short jet-

41

black hair styled in spikes tipped with bright blue. "This is Angie's life-long best friend, Willow, and her husband, Caleb. They are newlyweds also. It was a double wedding with Angie and Bruce."

Brandy shook hands with Willow and Caleb. *Faerie…but can't tell his. Magic signature is disguised.*

Hannah waved a hand toward three individuals still out on the deck. "That's Ruben standing next to the chaise, Terra is the woman walking toward the waterfall, and Bobby is leaning against the door. They are friends and co-workers.

"Birch and Freesia are Willow's parents and Tristian's surrogate parents after his were killed years ago."

Brandy glanced at Tristian, her expression softened. "Sorry for your loss."

"Thank you," Tristian said quietly.

Freesia hugged Brandy as Birch grasped her hand. "Glad to meet you," they said simultaneously, then looked at each other and laughed.

Freesia held Brandy at arm's length and smiled. "Your sister is the best thing that ever happened to Tristian."

Brandy nodded, not quite sure what to say given the circumstances. She decided to keep it general. "She's a great person. I look forward to getting to know Tristian." *Yep, they're both faeries. No disguising spell there.* She glanced back at Bruce. Power and confidence rolled off him, but he'd disguised his magic signature. *What in the world had Hannah gotten herself mixed up in?* Brandy shook her head.

"Oh, Tristian's a bit of a pain, but he grows on you," Freesia said with a wink and moved off toward the cake table.

Hannah led Brandy to the food spread on the table nearest the sliding glass doors that opened onto the patio. Brandy put prime rib, boiled red potatoes with the skins on them, and a couple homemade dinner rolls on her plate, then stopped to look out the door.

Hannah pointed to the small waterfall in the backyard. "Tristian built the waterfall for our wedding. We were married in front of it," she said dreamily.

"So the flowering plants, greenery…are all magic? It's not warm enough for all these blooming plants. Yet."

"Weddings are magical. Don't you think?" Hannah answered vaguely.

Brandy knew her sister was sidestepping the question but let it slide for now. They promised to fill her in, and she intended to make sure they kept that promise. *If I have to lie to Ma and Da, there better be a damn good reason.*

Brandy sat observing the individuals that had come to celebrate her sister's wedding. She kept the hurt to herself that she and her family had been excluded. These people seemed to care for Hannah, most of all Tristian, who was very attentive. The intimate touches and loving glances, relieved some of Brandy's trepidation upon her arrival. But why all the secrecy?

Brandy shook her head and rejoined the conversation, trying to ferret out any tidbit of information. The conversation was cordial, and nothing unusual came to light.

Finally, the guests said their goodbyes, and she was alone with Tristian and Hannah.

"Okay, spill. What the hell is going on here?"

Tristian raised a butterscotch eyebrow. Hannah's cheeks blushed red. "Brandy."

"No, it's all right, I promised an explanation and now is as good a time as any." With a sweep of his arm, he motioned to the large room with a stone fireplace that took up most of one wall. "Shall we convene in the family room? Would anyone care for wine?"

"Yes, please," Hannah said on a sigh and plopped on the couch with a pleading look to her sister.

"Sure…why not?" Brandy eased into the recliner nearest the roaring fire.

Tristian returned with a bottle of Cabernet and three crystal wine goblets. After setting the glasses on the table between them, he poured the wine and handed a goblet to Brandy. He lifted his glass. "To family."

Brandy frowned, shifted her gaze from Tristian to Hannah, then touched the rim of her glass to each of theirs in turn. "Okay…Now tell me why all the secrecy…Are you a spy or criminal?" Brandy took a gulp of her wine. *Wow, the expensive stuff.*

"Way to go, Sis, assume the worst." Hannah glared at her sister.

"Do I need to recap the recent events for you?" Brandy snapped.

"Ladies, this is my fault and I'll explain what I can. But you must understand that anything said in this room will go no further. Do I have your word?"

Brandy looked into her glass, swirled the red liquid around, and watched it wink in the firelight. "I guess so. Unless it's illegal. I am an officer of the law, you know." Her gaze touched lightly on Hannah, then shifted to Tristian and held his.

"I'm well aware of that. My requirements remain

the same. Our lives could depend on it." His scalpel-sharp gray-blue eyes were unwavering. The silence in the room was deafening.

Brandy sucked in a breath. "What are you...Hannah, what have you gotten mixed up in?"

"Please, Brandy," Hannah said in a soft voice.

"Your word." Tristian remained standing, his expression unreadable.

Engaging in a test of wills seemed futile, so she relented. "Okay—fine. I promise."

Tristian shifted his intense gaze from Brandy to Hannah. His expression softened, and he settled next to his wife on the couch.

He shook his head and sighed deeply. "The people that you met are part of a private security force. I am the top enforcer and manage the security teams. Terra, Bobby, and Ruben are my team leaders. Naturally, in my profession you make enemies who will stop at nothing for revenge. It's a dangerous profession. Moreover, it was responsible for the death of my parents, leaving me to raise my sister, Angie, who was twelve years old at the time. Hannah came into this relationship with her eyes wide open to the danger."

Brandy blanched. "So you say."

"I did, and I've never been happier. Please listen to what he has to say without judging," Hannah said softly.

Leaning back against the lounger, Brandy nodded, her lips drawn into a tight line.

"Coming to terms with loving another and protecting her was a big step for me. Extending protection to her family I haven't worked out. Not yet. Therein lies the problem and why we were married with our circle of friends and family that know and keep my secrets. Now that protection must be extended to you."

Brandy bristled. "If she'd…"

Tristian held his hand up. "It was at my request that she keep you at arm's length. In retrospect, maybe not one of my best decisions. But we're here now. The details of my profession will remain confidential. I have told you all you need to know. Someday in the future, I'll deal with Hannah's parents and extended family. I've promised Hannah we'll celebrate our wedding with them in Ireland. Until that time, I respectfully ask you to keep our secret."

She pushed up from the chair and paced, thinking better on her feet. Whirling around, she planted both feet and shifted her gaze from Hannah to Tristian. "Extended family I can handle. But expecting me to lie to Ma and Da—It's out of the question."

"Not lie, just omit a few facts. Only for a little while. I'll tell them I'm seriously involved with someone and plan to marry. We'll decide how much to tell them by phone to appease them," Hannah said. "Just back me up. That's all I ask. Can you do that?"

Chewing on her bottom lip, Brandy turned and paced again. "I guess so, but you had better tell them something soon. They are so worried about you."

"We will. I'll call them this evening." Hannah glanced at Tristian, who nodded, though the muscles at his jaw worked overtime.

"I don't want to intrude on your wedding night, so I'll let myself out and find a hotel."

"You'll do no such thing. You came for a visit, so stay with us. We'll catch up tonight. I'll show you around the town tomorrow. We'll stop by my cottage."

"Are you going to keep the cottage? I assume you will be living here from now on."

"Yes, I may rent it out or keep it for when friends and family visit, depending on what the future holds."

Chapter Five
Finding Brandy—A Blow to the Ego

It was clear to Stefan that Brandy knew Glacier as well as he did, if not better. He decided the visitor center or ranger station was the best place to start. If the straightforward approach didn't work, he wasn't above using vampire persuasion to get information.

Arriving at the visitor center, he stepped quietly inside and scanned the area. A female ranger walked through the doorway from the office to the main lobby. He stepped directly into her path. "Excuse me. Could you help me?"

"Oh my." She swerved to avoid running into him and put a hand on her chest. "You scared ten years off my life." Eyes wide, she took a deep breath and blew it out slowly. "Okay, now what can I do for you, sir?"

"I'm looking for a friend of mine. Her name is Brandy. She has a slight Irish lilt to her voice, and she's tall." He held his hand up even with his nose. "A slender build with long, curly hair, bright-green eyes. She knows this park like the back of her hand. Any chance you know where I might find her?"

The ranger paused for a moment, then slowly shook her head. "No, I'm sorry. I'm kinda new here, but Randy will be in shortly. He's been here forever and knows absolutely everyone. If anyone can help you, it's him. You don't mind waiting around a few minutes?"

A smile spread across Stefan's face as he nodded. "Not at all."

"Good. I'll see if I can raise him on the radio and let him know you're waiting."

"That would be great." Stefan paused, reading her nametag. "Sharry."

She hurried toward the counter, then stopped. "Your friend isn't missing or in any trouble, is she?" Sharry's forehead wrinkled with concern. Her gaze searched his.

"No, I don't think so. She was supposed to meet me at the Highline Trailhead this morning around dawn and didn't show. That's not like her, but she may have gotten busy and forgotten our appointment. I just want to make sure she is okay. Unfortunately, the piece of paper she wrote her address and phone number on was in my jeans pocket when I washed them. Stupid mistake." And the oldest excuse in the book, but it was all he had.

Sharry eyed him suspiciously, crossed her arms over her chest, and straightened. His dark gaze held hers, and then he smiled, ensnaring her with a little vampire thrall.

Slowly, she returned his smile. "It'll be just a minute." She walked behind the counter and keyed the radio.

"Thanks, I appreciate it," he said smoothly.

While waiting for a response, she asked the girls behind the counter if they knew a woman meeting Brandy's description.

"Maybe," one girl piped up, but she wasn't certain.

The radio squawked to life. Sharry took the handset

and walked into the office, closing the door. She was gone only a few minutes, returning with a big smile on her face. "Good news. He knows Brandy Shaughnessy. She works with the National Park Service as a park ranger and volunteer trail guide here. She works out of the West Glacier sub-office. Randy is on his way in, so you can talk to him yourself. Anything else I can do for you, sir?"

"Nope, you've been very helpful. Thanks." Stefan turned from the counter just in time to see an older man in a park ranger uniform walking up the path to the door.

The ranger removed his hat and sunglasses, then yanked open the door and strode into the building. He looked around until he spied Stefan. Smiling, he walked over to Stefan, hand extended. "The name's Randy. You looking for Brandy?"

"Yes, sir." Stefan shook Randy's hand firmly.

"Sharry tells me Brandy was supposed to meet you this morning at Highline Trail. Are you a relative?"

"No, just a friend."

"Policies prevent me from giving you any personal information about her. What I can tell you is she's been gone for a couple weeks but is on the schedule for tomorrow. You can probably catch her here around five in the morning. I think she's leading the sunrise hike."

"Thanks for your help. I'll catch her early tomorrow and give her a hard time about forgetting me." Grinning, Stefan shook hands again with Randy and nodded to the girls behind the counter. "Ladies."

On his way out the door, one young blonde called to him from behind the counter. "Hey, you'd be the last thing I'd forget."

"Thanks, I'll keep that in mind." He turned and kept walking toward the door. *How am I going to be here at five in the morning when I don't get off until six? By that time her group will be well on their way. Asking Russ for time off is out of the question.* In a small town like Whitefish, the rumor mill already knew more of his business than he liked. Asking for time off would add more fuel to the fire.

Two hours before his shift, he walked into the control room with a plan, one he hoped would keep the rumor mill at bay. "Hey, Cody."

"Hiya, Stefan. Still looking for a life, I see." He glanced at the clock and back to the vampire.

"Nope, not tonight. I need a favor."

"You, Mr. I-Don't-Need-Anyone?" Cody lowered the magazine he'd been reading. His gaze met Stefan's. "Only kidding. What's up, kid?"

Asking favors of any kind rankled. He'd got along just fine without anyone's help until now. *At least in the mortal world.* This time, he didn't see any way around it. He'd just have to suck it up and ask. "I need to leave an hour early tomorrow morning to take care of personal business. Russ would probably come in, but I really don't want to ask. He's my boss. I was hoping you'd be able to cover for me. I'd be happy to return the favor anytime."

Cody's salt-and-pepper eyebrows arched mischievously, and his lips twitched as if trying to hide a grin. "If it's about matters of the heart and that beautiful redhead, I'll be happy to. If it's about you being a stubborn SOB, I'll simply kick your ass. Now, you don't have to tell me which it is. But if I don't see her with you soon, I'll assume the latter and stomp your ass into a dry mud hole and then kick the dirt out. Got it?" A grin spread across Cody's face as he reached for his coat, then slapped Stefan on the back on his way out the door.

"Got it. Thanks, Cody." Stefan shook his head. *That Cody is a strange one.* The vampire went about his duties feeling better than he had in recent weeks.

The next morning at four-thirty sharp, Cody strolled in the control room door. "Go get her, boy." He grinned wide as he shoved Stefan out the door.

Stefan jumped in his truck and peeled out of the parking lot, sending gravel and dried leaves flying in all directions. It was still dark when he arrived at the visitor center and parked next to Brandy's yellow four-by-four, the same one she'd driven to the baseball game. She was the only one there. He walked to the door and watched her through the glass, appreciating her curves and long slender legs. *I'd love to have those wrapped around me.* A jolt of pure lust shot straight to his loins, causing a tight uncomfortable fit in the crotch of his jeans. *It's been too damn long.* He got up and walked around a bit. He couldn't greet her in this condition.

Under control again, he knocked on the window to get her attention. Busy perusing paperwork on a clipboard, she absently pointed to the clock on the wall. Another tap and she looked up. He felt her heart skip a couple of beats and smirked. *Sometimes being a vampire is pretty cool.*

Flustered, she dropped the clipboard, flinging papers all over the floor. Frowning at him, she bent down and picked up the scattered documents.

He rapped on the window again. "Brandy, let me in

or step out here. We need to talk."

She walked to the counter, picked up the keys, and unlocked the door, pushing it open just a crack. "I don't have time right now. I have a sunrise hike in a few minutes. Besides, I'm not sure I'm ready or even want to have a conversation with you."

"Well, I want to talk to you. Guess I'll have to join the hike."

"Suit yourself. We can't talk during the hike. I've a job to do."

"I know." Giving a half shrug, he straightened, taking a step closer and wedging his boot in the door. "We can talk later, but I won't let you out of my sight until we do."

Lips pressed tightly together, she narrowed her eyes and frowned. "What? Are you threatening me?" Her knuckles turned white, gripping the door handle so tight.

Yep, all the signs are there. She's pissed. He blew out a breath and threw his hands up in frustration. Then, remembering this situation was one of his own making, he relaxed his stance and grinned. "No, not at all. You have a habit of disappearing into thin air, and I can't risk that. Cody's going to kick my ass if I don't straighten this out with you. He's covering my shift right now, no questions asked but a lot of guessing on his part." Stefan removed his booted foot from blocking the door.

She threw up her hands, letting them fall limp to her sides, and sighed. Pointing to a bench against the brick wall, a faint smile crossed her lips. "Wait there for the other hikers. Don't expect special treatment either." She tugged the door closed and clicked the lock.

He walked over and sat on the bench. She wasn't going to make this easy, but he couldn't let her slip out of his life either.

It wasn't long before a young man and woman walked up. The man had a sleeping toddler in a child carrier backpack. Stefan stared up at the man, and he took a couple of steps backward, putting his hand behind his back and closing his fingers over his wife's arm protectively. He narrowed his eyes and watched Stefan and then cautiously asked, "Is this where we meet for the Iceberg Lake Trail hike?"

"Yep, it is. Have a seat," Stefan said absently.

Several people of different nationalities arrived. They all kept their distance from him. *This is going to be an interesting but crowded hike. Too bad. Small and intimate would have worked better.*

Brandy came out of the office, smiling brightly. Her gaze swept over all the hikers, totally ignoring him. "Good morning, everyone, I'm Brandy Shaughnessy, and I'll be your guide today. If you have any questions, please don't hesitate to ask. Are we all set? Cameras ready? The sunrise will be spectacular this morning. The views are tremendous on the lower section of the trail."

Several of the hikers smiled and murmured in agreement.

"The trail to Iceberg Lake is an easy hike in comparison to others in Glacier National Park. The first two hundred yards are the toughest," Brandy said.

He watched her with a wrenching pain in his gut. *Iceberg Lake. How appropriate. With the others, she's Little Miss Sunshine. Me—not so much. She's professional, but the warmth is gone out of those beautiful green eyes. Not a good sign.*

"The wind can have a bite to it. Does everyone have a warm jacket?" She assessed each hiker. "Appropriate hiking shoes are required. Sandals are not acceptable." She looked directly at a dark-haired girl, whose partner shot her an "I told you so" look.

The girl's face turned bright red as she wiggled her toes in her sandals. "I have other shoes in the car. It'll only take me a minute to change. Okay?"

"Sure," Brandy replied easily. "Sunscreen, sunglasses, bear spray, and water are also important. I see most of you have a hydration system. That's great. For those of you who don't, there are bottles of water for sale in the office. A couple of quarts should do. You can refill them at Ptarmigan Creek, which crosses the trail about halfway up. Who needs water?"

Only two of the hikers raised their hands. Brandy motioned them to follow her into the office. She took care of their needs and returned.

"Everyone bring lunch?" She surveyed the crowd.

All hikers nodded except Stefan, who gave her a cheeky grin and shook his head. She glared at him and whirled around on her heel, keeping her back to him.

The young woman with the man carrying the toddler said, "We've enough to share, if anyone gets hungry."

"That's fine then," she said more sharply than intended. Adjusting her backpack, she smiled at the dark-haired girl who had exchanged her sandals for hiking boots. "The weather here can change quickly. Keep an eye to the sky and that rain poncho handy. Grizzly bears frequent this trail, so stay together and alert. You'll also see bighorn sheep, mountain grouse, ground squirrels, and, if we're lucky, a mountain goat or two. Let's be off."

Bright streaks of orange, red, and pink crept across the dark-blue and purple of the breaking dawn. Resembling a prism, all the colors blended seamlessly into each other as the sun peeked over the mountaintops, its brilliant golden rays warming the crisp morning air. It had been a long time since Stefan appreciated such a spectacular sunrise. Still, he kept to the shadows as others stepped into the bright sunlight. Thanks to his grandfather's enchantment, the sun had very little effect on him, but he felt safer in the shade.

During the hike, Stefan mulled over the situation with Brandy and found that he was comfortable pursuing a relationship with her. But having to grovel didn't sit well at all. If there was a knot in his gut, it was only because it had been a long time since he'd gone out on a date.

Vampires were carnal creatures. He had enjoyed the occasional one-night stand with a female vampire, which satisfied both of their needs and desires but nothing more. The meetings were always discreet and out of town. He hadn't indulged in that pleasure for quite a while.

The fact that Brandy was something other than human nagged at him a bit. If she intended him harm, she'd had several chances as they hiked the deserted trails. He tucked that thought away for another day, hoping it too would sort itself out eventually.

Views along the trail were fantastic. The mostly open terrain had only a few forested spots in the middle of the hike. From a steep cliff, a couple of bighorn sheep stopped momentarily to watch the hikers, then returned to grazing. A lone grizzly bear lumbered across the meadow, paying little attention to the hikers and keeping a safe distance. Ground squirrels scampered through the vegetation and up the trees as the group passed alongside. A mountain goat clopped across the path and disappeared into the forest.

Upon reaching Iceberg Lake at lunchtime, the trekkers spread out on the rocky beach of the crystal clear lake as waves lapped at the shore. The air filled with lots of friendly chatter. Several people commented on the Irish lilt to Brandy's voice and asked her about Ireland. Alex and Pam, the couple with the toddler, set the child on the ground with a wrapped sandwich grasped tightly in her little fist. She wobbled on her short, chubby legs over to Stefan, offering him the sandwich.

Smiling, he took the sandwich, thanked them, and ate the sandwich, though his digestive system would make him pay for it later.

He walked away from the group, heading to the lakeshore, and skipped a rock across the surface, hoping to maneuver Brandy away from the crowd. Pointing out into the lake, he asked, "Ms. Shaughnessy, is there floating ice in the lake year round?"

"Very good question. Did everyone hear what Stefan asked?" She repeated the question, walking closer to the lake and him. "Yes, even in August the lake is generally full of floating ice. Because it's on the northern flank of Mount Wilber, it receives very little sun. The lake is left in shadow most of the year due to the three-thousand-foot vertical cliffs of Ptarmingan Wall that surround it."

All heads tipped backward to stare at the tall cliffs.

She pointed to the rugged terrain surrounding the lake, then continued. "During the winter, a thick coat of ice develops that slowly melts throughout the summer. The permanent snowfields above it also drop chunks of ice into the lake."

He snagged her arm as she passed by and whispered, "Brandy, I've thought a lot about what you said."

She watched him intently for a moment, nodded, and turned her attention back to the group. The bright-blue sky of the morning filled with dark ominous thunderclouds. "Let's get cleaned up and start back. Looks like a storm is brewing."

The trek downhill seemed shorter than the four and a half miles up to the lake. Large raindrops splattered on the ground as the hikers returned to the trailhead. They hurriedly boarded the waiting shuttle or ran for their vehicles.

Brandy waved to the departing hikers, then ducked inside the office with Stefan close behind her. Randy was standing behind the counter smiling "I see you found her."

"Yes, I did. Thanks for your help, sir."

The blonde-haired girl grinned at Brandy. "If I were you, I wouldn't forget about him too often, or someone might just lure him away."

Her light copper brows drew together, a little line digging itself between them. Brandy tilted her head up and looked at him quizically.

"I stopped by here looking for you when you failed to show at the Highline Trailhead the other morning. Guess you forgot me." He shrugged and tilted his chin toward the counter. "The girls gave me a hard time about it."

"Oh, is that the way of it?" Her mouth set in a thin line, she stared up at him, then looked sharply back at the girls. "I don't think any of you know what you'd be getting into with this one." Brandy jerked her thumb toward Stefan. "Don't let his handsome face fool you. He's a devil." She wound her hand through his arm, turned, and led him out the door.

Chapter Six
Talking Is Over-Rated

"Okay, Mr. Talltree, what did you want to talk about?" Brandy said, her voice dangerously calm. Stepping off the path, she walked toward a bench nestled in a clump of trees a few yards from the building.

"Us." He followed, then turned her to face him and experimentally ran his hands slowly up and down her arms. She didn't stop him, so he took that as an encouraging sign.

"Relationships. I'm no good at them." He shook his head. "I've had some very bad experiences. It's no excuse, but that's why I acted so badly the last time we were together. There's a lot of truth to what you said at the rock." Stefan stepped away from her and unconsciously dug the toe of his boot in the soft ground.

"Sure, and what are you going to do about it?" she said, flipping her long, curly red hair over her shoulder, her chin jutting a little higher than necessary.

He sighed quietly. "Let's start over. I'd like to take you up on your offer to teach me to hunt. You're aware it won't be pretty. Probably much like an addict's withdrawal from his drug of choice."

He wasn't sure this was the way to go. However, trying to get blood from a hospital or mail order was more difficult here than where he'd lived previously. The necessary forms and permits were a lot tougher to get post-September 11th. Questions he couldn't answer or tracking he didn't want to participate in left him in a quandary.

"Don't doubt it a bit, but like an addict, the choice is yours. You have to want to change your lifestyle. No one can do it for you."

"I know." He linked his fingers through hers as they walked to the parking lot. Stopping at her SUV, she leaned into him, brushing a soft, lingering kiss across his lips.

Encouraged, he banded a heavily muscled arm around her. "How about we meet for a moonlight walk before I go to work?"

Tugging free of his embrace, she took out a piece of paper and a pen from her backpack. She scribbled down something, then handed it to him. "Here is my address and phone number. Why don't you pick me up about seven tonight?"

A wide grin spread across his face. He tucked the paper in the front pocket of his jeans. "Great, I'll see you then." He opened the door, and she slid in the driver's seat. Giving her enough time to settle in, he closed the car door, watching her drive off before climbing into his truck.

****

Stefan opened the door to his cabin, toed off his boots, and strode across the hardwood floor to the bedroom. Stripping where he stood, he stepped into the shower to wash off the day's grime. He reached for a towel to dry off and walked to the closet, looking for something to wear. *Man, I'd better do laundry or I'll be running around naked.* The dirty clothes hamper was full, and the closet was empty except for one pair of jeans and a dark burgundy sweater.

Dressed, he picked the pace up a bit, grabbed his truck keys off the dresser, and drove over to Kalispell. Brandy's cottage was small, painted light blue, and accented by white shutters. A multihued stone walkway meandered its way to the front door. Colorful irises followed the contour of the walkway. Pansies brightened the planter beneath the purple ash tree on the left side of the yard. Red and white geraniums overflowed from the window boxes.

I wonder if she did the landscaping herself. Glancing at his watch, he noticed it was only six. *Hmmm, do I go back to the truck and wait, come back later, or knock on the door? Aw hell, I am already here. I want to see her, early or not.* He knocked on the door. She answered in black sweat pants, a thin pink tank top, and wet hair dripping all over the floor. *Christ, she was beautiful.*

"You're a bit early, aren't you?" She opened the door wider, inviting him in. "Sit wherever you like. I'll be ready shortly."

"Need any help?" he offered hopefully, watching the way her curved hips swayed. Her unrestrained, firm breasts bounced under the thin top as she turned and crossed the carpeted floor, barefoot, on her way to the bedroom. *God, what a great ass.*

"No, I can still dress myself, but thanks." She shut the bedroom door firmly.

"Yeah, but can you undress yourself?" he muttered under his breath. *That girl knows what I'm thinking before I do.* While it was a little disconcerting, surprisingly he didn't mind the feeling.

"Okay, I'm ready." She brushed by him, smelling of flowers and cotton candy. Dressed in black jeans and a snug red scoop-neck sweater, she'd used a red ribbon to tie her hair back in a ponytail.

He drew in her scent as she passed by him. *She smells good enough to eat.* Then he attempted a nibble at her neck. Brandy giggled and shooed him away. It never seemed to cross her mind to be afraid.

****

They took his truck to the Avalanche Lake trailhead. Walking hand in hand under the rising full moon, they stopped at the rock across from the trail where they'd met and had their first fight. Stefan slid a sideways glance at her.

Brandy leaned back on the rock, one foot propped against it. She sensed that he was less at odds with himself than when they'd first met. *Why can't I just walk away? Now I understand where Hannah was coming from.* There was something strong drawing her to him. *Lord knows this won't be easy.* She felt the anger and terrible sorrow that he carried and wanted so badly to soothe him but recognized that was something his male ego wouldn't allow. She'd play it his way, for now.

Standing in front of her, he braced his hands on each side of her waist, effectively boxing her in as he had that first night. Leaning in, he pressed his lips against hers. Her warmth pressed against his cool made her shiver. He gently covered her mouth, kissing her slowly. Her heartbeat quickened.

She wrapped her arms around his neck and relaxed into him, feeling the growing excitement beneath the denim he wore. Easing back, he ran his tongue over her soft, full lips, then trailed down her neck to the pulsing hollow of her throat, kissing her gently. She stiffened.

Tilting his head back slightly, he looked into her green eyes, his voice thick with desire. "I won't hurt you."

"I know." She snuggled up tighter, running her hands under his T-shirt, tracing the well-defined muscles across his back. The wicked glint in his eyes made no difference to her.

****

Watching Brandy's eyes go dreamy, he took her face in his hands, inching them slowly up to her temples, stroking the soft, baby-fine hair there. His fingers entwined in her hair until they fisted, and he took her mouth with his again.

She moaned softly as he slid his tongue between her lips. She answered, her tongue dancing sinuously alongside his with a passion all her own. He wanted to devour her in small greedy bites. As his fangs pushed through, he pulled back. "This is never going to work. We're going to drive each other crazy."

"I believe you're right," she purred quietly, making no attempt to move away.

She'd taken him right to the edge with a kiss and the feel of her warm body against his. He sucked in a deep breath out of habit rather than need. Her tantalizing scent filled his nostrils. *Damn, I didn't need that.* He exhaled slowly and closed his eyes, trying desperately to regain control. Finally, his fangs drew back as the bloodlust waned and the burning in his throat became manageable. When he opened his eyes, she was staring at him, not in horror as he'd expected but with curiosity.

"Unless you want to find a more secluded place to continue our activities or allow me to sink my fangs into you and feast…" He grinned wickedly. "I strongly suggest we get moving." Reaching for her hand, he entwined his fingers with hers, tugging her toward the trail. Bringing her hand up to his lips, he kissed the back of her hand, then quickly released it and took off running at top speed, knowing she'd try to keep up. Instead, she paced herself well behind him. At the top of a hill several miles up the trail, he stopped and waited for her. She increased her pace to catch up.

"Better?" She looked up at him through long copper lashes as a shy smile played at the corners of her mouth.

"Yes, thanks." Leaning over, he kissed her forehead and then held her at arm's length as if memorizing every feature. She slid her hand into his, and they walked in comfortable silence, listening to the gurgling stream, chirping crickets, and the occasional wolf's song.

"Brandy, we gotta head back. I need to get ready for work. Tonight was great. I'd like to do it again…soon." Unable to stop himself, he pulled her roughly back against his chest and held her there, listening to her thundering heart.

His chest crushed against her breasts. He felt her tremble in his arms. She buried her face in his neck and breathed deeply.

"You smell like pine and campfire smoke. It's very alluring." Smiling, she wriggled away from him and tilted her head up. "How about your next night off we hunt? It's really not hard…"

Oh, darling, it sure as hell is. Stefan shifted his stance to allow a little more room for his growing problem.

"You just need to let your instincts take over," Brandy said with a wink.

Believe me, that's the last thing you want me to do right now. His lips twitched as he stood listening to her.

"Stefan, did you hear me?"

"Yeah, sorry. My mind wandered there for a minute."

"The trick is to learn to control those instincts even while feeding. Self-control you've learned while working around humans will make hunting a snap. You'll acquire a taste for the wild game. I promise." Stepping forward, she wrapped her arms around his neck. Standing on tiptoe, she touched her lips to his, then slowly eased away. "Don't want to stir you up again, now, do we?" she taunted.

"Woman, you're playing with fire, and you know it." He raised a dark brow and leaned in to nuzzle her neck teasingly, knowing he was in complete control. She didn't even flinch. "As far as hunting goes, I have Friday and Saturday nights off. Friday night after you get off, will that work? That way if I screw up, I have Saturday night to get it right or recuperate."

"I don't think that will be a problem." She chuckled and nodded her head in agreement.

The weekend seemed too far off, so on impulse he asked, "Hey, would you like to come over tomorrow evening and watch movies? I have a great home theater system. We could get to know each other, maybe play ten questions. I'll answer questions you have about me if you'll answer ten questions I want to know about you?"

"Sounds fair, but I have one stipulation—no subject is off limits."

"Nope, won't agree to that." He wasn't ready to go there yet.

"Then no deal." She paused. "But I'll come over and watch movies anyway. Fair enough?"

"That works. What time do you get off work?"

"Usually by four. I'll pick up a bite to eat and come on over. You don't mind if I eat in front of you?"

"No, not at all." He gave her directions to his cabin and then drove her home.

****

The streetlights cast amber pools of light on the darkened street as Stefan strolled down the sidewalk to work. At 11:48, he sauntered into the control room.

Cody looked at him and deliberately glanced at the clock. "I see you got a life again. Glad to see it was worth me getting up at an ungodly hour this morning to cover for you. You gonna tell me how it went, or do I have to drag it out of you?" Cody took a menacing step toward Stefan, grabbing for his arm, but only caught hold of his coat sleeve.

An amused sneer formed on Stefan's lips. *Hell would freeze over before you would be able to drag anything out of me.* He liked Cody in spite of himself, so he played along.

"Okay, okay, I'll tell." Stefan brushed Cody's hand off his coat, feigning fear. *If he only knew.* He smiled to himself. "It was good. A little uncomfortable at first, but by the end of the night…well, let's just say things look promising."

"You're going to ask her out again, right?"

67

"It's none of your business. But yes, she is coming over to watch movies tonight."

"At your place? Wow, you prepared for company? Place cleaned up, food and drink in the fridge? How about romantic music and flowers? Maybe a few candles sitting around. You know...set the stage." He grinned, winking knowingly.

"I'll be ready, but flowers and candles aren't my style." Sounded good, but Stefan really didn't know what his style was anymore, especially now that it really mattered.

The six-hour shift flew by. He made sure Rocky's music and playlist were ready when the skinny kid came in for the morning shift. Stefan walked out the station door at five minutes after six.

It was too early to head into town to pick up a few things, so he decided to go home, finish the laundry, and put it away. It didn't take long to clean up the cabin. Remembering what Cody said, he looked around, wondering if he should set the scene. Unfortunately, there wasn't much here to create any kind of ambiance. He never saw the need for more than the essentials until recently.

Pictures that hung on the cabin wall were of Stefan's favorites places in Glacier. Russ, an amateur photographer, provided the framed photos. After hanging pictures, Russ claimed it looked more like someone actually lived here rather than just existed. Toward that end, Stefan splurged and bought a theater system with surround sound and a sixty-inch 3D HD TV. The system could rattle the walls when he was in the mood.

Turning his attention back to the problem at hand,

he considered perhaps Cody was right and drove into town. First stop was a flower shop where the clerk helped him pick out a bouquet of wildflowers with a few yellow long-stemmed roses mixed in. She arranged them in a tall crystal vase, tying a burgundy ribbon near the top. Next, he visited the market, bought a couple of six packs of soft drinks, and several bottles of iced tea. Brandy always had a bottle of iced tea or bottled water in her hand. Passing by a display of fragranced candles of various colors, sizes, and shapes, he decided it couldn't hurt. Picking out a few candles with holders, he paid for everything and headed home.

While putting the purchases away, someone knocked on his door. Stefan yanked open the door. Cody stood grinning on the doorstep with a bag of ice, a bottle of wine, and a covered basket.

"What the hell are you doing here?" Stefan asked, slightly annoyed. The people he'd kept at arm's length for several months seemed to be swarming around him like mosquitoes. What was their deal?

"Tracy brought in some of her world-famous cinnamon apple tarts especially for you and Brandy." Cody held up the covered basket sheepishly. The mouth-watering scent wound around Stefan and wafted into the cabin.

Too bad that type of food doesn't taste as good as it smells anymore. Another downside to being a vampire.

"I kinda told her you were having Brandy over tonight. You can't have dessert without wine." He raised the bottle of wine, wiggling his eyebrows, grinning. "Last, but not least, you have to chill this wine, so I brought ice and a bucket to put it in."

Stefan opened the door wider to allow Cody inside the cabin. "I do know what I'm doing. This isn't my first rodeo," he said stiffly, then his voice softened. "But I really appreciate all this, and I'll thank Tracy tomorrow. Now, Brandy will be here soon. You can't be here when she arrives. Got it?"

"Yeah, yeah, we just wanted to make sure you didn't screw it up again." He hooked his thumbs in his belt loops, rocked back on his heels, and looked around. "You fixed this place up nice."

"I know. Now get out!" Stefan grabbed Cody's arm, spun him around, and shoved him out the door, closing it behind him. Stefan watched out the window as Cody strolled down the path whistling, hands in his pockets. Stefan shook his head and blew out a breath. "Shit, there's just no discouraging that man."

Stefan held a couple of candles in one hand, wondering just how to…set the scene. He decided to put a candle on the tables at each end of the leather couch, one candle in the middle of the breakfast bar, and he set two on top of the entertainment center across the room. Opening the DVD player, he found one of his favorite CDs still inside. He pushed play and the room filled with strains of a soft, relaxing guitar instrumental.

Candles lit, he stood back to admire his work. The flames cast shadows against the wall, seeming to sway in time to the music. *Not a bad start.* He walked to the fireplace, struck a match against the stone hearth, and tossed it into the crumpled newspaper. Flames curled out of the paper, licking the sides of the dried kindling. Smoke billowed up the chimney as the blue-tinged orange flames raced to the larger pieces of pine, crackling and hissing as the blaze reached higher, warming the room.

Movement outside the front window caught his attention. Brandy picked her way up the path. Large wet snowflakes swirled around her. He greeted her at the door, reaching for her elbow as she stepped inside. She stopped and leaned over to remove her boots. When she bent over, he couldn't help but notice her backside. *Round, firm, and...this kind of thinking will get me in all kinds of trouble.* He averted his eyes, tuning into what she was saying.

"Boy, this snow storm came out of nowhere. Wasn't it just yesterday morning we enjoyed a great hike in the sunshine?" She laughed, shaking the snow out of her hair. "Springtime in the Rockies."

He took her parka and hung it in the closet. "I'll get you a towel to dry your hair," he said over his shoulder, walking down the hallway to the bathroom. Grabbing a towel, he silently returned, stopping in the doorway, and leaned his shoulder against the doorframe, watching Brandy.

She wandered around the room. It was tidy but masculine with polished hardwood floors and lodge-style furnishings. Brandy touched the vase of flowers as her gaze wandered to the lit candles placed around the room. Her eyes lingered on a guitar sitting in its uniquely carved wooden stand in the corner.

"What a wonderful place. Do you play?" She nodded toward the guitar.

"Thanks. Yes, I do."

She crossed the room, kneeling in front of the guitar. "Gibson? Is that mother-of-pearl inlay on the neck?"

"Sure is. Do you play?"

"No, I tried several times but just didn't seem to have a talent for it. Enjoy listening though. Would you play something tonight?" she asked, getting to her feet.

"Maybe later." He eyed the bag in her hand. "Your food is getting cold." He motioned to the breakfast bar. "Have a seat and enjoy your dinner. I've cola and root beer in the fridge along with regular and raspberry iced tea. What's your pleasure?"

Eyeing him speculatively, she asked, "Since when does a vampire have soft drinks and iced tea in his fridge? Blood, yes, but soft drinks?" She raised a sleek red brow in question. A teasing smile played at the corners of her mouth. "Thanks. I'll take a raspberry iced tea."

"For the record, I keep my blood in the freezer in case my guests are squeamish." A laugh rumbled deep in his chest.

"And just how many guests have you lured to your humble abode?"

"Oh, let's see…at last count…one," he said dryly.

She sniffed, looking around the kitchen. "Do I smell…" She sniffed again, one eyebrow raised. "Tracy's world-famous cinnamon apple tarts?"

"Yep, sure do. She baked them especially for you, actually." He shrugged again and shoved his hands in his pockets.

"For me?"

"Apparently my coworkers have very little faith in my ability to entertain a woman. Earlier this afternoon, I opened the door to find Cody standing on my porch with a bottle of wine—dessert wine, he claimed—a bag of ice, an ice bucket, and Tracy's homemade tarts."

Brandy burst out laughing, then covered her mouth,

trying to stifle the laughter. "Do you have any idea how hard it is to get those tarts? You have to order several days in advance." She waved her hand toward the counter where the tarts sat in the basket. "And you get them in one day. She must really like you."

"Or feel sorry for me. I've gone from being the strange, scary midnight DJ rarely seen during daylight hours to everyone's favorite charity case. You're to blame, you know. It all changed when you attended the ball game."

She hopped up on the stool, reached into her bag, pulled out a chicken sandwich, and took a bite, smoothing out the bag to set the sandwich on. "You're welcome," she called over her shoulder. "You're the one who invited me to the softball game. It is a small town, after all."

Moving around the breakfast bar, he said sarcastically, "I have plates." Taking a plate out of the cupboard, he slid the sandwich from the bag to the plate, crumpled the bag, and tossed it in the garbage.

"Sorry. I wasn't sure what creature comforts you'd have."

"I have glasses too. Wine glasses, to be exact, just in case you were wondering." He winked at her and walked around behind her, laying his hands on her shoulders, slowly sliding them down her arms. Stefan leaned into her, enjoying her warmth. "I'm glad you came," he whispered against her ear.

He sauntered back into the kitchen and grabbed a crystal glass from the cupboard and a bottle of iced tea out of the fridge. Setting the glass in front of her, he added a few ice cubes and poured the tea over the ice with a flourish. Then he handed her a napkin and sat across from her. "What brought you to Montana?"

She took another bite of her sandwich, chewed thoughtfully, then took a sip of iced tea. "The desire to travel, I suppose. See new things and get away from a controlling, possessive Irishman."

"Oh, so you have a boyfriend?" he asked, a knot forming in his stomach.

She'd taken another bite of sandwich and nearly choked. "No!" she sputtered. "We were high school sweethearts. After graduation, he expected to marry me. He wasn't what I was looking for in a mate…ah, man. Like my sister, I applied to a college in America, was accepted, and I left."

"You're not involved with anyone in Ireland or here?" Stefan felt that knot ease.

"Relax. I'm not involved with anyone at the moment but you. Is that what you want to hear?" She narrowed her eyes, watching him over the rim of her iced tea as she took another sip.

"Sure is." He shifted in his seat, glad to get that out of the way. "Your sister still in the States?"

"Aye, she lives in Maine. Hannah attended Yale as an exchange student. A cyber security firm grabbed her up right after college. She's been there ever since." Brandy popped the final bite of her sandwich in her mouth, picked up the plate, and put it in the sink.

"Wow, I'm impressed. That's not an easy college to get into."

Brandy padded back to her seat and settled in. "Ma and Da always insisted on a good education for us. We've relatives that are well connected. They pulled strings to get her admitted. She was an excellent student. Even before graduation, she got the job offer of her dreams that she couldn't refuse—working for Black Hawk Cyber in Maine. She never returned to Ireland. When she was out on her own, she called every week with tales of what she'd seen and done. Then she met a man, and everything changed. Her calls were sporadic. She became secretive."

Stefan washed and dried the dish, sliding it back in the cupboard. "What happened?"

"It got to a point where she rarely returned my phone calls. When she did call, she was distant and evasive. Three months passed. Ma and Da didn't hear a thing from her, and they were worried. I went to check on her."

"I don't mean to pry. The couple of weeks you were gone, did that have to do with your sister?"

"It did. I could tell something was up the last time she called. My job was crazy, but as soon as I could, I caught the first plane to Misty Harbor for a surprise visit. But the surprise was on me. I arrived on her wedding day immediately after she'd said 'I do.'"

"Wow, that must have been a shock. Did you know the relationship was serious?"

"Not exactly, but she seemed glad to see me. Tristian, her husband, was cordial enough but distant. It was a small wedding with his family and friends in attendance." Brandy paused. *Better not tell any more about what I actually learned.* "Hannah introduced me, assured me everything was fine, and promised to call more often. She seemed happy. I left it at that and flew back."

Stefan nodded, rounded the counter, and sat in the chair next to her.

Brandy shrugged, her forehead creased. "She won't

let me tell Ma and Da about her marriage. That bothers me. Hannah says she'll tell them when the time is right. She swore me to secrecy."

"Won't they be upset when they do find out?"

She threw her hands up in the air. "Oh, upset doesn't begin to describe the fireworks that will go off. Not to mention how hurt they'll be. In Ireland, a wedding is a big deal, a huge celebration."

Brandy's eyes clouded with sadness and worry, but Stefan said nothing.

Shaking her head as if to dislodge unpleasant thoughts, she shifted in her chair. "Okay, enough about me. I want to hear about you."

"You're much more interesting than I am."

"Don't think so." Brandy grinned. "Tell me about your family."

"I don't really have one." He got up and walked across the room to the entertainment center that spanned the entire living room wall. "Last winter, I built this and that corner hutch over there out of aspen during a snow storm that nearly buried us." Stefan slid his fingers over the smooth wood.

"I remember that one. It was just before Christmas last year."

"That's the one."

"I'd planned to fly to Ireland for Christmas. The frigging storm made travel impossible. Ma and Da were so disappointed. Now, tell me about your family," she insisted.

"No," he said flatly. "I don't have any family. End of story."

Her eyes rounded in surprise, but she didn't miss a beat. "Okay, tell me what brought you here."

"Why don't you pick out a movie for us to watch? They're in the corner cabinet, arranged in alphabetical order." He waved his hand toward the cabinet in the corner.

She sighed, moving toward the cabinet, then abruptly turned around to face him. "I'd rather hear you play." Pointing toward the other corner where his guitar stood.

Relieved that she'd dropped her line of questioning, he reached over, turned off the DVD player, and picked up the guitar.

Brandy plucked a coaster from its holder and sat her tea glass on the oak table in front of the couch. She sat down and curled her legs up under her.

Stefan sat cross-legged on the floor just below her, leaning against the couch. "What would you like to hear?"

"Anything. I liked the instrumental that was playing when I arrived. Can you play something like that?"

"I can." He played a couple of the songs that were actually on that CD, then several more that were not. She seemed to enjoy the music so much that he decided to risk playing a song he'd been working on. "Stay right here. I'll be right back."

He ambled to the entertainment center and opened the side door. Several sheets of music fluttered in the air, landing lightly on the floor. He gathered the sheets, thumbing through them until he found the one he wanted. "This song still needs some work, but I'd like to know what you think."

As she watched him, her eyes lit up with understanding. "You write your own music?"

"Sometimes." Checking the notes on the sheet of paper, he closed his eyes and concentrated on the song, its feeling and story. His callused fingers slid over the strings, coaxing out a haunting melody. Finished, he slowly opened one eye, then the other, to take in Brandy's expression. Her eyes were closed, her body swaying to the final chords of the song.

A little sigh slipped from her lips as she blinked her eyes open. "It doesn't need any work. It's beautiful. You are very talented." She was silent for a couple of minutes. "That was you playing on the CD."

"Guilty. Music is the one thing that brings me peace." Reaching out, he placed his guitar gently in its stand and leaned back against the couch.

She stretched her long slender legs out in front of her, then in one fluid movement, slid from the couch to the floor next to him, shoulder to shoulder. Drawing her legs up in a triangle, she wrapped her arms around them and laid her cheek on her knees. She looked up at him from under long copper-red lashes as the tip of her tongue slowly traced her pouty lips.

"You know, Stefan, every experience you've had up until this moment makes you what you are, what I find so fascinating. Any woman alive would consider herself lucky to be sitting here with you."

He raised a dark brow in disbelief. "Glad you feel that way but doubt others would. Not that it matters."

"That would be their loss." Her voice was firm and final.

Scooping an arm around her, he brought her into his lap, enjoying her delicious warmth, oddly comforted by the constant beat of her heart. He wrapped his arms around her and held her against his chest, existing only in a moment where nothing else mattered.

Unsure of how long they'd sat there, her regular breathing told him she'd fallen asleep. Stefan knew she'd been up long before sunrise this morning to lead another morning hike. It must have caught up with her. He didn't mind. This way there was no pressure or questions he didn't want to answer. Just her wonderful scent and body cuddled against him. *Could I really make this work?*

Chapter Seven
Snowbound without a Shovel

She awoke with a start and blurted, "Don't you have to be at work? I probably should start toward home."

He reluctantly released her, and she crawled out of his lap, stood, stretching her arms above her head, and rolled her head from side to side. She padded over to the window and pulled the curtain aside. "Wow, it's really snowing hard."

The snow had piled up quickly since she'd first arrived. He let out a low whistle as he joined her at the window. "I don't think you're going anywhere."

"I'm leading a sunrise hike tomorrow." She twisted the curtain in her fingers, then released it.

He shook his head. "That'll be canceled."

"I'd better call Randy anyway. See what he wants me to do."

Stefan stood behind her, his arm wrapped around her waist, mesmerized by the large feather-like snowflakes falling through the frosty air.

She ambled over to the couch and pulled her cell phone out of her purse. "I can make it home even if I can't drive."

"And just how do you propose to do that?" His raised brow formed a question mark as his inquisitive eyes continued to watch her.

She reached up, rubbing her forehead lightly with her fingertips. "Ah, I guess I was just thinking out loud again. I'm not sure what I meant. Just tired mumbling."

"It wouldn't have anything to do with your disappearance a couple weeks ago, leaving bits of your clothing on the forest floor, would it?" A sly grin tugged at the corner of his lips.

"I'm sure I don't know what you're talking about," she said primly, putting her cell phone to her ear and walking away.

While she was talking to Randy, Stefan's cell rang.

He glanced at the caller ID, frowned, and picked it up off the table. "What's up, Cody?"

"Hey, Stefan, you're coming in, right?" Cody asked anxiously.

"Of course. I'll be there in a few minutes. But you aren't going anywhere," Stefan said flatly. "Brandy's still here, and we're discussing whether she'll be staying or try to make it home."

"Don't let her leave. The roads are all closed. It's bad out there."

"Well, that makes it a moot point. I'll be in soon." Stefan disconnected the call and turned back to Brandy. "Well?"

"Randy doesn't want me going out in this storm. All the roads are closed anyway." She glanced at the phone in his hand, her brow raised.

"That was Cody. He wanted to make sure I was going to relieve him. The station is only a few hundred yards from here. Wanna come along? Otherwise you can stay here while I do my shift, then we'll see about getting you home when I get off. These spring storms don't usually last long, do they?"

She shook her head and considered his offer for a moment. "Sure, it might be fun if you won't get in trouble."

"Not a problem. Russ lets me do pretty much what I want as long as I follow the playlist. If you get tired, you can nap on the couch just outside the control room. I'll send Cody over here to crash. That way he won't bother you all night long."

"Don't want him flirting with me, huh?" She grinned wide, batted her long lashes, and flipped her cascade of long red hair over her shoulder.

"Nope, just don't want him bothering you." He took her parka out of the closet and held it out for her. "We need to get going."

Big, wet flakes fell steadily as they walked through the half foot of heavy, wet snow already on the ground. It was a quarter to midnight when Brandy and Stefan walked up to the radio station door, stomped their boots on the mat, and stepped inside. They slipped their snow boots off, leaving them in the little alcove just inside the reception area. Stefan took Brandy's coat, hung it on the rack above their boots, and motioned her forward where the lit sign over the control room door said "On Air." The light flicked off and they entered the control room.

Cody glanced up from the computer, his tired eyes filled with relief. "Finally. Good thing it's not blowing, or we'd have whiteout conditions and you wouldn't have made it in either."

"Yeah, the snow's piling up fast." Stefan shook his head, his hair slinging snow everywhere, including all over Cody. Ice crystals glistened in Cody's hair and eyeglasses.

He took his spectacles off, wiped the lenses off with a tissue, and glared at Stefan.

A smirk turned up the corner of his mouth. "Are we getting many calls about the closures and road conditions?"

"Hey! You did that on purpose." Cody glared at him, brushing the melting snow from his clothes, then stared at the puddle forming on the tile where Stefan stood.

Stefan bit back a grin, grabbed a roll of paper towels, and mopped up the floor.

"We did earlier in the evening, but they've tapered off. Seems the storm is making people nervous. It's mostly just the tourists and newcomers." Cody looked around Stefan to where Brandy was standing and winked. "Hi, Brandy."

"Nice to see you again, Cody."

He shoved Stefan out of the way, took her hand, and brought it up to his lips. "The pleasure is all mine," he said in a deep, sensual voice while he made a low sweeping bow and kissed the palm of her hand.

She batted her long eyelashes and smiled at Cody, gingerly slipping her hand from Cody's grip. If the expression on her face was any indication, she enjoyed the interaction. Stefan scowled.

"Okay, that's enough, Casanova." Stefan tossed him the keys to the cabin. "You can crash at my place tonight. That way you can shower and change before relieving me in the morning. There's leftovers in the fridge, and only eat ONE of those tarts. Understand?"

"I make no promises where Tracy's tarts are concerned." Cody smirked. "Who says I'm coming back?"

"Suit yourself, but you're not staying here." Stefan shoved Cody out the control room door and locked it.

Cody grinned through the glass door, dangled the keys and mimed laying his head on his hand, eyes closed, then mouthed, "See ya."

"That was rather rude," Brandy said sternly, then burst into giggles. "Does he always act like that?"

Still slightly irritated, Stefan shook it off and walked to her. Cupping her face in his hands, he looked into her trusting green eyes. God help him, she stirred something inside him that he thought was long dead. Leaning over and brushing his lips over hers, he whispered, "Only when females are around."

She whispered back, "If I didn't know better, I'd say you were jealous."

Stefan roared with laughter, composed himself, and asked, "Of what?" Reluctantly, he let go of her and turned back to the console, checking the time left on the song. "Hey, I have an idea. Since you're here, I could interview you at each stop set about the interesting aspects of being a park ranger in Glacier. Then we could open the phones for questions. That'll take the listeners' minds off the storm and we could have a little fun. When you get tired, I'll tell the listeners question and answer time is over and go back to regular programming. How about it?"

She rubbed her palms down the side of her pants and nibbled on her bottom lip for a beat. "Do I have to talk into the mic?"

With a half laugh, he said, "Sure, there's nothing to it. It's no different than talking to the crowd of people you take on hikes every day or just talking to me. You'll be great!"

She hesitated, twisting her hands together, picking at her fingernails. "I'm game, but personal questions are off limits, and only if you won't get in trouble."

"Russ will be fine with it. May even raise the ratings." He turned back to the console, checking the time left on the song playing and making sure another was in cue. A quick glance at the computer screen told him when the commercials were set to run, so he flipped on the mic. "Gooood morning, Whitefish. Stefan here with you on the Big Fish this stormy night. I have a special treat for you right after this." He flipped the mic off and pushed the button to play the commercial load. Watching the timer count down, he checked the songs set to play and flipped the mic switch back on. "Single-handedly, I captured a park ranger for a few hours. In return for her release in the morning, she has agreed to an interview. She'll also take your questions. Call us at 555-BIG-FISH. Until then, Fleetwood Mac on Big Fish Radio" Cutting power to the mic, he took off his headphones and turned back to Brandy, who was staring at him. "What?"

She tilted her head toward him and grinned. "What is a stop set?"

Returning her grin, he said, "A stop set is what you just heard. Normally, we back sell or front sell the songs coming up or already played, do a station ID at the top of the hour, and make sure the commercials run when scheduled. During storms, we pass along road conditions and closures. There are usually four stop sets per hour. The one at the top of the hour includes the station's call sign."

She turned in a slow circle, looking at all the equipment, then walked to the console, lightly fingering the buttons, toggles, slides, and blinking lights. "Looks like a lot to learn and remember."

"Not really. The computer handles most of it. Now, I have a question for you."

She caught her bottom lip between her teeth and narrowed her eyes. "Okay, what?

"Don't look at me like I'm going to bite you or something. I'd still like to know about your disappearance a couple of weeks ago. You dodged behind the rock and trees, then something large flew out of that area and soared across the sky. Bits of your clothes were scattered all over. Is there something you're not telling me?"

"You have your secrets and I have mine. You avoid my questions, so why should I answer yours?" she said pointedly. "Now, if you're willing to try a shot of honesty, I might be inclined to satisfy your curiosity." She tossed him a sassy smile and stepped back.

"Hey, now wait just a minute. You knew my secret without asking me. Therefore, I am assuming you're not merely human. Am I right?"

She shook her head as she drew her bottom lip through her teeth. "I'm not telling."

Ignoring her refusal to answer, he continued. "From the scattering of shredded clothes, I'd say you are a shapeshifter." He looked up at the clock. "Shit." Time for the stop set. He grabbed his headphones, flipped the switch, and motioned for her to step closer to the mic. "You're back on the Big Fish. That's quite a storm we've got raging out there. Good news though—weather service says it'll be out of here shortly after sunrise. Until then, state patrol asks that you stay off the roads. Now, as promised, Brandy from the park service is here to answer questions and tell us some of Glacier's secrets. Brandy, what's your favorite part of the job?"

She flinched, drew in a breath, then stepped closer to the mic. "Meeting new people and showing them the wonders of Glacier National Park. Protecting the environment and wildlife is also a big part of my job."

"Ever shoot anyone?"

Her eyes narrowed and she sent him a hostile glare. "No, not yet." Her eyes flicked up to his menacingly. "But that could change. Only kidding. I take that part of my job seriously and am very thankful that I've never had to draw my weapon."

"Me too," Stefan said with an exaggerated sigh.

The response from the listeners was overwhelming. Stefan and Brandy took calls until four thirty in the morning. When he looked across the counter, she was asleep in the chair, elbows braced in front of her on the counter and chin leaning on her hands. He crept quietly to her side and swept her into his arms. She reached up, put her arms around his neck, and kissed the side of his throat sleepily as he carried her to the couch just outside the control room. Laying her down gently, he covered her with the bright-orange, white, and yellow handmade afghan slung over the back of the couch.

Returning to the control room, he flipped the mic on. "It looks like question and answer time is over. Our guest has succumbed to sleep. Thank you all for your questions. I hope you enjoyed the impromptu programming tonight. Now sit back and relax with the unique blend of your favorite local and independent artists only here on Big Fish Radio."

There were several more phone calls wanting to

know when the park ranger would return. In the morning, he left a note for Russ, telling him what he'd done and suggesting there may be interest in such programming. The blue light started flashing and he picked up the phone. "Big Fish Radio, what's your pleasure?"

"I believe you've detained one of my park rangers and kept her up most of the night. Consequently, I don't think she'll be much use to me this morning." Randy laughed. "Stefan, let her know she's got the day off. I'll expect her bright and early tomorrow morning. After you get off, you two get some sleep and enjoy your day."

"Randy? You caught the show?"

"Yeah, I caught most of it. Great idea. It sounded like there was a lot of interest among the listeners too. Tell Russ I'll be talking to him."

"Will do. You have a great day and get some sleep yourself." Stefan signed off, checked the playlist, and pulled up the current weather and road reports for Cody just as he came waltzing in the door.

"Thought I'd relieve you a bit early so you could enjoy some quality time with your woman." He looked back at the sleeping Brandy and winked. "Take her home."

"She's not my woman yet. We're just…" Stefan trailed off, trying to figure out just what it was that they were doing. He knew Cody wouldn't let it drop. The man was standing there with his arms crossed, leaning back against the console and staring at Stefan with raised brows. Stefan figured he'd better come up with something quickly.

"…Enjoying each other's company." Stefan finally

said to appease Cody.

"That woman is in love with you, kid. Whether you want to admit it or not, the feeling appears to be mutual. I don't know what happened to you in the past to scare you off women or, for that matter, the human race. Don't let it ruin what you have with her. You're one lucky bastard, and you don't even know it. Everyone but you can see that the two of you are meant to be together. Now get outta here."

Stefan opened his mouth to argue with Cody, but he'd already turned back to the console and was preparing for his shift. Stefan opened the control room door and walked out to the couch where Brandy lay sleeping. He sat down gently on the couch. Not wanting to disturb her, he just watched her sleep as the wind howled outside the station. *What is going on between us? Affection? Attraction? Yeah, there is some of that. Lust and Passion? Yep, there's a lot of that. Neither of us is looking for happily ever after. Or are we? Hell no, I've seen what even trying for that dream does to people, and I want no part of it.*

He kissed her cheek, and she opened her eyes. "Are we done?"

"Yes, we're done. Let's head to the cabin and you can go back to sleep. Randy called and said you're off today, but he expects you early tomorrow morning. He also said he liked the show." Helping her put her coat on, he slid his arm down her back and under her knees, then put the other one around her shoulders, bringing her to his chest.

"Stefan, put me down," she squealed. "You're not carrying me all the way to the cabin." She wriggled out of his hold and put her feet on the ground. "What would people think?"

He bit back a grin. "They already know we spent the night together. What difference does it make if I carry you to the cabin? Would they think I drained your blood until you were too weak to walk?"

She slapped at him as a laugh bubbled out between her lips. "You guard your secret too well for that."

He slung his arm around her and nudged her toward the door. "Speaking of secrets, when we get back to the cabin, I want to hear all about yours." They pushed open the door and were surprised to see that a deep blanket of sparkling snow covered the rooftops, surrounded cars, and piled a couple feet deep against fences. Cody's footprints were the only marks in the snow.

"What a beautiful morning," Brandy said, her warm breath frosty in the cold air as they walked toward the cabin, their boots crunching on the freshly fallen snow.

By the time they reached the cabin, they were soaked to the skin, and Brandy's teeth were chattering.

"Take off your clothes..." Her eyes flew open as a crimson blush crept to her cheeks. He laughed and finished the sentence. "...in the bedroom. There should be some clean sweats in the top dresser drawer. Might be a bit big, but you can cinch up the drawstring. At least they're dry and warm." While she dressed, he tossed several pieces of wood into the fireplace, then coaxed the glowing embers from the night before to life. By the time she returned, a crackling fire warmed the room.

She grabbed a pillow off the couch and lay down in front of the fire. "I'll watch the fire. You go get out of those wet clothes. There was another pair of sweats in the drawer, so I tossed them on the bed for you."

In the short time he took to change and return to the living room, she was sound asleep. He scooped her up and carried her to his bedroom, gently laying her on the bed and pulling a comforter over her. Leaving a blanket between them, he lay beside her and wrapped his arms around her, enjoying the feel of her warm body next to his, imagining her naked body under him. She moaned, rolled over, and cuddled against him as she continued sleeping.

The sun was high in the sky when Brandy awoke, draped across Stefan's bare chest, their legs entwined. He'd simply held her, nothing more. Not because he didn't want to, but because the chances of getting what he wanted were better by not taking advantage of the situation.

She sat up quickly, holding the blanket around her. "What are you doing?" She demanded, then glanced under the blanket.

"Just laying here waiting for you to wake up. Relax. We are still completely dressed, and your virtue is still intact, in case you were wondering." He grinned outrageously and blocked her arm as she attempted to swipe at him.

"You've only your sweat pants on," she pointed out, watching him warily.

"Yes, and you seemed to enjoy that this morning." He raised his arm up to fend off another attack if necessary.

She laughed, absently running her soft delicate fingers across his chest. "That I did. Still do." Her hand wandered lower to the waistband of his sweat pants.

"Better be careful. You're treading on dangerous ground," he warned, laying his hand over hers. "I'm more than willing to continue this, but I don't think you are."

"What? Oh!" She was concentrating on his eyes, not where her hand was going. She jerked it back, color rising in her cheeks.

Resisting the desire to smile, he rolled over on his side, propped himself up on his elbow, and blinked at her. "Are we still going hunting this weekend?" She settled against him, comfortable that they were both mostly dressed and that he'd made it clear the next move was hers.

"Sure, the snow will probably be gone by then. It may be muddy, but that makes it easier to track our prey." She shifted, peering up at him.

On a hunch, he asked, "Will you be hunting in your human form or shifting into the form you won't discuss with me?"

"Ah, well, I always hunt as…" Her eyes widened. She stared at him and slid out of bed. "You tried to trick me." She turned, standing stiffly, teeth clinched, hands fisted on her hips, green eyes glittering with malice.

"Oh, come on, Brandy," he said smoothly. "If you don't hunt in human form, I'll see for myself this weekend. What are you afraid of, my reaction? I'm a bloodthirsty vampire for God's sake. Whatever you are will make no difference to me."

"It might," she said nervously, gnawing on her bottom lip.

"Damn, woman. I knew you weren't human that first night I saw you. Then you disappeared behind the rock and flew off into the night sky too quickly for me to make out exactly what you were. I'm still here. Even went looking for you, didn't I?"

"Aye, you did. It's just that I've not...shown that part of myself to anyone since I left Ireland. I'm not sure where this relationship is going, but I'd like to give it a chance. But if you...I mean...if..."

"It seems we both have a problem with trust. I understand, but we can work through that and see where it leads us. Your instincts told you I was a vampire. To me that was a dead giveaway you weren't human."

She sighed deeply and gazed into his dark eyes. "I'm a gryphon, complete with beak, talons, paws, tail, and rainbow-hued wings. Happy now?"

"Wow!" he paused for a beat. "Ecstatic, actually. I've never seen one. Thought they were myths." He got to his feet and took a step toward her. "Gryphons are real?"

Surprised by his reaction, she put her hand up to stop him. "I could say the same about vampires."

"You knew better and weren't the least bit shaken when you confronted me. When do I get to see you shift?"

Totally ignoring his last question, she continued, "That's because, being from Ireland, myths, legends, and magic are all intertwined. Growing up, you're never sure what is fact or fiction. What most consider fiction, I know to be fact. No, you didn't surprise me. But interest me you did."

"Ah, so you have a taste for the unique, maybe even the dangerous?"

"That I do, and not ashamed to admit it." She coyly batted her beautiful green eyes at him, her heart rate increasing.

The corner of his mouth twitched as he heard her heartbeat and scented her arousal.

He had all those feelings churning inside him again, desires he had no business having toward her. Nevertheless, he couldn't help himself. He reached out to her, and she slithered against him, wrapping her arms around his neck, breathing a lingering kiss there. Holding her tight, he felt the curve of her breast and the firmness of her nipples against his bare chest. The heat of her intimately against his growing problem was more than he could handle after spending the night with her wrapped around him. "Brandy," he whispered huskily, "You are driving me insane. Vampires are extremely carnal creatures. I want you. Don't deny me or yourself." Stefan traced her jawline with his finger, watching the desire burn in her eyes. He leaned over and nibbled along her jaw and flicked the tip of his tongue along the side of her neck.

****

Oh God... Brandy rubbed her body against him, then paused before she shoved hard against his chest, then pushed him away. Talk about mixed messages. Confused, she needed to stop, she had to stop, but she didn't want him to stop. She wanted to feel his hands caressing her body, his mouth on hers, and she wanted him, all of him. With tears threatening, she blinked rapidly and wiped her eyes. "I can't. I just can't. You don't understand."

He dragged his hand through his hair and rubbed at the tension knot at the back of his neck. "Then for God's sake explain it to me. You want me as bad as I want you. I can feel your heat, smell your arousal, and hear your heart race when we touch. There's an attraction, something primal between us. What's stopping you? Are you afraid of me, of what I am?"

"No, absolutely not. I've never felt like this about anyone. For my kind, these feelings must be mutual before I can give myself, and they're not, at least not on your part." She felt his desire and confusion, yet she couldn't...just couldn't.

"What the hell is that supposed to mean?"

"Gotta go." She moved the curtain aside and peered out the window, blinking at the bright sun. "The roads are passable, and the snow is melting quickly."

"No, wait. Don't leave like this."

"I have to," she insisted. "We both need some distance right now. See you after your shift on Saturday morning. Meet you here." She reached up, touching her lips to his, lingering longer than she meant to, then turned and sprinted out the door.

Grabbing the broom and snow shovel, he followed. "You can't go anywhere until we dig your car out."

She brushed the snow from her vehicle, and he dug a path to the street in silence. He opened the car door for her. As she started to climb in, he grabbed her arm, pulling her to him, and brought his mouth down hard on hers and lingered there, then shoved her back. "Don't tell me how I feel." He whirled around, and without a backward glance, he strode back to the house and slammed the door. Snow whooshed off the roof and covered the newly scooped path in his wake.

She sank into the car seat, leaning her elbows on the steering wheel, and put her head in her hands. *Sweet Jesus, what am I going to do?* He was her future. She knew and accepted that fact. Getting him to a place where he could believe and accept it too would be the most difficult thing she'd ever done. He trusted no one. The previous women in his life had left him scarred and bitter. This was the only explanation she could come up with that would garner those kinds of reactions. He deserved better, and she was determined to see that he got it, one way or the other. But she wondered at what cost to both of them.

A soft rap on the car window made her jump. Stefan stood outside the window, hands shoved in his pockets and eyes cast downward. She rolled the window down. His gaze flicked up to hers.

"Brandy, I'm sorry. I had no reason to snap at you."

Pleased yet surprised, she reached up and placed her warm hand on his chilled cheek. He put his hand over hers and squeezed, rubbing his cheek against her palm. What she knew of vampires was at this point very little, but she knew that they never showed weakness or vulnerability nor humbled themselves.

Strength and power equated to respect in the vampire world. If a vampire wavered on either, he was killed by his own kind. At least that's what she'd learned from her recent research. He was a lone vampire as far as she could tell, and that was rare, but when it came to Stefan, nothing surprised her.

She knew apologies didn't come easy from him, so they meant more. "It's all right. We'll forget that part and remember the wonderful time we had together."

"Thanks. I'll see you on Saturday, if not before," he added hopefully.

By the way he shifted from foot to foot, she could tell he wanted to say more. But for some reason he said nothing else. "I think we both need a couple days to cool off and calm down. Then we'll talk. Even if the subjects make us both uncomfortable. See you Saturday."

Chapter Eight
Born to Screw with a Man's Head

It wasn't what he wanted to hear. His temper flared, but this time he ruthlessly shut it down. She wasn't like anyone he'd ever known, and he'd just have to learn patience. He watched her drive off. This time he strode up the snow-covered walk to the open door, stepped inside, and closed it quietly.

Frustrated with himself, her, and everyone in general, he ran the trails, then walked to work. Arriving at the station, he shoved the control room door open. "What is it with women? Are they born to screw with a man's head?"

Cody shrugged. "Well, hello to you too. Man's asked those questions since the dawn of time. As far as I know, no one has ever solved that particular puzzle. Though I think it is better to have one causing you problems than no woman at all. Right?"

"Not necessarily." Stefan yanked the programming sheets off the counter and plopped down in a chair.

"What's Brandy done now?"

"Nothing really. I think it's more me and my reactions that set off fireworks between us."

Cody nodded his head in agreement. "If you need to talk, I'm always available. By the way, Russ wants to see you after your shift. Would you mind taking the control room a bit early? I've got a shitload of commercials to cut."

"Not a problem. Better you than me." Stefan grinned wickedly.

Cody flipped him off and disappeared out the door.

The rest of the shift was uneventful. Russ arrived at five in the morning with the tall, skinny kid in tow. He opened the door quietly and nodded toward the kid. "Rocky's going to cover the rest of your shift and part of mine. Join me in my office, would you?"

Entering his office, Stefan asked, "What's up, boss?"

Russ motioned to a chair against the wall. "I spent a lot of yesterday fielding calls about your park ranger segment. You generated a lot of interest with that show. Nice job."

Relaxed, Stefan settled into the chair, relieved he wasn't in trouble. "It was just a spur of the moment thing. The storm stranded Brandy at my cabin, and she didn't have to work today. She opted to come to the station with me. We had fun with it and thought the listeners did too."

"Are you planning to have her on again?"

"Not really sure. I didn't know whether it was something you'd be interested in."

"Hell yes, we're interested. Ratings, man. Can't remember the last time something generated so much listener response, especially during the midnight shift."

"I'll talk to her about it this weekend and let you know."

"Fair enough. It's six. Go on home and get some sleep."

"Thanks. I'll get back to you."

A couple of days passed. Stefan ran extra laps on

the trails. It helped him sort out the situation with Brandy. How could a woman make a man so miserable? He'd chosen the solitary life for a reason.

No vampire politics or death orders and no chance he'd ever run into Serena, the vampire that turned him, again. He was sure he'd rip her throat out. This would subject him to severe punishment by the Vampire Council for killing one of their own.

He was surprised at the hatred that boiled up within him, especially after the love they'd shared. Scratch that—he'd thought he'd felt. To her, he was just a toy, and in the end, he'd paid a terrible price.

He'd learned the vampire rules the hard way. Captured, beaten, and dragged before the Council as a rouge vampire, they recognized him as a young vampire without a responsible sire. Because of his emerging talents and bloodline, the Council assigned him a mentor to ensure he understood the rules he must abide by or die.

His mentor was the Council's vampire assassin. At his hands, Stefan learned the Vampire Code, studied the value of silence, speed, and agility, and acquired a cache of deadly weapons along with the ability to use them. He learned to take orders, perform without question, and wield the magic borne in his blood, which resulted in handsome rewards.

When he turned from that way of life, he took his cache of weapons and secreted them away in a hidden closet in his cabin. That part of his life was long over, and it was the last time anyone had required his obedience or tried to control him. Not that Brandy fell into that category, but answering to anyone for his behavior or having anyone defy him was simply…

difficult. That was something he would have to learn to accept if he wanted Brandy in his life.

He pulled out his cell phone and called her. After four rings, her voicemail picked up. He left a message. "If you'd like to join me for a trail run, there's no pressure. Meet me at the rock around eight tonight. If not, I understand." As an afterthought, he added what she would consider a challenge. "You're only a gryphon and not fast enough to keep up with a vampire." He paused for a beat. "If nothing else, see you Saturday morning." Touching the screen, he ended the call, hoping the challenge would be too much for her to resist.

That night, she wasn't at the rock. Disappointed, he started his run. Behind him, a burst of wind and the thunderous beat of large wings spun him around. A large gryphon landed gracefully on the trail, tucking her multicolored wings at her side. He let out a low whistle. She was absolutely beautiful.

Brandy had the head, shoulders, and front talons of an eagle, the rest of her body and hindquarters of a lion, covered in coppery-colored fur and feathers. Her huge green eyes stared at him.

Standing about a foot and a half taller than Stefan's six foot seven, she unfolded her wings and took flight again, circling overhead in a challenge for him to chase her. He took off running up the trail at top speed. She flew above and slightly in front of him.

They spent a couple of hours on the trails. She landed in front of him, folded her wings over her back, and padded over to him. Gently, she laid her beak on his shoulder and blinked at him. He raised his arms and wound them around her, burying his face in the soft feathers of her neck. "You are ravishing," he murmured, inhaling the clean, fresh scent of pine wafting from her.

She nuzzled against him and stepped back. With two powerful beats of her wings, she was airborne. The breeze that swayed the treetops in the forest below swirled around her as she soared over the canopy. Stretching her wings further, she pulled out of the glide to spiral higher and higher into the star-strewn sky. Up there, she was free, leaving any earthbound problems behind. He envied her. *Be careful what you wish for, Stefan!*

Shit, did she just say that in my mind or what? Damn, she's full of surprises. How cool. As he watched her disappear into the night, pride swelled within him along with protectiveness and a long-buried desire to possess her completely.

****

A half hour before midnight, he yanked open the control room door and strolled in. "Hi ya, Cody. What's shak'n? Sorry about the other night."

Cody glanced up over the newspaper he was reading. "That's okay. Women will do that to you. Not much happening here. Computer giving me fits again, but that's nothing new." He grinned. "Things better?"

"Yeah, I think so. Who the hell knows with women?" Stefan shrugged and picked up the playlist.

"If you don't mind a bit of advice, need to control your temper. Be open and honest with that beautiful lady of yours. Keep messing around and you'll lose her."

Stefan raised a brow and narrowed his eyes, studying Cody intently. "This from a confirmed bachelor?"

"No, from a man who lost the only woman he ever loved. Watching you these past few weeks reminds me of myself years ago. Don't make the same mistakes I did, son."

Stefan couldn't believe his ears. Cody in love with only one woman? He opened his mouth to speak.

Cody shook his head. "Don't ask. It's something I never discuss. But I can't stand by, watching you screw up, and not say anything." He picked up his coat, slung it over his slumped shoulders, and walked slowly out the door without another word.

Chapter Nine
A Meeting of Fangs and Wings

Saturday morning, Brandy sat on the porch step dressed in jeans, a dark-blue sweater layered over a navy T-shirt, and well-worn hiking boots as Stefan arrived home after shift.

"Good morning, beautiful. You're up early." He leaned over and kissed her, giving her ponytail a tug. "Glad you could make it."

Her eyes lit up as she laughed. "Me too."

"Give me a second to change into my hiking boots, and I'm ready to go." He unlocked the door and held it open for her. "Wanna wait inside?"

"No thanks. It's a glorious morning. Just listen to the birds and smell that crisp, clean mountain air. I love it here." She took a deep breath and watched as a pair of red-tailed hawks screamed, declaring their territory and soaring high over the meadow in search of their morning meal.

"Be right back." He sped into the house, leaving the door open, and switched into hiking boots he'd left by the front door last night.

Returning to the porch, he locked the door behind him. "Where we going?"

"Just outside the northwest boundary of the park. I'll drive. It's about an hour from here." She reached into her pocket and pulled out the keys. "We'll have to hike part of the way in. That will give us plenty of time to explore the area during the day—there's plenty of cover—and then hunt at dusk."

"Fine by me." He opened her SUV door and waited for her to get in, then vaulted over the hood and got in on the passenger side.

"Show off." She grinned.

"Guilty as charged. Just trying to impress my lady," he said with a sly smile.

Surprised at his change in attitude and candor, she chuckled as blood rushed to her cheeks. "Your lady, huh? I don't impress easily, so save it for the hunt."

Brandy turned the vehicle onto Highway 93 toward Eureka. She drove with the window partway down, the wind whipping a few strands of hair that escaped the ribbon she'd tied around her ponytail.

Stefan reached out and wound a curl around his finger, watching the sun glint off it, then let the strand fall and tugged another piece loose. "Don't know why you tie it back. I like it free, falling over your shoulders and down your back."

"Just like a man," she scoffed.

Holding the strands between thumb and forefinger, he brought the wisps of hair to his nose. He closed his eyes, nostrils flared. "It's so soft and smells like fresh lemons and honeysuckle. I like running my hands through it."

"Aye, and you don't give a thought about the wind tangling it into knots that will take me an hour or more to brush out before I can shower and go to bed."

"I'd be happy to brush it out for you before we go to bed."

She glanced over at him and lifted her chin.

"That's not going to happen. Why is your hair always pulled back into a ponytail or braided?"

"Because I don't want it in my face."

"Exactly!" She tossed her head in triumph.

"It's not my hair I want to run my fingers through; it's yours. Besides, mine doesn't curl and wave as it cascades down my back." He tugged on the end of the blue ribbon, letting her hair free.

"That's fine then, but I'm tying it back as soon as we get out of the car." She huffed.

He nodded, rubbing his knuckles gently across her cheek, then let his fingers slide through her flowing red hair. His hand fell, brushing down her arm. The tips of his fingers feathered lightly on the side of her firm breast.

She shot him a warning glance, her mouth set in a grim line. "That's enough, Stefan. I'm driving here. I don't think we want to go where you're headed."

****

"Maybe you don't, but, ah, well, okay, probably not." Stefan smiled sheepishly. *Hell, who am I kidding? That's exactly where I want to go. Feel the weight of her firm, round breasts in my hands and run my tongue over her nipples until they are hard... reach between...*

Without taking her eyes off the road, she attempted to swat him upside the head and missed as he ducked. "Not there either. Wipe that grin off your face."

He caught her hand and brought it to his lips, then released it. "What! You don't know what I'm thinking." Trying his best to look innocent, he settled back in the seat, letting his eyes wander over the graceful curves of her body.

"I don't need to. You're male with a one-track

mind."

"Gee thanks for noticing. Well, the male part anyway."

A worn wooden sign welcoming them to Eureka stood just ahead. She turned onto a small dirt road—no, a wide trail was probably a better description—and stopped.

"This is the end of the road. We'll need to hike in from here."

Quick as a wink, he hopped out of the SUV door, jumped over the vehicle, landing lightly on the balls of his feet, and opened her door, bowing ever so slightly.

Brandy giggled as she placed one foot onto the gravel road. "And they say chivalry is dead." Reaching for the hand he'd extended, she stepped out, catching the toe of her shoe on the doorsill plate, and fell into his arms.

"Well, isn't this convenient." Slipping his hands around her waist, he pulled her tight against him. She felt so good. Her warm, womanly curves pressed against him made him hard, and he couldn't do a thing about it. He wanted her naked and under him but knew better than to try or even suggest it. That move had met with resistance and bitter disappointment a week earlier. *Don't want to go there again.*

He leaned away just enough for their eyes to meet. Hers were dreamy. She tucked her head under his chin, laid her cheek on his chest, and cuddled closer. Brandy tilted her head and brushed a kiss across his throat. Her heartbeat increased, and the blood pulsed through her veins like a drumbeat in rhythm with her heart.

As her vitals changed, his fangs tried to break through his gums. *No, not going to happen, not going to spoil this moment.*

"We should get going," she said slowly, her voice thick, but she didn't move out of his arms, almost as if she liked feeling his arousal pressed up against her belly.

He'd never felt this way, and it worried him, maybe because it had been several months since he'd had a woman. Now all he wanted was her, all of her and not just her body. Yes, he wanted her in his bed, but there was more to it—a need to be near her, to enjoy her company, to understand and know everything about her.

He'd never cared for a woman like this, not even Serena, the creature of the night he'd thought himself in love with before she brutally attacked and turned him. The last thing he wanted to do was to start now, but it was too late. He was sunk, and though a part of him battled with the concept, down deep he knew it.

He gripped her arms and held her away from him. "Have you ever felt like this, Brandy? Be honest."

"Can't say as I ever have. I've never felt like this with anyone—but you." A small sigh escaped her lips. As he released his hold, she relaxed against him.

That was all it took. His hands caressed her back. His mouth moved over hers, devouring its softness. When her lips parted as he nibbled on her bottom lip, he hesitantly explored her tongue with the tip of his.

She tenderly reached up and cupped his face in her hands as their tongues joined in a sinuous dance.

He drew back, gently taking her hands in his. Much more of this and he'd have no choice but to take her in the cool, wet grass beneath their feet. "Brandy, we better get going, unless you have changed your mind about being intimate."

Reluctantly, she backed away. "I can't. I just can't."

Deciding to push the issue, he probed carefully. "Can you at least tell me why?"

"Eventually." She twined her fingers through his and ambled toward the trail.

As they walked, he decided to touch on the other night. "Brandy, your gryphon is the most beautiful creature I have ever seen—next to your human form, of course. I don't know why you were so uncomfortable about telling me. Afraid it would change things between us?"

"Maybe. It's not something you see every day, and most find it disturbing. Since you are Native American, I hoped you wouldn't feel that way. You probably grew up with legends of shapeshifters."

"I did. My grandfather used to weave bedtime stories about the legends and shapeshifters of our people." It was probably not a good idea to tell her just how familiar he was with shapeshifters. No, he wasn't ready to bare his soul, if he had one, to her yet.

"Did we just have a serious conversation? Huh, there may be hope for us yet." She laughed and took off running. He raced after her, negotiating the narrow trail, hopping over the bared tree roots and jagged rocks.

Stefan spent the rest of the day learning the area where Brandy indicated they'd hunt come nightfall. Trails wound in and out of the dense forest and over steep rocky cliffs. The cliffs and valleys were breathtaking during the day, but the mountainous terrain would be treacherous at night. Snow-covered patches still dotted the northern slopes, which didn't get much sun during the day. Those trails would be icy in spots.

Brandy stopped and sniffed the air, glancing toward Stefan. "Catch the scent of elk on the wind?"

His nostrils flared, and he nodded.

"When the time comes, let yourself go. Your survival instinct will take over. Just stay aware of your surroundings. Don't go completely feral on me. I wouldn't want you to mistake my gryphon form as prey. The elk are our prey tonight. You'll want to take them down quickly, sink your fangs into their jugular, drain them, and move on till you're sated. The scavengers will take care of the carcasses. We'll follow the herd downwind for a couple of miles, then strike. I'll check the area for campers or hikers around dusk, then we'll hunt."

He took a deep breath and blew it out. Not because he was nervous, only trying to release the desire that was building inside him again. He shook his head, attempting to concentrate on the matter at hand. "Okay, doesn't sound like a big deal. I know how to drain a creature's blood."

"It's not. Trust me. Bet I can make this a challenging and enjoyable experience. At least you will feel better about yourself. Right?" She winked and sauntered down the trail in front of him, swaying those sexy hips.

Shit, if she doesn't stop doing that, I'm never going to get myself under control.

The sun set behind the mountains in a fanning display of oranges, yellows, and reds melting into the blue sky as Brandy disappeared into the forest, promising to return shortly. He heard the beat of wings as she took flight, and then he settled down to wait. Returning an hour later, she circled and landed in front of him, folding her wings against her back. *No humans within a hundred-mile radius. Let's hunt.*

That is so damn cool. He could hear others' thoughts but never tried to communicate inside their minds. That was something he might try. He'd learned his strengths and talents by trial and error, but listening in on thoughts could be hit or miss. Maybe he should have stayed with his mentor longer, learned what else was possible. That train of thought was only going to spoil the night, so he turned his attention back to the current task.

His first attempt at taking down an elk was awkward and embarrassing to his male ego. Thankfully, gryphons couldn't laugh out loud. Brandy had her catch down and torn apart in a matter of seconds without a spot of blood anywhere on her.

He eventually took an elk down but not without a fight and blood everywhere. The second time went much smoother. Landing on the elk's back, he grasped its neck, latched on to the jugular, brought the animal down, and drained it with little effort. His thirst satisfied, he scanned the area for Brandy, finally locating her fully clothed and sitting on a rock a few yards away.

He strolled to where she sat. "That wasn't too bad, was it?

"Nope, you're a natural predator, as you have reminded me several times lately." She looked at his blood-stained clothes and tossed him clean jeans and a sweatshirt. "I figured you might need these, so I picked them up for you yesterday in case we meet anyone on our way back. Don't want someone to get the wrong idea."

Crossing his arms across his chest, he stared at her. "It's three in the morning. Who the hell are we going to meet"—he held his arms out wide and turned in a complete circle—"here?"

She watched him with smug delight, ignoring his sarcasm. "There's a lake down the path about a half mile. Want to wash up?"

It was impossible to be upset with her. He'd just chalk this one up to wounded male ego. Out-hunted with ease by a female. Didn't matter she was a gryphon. It felt wrong on so many levels. "Yeah, I do. You're loving this, aren't you? You're so much better than I am."

"Oh, your male pride will survive. It takes practice, but you did very well tonight. How do you feel? It's not what you're used to, but easier to obtain and helps your self-image. Does it satisfy your lust for blood?"

Her ability to know what he felt was disconcerting. "Brandy, how do you do that?"

"Do what?"

"Don't give me that innocent crap. You know exactly what I mean."

"I've lots of talents, and when you're willing to open up to me, I'll tell you about them. I don't need your deep, dark secrets. I just want to get to know the man in here"—she jabbed a finger at the left side of his chest—"under all that bullshit you've piled up for protection. Is that too much to ask?" She tilted her head as she sucked in her bottom lip and waited silently for his reaction or answer.

He grabbed her hand and twisted slightly, grinning

as the moonlight glinted off his fully unsheathed fangs. "If you don't quit poking me in the chest, I'm going to show you what these are for. Understand?" He opened his mouth wider, fangs unsheathed, and leaned in toward her neck.

"Go ahead," she said, undaunted, then bared her neck further to him. "Or would you rather feast from my wrist that you have captured?" She worked the inside of her wrist around in his hand and brought it close to his mouth.

"Woman, do you have a death wish? Even though I've just fed, your blood is so much sweeter. Don't tempt me like that. It isn't safe. I do have limits." He released her wrist and pushed away from her as they arrived at the lake. The water was chilling as he knelt and washed up.

She jumped up on a rock, balanced for a moment, then sat. "I know you won't hurt me. That's called trust. Ever heard of it?"

Finished rinsing out his shirt, Stefan scrubbed at his face, then turned to look at her. "Yes, but taunting an apex predator is never a good idea." He'd never known anyone like her. If he was going to give this relationship a chance, learning to trust her was the key. He shoved his hands in his front pockets and paced away from her, then back. "Okay, what do you want to know?"

Her tight expression relaxed into a smile. She crossed her legs at the ankles and swung them back and forth. "Let's start with where you were raised. Are your parents still living? Any siblings?"

Closing his eyes, he tried to shut out the wave of long-buried emotions washing over him. "I was raised on the Wind River Reservation in Wyoming by my paternal grandfather. Dad died when I was four. Mom abandoned us when I was two. Never saw her again. I don't have any siblings."

"I'm sorry for your loss," she said softly. "Were you born on the reservation then?"

"No, in Cambridge, Massachusetts. My parents met and married while attending Harvard. My mother was an exchange student from Italy, studying law, and my dad was in medical school."

"Oh. Wow."

That was enough questions. He plucked her off the rock, grinning when she squealed and locked her arms around his neck. "What's the matter? Afraid I'll drop you now that I've got you? You don't know me very well. I take care of things that are mine."

"Yours!" she said with a snort. "Now, that's a different tune than I've heard before."

"I know lots of diverse tunes." His grin flashed briefly against his bronze skin. "My turn. Now, tell me why you won't sleep with me. I know you want me."

"That's complicated. Ask something else." She straightened her back and clenched her jaw.

Seeing her reaction, he figured pursuing that subject would get him no closer to the answer right now, so he moved on. "Can you only communicate in my mind when you are in gryphon form? How did you know I was a vampire, and how do you know my feelings? Can you read my mind?"

"All fair questions. No one outside my family has ever seen me in gryphon form. Since you are the first person I tried to communicate with as a gryphon, I guess the answer is yes. I can't do it while I'm human.

At least, I don't think so. No, I can't read your mind but can feel your emotions. As far as being a vampire, I just knew…not sure why, but I've always been able to do it. All I need is to touch the person."

He sat her gently on her feet and brushed the damp curls from her face while keeping his other arm wrapped tightly around her. He could listen to her talk for hours, but the arousing effect her intoxicating Irish lilt had on him was damn inconvenient.

She brought her face closer to his, running her hands up his chest. In a soft voice, she asked, "Who turned you and left you alone?"

"What?" Her question snapped him out of his sexual haze. His temper spiked and he growled. "There you go again, knowing things you have no right to know. Asking complicated questions when you won't answer mine."

"All right, I'll answer yours, if you'll answer mine." She moved closer, wrapping her arms around his neck like velvet chains, and touched her lips to his, drew back, and sighed. "Aye, you deserve an explanation. Just didn't want to scare you away. Gryphons take only one mate, and that is for eternity. If something happens to that mate, the other will spend the rest of her life alone and never search for another."

He nodded, mesmerized by the emotion in her eyes.

"Some choose to follow their mate in death. The act of lovemaking seals that bond. It's a hell of a commitment for anyone other than a gryphon to understand, let alone agree to." She paused, watching him intently. "I don't expect that type of commitment from you, but that's the reason I can't be intimate with you." Tears glistened in her eyes. She blinked them away before they could spill down her cheeks. "Now it's your turn. Who turned you and left you alone?"

Feelings churned inside him. He didn't want to deal with them, let alone explain. He blew out a breath. "I loved Serena, but I didn't know she was a vampire until the night she turned me. She laughed at my innocence and left with a group of friends that had joined her to watch me suffer. Angry and betrayed, my fury and lust for human blood was uncontrollable, and I went…" He drew in a long breath and blew it out slowly. "The rest I don't want to discuss. Please don't ever ask me again."

She nodded solemnly.

They stood in silence, wrapped in each other's arms, neither one knowing what to say or how to comfort the other.

Where did he go from here? The thought of being committed to one woman for eternity was interesting, if such love existed. He couldn't allow her to commit to him not knowing what he was capable of. She'd never seen the beast within. What if someday he lost control and hurt her? He couldn't take that chance.

Brandy liked to walk on the wild side by her own admission. He could see the romance of her wanting a relationship with a vampire. But at the end of the day, would he be the person she would want to walk through life with, especially when that life was for eternity? Eventually, she would learn of his past as a vampire assassin, and he couldn't give her a family. Unless more of the legends he'd studied were true. Even then, he couldn't put her through that.

She deserved more—a man that could make her

happy, give her children, and make her dreams come true, not force her to live in a damn nightmare. Yet…being with her felt so right, as if she completed him somehow. He shook his head to dislodge the possibilities.

As if reading his mind, Brandy backed away, breaking their hold. "You can tell me all the terrible things you have done, even in graphic detail if necessary. It won't change how I see or feel about you. I sense a great compassion within you. That doesn't mean I don't see the emotional scars, bitterness, and the beast inside."

He started to say something, but she held her finger up.

"Let me finish. Behind that protective wall you've built, you're like any other man. You want to be accepted, loved, and give love in return. But you're afraid. Afraid of being hurt like your father. Like you were when Serena betrayed you. And like the hurt you saw in your grandfather's eyes when you left. You worry about inflicting pain on those you care about. Gee, I don't know, does that sound like a monster to you?" She tilted her head up to gaze into his eyes. "It doesn't to me."

He balled his fists at his sides and shoved them in his pockets. She could be so damn stubborn—rationalizing everything. "What you're suggesting could have deadly consequences for you. I'm not willing to accept that responsibility."

Sadness reflected in her green eyes as her lilting voice wavered. "You've decided that continuing our relationship will endanger my existence. You couldn't be more wrong. If you refuse to give us a chance, you might as well destroy me now."

Taking a moment to gather his thoughts, he rubbed his eyes, and Brandy yawned behind her hand. They were tired, and this subject would look better to both of them tomorrow. He flashed a grin, reaching for her. "Bit of a drama queen, are you?"

She hesitated for a minute or two and studied his face. "Maybe. At least I know what I want and have the guts to go after it. Unlike a big, bad vamp I know."

"You win. We'll discuss it tomorrow. With your permission, I'll drive back to Whitefish since you're exhausted." He brushed a strand of hair from her face, lingering for a beat. "You can drop me off and drive home, or you can sleep at the cabin. It's up to you."

Yawning again, she blinked several times. "I'll stay with you. Thanks."

By the time they arrived at the cabin, she was sound asleep, her head resting on his shoulder. Careful not to rouse her, he carried her in, took off her boots, and laid her gently on his bed, pulling the patchwork quilt over her. As he watched her sleep, he considered his next move. Kissing her cheek gently, he got up and walked silently into the living room. Rolling his shoulders, he rubbed the back of his neck and sat down on the couch to think. *I swore I'd never...yet here I am.* He gazed at the ceiling as if he could see though the logs to the heavens above. *Grandfather...I wish...*

Chapter Ten
Vampire to the Rescue

To clear his head and sort out his feelings, he walked into town, leaving a note for Brandy in case she woke up before he got back. Impulsively, he'd grabbed a flower out of the vase sitting on the kitchen counter and laid it across the note.

The cool night air tousled his hair as he ambled down the sidewalk. He paused at the intersection of Main Street, where a lone car rumbled by. Thin clouds floated across the dark sky. A translucent, colorful corona ringed the full moon. Russ claimed that meant there would be a change in the weather. Maybe spring had finally arrived. Another mile or two and he still was no closer to a resolution to his current dilemma. Women were such puzzles. He spun around on his heel and trudged back the way he'd come.

Upon his return, her car was still out front, but the note on the counter was gone, so he peeked in the bedroom. She was still asleep in his bed, her hand closed around the flower with the petals resting against her cheek. An empty glass with melting ice cubes sat on the nightstand.

Rather than wake her, he backed out and closed the door softly. In the living room, he tossed logs into the fireplace on top of crumpled newspaper and struck a match. He dropped it into the combustible material.

The flames raced up the newspaper, turning to black soot. A slow orange flicker caught at the edge of the logs and quickly engulfed the dried wood. Stefan eased onto the floor cross-legged and reached for his guitar. No matter what happened in his life, music centered him and washed away the terrible memories for a time. Then he could think through a problem rationally and come to a solution he could live with. After just a few chords, he heard bare feet padding on the hardwood floor behind him.

She leaned over him, the flower tucked in her hair behind her ear. Brandy's arms skimmed over his shoulders as her fingers traced the sculptured muscles of his chest. She gently bit his neck, then soothed the bites with her tongue. "I like it when you play. The music is so emotional, reflecting, sad, angry, happy…I can feel it all through your music." She raised an eyebrow and peered at him. "That's quite a talent."

He laid his guitar aside and reached for her, knowing they would make this relationship work or die trying. "I don't know about talent, but it keeps me sane and somehow on an equal footing." His arm circled around her shoulder and under her arm, fingers brushing lightly against the side of her breast.

She slithered over his shoulder and into his lap. Snuggled against him, she turned her face up and touched her lips to his, once, twice, then fully took his mouth with hers. He returned the kiss, parting her lips with the tip of his tongue, and penetrated the lush softness of her mouth.

Trailing his lips across her jawline, he brushed kisses along her throat as she continued to feather the contours of his chest with her fingertips. He loved the feel of her soft, warm hands on his cool skin. Sliding her fingers up the sides of his neck, she fisted them in his hair as he began to explore her body's sensuous curves with his hands. She moaned and arched toward him, pulling him closer.

The soft contours of her ass fit nicely around his hardening ridge. He unbuttoned her shirt and slid his hand inside to caress her firm, full breasts, captured beneath the wisps of silky material.

Fingering the front closure of her bra with his fingers, he hesitated for a moment. When she didn't try to stop him, he flipped open the clasp and freed those beautiful mounds of perfumed female flesh. His mouth closed over her bare breast and feasted on it. His tongue stroked her nipple until it hardened, then moved over to explore the other one.

Kissing his way back to the hollow of her neck, his hand moved in slow circles over her flat belly, then slipped between her legs. She shifted slightly, allowing him full access to caress her intimate areas. Even through her jeans, he could feel her heat, sense her arousal.

Brandy rubbed her fine, firm ass against the hard ridge under the fly of his jeans and moaned. She had to know what this was doing to him and to herself. He wanted her, all right. And though she'd survive their throes of passion, that commitment hung over him like an ominous thundercloud.

Before he knew what had happened, his fangs slipped free, raking across her delicate throat. He drew back and watched, mesmerized, as a thin line of blood seeped from the wound. Leaning in, he licked at the blood, reveling in the sweet taste of her and, at the same time, appalled at his lack of control. He licked at the wound once more, sealing it. "I'm so sorry. This is why our relationship puts you in grave danger. I wouldn't mean to, but…"

"Stefan, it was an accident. You could have sunk your fangs into my jugular, but you didn't. Instead, you stopped the blood flow and sealed the wound." She ran her warm hand over his cheek and breathed a kiss there. "Dangers of dating a vampire," she said flippantly, touching a finger to the tender wound.

"Not before I had a taste." He shook his head in disgust and looked away.

Cupping his chin, her heart still thundered, she forced him to look at her and whispered, "It was… strangely stimulating, and you didn't hurt me." With a slight tremor in her voice, she gave a half laugh and said, "Kept things from getting out of control."

"You got that right*." Guess it was a good thing she refused to sleep with me. I just proved that I don't have the control to keep her safe.*

****

As Stefan got ready for work, Brandy left the cabin and took the long way home. She needed time to think and shuddered at the realization she'd been seconds away from surrendering to him completely. Brandy pushed the thought away and tried to calm her jangled nerves.

The truth was she simply didn't want to walk into an empty house alone. The sanctuary of her nice, quiet home now made her irritable. *I don't need to be near him all the time.* A smile tugged at the corners of her lips. *Who the hell am I kidding? I like having him around.*

Suddenly, the hairs on the back of her neck stood on end and a shiver shot down her spine. She let the car coast to a stop in front of her house. Walking hesitatingly up the path, she sniffed the air and looked for anything odd or out of place. Nothing. *I'm letting my imagination run wild.* Still, she strolled around the house's perimeter to make sure there was nothing lurking out back or signs of forced entry. Again, nothing.

As a precaution, she put her purse inside the car, locked it, and held the keys in her hand. She shoved her cell phone in a pocket and climbed the steps to the porch. Turning her key in the lock, the door creaked slowly open. A sulfur stench immediately assaulted her senses. Standing in the doorway, heart pounding, she pushed the door open wider and stepped inside.

The couch lay upside down in the center of the room. Stuffing torn from the pillows covered the floor. Books and movies thrown from their shelves were scattered around the room. Thin tendrils of gray smoke curled in the air above a large scorched area in the center of the living room floor. Brandy stood and stared, then picked her way to the hall. Her heart sank. The Irish crystal lamp her mother had given her as a house-warming gift lay shattered on the hallway floor. Bile rose in her throat as she whirled around and barreled out of the house. Tears burned her eyes as she fumbled with her keys, trying to unlock the car door. Once inside, she locked the doors, shoved the key in the ignition, turned it, and the engine roared to life.

Gasping for breath, she pulled the cell phone out of her pocket and dialed 9-1-1, then ended the call. *What the hell is wrong with me?* Disgusted, she shook her head, pushed back against the seat, took several deep calming breaths, and blew them out. *That's better.* She hit 9-1-1 again and put the phone to her ear.

"9-1-1, what's your emergency?"

"Someone broke into my home and vandalized it." Brandy gave the dispatcher her address and a description of the damage.

"Are you still in the house?"

"No. I'm sitting in my car parked outside the house. It appears the perpetrators are gone."

"Okay, officers are on their way. Is there a neighbor's home you can go to and wait for their arrival?"

"Not really. I'll just wait in my car for the officers. If things change, I'll call back."

"I'll stay on the line with you."

"That's not necessary, but thanks." She disconnected the call before the operator had a chance to object and dialed Stefan's cell phone number.

His smooth, seductive voice rumbled over the phone. "Hey, Brandy, miss me already?"

"Stefan." She breathed into the phone, her voice shaky.

"What's wrong? Where are you?" Stefan asked.

She gripped the phone so tightly, her knuckles turned white. "Someone broke into my house and tossed the place. They smashed the crystal lamp my mother gave me. The house reeks of sulfur, just like at the scene of the animal attack a month back. It's awful." God, she couldn't stop talking. She shouldn't have told him anything about the ongoing investigation. She knew better than to react like this. But her home had been violated. She felt violated, and that's different—it's personal. Taking a deep breath, she tried to compose herself again and continued. "I'm sitting in my car in front of the house—waiting for the police."

"I'll be right there. Drive over to one of your neighbors'. DO NOT stay in front of your house." Before he disconnected the call, she heard part of his conversation. "Cody, please cover for me for a couple of hours. Brandy's house was broken into and vandalized. She is upset but all right—I think."

"Go ahead. I've got this. Call me when you know more."

"Thanks." Stefan paused. "Brandy, you still there?"

"Yes."

"I'm on my way." In a matter of minutes, he pulled in behind her car. Jumping out of the truck, he yanked open her SUV's door, hauling her into his arms. "Are you okay?" He brushed the hair out of her eyes, his gaze swept over her. When he held her tight against him, beads of sweat trickled down her face and nape of her neck, dampening his shirt.

"Aye, I'm okay, just embarrassed about my initial reaction. You should be at work. Sorry." She relaxed against him. Like it or not, he'd become an important part of her life. His fingertips gently caressed her cheekbones, the careful touch so different from the raw-edged anger she felt, barely contained, pulsing off him.

"Don't worry about it," he murmured against her hair. "Cody's got it handled till I get back. Now what's this about an animal attack?"

She drew back and peered at him. "I shouldn't have told you about that. It's an ongoing investigation. Well, I guess it's closed now, but I don't think they got it right."

"Like hell you shouldn't have," he growled. "If you're in danger, I want to know. How can I protect you when you keep things from me?"

She sensed his temper spike, but he didn't act on it. Instead, he squelched the urge and pulled her tighter against his chest, stroking the back of her hair gently.

Red-and-blue flashing lights announced the arrival of Kalispell's finest. The officer pulled along Stefan's pickup that was double-parked beside Brandy's SUV and stepped out of his vehicle. "Is she all right?"

"Yes, no thanks to you. What took you so long?" Stefan demanded as Brandy wriggled against his strong hold to break free and handle the situation herself.

Realizing that she was no match for Stefan's strength, she whispered, "Please, don't embarrass me any more than I already am. I can handle this."

He released one arm, allowing her to turn toward the officer, but kept the other wrapped protectively around her waist. She glared at him and he reluctantly released his hold.

Stepping forward, she extended her hand and smiled. "I'm Brandy Shaughnessy." Motioning across the street, she started to walk to her house. "Shall we see the extent of the damage to my home?"

Stefan's arm snaked back around her waist, stopping her forward motion. She shot him an icy stare and he merely smiled, relaying his thoughts in her mind. *You're not going anywhere near the inside of that house until the officer clears it. Relax and let him do his job.* Her eyes flew open wide and she gawked at him, so he knew she'd understood.

This little experiment worked even under stressful conditions. She stared at him defiantly. He smiled. *Yep, communication in each other's minds works in either form. Better we communicate this way than in front of the officer.*

She jerked away from his hold.

Officer Cobb shifted his gaze from Brandy to Stefan. "Ms. Shaughnessy, I'd prefer that you stay here until I've made a sweep of the inside of your house and surrounding area. Did you see anyone run from the house after you exited the premises?"

"No, but I wasn't really watching. Someone could have left out the back, and I'd never seen them."

As soon as the officer was out of hearing range, Brandy turned to Stefan. "How did you do that?"

"I'll tell you later. When it's safe to go back in your house, I'd like you to gather enough things so you can stay at my cabin for a couple of weeks. I want to know exactly what is going on with the animal attack and what it has to do with your break in."

Staying in the house tonight was out of the question. There was no sense arguing with him. "I'd like that. We can't leave the house unsecured."

"I'll make sure it's secure before we leave. Tomorrow, we'll come back during the day and assess the damage."

Given the all clear by Officer Cobb, she stepped gingerly through the debris and gathered her things. Stefan boarded up the front door from the inside, then dead bolted the back door as they left. The place needed to be aired out and thoroughly cleaned before she would be able to move back in. At first glance, it looked like she'd have to replace all her furniture. *Who could hate me enough to do such a terrible thing?* Tomorrow, they'd see if anything was missing.

****

When they returned to the radio station, Stefan filled Cody in, then settled Brandy in a chair beside him inside the control room for the duration of his shift.

The sun broadcast bright-yellow rays above the horizon as Stefan's shift ended. Russ strode in, followed closely by a petite raven-haired beauty with a face like a pixie. She wore tight designer jeans, a sequined sweater, five-inch spike heels, and looked so out of place that Brandy openly stared for a moment, then, remembering her manners, smiled at Russ. "Good morning to ya. How's it all going?"

"Fine, Brandy, good morning to you. Doing another ranger segment?" He sniffed and wrinkled his forehead. "Smells like fireworks in here."

"No, unfortunately, my home was vandalized last night. I couldn't stay there. Stefan came by and picked me up while Cody covered his shift. Stefan returned to finish his shift. For the sake of time, I came along. Sorry about the smell. After the break in, my house reeked of sulfur." She sniffed and tugged at her sweater. "Guess our clothes absorbed the odor."

"Oh, wow, sorry to hear about your house. If there is anything I can do, just let me know."

"Thanks. We've got it handled."

Russ glanced from Brandy to Stefan and back to the girl who came in with him. "Brandy, this is Synn. She is going to be filling in at the receptionist position while Jody's out. Synn, Stefan is our overnight guy. Brandy is a ranger in Glacier. She occasionally does some in-studio public service segments on Glacier with Stefan."

Stefan looked up from his paperwork and nodded.

"Welcome aboard, Synn." He looked her up and down with male interest, then returned to his paperwork, obviously anxious to get out of the station.

Synn stepped forward, nodded curtly to Brandy, and let her glance linger over Stefan. To Brandy's mind, it was nothing short of an invitation, and she'd caught Stefan's covert glance at Synn. She couldn't fault him for it. After all, he was male and Synn exuded sex. That didn't mean he wasn't going to hear about it when they left.

Something else about her bothered Brandy, but she just couldn't get a handle on it. She blew it off, thinking it was just the way Synn looked at Stefan that got her hackles up. Brandy shook off the feeling. There were more pressing matters at hand.

Russ didn't seem to notice Synn's blatant behavior as he watched her walk provocatively out of the control room. "She recently moved here from L.A., where she was a receptionist and production assistant for a large radio station there. We're lucky to have her while Jody is out on maternity leave. I'll be right back after I get her settled. Stefan, you don't mind covering for me for a few minutes, do you?"

Stefan shook his head and continued prep for Russ's shift.

Russ followed Synn out, introducing her to the rest of the staff and showing her around.

"Boy, is that girl trouble with a capital T." Brandy pursed her lips.

Stefan frowned and looked over at Brandy. "Huh, what?" He followed her gaze. "Oh, yeah, she's a looker, all right. Just Cody's type."

"She's got her eye on you. See to it that you stay

away from her." Brandy stared menacingly at him.

"Oh, Brandy, get real. She's not my type and you know it." He reached over and pulled her to him, nibbling on her neck. "I've got what I want right here. Now tell me about the animal attack. What does it have to do with your break in? Why does it have you so spooked?" Stefan checked the timer on the console as it counted down the triple play, then turned his attention back to Brandy.

She let out a heavy sigh. "The night we met, after you left, the scent of fresh blood led me to a gruesome scene. A body lay torn apart on the trail. There were bite and scratch marks all over it. A strong odor of sulfur hung in the air, and the ground was scorched beneath the body. I secured the scene and called Randy. He called the proper authorities, who brought in crime scene investigators. They determined it was just an animal attack. There was definitely more to it than that. The scorching and strong sulfur smell would have driven animals away from the area, and there were no animal tracks."

Stefan nodded but said nothing.

Angry and frustrated, she continued. "They wouldn't listen to me and explained it all away by blaming the victim, even for the scorch marks. Claimed he was probably smoking and tossed a lit cigarette that started a small fire. Or a spark caught from the illegal campfire set a few feet away or maybe fireworks." She shook her head vehemently. "They didn't find any evidence of fireworks at the scene. The sulfur smell in the air was mostly gone by the time the investigators arrived. But remains of the body still reeked. Again, they chalked it up to illegal fireworks."

Her pent-up fury now was a living, breathing thing. "My home vandalized. My clothes and belongings stink to high heaven. Now the scorched area is in the middle of my living room, and no one is listening to me. There were no fireworks or cigarettes involved in my home. These cases are related."

Stefan stood back and listened, letting her get it all out, and then held up his hand. "Hold that thought. Russ is coming, and I need to do a station ID, sign off, and intro him. Let's continue this conversation outside in the truck."

Russ knocked lightly on the glass door to the control room. Stefan finished the stop set and flipped the mic off, motioning Russ to come in. Brandy bit her lip, her body still quivering with emotion. She took a deep breath and forced a smile.

Russ opened the door and stepped in. "Got Synn all settled and introduced around. She's quite a looker, don't you think?" he said, winking at Stefan.

"What I think doesn't matter. It's what your wife thinks when she gets a load of Synn that should concern you," Stefan said, grinning wickedly. "As for me, I'm glad I'll be gone before she comes to work. Don't need that kind of distraction. You're gonna have a tough time keeping Cody off her though." Stefan walked toward the door, wrapped his arm around Brandy's waist, and playfully nudged her out the open door.

Synn narrowed her eyes as they passed by the reception desk.

Once outside the studio, Stefan's forehead creased in concentration. "If the two incidents are connected, why?" He leaned against the truck facing her.

"I don't know. It's just a strong feeling. What if I'd

131

been home?" She shuddered as if a cold chill ran down her spine. "Is this thing after me?"

"Brandy, just stop. It's been a traumatic night. You're tired and need sleep. Once you've gotten some shut-eye, we'll continue this discussion. See if we can figure out how they're linked." He gathered her into his arms and held her for a beat.

"Okay, but everything I own reeks of sulfur." She glanced in the bed of his truck, where they'd thrown all her stuff last night. "You'd probably better leave the bags of clothes and things in the back of your truck. I'll get them when they've aired out a bit." She wrinkled her nose at the stench.

He opened the vehicle door and grasped her by the waist, lifting her into the truck. Before letting her go, he pulled her to him and nuzzled her neck. The intoxicating fragrance of blood pulsing under her delicate skin nearly overwhelmed him, but he breathed only a kiss at the soft juncture of her throat.

Her arms encircled his neck and held him there as he started to draw back. A single tear trickled down her cheek and plopped on his face.

"It's all right," he murmured, trailing kisses up her neck. "You're safe." His arms encircled her as he slipped in beside her and closed the door.

All the fear, anger, and frustration she held inside exploded in a flood of tears.

He lifted her into his lap and held her tight against his chest, his cheek resting against the top of her head until she was quiet.

"Ready to go home?" he whispered, brushing the hair out of her eyes and kissing her forehead.

She nodded. He slid over to the driver's seat and

started the truck, his arm wrapped tightly around her shoulders as he pulled away from the curb and headed for the cabin.

She wiped the back of her hands across her face and looked over at Stefan shyly, the corners of her mouth turned up slightly. "Sorry about that. I guess it'd been building up all night, and the floodgates opened when we were alone. I'm not usually a blubbering idiot."

"I know that." Arriving at the cabin, Stefan smiled at her and stepped out of the truck. In a blur of movement, he bounded over the cab and opened her door, offering his hand to help her out of the truck. "We all have our limits. Feeling better now?"

"I am, thanks." She grasped his hand and jumped out of the truck.

He tossed the keys for the cabin to her. "Go on in and take a nice hot shower. It'll relax your muscles. There are a couple of clean flannel shirts in the closet. Plastic bags are in the cupboard under the sink. You can sleep in the shirt today, stuff the clothes you're wearing in the bag, and worry about washing your things when you wake up." He hefted two of the bags out of the truck and slung them over his shoulder. "The bags will be in the backyard...airing out."

Steam billowed out of the open bathroom door as she showered. When the water stopped, she appeared in the doorway wrapped in a large, purple towel. He glanced at her, finished clearing out a couple of drawers, and made room in his closet for her clothes. Pausing only a beat, he sauntered out into the living room.

****

Her damp hair clung to her white shoulders and spilled down her back as she padded out to where he was sitting on the couch. "You said I could borrow one of your flannel shirts to sleep in?" She yawned wide and blinked innocently at him.

Warm and fragrant from her shower, he wanted to eat her alive. "Woman, you're treading on dangerous ground. We are going to have to set some rules while you're living here. First one is 'no running around naked.'"

She blinked at him again and looked down at her towel.

"…'Or almost naked in my presence,'" he corrected. "You'll have me in a constant state of arousal, and that's not safe for either of us. The shirts are in the bedroom closet. Just pick one."

Smiling sweetly, she purred, "You didn't say which closet, and I didn't want to go snooping around in your things."

Laughing, he got up and grabbed her hand, pulling her into the bedroom, secretly hoping the damn towel would fall off. He opened the closet door and waved his hand toward the clothes hanging there. "Pick one."

She slid around him and plucked out a red plaid shirt. Facing him, she raised a brow while looking out from under her long copper lashes. "You want to watch me change?" She reached for the edge of the towel tucked between her breasts. "Doesn't that go against rule number one already?"

"Sure does, and no, I don't." He turned on his heel and strode out. "Women!" He sat down at his computer and stared at the papers scattered over the desk. God, he absolutely hated paperwork, and his procrastination had led to this mess. The bright side of the situation was that the investments generating the paperwork allowed him to live quite comfortably. He preferred to keep busy, which was why he had taken the DJ position. Unable to concentrate, he pushed back from the desk. He needed to release all the pent-up energy she'd roused in him. A long, hard run should do the trick, and then he'd tackle the unfinished piles of paper.

Chapter Eleven
It Could Be Worse

Shimmering slivers of silver moonlight spun over her as she awoke, slightly disoriented. Where was she? Then memories of the past twenty-four hours came flooding back. This was Stefan's house. Hers was, well, uninhabitable currently. The vivid blue numbers on the bedside clock read 12:05 a.m. *I've been asleep for nearly eighteen hours.* A loud rumble from her stomach confirmed the thought.

Sitting up in bed, she wrapped her arms around herself and snuggled into the warm flannel shirt he'd given her. She pulled the shirt around her face and sniffed. His spicy, outdoor scent remained in the shirt and was somehow comforting.

The room had a chill to it. He probably kept the cabin cooler than she was used to and forgot to turn the heat up before he left for work. Leaning over, she turned on the bedside lamp. Silhouettes of moose, bears, and wolves danced across the walls, the soft light escaping through the lampshade cutouts. She glanced around the room for the clothes she'd worn this morning. Dressed in only a flannel shirt, she decided it wouldn't be a good idea to go outside and retrieve her bags of clothing.

Gingerly, she touched her bare feet on the cold tile floor and walked over to the dresser where Stefan kept his sweats. Opening the top drawer of the dresser, she stared down at her lingerie neatly folded where the sweats had previously been. Her cheeks heated, when she imagined his large hands folding her delicate lingerie. She sniffed hesitatingly. No ode-to-fireworks smell. Just a freshly laundered fragrance drifted from the open drawer. Apparently, he'd washed them too.

In the carved oak chair next to the bed, neatly folded, were a pair of clean jeans and her favorite purple cable-knit sweater. On a hunch, she opened the closet door. The scent of laundry soap and fabric softener wafted into the room. Her clothes hung neatly on one side of the closet. *Huh, he was busy while I slept.*

She sat on the edge of the bed and pulled on her jeans. This living arrangement would make keeping her hands off that sinful body of his difficult. *He is so damn sexy and instinctively knows how to touch me.* A shiver of desire shot through her all the way down to her toes and back to…to…well…She shook her head vehemently. The final act of intimacy was unthinkable, not to mention forbidden, without the love and commitment of both. Yet so was commitment of one without the other, and she'd already failed that requirement miserably. Now she could only hope he'd come to realize what was in his heart for her and act on it before she surrendered completely to him.

Knowing the carnal ways and needs of the vampire, she was aware that withholding herself from him could eventually drive him to satisfy his needs elsewhere or, in the heat of passion, insist on her submission to that final act, which would bind her to him for eternity without his commitment.

She had to break through that damn wall he'd constructed around himself. She could feel his yearning and seeking heart even through his barrier. Even if he wasn't aware, his support and thoughtfulness last night confirmed what she already knew, making her more determined to destroy that barrier and claim every part of him.

Smiling to herself, she wriggled into her sweater, noticing his faint scent on it, and reached for her phone.

****

After finishing most of his personal paperwork, Stefan whistled his favorite tune as he walked out the door on his way to the station. When he approached the control room, his sunny disposition disappeared. The backup CD players were haphazardly stacked on the counter next to Cody and the computer screen was dark. Synn perched on the guest chair across the counter from Cody, filing her long red fingernails. *God, this is the last thing I need. She sure as hell better be leaving with Cody.*

"Morning, everyone," Stefan said cheerfully as he glanced at the play logs scattered all over. He flashed a quick smile. "What's wrong, Cody?"

His jaw clinched, Cody jerked his hand toward the blank monitor. "Damn computer system just quit, so there is no programing. Pulled out the reliable backup CD players but can't find the damn CDs."

Synn sauntered across the floor and stood next to Stefan, reaching her hand out to stroke lightly up and down his arm. He merely gave her an icy stare and roughly brushed her hand aside. Standing beside the control room door, he motioned her out the door. "Only jocks allowed in here. If you have production to do, better get it done, otherwise leave. No one allowed in the station after midnight except authorized personnel."

Synn straightened, jutting out her chin. She tossed her head defiantly and flounced out the door. "I'll get authorization."

"You do that." Stefan crossed to the cabinet standing just outside the control room and unlocked it, throwing both doors wide open. "Pick your poison, Cody. Remember Russ told us they'd put the CDs in here under lock and key so they wouldn't walk off after we converted?"

Color rose in Cody's cheeks as Stefan tossed him a couple CDs, and he loaded them in the players. "If I'd remembered, I wouldn't have asked," Cody said sarcastically. "Thanks. I should've simply called you."

"I'd really rather you didn't. I do have a life of my own now and don't care for interruptions. But it looks like your mind and bod…ah…was otherwise engaged." Stefan winked at him and grinned. "Have an interest in the station's newest employee?"

"Yeah, I wish. All she wants to do is talk about you. I told her you were not available. Then she asked about Brandy."

Stefan stiffened and snarled, "What did you tell her?"

"Oh, relax, stud. I told her that was none of her business and changed the subject back to me. For all the good it did." He waved his hand in the air as if to wave the whole thing away.

"Look, I don't mean to be difficult." Stefan raked his fingers though his hair. "I don't care what you do, but if she's here with you, she needs to be gone long before I come in. Okay?"

"I got your back. No problem." Cody raised his eyebrow in question, but didn't say anything more.

Stefan's phone vibrated in his back pocket. He yanked it out, groaning, and checked the screen. His lips curved into a smile, and he flipped it open. "Hiya, Sleeping Beauty, awaken without your prince?"

Brandy giggled. "Sure did. I really appreciate everything you did, but it's a little chilly in here. How do I turn the heat up?"

"Oh, sorry. The thermostat is behind the entertainment center to the left. Just flip the switch to heat. It's set at seventy from the last time you were there. It'll warm up quickly. If not, there's wood set up in the fireplace. Toss a match in the crumpled-up newspaper below the logs, and you should have a roaring blaze in no time. By the way, I picked up your car this afternoon. Didn't think it was a good idea to leave it there. Thought we'd run by your house today when I get off, if you're up to it?"

"Sure, I'll be ready." Brandy's voice held a note of concern. "Stefan, is everything all right? You sound kinda tense."

"Fine," he snapped, his voice sharper than he'd intended. "Just computer problems at the station. Nothing to worry about."

"Okay." Brandy paused for a couple beats. "I'll see you in the morning."

Synn left with Cody, under protest, and the rest of the night crawled by. *Synn is going to be a problem.* He wasn't sure what her deal was but sensed the attraction she was displaying to him wasn't genuine. He'd tried to read her thoughts, but she'd blocked him before he got more than a feeling, and that was unusual. There were few human thoughts he couldn't read. Now, Brandy was another story. She allowed him in on occasion, but usually just shadows of her thoughts were available to him. It wasn't intentional. Seemed more an unconscious effort on her part.

The remainder of his shift was uneventful. He prepared the incoming DJ's first hour of music and was ready to bolt when Russ arrived.

Stefan snuck in the door to the cabin and saw Brandy standing in front of the roaring fire. Soundlessly, he crept up, caught her around the waist, and pulled her to him. His cool breath behind her ear made her shiver as his lips brushed the base of her neck. "Good morning, beautiful," he murmured.

"Good morning to you," she purred, turning around to face him. "Did you have a good night?" Her gaze was as soft as a caress and set his mouth to watering.

"I did." He brushed aside his suspicions regarding Synn for now. Brandy had enough to worry about with her house and the ongoing investigation. The subject of Synn could wait until another time. He grabbed Brandy's jacket and nodded toward the door. "Let's get this over with, then come back here and enjoy a quiet evening together."

****

"Sounds perfect." It was too easy to get lost in the way he looked at her. Brandy slid her arm into the jacket he held out and followed him out the door.

He opened the truck door, grasped her around the waist, and lifted her in the truck, giving her nose a little tweak before he kissed her reassuringly. "This won't take long."

Growing uneasy and restless the closer they got to

her house, she shifted in her seat several times, trying to dispel the feeling of foreboding. *This is just plain silly.* She lectured herself. *I'm a grown woman with law enforcement training. Someone merely vandalized my home, nothing more. We'll clean it up, and I can move back in tonight.* She felt better with a plan.

Stefan parked in front of the house and reached for Brandy's arm as she opened the truck door. "I want you to stay here until I check out the house."

"I will not. It's my house and I'm going with you." She yanked her arm out of his hand and hurried toward the house.

He vaulted out of the truck, landing directly in front her. "You are not going in there until I have checked the place out top to bottom," Stefan said in a dangerously quiet voice. "As you reiterated several times, this is too much like the scene in the woods to be a coincidence. A bit of caution is appropriate. Wouldn't you agree?"

"No," she declared, her hands fisted on her hips.

"Oh, come on, Brandy, we can do this the easy way or the hard way, but you're not going into the house until I make sure it's safe."

Standing with arms crossed over her chest, she took another step around him.

He shrugged, grabbed her at the hips, and threw her over his shoulder.

A wave of shock flowed over her before fury set in. She kicked and pounded her fists on his broad back as he strode back to the truck.

Lowering her feet to the ground in front of the open truck door, he held her firmly by the shoulders and said calmly, "Now, if you'll wait five minutes, I'll be back. Then we'll go inside together, if it's safe. Otherwise I'll use vampire persuasion, and you'll stay here anyway. Your choice."

She struggled under his grip, jerking her shoulders back and forth. Would his vampire's thrall have an effect on her? Did she want to find out? Of course not. She conceded, attempting to reign in her temper.

"Think about it rationally. I know you'll agree with me." He smiled down at her, releasing his hold slightly.

If looks could kill…but she finally relaxed her stance. "Okay, I'll give you five minutes, then I'm going in…" She looked at her watch to emphasize the point.

Stefan raised an eyebrow and gave her a hard stare. "Ten and, I'll be right back."

She nodded.

Because they'd sealed the house when they left, the strong stench of sulfur burst through the door when he shoved it open. She wrinkled her nose as the smell wafted through the air. Searching every room as she watched from outside, he opened all the windows and doors as he passed through.

Finished, he stepped outside, motioning her in. She had moved to the sidewalk and was talking to an older couple, pausing to glance at him as he motioned for her.

He walked out to join them as she said, "Yeah, someone broke into my house and apparently tried to start a fire. The living room rug appears burned in several places, the floor scorched, and sofa cushions ripped apart. We didn't have a chance to see if anything was missing last night. That's why we're here today." She turned. "Oh, Stefan, these are my neighbors, Janet and Max. This is my friend, Stefan. He was kind enough to take me in last night, but I'll be back tonight."

Stefan smiled in greeting.

"They were home all day yesterday and didn't see anyone come in or out of my house. Strange, isn't it?"

He reached his hand out to shake the one offered by Max and nodded in Janet's direction. "Nice to meet you. Hope to see you again under better circumstances. Didn't see anything, huh?"

They shook their heads with a frown. Max stared down at his hand, wiggling his fingers.

"Hope you'll continue to keep an eye on Brandy's house. I don't believe it will be habitable until we get a repair crew in here. If you'll excuse us, we've got an awful lot of work to do before sundown." He smiled graciously at the couple and placed his hand on the small of Brandy's back, guiding her toward the house.

She whirled around, teeth bared, and hissed, "What do you mean? I plan to get this place cleaned up and bring my things back later tonight."

Stefan glanced behind them as Janet and Max walked back to their house. Brandy followed his gaze, her lips pursed.

Keeping his voice low, he said, "Well, first of all, the place is going to need to be professionally cleaned, new carpet installed, and minor repairs completed before you can stay here. With your permission, I'll make those arrangements. Second, as you stated yourself, this is way too close to the earlier scene to be a coincidence. I don't want to scare you, but finding your body in pieces next time I stop by would really piss me off."

Stefan stepped through the doorway first and put

his arms around her, drawing her close even as she fought against his hold.

The corners of her mouth finally turned up in spite of herself. "I guess you have a point, but I'm moving back in as soon as all that's done." She finally relented and leaned against him for a moment, feeling safe and enjoying his strong arms around her.

"Sure," he said a little too quickly.

They spent the rest of the afternoon sweeping up the debris, wiping down the walls, and taking the broken furniture to the dump and another load of her stuff to his cabin. On the way back, he paused at a stoplight and looked over at her. "Hungry?"

She shook her head. "Not really."

"You should eat something." He pulled into a fast-food drive-through and ordered a burger, fries, and chocolate shake. "Don't want you starving to death on my watch." Stefan grinned and handed the food to her, pulling into a parking space.

To her surprise, the delicious aromas made her mouth water when she opened the bag. She took a big bite of the burger and chewed slowly.

"I'm going to call a professional cleaner that advertises on the station, then call a contractor Russ recommended. Maybe they can meet me at the house tomorrow at first light."

Brandy agreed he should oversee the work himself since he was off during the day and he didn't want her anywhere near the house.

Once they returned to the cabin, he built a warm, crackling fire and sat down on the couch, patting the place beside him. "Have a seat."

She walked over and settled in next to him with her

legs tucked up under her, glad to be back at his cabin. "Play for me, please."

"You read my mind." Smiling, he reached for his guitar, shifting on the couch to face her. His fingers strummed across the strings, teasing out the melody of the latest song he was working on. He cocked his head and frowned, listening to the song. "This doesn't sound right." Stefan walked to the hall closet and took out a large hard-shell guitar case. "I think this part of the song needs a fuller sound. See what you think of the twelve-string rather than the six." He returned to the couch and ran his thumb across the strings, twisting the tuning pegs until he brought them into tune, then played the song again.

Brandy leaned her head against the couch and closed her eyes, listening. "You're right. That sound fits the song much better. Do you play other instruments?"

"Keyboards. They're set up in the corner of my office next to the computer. I use them sometimes to finish the song after working out the basics on my guitar." He played several more tunes before the tension of the day began to fade away. Brandy's tight, drawn lips relaxed into a slight smile. Stefan put the guitar away and gathered her in his arms.

Resting back against the couch, he slid an arm around her shoulders as he curled a soft strand of her red hair around his fingers. "Rough day, huh?"

Without opening her eyes, she laid her head on his shoulder and sighed, "Uh-huh, but what a wonderful way to end it."

"Why don't you hop in the shower while I tend to a few loose ends in the office? I'd like to get you settled before I head into work. When I leave this time, I'll turn the security system on. You can move around anywhere inside, but it will go off if any of the doors or windows are breached, notifying the local authorities and me. I didn't set it last night because I was afraid you'd go outside or open a window and set it off, being unaware it was on."

"I have a sunrise hike tomorrow, so show me how to disarm it. I may be gone by the time you return." She glanced at the alarm panel.

He frowned, narrowing his eyes. "Do you think that is a good idea?"

"I have a job and I want to keep it."

The muscle in his jaw twitched as he clinched his mouth shut. Finally, he let out a heavy sigh and reached for a pen and pad, scribbled a set of numbers on the paper, then demonstrated disarming the security system. "Please check in with me when you leave. I'll see you after you get off."

"You got it."

Chapter Twelve
Don't Turn Your Back on a Synn

During the ensuing weeks, when Stefan arrived for work, Synn was always with Cody under the pretense of doing production work. True to his word, Cody insisted she leave with him amid her protests or excuses why she should stay. Stefan aggressively spurned her advances.

That evening, when Stefan arrived for his shift, Synn wasn't there.

"Hey, where's your shadow?"

"I cut her loose. Let me shuffle a couple of songs here for a longer play. We need to talk."

Working at the computer, Cody rearranged the playlist, appearing deep in thought.

Whatever was bothering Cody, Stefan surmised it was bad. He leaned back against the counter, elbows resting against the counter's top, foot propped against the front of the cabinet. "What's up?"

Cody turned from the computer, eyes dark and forehead lined with deep creases, the vein at his temple pulsing in time with his heartbeat. "That woman is scary. The look in her eyes when she doesn't get what she wants is unnatural. I'm telling you." He ran his hand through his hair and rubbed at the back of his neck. "She's way too interested in Brandy and you. She tried to wheedle confidential information about you two out of everyone at the station. Son, you two don't have any connection to her, do you?"

"Nope, never saw her before the morning Russ introduced us. If Brandy knew her, she would have said something." Stefan shifted against the counter uneasily.

Cody blew out a breath and shook his head. "Watch yourself and Brandy too. That woman is up to no good. I've had a word with Russ. She's can't be in here after hours anymore. But I don't think Russ is taking me seriously. She's got him wrapped around her little finger."

Stefan cocked a dark brow and studied Cody. "Thanks for the warning. She's not here now?"

"No, I walked her outside at the beginning of my shift and locked the door after her." Cody picked up his jacket and walked toward the control room door. "I'll do another check of the offices and production room before I leave. Have a good night."

For the first couple of hours of his shift, Stefan paced the control room floor and watched the windows and door. Something wasn't right, but as the night wore on, he relaxed some.

Using his cell phone, he checked on Brandy, then settled into the rest of his shift, leaving only once. He thought he heard a phone ring but couldn't locate his cell. Maybe he'd carried it into the office when he'd picked up some paperwork earlier. He'd check after this stop set.

****

As Stefan flipped on the mic, he saw a shadow move out of the corner of his eye. He rushed through the stop set, yanked off his headphones, and started toward the door. She stood outside the glass door to the control room, holding his cell phone up, waving it from side to side in her hand.

Turning the knob, she sauntered in. "Good morning, Stefan," she purred, continuing toward him until she was standing in front of him, her breasts brushing against his muscular chest. The woman wrapped her arms around his neck in an attempt to bring her lips to his. Cody's warning reverberated in his brain. He carefully brought his arms up through hers and broke the hold. "Synn, you're a beautiful woman, but I'm already in a relationship."

"Pity." She didn't back away. Instead, she held his phone and toggled it back and forth in her hand again. "We had a really nice talk earlier. Told her you were too busy to talk to her." Synn shrugged. "She hung up."

Lunging at her, he grabbed for the phone. It slipped out of her grasp and clattered to the floor. She drew a bloodied dagger from her coat pocket and threw herself at him, straining for his throat with the weapon. In a blur of motion, he stepped sideways, caught her by the shoulders, and shoved her across the room.

The chair he'd been sitting in moments before crashed against the opposite wall. The papers he'd held in his hand fluttered to the floor. Stefan slammed her viciously against the wall, knocking the dagger to the floor. He stepped on the dagger with his booted foot and forced his forearm against her throat, holding her up against the wall.

"I like the rough stuff, but we probably should wait until you're off shift," she cooed seductively, completely unaffected by the situation.

In a split second, his fangs unsheathed and claws pierced his fingertips, raking against the wall as he rasped menacingly, "I'm tired of your games. Whatever you're offering, I'm not interested in your kind. Get the hell out of here. Leave Brandy and I alone, or you won't live to regret it. Am I making myself clear?" In his anger and frustration, the fear of his secret being discovered was gone. "Crystal," she snarled, her lips curling to show sharp, pointed teeth as she struggled to loosen his hold and said sweetly, "Tell Brandy it was nice talking to her." Before he could crush her windpipe, she disappeared from his hold and the room without a trace.

He briefly considered searching for her but instead snatched up the station phone to call Brandy. There was no answer, and he waited for the beep. "Brandy, don't answer the door and deadbolt it. Make sure all the windows are locked. We need to talk. I'm leaving now." He switched the computer to program so it would play all the commercials and songs automatically without his intervention. Russ could fire him for leaving the station unattended, but he had to make sure Brandy was okay. He grabbed his coat just as Russ strode in the door.

Russ stared at the damage inside the control room. "What happened in here?"

Stefan stopped midstride and paused to glance at Russ. "No time to explain." He pushed past Russ.

Russ grabbed his coat sleeve. "The side door was breached. The alarm company called to say they couldn't reach anyone here at the station. Did the phone ring?"

"No, not once all night." Stefan paused. Had Synn cut the phone lines? He jerked free. "Brandy isn't answering her phone. I gotta get home. I'll come back later to clear out my locker if necessary. Or have Cody collect my stuff. I'll contact him to pick it up." He stopped long enough to look Russ in the eye. "I'm sorry for the way things turned out."

Stefan sprinted out the station door into the inky darkness and was at the cabin door in seconds, his key in the lock. Before he flung open the door, he felt the fury of her mind. Yet he was unprepared for what greeted him.

Brandy stood in the center of the room, face flushed with fury, her green eyes rimmed red, and coppery feathers sprouted around her face, which began to blur. "Couldn't wait, could you?" Brandy raised her hand as her talons emerged, blood dripping from her fingertips. She slapped him. The blow aimed at his face caught only his shoulder as he turned away, wincing.

"What in the hell are you talking about?" Surprise, shock, then anger vibrated through him. He stepped back, arms at his sides. "Brandy, you don't understand. Synn stole…"

"Like hell I don't." She swung again with such fury that she lost her balance and fell against him.

As he reached for her, his claws broke though the calluses on his fingertips. He grabbed for her shoulders to shake some sense into her, but she twisted, again falling forward into his claws, slicing her shoulder. A dark-red stain seeped through her white shirt as the sweet scent of her blood filled the air.

He hadn't hunted recently, and the scent of her warm, fragrant blood drove his desire for blood out of control. Pinning her against the wood paneling, his hand fisted her hair. He yanked her head back and bared her neck as his fangs pricked the smooth skin over her jugular.

"Stefan, stop!" she screamed, her panicked voice finally cutting through the red haze of bloodlust in his brain.

He released her. She slid to the floor, then scrambled to her feet, backing away from him. They looked at each other, eyes wide in shock and disbelief as both returned to their human forms, appalled at the damage they'd inflicted on each other.

Stefan moved toward her. She held up her hand, her entire body shaking, face pale as she pointed toward the door. "Get out."

The last thing he'd wanted to do was hurt her. But he had. She was wrong about him, and she'd paid the price. He sprinted to his truck and yanked open the door. By the time he paused to take one last look, the door was already closed. He shoved the key in the ignition. The engine roared to life. He stomped on the gas pedal, and the truck fishtailed down the road, throwing gravel in its wake.

****

Brandy stood in the cabin, watching the blood seep through her shirt. How had things gone so terribly wrong so fast? She wanted to sob, scream, and curse. She wanted to blame Stefan but couldn't, knowing that it wasn't his fault any more than it was hers. She was so angry—with him and herself for letting someone else fulfill his needs when it should have been her. No, she wasn't thinking clearly.

Peeling off her shirt, she walked into the bathroom, turned on the shower, and stepped inside, letting the warm water wash over her. It stung as she watched the crimson water flow down the drain. The gashes were

153

Tena Stetler

not serious, not like the damage she'd caused to their relationship.

As her anger subsided, a devastating realization dawned. In her fit of temper, she'd never given him a chance to explain what really happened. She remembered him saying Synn stole…stole what? *Oh God, what have I done?*

The grim reality sank in. They were two magical creatures with inherently dangerous abilities and tempers to match. Yet, at the peak of his bloodlust, he'd stopped because he'd heard her pleas. He cared deeply for her. Would he ever admit it to himself? She didn't know and, right now, didn't care. What she did know was that they both needed time and space to heal the emotional wounds as well as the physical.

Chapter Thirteen

Life Sucks, Then You Die—Unless You're a Vampire.

Using his parks pass at one of the unmanned entry points to the park, Stefan drove the familiar roads. Finally he pulled to a stop at an isolated area near Glacier Lake. He slumped in the seat, closed his eyes, and held his head in his hands as he let it fall back against the headrest. *How did I let this happen? I've done nothing wrong. Never even considered accepting what Synn had offered for weeks. Yet Brandy assumed the worst. Why?* Whether he liked it or not, the answer stared him right in the face. He'd been afraid to tell her what was in his heart, afraid of being hurt. He snorted. *What a fool.* Trust. In the end, it was something neither of them would risk.

His shredded T-shirt was stained crimson and sticky against his skin. The wounds were already healing, but they had a strange golden tinge to them. He wound his way to the back side of the lake, stripped off his shirt, and rinsed it in the lake.

The blue sky filled with fingers of orange as the sun set behind the mountains. He slowly returned to the truck, started the engine, and turned toward the main road leading back to the cabin. Her car was still there. Hope surged inside him. Could they fix this? No, he couldn't put Brandy in danger any longer. He might have killed her.

Trudging up the path to his cabin, he decided to pick up a few items of clothing and give her time to gather her things to clear out.

As he climbed the stairs onto the porch, Brandy shoved open the door, duffle bag slung over her shoulder. He stepped out of her way, holding the door open, allowing her to pass. Voice tired and strained, she said, "Stefan, I'm going to my sister's home and maybe on to Ireland. I'm not sure yet. You need to decide what is important to you and what you are willing to do to get it. I know what I want, but it's not good for me. The feelings I have for...well...I've got some decisions to make also, and I can't do it here, not now." Her eyes, clouded with sadness, shifted to his and back to the ground. "I've talked to Randy and taken a leave of absence. Please don't look for me."

She walked down the path and out of his life. She was right, and he knew it. Standing in the doorway, he watched her get into her car and drive away until her car's taillights became tiny red dots bobbing in the darkness. He closed the door and with it his heart, his life, and any chance of happiness.

Walking over to the couch where they'd sat hours earlier, so happy, he eased down and slumped over, his elbows resting on his legs and head cradled between his hands. He let out a low, guttural sound and leaned back, pressing his fingers to his eyes. *Time to move on. There's nothing left for me here.*

As he got to his feet slowly and headed toward the bathroom, a loud knock sounded at the door. *Fuck, what now?* He yanked open the door and stared in surprise at Russ standing on the porch.

Russ's eyes widened, jaw dropped, and he took a couple of steps backward. He inhaled sharply and stared openly at the healing wound on Stefan's neck, his damp, shredded shirt, and stained jeans. "God, man, what happened to you?"

Stefan sighed deeply, shook his head, and said in a low, gravelly voice, "You don't want to know. What can I do for you, Russ?" Stefan stepped out on the porch with Russ and closed the door.

Russ's forehead wrinkled and his eyes filled with concern. Stefan's voice had never sounded so rough nor had such despair in it. "I came by hoping you could shed some light on what the hell happened this morning. We found Cody unconscious in the production room after you bolted out the door. He didn't remember much except seeing Synn standing in front of him."

An incredulous look crossed Stefan's face as his eyes narrowed. "You what? Is he all right?"

"Yeah, he'll be fine. Nothing more than a bad headache and a row of stitches. Her knife didn't penetrate very deep. He's hoping you'll be along shortly to relieve him." Russ grinned uncertainly at Stefan. "He insisted on returning to work while I came to talk to you. After what you said, I wasn't sure what to tell him. I can go back and relieve him, call Rocky in if I have to, but I don't want to explain what happened to everyone yet. Telling Rocky will be like broadcasting it over the radio waves. The boy gossips worse than a bunch of old women." Russ grimaced and shook his head.

Stefan grunted and wiped the back of his hand across his face. "I'll be there," he said on a sigh. "But I can't tell you any more than Cody already has."

"Yeah, he made the situation pretty clear. I've terminated Synn, called the police, and got a temporary restraining order against her. It'll be permanent at the next court hearing. She can't come within one hundred feet of the station or any of its employees or their families."

"Good. Now, if you don't mind, I really need to get ready for work." A slight smile formed on Stefan's lips. "I'll finish Cody's shift, pull mine, and see you or Rocky in the morning as usual. And thanks for respecting my privacy." He turned and walked back into the house, closing the door behind him.

****

Stefan walked through the control room door and stared at Cody. He had a bald place with stitches above his right ear that ran up to his temple. Stitches crisscrossed the back of his hand and arm. He had dark circles under his tired-looking eyes. "You look like shit."

Cody jumped and spun around. Apparently, he hadn't heard Stefan come in. "Thanks. Good to see ya too." Cody studied Stefan. "You don't look so good yourself but better than when Russ saw you a little while ago."

"She's gone, Cody."

"I figured. She loves you, and she'll be back. Just give her time." Cody clasped Stefan's shoulder and crossed the room to pick up his jacket. He winced as he threw it over his shoulder. Hand on the doorknob, he turned back to Stefan. "You're not like us, are you?"

"No," Stefan said flatly.

"Didn't think so. You know…it really doesn't

matter to me. If you need to talk, I'm available...anytime." Cody turned around and lumbered slowly out the door, shutting it quietly behind him.

Chapter Fourteen
Reunions Can Be Messy

As spring turned to summer, then to early autumn, Stefan grew restless. *How the holy hell did I wind up in this situation?* Irritable, Stefan walked toward the Alpine Game Center as he had every night for the past couple of months. One minute he'd had a satisfying career and a comfortable, if frustrating, relationship with a woman. *The next? I risked my job and lost Brandy. Why?* Because he was unable to control his explosive temper, his arrogance, and his bloodlust. He'd nearly lost everything. *Stupid bastard.*

The game room door banged open, and Stefan stepped inside just as a blinding streak of lightning shattered the midnight sky. Thunder shook the ground underfoot, and dark clouds covered the moon, matching his mood—edgy, erratic, and foul.

Inside the dimly lit game room, a woman brushed past him, the hot flow of blood pulsing beneath her porcelain skin. His fangs unsheathed, and he forced his mouth shut tight.

Imagining her terrible, piercing screams as he crushed her throat to let the fragrant, sweet blood flow into his mouth, made him pull back and move swiftly away. The almost-victim had no idea how close to death she'd come.

Thirst burned like fire in his throat. He was too

vulnerable to walk among warm-blooded humans tonight. He needed to hunt. Next to human blood, animal blood had all the appeal of rotten eggs, but it kept him sated and able to work among warm-bloods. Tonight he should've hunted, but he didn't give a damn.

He stepped out into the cold, misty night and closed the door quietly behind him. As he walked down the dark, wet street, he heard footsteps behind him and paused.

"Stefan, what happened back there?" A voice whispered out of the foggy night.

Crouched down ready to spring, he whirled around, sniffed the air, and then stood, relieved yet shocked to see Brandy glide out of the swirling mist into the shrouded moonlight.

"I could have killed an innocent girl. She was so close, the blood pulsing in her veins. I could smell it and almost took her." An involuntary shudder shot through his tense body as his shoulders slumped. He had no business staying among the humans. Returning to the service of the Vampire Council was what he should have done, where killing was his job description and rewarded.

"But you didn't. You need to hunt. Let's go." She reached out, wrapping a soft, warm hand around his arm. Her emerald eyes glittered with excitement.

Her touch brought a torrent of shame and guilt spinning through him. Yet it didn't stop the want—no, need—that clawed at him when she was close. *No, I can't take that chance again.* He shook her arm free. "Leave me alone."

Undaunted, she stood directly in front of him,

hands fisted on her hips, looking up into his unresponsive eyes disapprovingly. "I already did that, and look where it got you." She raised her arms up and let them drop to her sides as she glanced up and down the empty, wet street.

"I could have killed you. That's why you left. Remember?" he growled, glaring at her. This was the last conversation he wanted to have with her. The memories of that night still haunted him. "I've regretted that night every moment since you left."

"Yes, I remember the fight, but you're being melodramatic. Neither of us was critically injured except maybe emotionally. You know why I left, and it wasn't because I was afraid of you." Brandy's voice was defiant, her lips formed a grim line, and her green eyes watched him warily as she reached up, tentatively laying her hand on his shoulder. She let it slide slowly down his arm, taking his hand in hers and intertwining their fingers.

Calmer now, the bloodlust waning, he asked, "Why are you back? If it matters, I didn't touch Synn. It was a damn set up from the very beginning." He dropped her hand.

Her eyes rounded, and she drew in a breath. "Oh God," she breathed out the words and shook her head, glancing at the horizon. "Questions can wait. We've got a couple of hours before dawn. Let's hunt." Brandy tugged him toward the forest.

Secretly glad she was back, he shook his head stubbornly. "There's not enough time."

"Sure there is." She raised a brow questioningly. "Or would you rather risk another innocent victim that won't escape this time? Now, let's go!" She reached for his hand, tightened her hand in his, and jerked harder this time, breaking into a sprint toward the forest.

****

The afternoon sunlight was streaming through the windows as he relaxed on the recliner beside the bed where Brandy lay. Last night seemed like a dream and a horrible nightmare all rolled into one. A wave of relief flowed through him as he watched her sleeping peacefully, her head resting on a scrunched pillow, red hair tangled and body curled. It was no dream. He leaned over and inhaled her delectable scent. A day hadn't gone by that he hadn't missed her terribly. Questions swirled through his mind like the dark mist last night. *What is she doing here? Why has she come back?*

She stirred and tilted her head up to look at him, then reached up and ran her fingers through his thick, straight black hair, fingering several strands before letting them slip through her fingers. "Feeling better," she asked, eyes squinting against the bright sunshine, "this afternoon?"

"Yes." He leaned down and kissed her hair, rubbing his cheek against the softness.

"I thought so." She smiled.

In reply to his unasked questions, she answered, reaching up and framing his face in her warm hands, "I've been here for a week, watching you. You're far too dangerous on your own. I'm back for good, and it's the right decision. Nothing you can say or do is going to change that. We're both to blame for that incident. We've learned from it, and it won't happen again, so let's move on." She got up and reached for her sweater hanging on the back of a chair.

Stefan stood, stretched, and picked up his jeans off the floor and padded over to the closet for a clean shirt. "Brandy, are you sure? Look what trusting me got you." He glanced at the pink scars extending across her shoulder. He wanted to run his fingers lightly over those scars and caress them away along with that terrible night. Those scars would keep that night burned in his memory for the rest of his life.

"The scars we bear serve as a reminder of our mistakes." Her eyes traced the three scars that disappeared as he slipped into his shirt.

"If you're sure, I won't argue," he said, relieved.

"Is Synn still working at the radio station?"

Grimacing, he shrugged and shoved his hands deep in his pockets. "No. She attacked Cody that night, then disappeared. Still, I've caught a glimpse of her hanging around a couple of times. Russ terminated her the day you left and convinced the judge to issue a permanent restraining order against her. She has to stay one hundred and fifty feet away from the station and its personnel."

"Is Cody all right?" Brandy asked in a concerned voice.

"Yeah, he's a tough old bird. The encounter shook him up pretty bad. He had a huge knot on his head and defensive wounds on his hand and arms where she slashed him with a knife."

"No criminal charges filed?"

"Not until she is located. I don't think Cody wants to pursue the charges. Wants the whole thing to go away."

"Really? Think she was looking for you?" Brandy tilted her head up questioningly.

"I don't know. Maybe. Brandy, you've got to know I didn't have anything to do with her." He told her everything that had happened at the radio station.

"I am so sorry for not trusting you and giving you a chance to explain. I couldn't stand the thought of another woman...I was wrong." She reached her hand up and stroked his cheek. "None of this would have happened if..."

"Let's forget it and move on." He took her hand in his, brought it to his lips, and softly kissed the back of her hand.

Blinking up at him, she nodded and blew out a breath. "What have you been doing to keep yourself busy?"

"Other than work, not much. Hunting when necessary, though the memory of us hunting together haunted me." *This was another reminder of how bad I'd screwed up.*

"Nights off I usually spent in The Alpine Game Room. It's always empty after one or two in the morning except for the old man that runs it. Sometimes I help him out after midnight. He has a hard time keeping help during those hours and pays well. I don't know what happened last night..."

Brandy's voice hardened and her body stiffened as she retorted, "You do know what happened! You waited too long to hunt. The girl appeared out of nowhere and surprised you." She jabbed a finger in his chest. "You were unprepared!"

He took a step backward, watching her warily, keeping his anger in check.

Slowly shaking her head from side to side, Brandy sighed with exasperation. "You've spent the last few months undoing everything you worked so hard for over the past several years."

"Brandy, I didn't care anymore. The longer you were gone, the worse it got. I'm a creature of the night that needs blood to exist. Nothing will ever change that. You can't know what it's like," he said flatly, narrowing his eyes, staring as if he could look right through her.

Unwavering, she stared right back at him. "No, you're right." She conceded. "I don't physically know, but I watched you transition from human blood to animal blood, and that wasn't easy. You did it. Even continued to work with humans on a daily basis. If it was so hard for you to remain here, why didn't you leave?"

"Couldn't leave the station after all they'd done for me. Part of me hoped you'd come back."

"You didn't look for me," she countered matter-of-factly.

"You told me not to. Those were your last words," he said grimly, then brought his eyes up to hers and admitted sheepishly, "I did call your sister looking for you. She said I'd done enough damage, you didn't want to see me again, and not to call back." He shoved his hands in his pockets and paced back and forth.

"Yeah, Hannah can be rough." Brandy smiled knowingly. "I was every bit as much to blame as you were. I pushed you too far and knew it. It's no excuse, but I was hurt, angry, and not thinking clearly." Then she paused as if to consider what he'd said. "Wait a second. You called Hannah?"

He stopped pacing and shifted his eyes to Brandy. "I did. She made it quite clear you didn't want anything to do with me."

"Really? She never mentioned talking to you." Her forehead creased, and there was a steel glint in her eyes. "Hmm, need to have a talk with my sister."

"Is that where you've been?"

"Kinda. I spent time with Hannah and her husband, Tristian, in Maine. They insisted a visit to Ireland to see the rest of my family would be good for me. I took their advice but still couldn't get you out of my head. "She spread her arms wide, then dropped them to her sides. "I am back for good."

Tristian...Maine...No way. Shit. If that was the Tristian I met, he would've hunted me down and... The tone of Brandy's voice yanked Stefan out of his thoughts.

"Now put your shoes on. We are going out."

"Now? Where? Wait a minute. Does Tristian have a last name?" Stefan asked.

"Uh, what? Oh, sure, it's Shandie." Brandy looked over at Stefan inquiringly. "Why?"

Dammit. Stefan swallowed hard and forced himself to relax. *This is going to get complicated really quick. I'm going to have to tell Brandy about my previous life with the Council, and soon.* "No reason. Just wondered."

"Nice try, but changing the subject isn't going to work. We're going out. Now. You hunted last night, and you can't let what almost happened in the game room undermine your confidence. When is your next shift?"

"I've a couple of nights off." He pulled his hair back in a ponytail. Their eyes met as he turned around, and she watched him intently. A smile played around the corners of her mouth.

He continued to watch her as she slipped into jeans and pulled the sweater over her creamy white skin. She ran a brush through her long, curly hair and flipped it over her shoulders. Sunlight glimmered off the strands of red hair that cascaded down her back. The effect was mesmerizing.

Her eyes narrowed, and she turned to face him. "What are you looking at?"

"You, Brandy. I missed you…a lot," he admitted reluctantly, feeling as though he'd laid his soul bare for her examination.

Her eyes softened as her glaze swept over him. "Wow, that's different, admitting your feelings." Brandy padded across the floor in her bare feet and leaned against his broad chest. She slid her hands up his back slowly to the nape of his neck. Her fingers sifted through his hair as she removed the rubber band.

"You have such long, silky hair." She fanned the sleek black strands out across his shoulders and laid her cheek against them. "I love the silky feel against my skin."

He wrapped his arms around her and sighed quietly, smoothing her unruly curls with his large hand as he pressed her warm body against his cool chest.

She backed away, stepped into her shoes, and bent down to tie the laces. "Now let's go." Grabbing his hand, she pulled him out the door into the frigid air. Ice crystals danced on the breeze, coming to rest on her upturned face, sparkling like diamonds in her windswept hair and eyelashes. They walked hand in hand down the slick, crowded sidewalks. Thirst burned in his throat but not so much that it made him uncomfortable. A good sign.

Like kids, they ran through the park laughing and leaving footprints in the newly fallen snow. He'd never thought he could feel like this again. Grinning wickedly, he scooped up a handful of snow and threw it at Brandy.

She ducked as it sprinkled over her back, then bent down with her back to him, turned, and lobbed a snowball at his face. Her aim was much better and more deliberate than his, and the packed snowball found its mark as he grinned back at her through a face full of snow.

Pay back later, when she least expects it. He grinned mischievously at her. At last, they found an empty park bench in the shadows and sat down.

Brandy turned to him. "How you doing?"

"Good. The thirst is there, but manageable. It's not like I've been stalking humans since you've been gone," he said indignantly. "Not saying I haven't had a few close calls."

"Okay, let's go back to the game room."

"No," he hissed. "Not during the day and especially not when it's crowded."

"Yes. You've fed and need to know you can handle being in a crowd again. I know you can. Besides, that's what you get for becoming a recluse while I was gone."

She was right, but he sure didn't relish the idea. They walked to the entrance of the game room. He took a deep breath and walked in. The place was crowded with kids playing video games, running around, and shouting. The sound of blood coursing through their veins filled his ears. He shook his head and wiped his brow. Thirst burned like red-hot pokers jabbing at his throat, renewing his desire for human blood. As if she'd read his mind, Brandy grasped his hand, holding him back.

"You're doing fine. Relax."

Fine, hell. His gums burned as his fangs descended and the beast within strained to get out. He clamped his mouth shut tight, closed his eyes, and willed his mind to block out every sound and smell around him, as he had in his assassin days. At last, his fangs began to retract and relief flowed through his tense body. In control again, he opened his eyes and squeezed Brandy's hand. Stefan nodded to the old man sitting in the back as they left.

Once outside, he disgustedly blew out a breath. "Are we through?" He wanted to put his fist through something but resisted. If he was going to win Brandy's heart, he had to control his temper, behavior, and the beast.

"Yes, for today. Let's hunt and then head back to your cabin."

"Sounds like a plan." Deciding to push his luck, he asked, "Will you be staying with me?"

"It depends." She looked up coyly, batting those long copper lashes at him. "Do you want me to?"

"You bet." He was tired of playing games, of being alone. It was time to settle down, and Brandy was the one he wanted to come home to at the end of the day. Funny, he'd never considered building a life, a future, with anyone. Now he thought about it all the time. Still, he couldn't tell her what was in his heart, not yet. The risk of rejection was still too great.

Brandy studied his face for several minutes. Little lines creased her forehead as she asked, "What has changed you so much?"

"Realizing what life would be like without you. And that damn Cody reminded me how bad I screwed up every single night I came to work. More than that, I got a glimpse of what it could be like with you by my side."

Her eyes twinkled, and she stifled a laugh. "Is that the truth, then?"

"It is. Well, to be fair, Cody has been very understanding. I haven't been much fun to be around. He said you'd come back when you were ready." Stefan stared down at her with an appreciation he never realized before. "Smart man."

They headed for the deep forest to hunt. Brandy ducked behind a tree, slipped out of her clothes, and shifted into gryphon form. No matter how many times he watched her, he felt captivated by her transformation and graceful flight. It was rare that she shifted in broad daylight. When she did, the sun glinting off the bright copper feathers and tawny fur was a remarkable sight. And then—she spread her wings.

After he had gotten his fill and Brandy hers, they hiked back to town and up the wet steps to his cabin. It was snowing again. He held the door open for her. The daylight accentuated the condition of his once tidy home. The draperies were torn and dirty. He'd punched holes in the walls. A chair still lay in pieces under the breakfast bar where he'd smashed it after watching Brandy leave. Not caring about anything, his miserable existence had colored everything. After nearly losing Brandy, he was going to make damn sure she never had a reason to leave again.

****

Lost in thought, he stood in front of the frosty living room window, watching the curtain of darkness cover the newly fallen snow. Brandy's gentle voice and soft touch brought him back to the present. She laid her warm face on his cold back and wrapped her arms loosely around his waist.

She stood on tiptoe as her warm breath caressed his neck and whispered, "What ya thinking about?"

Her breath caused a shiver of desire to race up his spine. "You. Happy you're back." He reached down and put his hands over hers, entwining their fingers. Slowly, he turned to face her and watched her eyes as he touched his lips to hers and drew her against him.

"I'm not sure…" she murmured, leaning into him.

His mouth slid over hers and captured her gasp of surprise as his tongue slipped between her lips and danced sinuously with hers, arousing the beast within him. His fangs unsheathed as he felt the heat of the beast gaining control for the second time today.

Faced away from her, he pulled back slightly, his cheek slid across hers until it rested against the soft curve of her neck. She didn't see the changes he couldn't control. *Damn it.* This wasn't going to ruin his chances of a life with Brandy, and he ruthlessly shut down the beast. Being intimate with her was going to take more caution and practice than he'd thought, but on the flip side, the practice would be…Images of their naked bodies entwined flowed through his mind in vivid detail, causing the expected results.

Brandy shoved at him, "Stefan, you know the…"

"Rules," he finished for her and raised his head, gaze locked on hers. He sighed and brushed his lips lightly across hers. He loved that feeling. Not ready to relinquish his hold, he trailed kisses along her cheek and whispered, "Things are about to change." If she saw the struggle that had just ensued inside him, she didn't acknowledge it. *That's the thing about Brandy. She sees the best in everyone.*

A smile lit up her eyes as she tilted her head to look up at him. "Are they? I think I like this new Stefan. It may take some getting used to though," she teased and slid her hand under his T-shirt to massage his well-defined back muscles. He felt her tremble in his arms as he flexed under her fingertips. He loved that reaction. *Will she continue to fight the desire she feels each time I touch her?* He could scent her arousal.

"How about tomorrow we head to the mall. This place needs some sprucing up."

Surprised at her quick mood change, he shook off the cloud of desire that fogged his brain, leaned away, and looked amused. "What's wrong with it?"

Her eyes narrowed, and she swept her arms up from her sides and turned in a circle. "What isn't?"

He grinned sheepishly. "Okay, okay, things got a little out of control while you were gone."

"Aye, just a bit." She giggled and reached for his hand.

****

The next morning, they walked to the Mountain Mall, arriving early to avoid the crowds. Brandy found the fragrant candles she was looking for along with a crystal vase and a couple of crystal bowls. She perused the draperies until she found just the right shades of blue and handed them to him along with two sets of brightly colored kitchen curtains. "Those should add just the right touch."

"For who? Seems a bit feminine to me." Staring down at the kitchen curtains, he glanced up at her and winked.

"I'll be staying for a while; besides, they brighten the kitchen." She fluttered her eyelashes and smiled up at him.

"After we're done here, how about we go back to the cabin, get my truck, and take a ride over to Kalispell? I need to stop by Badger Building, out on Highway 2, and get sheet rock, mud, drywall tape, and paint to fix the holes in the wall. We can also check on your cottage. The construction is completed, but I didn't replace the furniture."

"Thanks for that. I didn't even give the house a thought when I left. I stopped by my place and discovered the repairs were complete, but like you said, no furniture. Since I wasn't sure what the future would hold, I stayed in a motel."

****

Walking toward the mall exit, Brandy stopped. The hair on the back of her neck stood on end. She glanced behind her and scowled, increasing their pace.

"What is it?" Instinctively, Stefan drew her closer to him and looked around. Synn stood in the shadow of the brick column. "Shit."

Brandy hesitated, then shook her head and frowned. "There's something about the woman that bothers me, other than the obvious. I don't know what she is, but I don't think Synn's human." Brandy shuddered, then gave her shoulders a quick shake. "I don't want to get close enough to find out."

"You're damn right you don't. She isn't human. She disappeared right out of my hold that night. I won't let her control our lives either." He slowed the pace and stared defiantly in Synn's direction. Abruptly, he stopped and sat on one of the mall benches, then pulled Brandy into his lap.

"What are you doing, Stefan?" she squealed, her cheeks blushing bright red as customers nearest them snickered and moved past.

"Enjoying myself. You got a problem with that?" He nuzzled into the back of her hair as he shifted her to his side.

She leaned her head back against his shoulder, her eyes drinking in his face. "Nope." A sigh escaped her lips. For the first time, she felt actual contentment inside him, tinged with anxiety. But given the situation, that was to be expected. The terrible despair and anger that simmered just below the surface was fading. Strong, proud, and defiant, yet somehow vulnerable—that was her vampire.

Absently, he tugged at a wayward curl that had come loose from the black ribbon she'd tied her hair back with.

Untying the ribbon, she shook her hair free and looked expectantly up at him. "If you are finished with your public display of affection, can we go?"

"Yep." Grabbing her hand, he stood, spilling her out onto her feet. They swiftly exited the mall. Her hair fell around her shoulders and down her back as they walked through the crisp morning air. Reaching for wisps of her hair, he ran his fingers through her beautiful mane. Suddenly, a gust of wind whipped her hair all around her face in a cloud of sun-fire. She dropped his hand and reached back to tie it up again.

In an instant, he took the ribbon from her and

grinned outrageously, stuffing it in his pocket. "I like it wild."

Exasperated, she huffed out a breath that hung in the air like a thin wisp of white smoke. "Okay, but you're going to brush it out for me tonight."

"Gladly," he murmured, slowly raising a brow as the corner of his mouth curved up seductively.

She popped him in the ribs with the back of her hand. "I will not be naked on your bed, nestled between your legs, while you brush my hair. Get that image out of your mind right now. Not going to happen."

He snickered. "We'll see." Dodging to the side, he caught her hand before she could pop him again, and her gaze darted behind them.

Chapter Fifteen
Family Can Be a Difficult Dilemma

After they returned from hunting, showered, and curled up on the couch together, Brandy looked over at him. "Stefan, there's something I'd like to ask of you."

"Okay, shoot." He nuzzled her neck, gently kissing her as his fangs accidently slipped free, scraping her soft skin.

"Stefan, pay attention," she chided, rubbing her neck. "I'd like you to consider coming to Maine with me to meet Hannah and Tristian."

"Uh-huh," he said absently, tracing his finger along her jawline. "Whoa. What? I don't think so. They don't like me."

"They don't know you. All they know is that we had some problems, like all couples."

"Only those problems stem from the fact that I'm a vampire and want to drink your blood." He smiled wide, the firelight glinting off his still prominently displayed fangs.

"Well, there is that. Now put those things away before you hurt someone." She grinned, surprised at her ability to tease him now without him getting defensive. "The only problem I see is that they are aware I am seriously involved with someone. They don't know who or what you are. This may present a problem at first." Chewing on her bottom lip, she added, "Oh, and

Tristian is a human. Will that be a problem for you?"

"No more than every other warm-blooded human on this planet on a bad day," he complained sarcastically, raising an eyebrow.

She watched a shadow of doubt cross his dark eyes and chalked it up to nerves. "I'll call Hannah and tell her we're coming." She pursed her lips and wrinkled her brow. "But I don't think it's wise to tell her you're a vampire over the phone."

"Probably a good choice." He stretched his long legs out in front of him.

"You should know that Tristian is not just a human. He is a demon slayer." She dropped her voice to just above a whisper. "And a warlock."

****

"He's what?" The words flew out of Stefan's mouth before he had time to gather his thoughts. He bolted upright. *Well, that confirms his identity. He is Tristian, the demon overlord's assassin. But why—how is this possible? I'm sunk.* Brandy's sister was with Tristian, the warlock he'd fought side by side with as the Vampire Council's assassin. This situation couldn't get more complicated if the demon overlord appeared himself. *Shit.*

Brandy's eyes narrowed with annoyance. "Oh, calm down, Stefan. You are not a demon. You have nothing to worry about."

Right. Nothing to worry about, only watching my life unravel before my very eyes. Stefan closed his eyes and calmed himself. When he opened them again, Brandy was staring at him expectantly. He cast a dark look in her direction. "The girls in your family don't like their own kind, do they?" Brandy jumped up, her hands fisted on her hips, her green eyes blazing. "No, vampires and demon slayers are much more interesting than gryphon shapeshifters. Get real, Stefan! I am sure that Hannah didn't plan to fall in love with a warlock demon slayer any more than I did with a stone-cold vampire. It just happened."

Staring at her, intrigued at how quickly his words ignited her Irish temper, he backed off. "Okay…okay…point taken. If your family can accept that you are seriously involved with a vampire, then I am willing to accompany you to Maine." He reached for her fisted hand and pulled her back down on the couch, gently straightening her fingers out one by one, laying her open hand on his thigh.

She huffed out a breath, settled down caressing his thigh mindlessly. Her hand wandered higher inside his thigh but stopped as if she'd reconsidered. A sly smile curved his lips.

His gaze traveled from her hand to her sparkling eyes. Her temper was quick but cooled just as fast. "You know what they say about people who play with fire." He grinned, teasing her. "You ready to get burned?"

"I'm sure I don't know what you're talking about." She gave one last caress of his thigh and used her hand to brush back strands of wayward hair from her face.

As if the recent revelations weren't enough, a jolt of remembrance came to mind. Serena was from Maine, in fact, not far from Misty Harbor. All those feelings of anger, betrayal, and helplessness churned inside him again. He tried to dispel the feelings before Brandy noticed. *Too late.*

Brandy's forehead creased in concern as she

wrapped her arm around him. "Stefan, are you all right?"

Damn her empathic abilities. He blew out a breath and tried to keep his voice nonchalant. "Yes, I'm fine. It's—the vampire that turned me, Serena, and her group of friends are from Collinsport, a small town about fifty miles outside of Misty Harbor. There are vampire covens and activity in and around that town."

"You've never heard from her again?"

"No. And that's a good thing. I thought myself in love with her, which now I know was only infatuation. Still, her betrayal and my own stupidity cost me everything. I was forced to leave my tribal home because I couldn't be trusted. It nearly killed my grandfather. For the longest time, rage and revenge…Never mind, you don't need to hear this."

"If it helps to talk about it, I'm a good listener," Brandy offered.

"Forget it. I'm learning to let it go."

"Okaaay…" She paused for a beat. "You know, my sister never mentioned anything about paranormal activity around their area. I would assume she and Tristian would know of such things. But then again, she hasn't confided in me a lot since her marriage." Brandy studied his face and rubbed her hand affectionately across his back. "Anything else you want to tell me?"

Oh, Tristian would know all right. I'm going to need to come clean about my past with the Vampire Council before Tristian outs me. Stefan rubbed his temple irritably. "No. I'm not a damn child you have to coddle. Just thought you should know. That's all." He paused and drew a deep breath he still didn't need. "When did you want to visit your sister?"

Her eyebrow shot up at the sudden change of subject "First of next week. I'll make the plane reservations and then call Hannah to tell her when we'll arrive. One more thing while we're about this, I'd also like us to spend Christmas in Ireland with the rest of my family."

He shoved up from the couch and stared incredulously at her. "Brandy, that's three thousand miles from here, fourteen—fifteen hours cooped up in a plane with a couple hundred warm-blooded humans. Not to mention being around your family twenty-four seven, or will we be staying in a B&B? I'm sorry, but that's asking an awful lot."

She tapped her finger lightly on her lips. "I'd have to arrange time off from work, but we're going into the off-season, so that shouldn't be a problem."

"Getting time off for me shouldn't be a problem. Russ hires interns throughout the year to fill in. He gets free labor, and in turn, they get hands-on training. It's a win-win for everyone. If I agree to go."

She blinked at him and smiled coyly from under her long red lashes. "Please," she wheedled.

"Let me think about it," he said sharply, his tone leaving no room for discussion.

Over the next few days, he repaired the holes in the wall and hung new draperies in the living area and kitchen. Just standing there looking around, it was apparent that Brandy had put her mark on the cabin. She had made a mark on his heart as well. He also, unbeknownst to her, arranged to take extended time off. The thing with Synn weighed heavily on his mind. Something wasn't right.

That evening, she warmed up a small frozen

lasagna and garlic bread and set them on the breakfast bar. He poured two glasses of wine and handed her one. "Will you be refurnishing your cottage before we leave, since the construction is completed? Or would you consider moving in with me as a permanent arrangement?" He took a sip of wine, eyeing her over the rim of the glass.

She stiffened for a moment, then relaxed a bit, chewing on her bottom lip as she took a seat in front of the lasagna. "I don't really want to give up my cottage—yet. I noticed you must've boxed up and labeled all the things that weren't damaged and the clothes I left behind. She forked up a bite of lasagna, blew on it, and popped it in her mouth. "Mmmm. This is really good. Want some?" she teased, scooping up another bite and offering it to him with a grin.

Wrinkling his nose, he carefully pushed the fork back at her. "Very funny. No thanks," He took another sip of wine. "Easier to move boxes during construction. Less chance of more things getting damaged. I'm not suggesting giving up your cottage. It makes sense to leave it unfurnished and packed up while we're gone. Less chance of vandalism and less for Cody to keep an eye on. We could actually store most of your personal things in the cabin while we're gone."

Her eyes widened and she put her fork down. "Hey, wait a minute. You're agreeing to the trip?" One corner of her mouth turned up in an unsure smile.

"Yes, if it means that much to you." He chuckled.

"That's wonderful. I'll make the reservations right now." Brandy hopped off the chair, stood on tiptoe, planted a smacking kiss on his lips, then pulled her phone out of her pocket.

****

They moved the few remaining items from Brandy's home to the cabin since Cody had agreed to keep an eye on the cabin while they were gone. Stefan had no intention of allowing her to return to her house, where he couldn't protect her. The trip gave him the perfect opportunity to take that situation out of the equation, at least until they got back.

Reluctantly, he ran his fingers over the fret board of his guitar as it stood in the wooden stand his grandfather had hand-carved. As much as he'd been through, he'd never left it behind. His music and guitar were the only things that provided comfort during his darkest days as a new vampire. Even now, playing relaxed him, so he was able to cope with a world he didn't fit in.

Brandy watched him, her eyes gentle and understanding. She rested her hand on his arm. "Stefan, bring your guitar. I'm sure there will be times during our trips your playing will be a comfort to us."

Arriving at the airport, they checked the luggage. Brandy sat down and picked up a magazine to read while waiting to board. Stefan shoved his hands in his pockets and paced, imagining all the things that could possibly go wrong.

She reached out and caught his hand. "Stefan, relax. Things will be fine. My family is very understanding. There won't be any problems, except maybe Tristian at first. He's a little overprotective where my sister and I are concerned."

"Yeah, I bet he is. Especially when he saw you after our fight," Stefan said uncomfortably.

It was miserably cold when the plane landed, and

the slushy rain turned to snow. While gathering their luggage, Stefan turned to see a young woman hurrying toward them that looked a lot like Brandy. The woman was a bit stockier and shorter with dark-red hair that framed her face and curled around her shoulders. A large, muscular man with shoulder-length, wavy dark blond hair and piercing gray eyes strode behind her. Stefan rubbed the back of his neck. It was definitely the Tristian that he knew.

Brandy rushed forward and threw her arms around Hannah. "It's so good to see you." Giving Tristian a quick hug, she kissed them both on the cheek, then twisted around to find Stefan standing behind her and smiled. "Stefan, this is my sister, Hannah, and her husband, Tristian."

Hannah hugged Brandy again and turned, reaching out to hug Stefan. Uncomfortable with the show of affection, he hugged her lightly. She backed away quickly and looked from him to Brandy questioningly. Tristian's expression turned to puzzlement when he stopped beside Hannah and extended his hand. Stefan took a deep breath and grasped Tristian's outstretched hand.

"This is who you are involved with?" Tristian asked incredulously.

Stefan gave an almost unperceivable shake of his head and leaned over to Tristian, whispering, "I'll explain later."

Tristian's eyes darted from Stefan to the back of Brandy's head before turning to face Brandy and Hannah, who were chattering away. He mouthed something to Hannah and turned on his heel.

"The baggage claim area is this way." Tristian

strode quickly down the concourse, Hannah at his side.

Stefan took Brandy's hand and followed the couple to a huge area where a large group of people were waiting. With a groan, the conveyor belt began to turn, bringing with it bags of all shapes and sizes. Stefan grabbed his guitar, handed it to Brandy, and snagged the rest of their bags from the conveyor belt.

"Come on. The car's this way." Tristian walked briskly toward the terminal exit.

He opened the trunk of his luxury sedan. Stefan carefully stowed the luggage inside. Tristian closed the trunk lid and got into the vehicle. Stefan held the door open for Brandy, then slipped into the backseat beside her. Tristian's eyes narrowed as he watched Stefan in the rearview mirror and mouthed the words "this better be good." Stefan wrapped his arm around Brandy's shoulders and pulled her close. She looked up questioningly but said nothing.

Hannah twisted in the front seat, as much as the seatbelt would allow, so she could see Brandy as they talked. Hannah's gaze wandered in Stefan's direction occasionally.

"We have reservations at the motel just a couple of miles from your house. Could you drop us off there?" Brandy asked cheerfully.

"Absolutely not. You won't be staying in a motel when we've plenty of room in our home," Hannah said.

Brandy explained, "Tonight we will be staying in a motel, and that isn't negotiable. After we've a chance to talk and you get to know Stefan tomorrow, then we can discuss other arrangements."

Hannah glanced at Brandy, who shook her head adamantly. Disgruntled, Hannah finally agreed.

"Tristian, take them to the motel."

Stefan hefted the two large suitcases from Tristian with ease. Brandy set the guitar and her carry-on bag on the sidewalk and hugged Tristian and Hannah. "Goodnight. We'll see you in the morning."

"We'll be here bright and early to pick you up," Hannah said brightly.

Brandy let out a heavy sigh. "Hannah, we've just endured a long trip. We're tired and want to unwind before trying to go to sleep. Bright and early is not on our agenda. We'll call you in the morning when we're ready to go."

That was the final straw. Hannah's blue eyes filled with tears that threatened to spill down her cheeks, rosy from the cold winter air. "Why are you being so difficult?" she demanded, her gaze darting between Stefan and Brandy. "We are so excited to have you visit. Now you're closing yourselves off and sending us away." She drew in a breath. Tristian reached an arm around her and whispered something.

Brandy leaned over and put her arms around her sister. "I don't mean to be difficult," she said softly, weighing her words carefully. "I just think it's best that you and Tristian get acquainted with Stefan when we're well rested. That's all. Stefan doesn't know you nor you him. That could be a very uncomfortable situation, especially if we are staying in the same house. We need a little breathing room."

Brandy winked at Hannah and whispered, "Besides, Stefan and I would enjoy alone time before Tristian interrogates Stefan. You know how he is."

Hannah brightened, nodding in agreement. She blinked up at her sister and Stefan, then smiled knowingly, giving him a wink.

Stefan exchanged a look with Brandy and rolled his eyes as he swaggered to the office and registered. He handed Brandy a key card as they walked to the room. Once inside, Brandy padded into the bathroom to shower. She turned to watch him take off his shirt and shoes. He stretched out on the king size bed with a broad smile across his face. Closing the bathroom door, she felt him relax. This must be heaven for him after several hours cooped up in a plane with a couple hundred warm-bloods.

When she stepped out of the bathroom dressed in a long white satin negligee, which clung to her curves, deliberately leaving very little to his imagination, she grinned at the smoldering look he sent her.

Easing into the chair beside the bed, she leaned back, closing her eyes. Stefan got to his feet, bent down, and kissed her forehead, wrapping his arms around her, inhaling deeply.

"Are you sniffing me?" she said on a laugh.

"Keep those eyes closed for just a minute more." He took her wrist in his hand. She felt the cool metal of the bracelet circle it.

At the click of the clasp, she opened her eyes and stared wide-eyed at the delicate emerald and diamond bracelet. A small gasp escaped her lips as her other hand flew to her mouth. "Stefan, it's beautiful, but…"

When she brought her warm hand to his cool lips, she shivered a bit. *Fire and ice—that's what we are.*

The corners of his mouth curved into a smile as his lips skimmed over her knuckles. "To celebrate a new beginning."

"Since I returned, your actions have more than

shown your intentions." She reached up and touched her lips to his, though she was still waiting for his words.

He straightened and sat on the bed. "I know, but the next couple of weeks may be difficult. This will remind us what we are working toward."

Brandy arched a brow. "Trust comes more easily for some of us than others, boyo." She rose from the chair and curled into his lap. "Actually, it's a beautiful reminder of just how far we've come and where we are going. Maybe to Ireland for Christmas?"

Pausing for a beat, he said slowly, "Maybe." Stretched out the full length of the bed, taking her with him, he turned her so his lips brushed gently over hers, then took her mouth hungrily, wanting more but showing her he was willing to wait for now.

"Oh Stefan." She sighed sleepily as he arranged her against him in a cozy spoon position, his front to her back. She drifted off to sleep.

She shivered slightly as he lay quietly next to her. Sleepily, she watched him slide out of bed and his bare feet shuffle into the bathroom. He had a habit of taking a warm shower, then returning to the bed warm against her.

Chapter Sixteen
Bringing Home a Vampire

Steam rolled out of the bathroom door as Stefan stepped out, toweling his hair. He stopped and stared, surprised to find her sitting crossed-legged on the bed. Buck naked, he made no effort to cover up.

Her eyes went wide. Red patches bloomed on her cheeks. Still her gaze wandered over him and quickly returned to his face.

Finished toweling his hair, he wrapped the towel low on his hips. "Enjoy the view?" He sauntered over to the bed and eased in beside her, his hand caressing her arm as he leaned in to trail kisses up her neck, across her jaw, and trace her lips with his tongue.

"Uhh…maybe," she stuttered. "I mean, you said maybe about going to Ireland. Is that close to a yes? I need to get tickets. Call my parents with the wonderful news tomorrow, uh…today before we go to Hannah's. Do you have a passport?"

"Sure, I do," he said in a low, seductive rumble. "But when did maybe turn into yes?" He tilted his head and looked at her with interest, tracing his finger along the curve of her shoulder, around the swell of her breast, dipping into the cleavage bared by her negligee. "Will you tell them a vampire is coming to celebrate Christmas with them?"

She licked her lips, shook her head slowly, and

189

caught his hand. "Perhaps it isn't something I should spring on them over the phone," she said hesitantly. "Rather tell them in person."

"Probably a good idea." He kissed the side of her neck below her ear.

"Um…provided I can convince my sister to keep her mouth shut. Stefan, you are making it very hard to concentrate."

"Oh, sorry." A devilish grin spread across his face as he eased down beside her. "You were saying."

"My parents should hear it from me. Hannah probably has an idea what you are, but she won't say anything till she can confirm it."

"If your parents talk to her before we see them, she won't tell?" *Hannah may, but Tristian sure as hell knows what I am.*

"No, I don't believe she will. That's one reason I insisted on staying in a motel and left her with the impression that we're intimate. At that point they have no choice but to accept our relationship, and she no time to confirm what you are."

"She won't know that we're not? I mean, you seem to be able to tell anything about anyone when you meet them."

"That's true, but if you play your part well, she won't know for sure. She doesn't have the same abilities I do."

He raised his arms above his head and let them drop to his sides. "How the hell am I supposed to do that?"

"Just follow my lead. We're openly affectionate people when committed." She smiled shyly, stifling a yawn.

"Brandy, we're not. Not due to my lack of trying." He wiggled his eyebrows. "I won't let you lie to your family. Tell them the truth, or the trip is off. Or we can…"

Ignoring his innuendo, she protested. "I won't be lying." Her full lips formed a pout. "It's not my fault if Hannah jumps to the wrong conclusion. Trust me. It will be easier this way, especially with Tristian. I'll tell my parents and Hannah the truth when we arrive in Ireland. I promise."

"It is if you deliberately mislead her, especially when my scent is all over you," he muttered. "Are they coming to Ireland for Christmas too?"

A mischievous grin spread across her face. "Yes, they just don't know it yet. We've a very busy day tomorrow, and I need some rest. But I wouldn't mind a pair of strong arms around me as I sleep."

"I don't think that is a good idea. There's no guarantee I can control myself." His quick frown turned to a slow seductive smile. "Unless you are willing to…."

"I can't."

"What are we going to do about this physical impasse?" He leaned into her and trailed kisses lazily down her neck, unwilling to concede defeat yet. *If I have my way, she'll need a cold shower. Or maybe…*

"There is nothing to do about it," she said a bit testily, then gazed into his heavy-lidded eyes and murmured, "I guess we'll have to work on that."

Was he ready for the type of commitment a physical relationship required? But she wanted him badly. He could sense it. All he had to do was convince her.

He reached between her legs, gently unfolded them, laid her back, hovering over her, and whispered, "Let me pleasure you, my love. I can do it without us becoming one, but intimacy would be required. We'll go no further than you are comfortable with."

"Oh, you can, and what about you?" she said softly. Her fingertips caressed the muscles across his bare, sculptured chest as she moved her hand down his well-defined abs, finally sneaking her fingers beneath the towel.

He stilled as her fingers explored closer and closer to him. "Oh, we'll think of something." Nudging the strap of her silky negligee off her shoulder again, he slid his hand over her full, round breast. His other hand gathered her gown above her waist, and he slipped between her legs on bended knees as he caressed the inside of her thighs, spreading her wide, and leaned in. "You are absolutely beautiful."

He saw the war in her eyes, but her body had a mind of its own. She arched toward his touch, straining to accept more as his fingers gently teased and stroked. Eventually, she gasped in sweet ecstasy.

Her fingers wrapped around his hard, thick length as she learned what pleasured him.

****

The morning sun was warm, shining brightly through the window when her eyes blinked open. She stirred and peered up at Stefan through her thick lashes as the heat rose in her cheeks. Her body was draped across his bare chest as she recalled the pleasure they'd given each other until the wee hours of the morning.

"Good morning," she murmured.

"Good morning, sunshine. Did you sleep well?" He

brushed a strand of hair from her face and brushed his lips over her temple.

She stretched and sighed, turning her face up to brush her lips against his. "I feel wonderful." Snuggled against his chest, she took a deep breath, drawing in his musky sent, not feeling any of the anxiety she'd expected, only a warm glow of belonging. Whatever happened next, she would never regret last night and the pleasure they'd shared. Though he'd been the one to insist they stop short of mating as set forth by her people. "What time is it?" She wriggled and twisted, trying to look at the clock.

His arms held tight around her as if he wasn't ready to let her go or let the world intrude on this feeling. "A little after eleven a.m."

"Wow, it's late. Hannah will be pounding on our door soon if I don't call her." Brandy tilted her head and tried to concentrate. "It'll be about six o'clock in the evening in Ireland. Da should be home. I want to talk to Ma and Da at the same time and before Hannah shows up."

Reluctantly, he released his hold and sat up in the bed, leaning back against the headboard. The corners of his mouth turned up in a satisfied smile. Brandy slipped out of bed and padded across the room to pick up her cell phone. She scooted back to the bed and yanked up the blanket, curling up next to him, her head resting in the curve of his shoulder, letting the sun warm her.

She tapped the phone's screen, touched in the number, and waited for the connection, chewing nervously on her bottom lip.

"Ma, how are you?"

"Doing well. Are you okay? Is something wrong?"

"Oh...no...nothing is wrong. Everything's fine. Is Da there too?"

"Aye, that he is," her mother answered cheerfully.

"Stefan and I would like to come to Ireland and celebrate Christmas with you."

"You would? That would be absolutely wonderful! Then you and your young lad worked things out?"

"Aye, we did." Brandy felt Stefan's anxiety rise and knew he could hear the conversation.

"Ma, you were right. Things are much better, and I'm so happy."

"I'm glad. We so look forward to meeting your young lad."

Then Brandy hesitated and drew in a deep breath. "He's a good man, but he's not one of us."

Her father's gruff voice came over the phone. "We knew you weren't looking for one of your own when you left Ireland. You were looking for something else... I guess you found him."

"Funny you should say that, Da. Someone else made that very same observation recently." She rolled her eyes and glanced over at Stefan.

His lips twitched to keep from smiling. "Boy, is that a double standard. They didn't get in near as much trouble for that observation as I did," he whispered.

"We'll be pleased to meet him. When will you arrive?"

"Not sure yet. Haven't made the reservations. I'll let you know as soon as I do. I just wanted to make sure you didn't have other plans for Christmas."

"Is he like Tristian then?"

"No, Ma, he's not like Tristian either."

"She doesn't know the half if it," Stefan

commented in a low voice. Brandy reached to slap at him. Only a breeze of air brushed his face as he moved out of range, a wide smile on his face.

"Well, you are of legal age, and you know what you're getting into. Do you love him? Is he good to you?" Her father's voice boomed over the line.

"Da, we're just coming to visit, and yes we know exactly what we're getting into."

"You're not going to run off and get married like Hannah did, then tell us afterward. Are you?" Her mom asked anxiously.

Brandy laughed. "Ma, it's not like that." She sighed again. "No, I am not going to run off and get married."

"Thanks be to God for that. I want you to know, when you get around to planning your wedding, your father and I want to give you a traditional Irish wedding over here."

"Ma, Da, could you do me a favor?" She blew out a breath. The hair fallen over her face bounced to the side, where she tucked it behind her ear.

"Sure, darling."

"Stop talking of marriage. You're going to scare Stefan off. He is already nervous about spending Christmas with you. Let's take one step at a time, and don't embarrass me anymore. He's right here and can hear every word."

There was a long pause. "Are you planning to stay with your sister?"

"No, probably not. We're staying at a motel just a mile from her place. They don't know Stefan. To be honest, I don't feel very comfortable around Tristian right now. It's probably best if we get acquainted before staying in the same house."

Another long, uncomfortable pause and her mother said flatly, "I see."

Those two little words spoke volumes, and Brandy chose to ignore the implications. "Please don't tell Hannah we plan to spend Christmas in Ireland yet. We've just arrived in Maine and plan to spend the day with them. I'm kinda hoping to convince them to join us at Christmas time since you've never met Tristian." Laughing, she said, "You can call Hannah later and get the scoop on Stefan."

Her mother's melodic laugh flowed through the phone. "We love you."

"I love you too. Bye for now." Brandy tapped the screen to disconnect the call and sighed, holding the phone to her chest for a few moments, a faraway look in her eyes. Then she laid it on the nightstand.

"Well, how did it go? Your mother's tone of voice changed for a bit."

"Good, they're looking forward to meeting you." Smiling, she slid to the edge of the bed, leaned over, and picked up the jeans she'd laid out last night.

"So I heard. Are you sure this is a good idea?" He rolled his shoulders and rubbed the back of his neck nervously as he stood and dressed.

"It'll be fine. They'll love you."

"Yeah, until your parents learn I'm a creature of the night."

"Stefan, that won't matter once they meet you. I was heartbroken when I went home months ago, so they know we've had problems. Ma convinced me to try to work it out. She knew more about us than I did at the time. Besides, I'd like to visit with my family. We'll have a wonderful time. Even better if I can convince Hannah and Tristian to join us." She caressed his arm reassuringly in hopes of alleviating some of his anxiety.

"Brandy, are you forgetting I'm a vampire? I crave human blood. I've just now been able to control my thirst again. It's uncomfortable for me to be around warm-blooded creatures for a long time. Gryphons fall into that category. It's not safe. I am dangerous. You know that."

She felt his gaze on her scars and waved her hand in a dismissive gesture. "You won't hurt us."

He hissed out a breath. "Meeting your large family would be stressful enough without flying three-thousand miles in a plane full of warm-bloods to do it. I'm not ready for that. May never be..." He trailed off, shaking his head, and strode across the room, reaching for the doorknob.

"You don't have that much trouble at work," she pointed out, a slight challenge in her voice.

Stefan whirled around to face her. "That's different and you know it. I come in when Cody is ready to leave. Rocky or Russ comes in minutes before I leave. Other than that, I'm alone, just the way I like it."

"What about the baseball game?"

"That was for your benefit." A sly smile formed on his lips. "It worked didn't it?"

She grinned mischievously. "You know what I think?" Pulling him to her, wrapping her body around him, she brushed her lips against his and trailed them across his cheek, whispering, "I think my tall, handsome, ultimate predator is afraid to meet my family."

He shoved his fingers though his hair. "Brandy,

don't joke. You know what I am and what I am capable of." He turned and paced across the room.

"Yes, and I also know you can control yourself. We'll hunt often. Believe me, it won't be a problem," she said in a soothing voice. "Now, I better call Hannah to come get us. I don't want to give Ma and Da too long. They'll call Hannah and poke at her until they find out what she thinks."

"Do I have a choice?" He shoved his hands in the front pockets of his jeans, resigned to his fate.

"Nope! You said you were ready for all of this. A new beginning I believe you called it." She smiled radiantly and held out her wrist, watching the sunlight bounce off her bracelet, creating rainbows that danced across the walls of their room.

For a fleeting moment, a little voice in her head asked, was he ready to settle down? Would her family accept him for who and what he was, as she did? She straightened. They had to, so she pushed that annoying voice aside and picked up the phone and touched her sister's number. "Hannah we're ready whenever you are. Just so you know, we'll be staying in the motel at least one more night. See ya soon." She touched the screen and ended the call.

****

Stefan was thankful to be spending another night at the motel. The constant scent of human blood other than Brandy's made him extremely uncomfortable. Not to mention the thirst and burning would be difficult in addition to the fact that he didn't know Hannah. While he'd worked with Tristian once, talked with him at the overlord's wedding, he wasn't sure where they stood given the fight with Brandy. Stefan had seen Tristian's work firsthand. Regardless of Brandy's positive outlook, things didn't bode well for him.

"Brandy, we will…"

"Aye, Stefan, we'll hunt tonight." Brandy pulled the curtain aside and glanced out the window. "They're here."

Tristian pulled into the parking space in front of Brandy and Stefan's room.

"Let's go." Brandy put her arm around Stefan's waist and gave him a squeeze. "It's going to be fine."

Stefan sighed and kissed the top of her head, draping his long arm across her shoulders as they walked out. In the car, she scooted all the way over next to him. After she settled, he slipped his arm around her. Tristian frowned at Stefan again. *Yep, Tristian is going to be a problem*. When they settled into the backseat, Hannah turned around in her seat so she was facing them.

Hannah's eyes flew open wide as she caught sight of the bracelet. "Brandy, that's some bobble."

"Yes, it signifies a new beginning for us." Joy bubbled in her laughter and shone in her eyes.

"That's different, but it is beautiful. Do Ma and Da know about him?" Hannah jerked her head in Stefan's direction.

"Thanks. Yes, we talked to them this morning," Brandy said smugly. "Actually, Ma and I had a long talk about him before I returned to the states."

Tristian turned up the driveway to their home, his face unreadable, but the frown was now a smirk.

Wow, demon hunters must do well. Stefan surveyed the house and land it occupied. The home resembled a stone castle less the moat. It sat on a large piece of land overlooking the ocean to the front and bordering a lush forest in the back. Even in the autumn, you could tell the manicured lawn and gardens had been well cared for during the growing season. Stefan leaned over and whispered to Brandy, "You may want to reconsider your choice. You could do a lot better than me. All of our stuff won't fill up a small moving truck."

Brandy glared back at him and whispered, "No way. I put too much effort into you. Besides, material things don't guarantee happiness. You've never settled long enough anywhere to accumulate stuff. That could change." She reached over and caressed his face, brushing her lips over his right in front of her sister and brother-in-law.

Stefan returned the kiss, deepening it, and caressed his hand over her cheek. *I could get used to this.* Brandy usually was quite reserved. Public displays of affection were not something she engaged in until recently.

"All right, you two give it a rest." Hannah laughed. She seemed to be warming up to him.

However, Tristian remained aloof. His glances in the rearview mirror alternated between puzzlement and piercing.

Chapter Seventeen
Home Is Where the Heart Is—Sometimes

Tristian let them out in the front and went to park the vehicle. Hannah fished out her keys and unlocked the door. Stefan pulled the heavy wooden door open while the women walked into the foyer. Hannah paused and motioned for them to follow her down a hallway, leading the way to a huge family room.

Light oak paneling covered two of the walls with a smooth stone fireplace spanning the entire third wall. The hearth was set in matching stone. Warm, rich golden hardwoods covered the floor with southwest-design area rugs scattered for accent. The vaulted ceiling had open beams running the entire length of the room, with floor-to-ceiling windows that alternated between multicolored stained glass panels and regular windows.

Hannah sat down on the light-blue fabric couch. The front door groaned open under protest as Tristian returned and joined her on the couch. Brandy pulled Stefan down beside her on a matching love seat, curling herself under his arm, and snuggled into the curve of his body.

When Stefan looked down at her, his heart swelled, and he couldn't imagine life without her.

Tristian turned slowly to face Brandy and Stefan. "I imagine that Brandy has told you all about us. But our information about you is limited. Except that several months ago, she was here, absolutely inconsolable over the breakup of what I assume was your relationship. I don't mind telling you that makes you a very unpopular person around here, regardless of previous encounters."

Stefan met Tristian's gaze and again shook his head slightly.

"Previous encounters?" Brandy looked from Stefan to Tristian, then to Hannah.

Ignoring Brandy, Tristian continued. "The next thing we know, she calls to tell us that she is coming for a visit and bringing you with her so we can meet you. She indicated you both needed a change of scenery." Eyes narrowed, he asked, "Are you running from something or someone?"

"Tristian, you don't know the whole story. Please don't be rude," Hannah begged.

"Hannah, Brandy is your younger sister. Don't we have an obligation to protect her? We don't know anything about this person—I use the term loosely—she's involved with."

Tristian shot Stefan a menacing glance as he shoved up from the couch, pacing the length of the room in front of them. "What we do know is that he broke her heart a few months ago when she appeared on our door step with unusual wounds that even I had only encountered a few times.

"We nursed her back to health, both mentally and physically, and sent her to Ireland, only to learn that she returned to him" Tristian stopped in front of Stefan, his fists clinched, the veins at his temples bulging. "The type of life we lead requires that we know everything about anyone close to us. They also need to know everything about us. If Brandy, by way of Stefan, brings danger to our doorstep, I need to know. Secrets can get us and anyone we care about killed."

"Tristian, please" Hannah implored.

"No, Hannah, they need to know that if they decide on an extended visit, their way of life will be affected as well as our own."

It was apparent Brandy hadn't counted on this type of confrontation. Nor was she happy that Tristian was laying out exactly what occurred during their separation. Despite Tristian's unwelcoming manner, Stefan understood exactly where he was coming from.

He respected the guy for wanting to protect his family from what Tristian perceived as a threat. It was reasonable to advise them of the threat that he brought to the equation. Tristian's eyes lingered on the scars visible above Stefan's collar.

Emotionally, Brandy was in no condition to explain anything. Tristian had opened old wounds that she hadn't dealt with.

Stefan stood up, voice calm and body relaxed. "Hannah, Tristian is right. You both deserve to know the truth. Brandy and I had a rough time, but that's over. We're working out our differences and nothing is going to come between us again." He looked at Hannah, then to Tristian, before continuing. "You have been brutally honest with me and I respect that. I'll return the favor. I am a vampire. With Brandy's help, I've changed my ways so I am—for the most part—not a danger to warm-bloods." Stefan glanced at Tristian, watching for a reaction while hoping that Tristian would keep their secret a little while longer. Tristian was one hell of an actor. Stefan had to give him that.

Walking over to the window, Stefan looked out for a moment, hands behind his back, then turned to face them. "After quite a while together, a couple of months ago our world got as bad as it could possibly get. We made terrible mistakes. The scars Brandy bears I am responsible for, as I'm sure, Tristian, you have already figured out. I imagine that you figured that Brandy is responsible for the scars that I bear. Though superficial, they're grim reminders of things that we'll never let happen again."

Staring directly at Tristian, Stefan continued in a calm, serious tone. "As far as our way of life being affected by associating with you two, if it's what Brandy wants, I will gladly make whatever adjustments are necessary to make her happy."

Tristian nodded thoughtfully.

"I understand why you don't like me. For Brandy's sake, I ask that you at least get to know me before you pass further judgment. Now, if you will excuse me, I really need to take care of some necessary activities of being a vampire." *I've gotta get out of here and sate my thirst.*

"Fine, but I would like a few words in private, Stefan." Tristian motioned for Stefan to follow him.

Stefan stood rooted to the spot.

"It'll only take a minute." Tristian walked out of the room, through the glass doors, and onto the back porch. After Stefan stepped onto the porch, still within sight and hearing of Brandy, Tristian shut the doors firmly behind them, and he moved away from the girls' prying eyes, indicating Stefan do the same.

Stefan stepped to the side and opened his mouth to

speak.

Tristian held his finger to his lips and whispered, "In a minute." He continued to watch and listen through the glass.

Getting quickly to her feet, Brandy started to follow the men.

Without a word, Hannah put a hand on Brandy's arm and said firmly, "Don't. Let them work it out. I'm sure it'll be fine."

Brandy pushed Hannah's hand away. "But you don't understand."

"Oh, little sister, it's you who doesn't understand. Just let them be. Let's go check the kitchen and see if there is any wine left. Otherwise we'll have to go down to the wine cellar." Hannah gave her a little shove toward the kitchen.

****

"Okay, Stefan, what the hell is going on here?" Tristian clasped his hand and shook it vigorously. "It's been a long time. How have you been?"

"Not bad. You know I left the Vampire Council's employment."

Tristian nodded. "You told me when I saw you at the wedding. Was there a problem? Most vampires don't leave the Council and live to tell about it, especially in your position."

"I just wasn't cut out to live that life. Lady Rose was unusually understanding about my leaving. She stood by our agreement when I first joined the Council and allowed me a semi-permanent sabbatical unless dire circumstances require my return. So far that's not been the case."

"It went down as you expected. You simply walked

away? Unscathed?" Tristian's brows rose nearly to his forehead.

"Yep, I moved to Montana where I'm the overnight DJ in a little radio station," Stefan said proudly. "I'm sure Lady Rose still discreetly keeps tabs on me. Apparently I haven't done anything to draw her ire."

"You're kidding me." Tristian roared with laughter but quickly covered his mouth, not wanting to attract the girls' attention. "You went from the Vampire Council's assassin to a midnight DJ working among warm-bloods at a radio station? That must have been quite a trick."

"It was tough at first. But I couldn't continue the murder for hire. There was a difference of opinion within the Council. I was caught in the middle. Some of the vampires on the Council were issuing contracts without proof of wrongdoing. It was political and ugly."

Tristian's eyes rounded in surprise. "I thought Lady Rose was a strong and fair leader."

"She is, but others wanted to undermine her leadership. They were in the minority but caused a serious rift. After I left, it's my understanding that she and the majority of the Council tore the throats out and burned those refusing to follow the rules. Peace was restored. The human body count dropped dramatically."

"Wow, I didn't hear about that, only there was some kind of disagreement in the vampire realms," Tristian said, rubbing his chin thoughtfully. "Now, what are you hiding from Brandy?"

"Not hiding. Omitting. She doesn't know I was an assassin. Thanks for covering for me. You're a damn good actor."

"And you are seriously involved with my sister-in-law. You need to straighten it out now, or I will," Tristian said firmly, glancing back inside in an effort to locate the girls.

"Agreed."

****

Stefan strode into the room with Tristian trailing behind.

Brandy met Stefan as he entered the room, wrapped her arms around him, and glanced from Hannah to Tristian. "We'll be back in a few hours to continue this discussion." She turned toward Hannah, her face lined with concern. "Please don't tell Ma and Da anything that would upset them. I realize the brutal truth was necessary between the four of us, but not for them...not yet."

The muscle in Hannah's jaw twitched, but she nodded in agreement.

Stefan and Brandy walked past her sister and brother-in-law, then into the deep forest behind the house, traveling several miles to hunt. After Stefan sated his thirst and Brandy's hunger, they headed back.

She touched his arm. "Stefan, I was so proud of the way you handled that situation at the house. Tristian caught me completely off guard, and I was at a loss. Sorry it was left all to you."

"That's okay." He patted her hand, leaving his laid over hers. "It was apparent he opened wounds that you weren't prepared to discuss. I figured it was only fair to take responsibility and clear the air. Tristian had every right to say what he did. His only interest is to protect you. From his point of view, I'm a danger to your well-being. Hopefully, he will reconsider that position eventually."

"If he doesn't, it will be his loss. I know Hannah will accept you," she said determinedly, tiliting her head up, a mischievous smile spread across her face. "There's always the rest of my family in Ireland."

Approaching the house, Stefan stopped. *It was now or face her while Tristian did.* "Before we make any other plans, there is something I need to tell you." Stefan intertwined his fingers with hers, holding on tight, motioning to the bench on the patio.

"What is it?" She glanced at their hands as the tips of her fingers turned purple. "Stefan, please loosen your grip just a bit."

"What—oh—sorry." He loosened his grip slightly, rubbing her fingers to restore the blood flow. "I...uh...well. Aww hell." Stefan ran his fingers through his hair and rubbed at the back of his neck. "Before taking the job as a DJ..." He paused for a beat, swallowed hard. "I worked for the Vampire Council. I was discovered trespassing on their territory. The Council didn't take kindly to a lone vampire with little training and even less control complicating the difficult peace they were trying to forge between themselves and the humans. Captured and beaten into submission, I was given a choice by Lady Rose, head of the Council— death or join her clan and work for the Council. It was a no-brainer. She assigned a mentor to me since my sire had abandoned me. Which, if you were wondering, was Serena."

Brandy nodded, caressing his arm with her hand.

"The mentor was an elder of the vampire hierarchy and served as the Council's assassin. As his apprentice, I learned quickly what he expected. I excelled in my position, earning the trust and respect of the vampire community. I took assignments on my own. On one of those missions, I met Tristian." Stefan paused to gauge Brandy's reaction.

Brandy sat with a hand covering her mouth, listening. Now her eyes met his and she folded her hands in her lap. "You know Tristian. Why didn't you tell me?"

"Because I'd have to tell you everything. I was afraid you wouldn't be able to forgive my prior life."

She rose and walked around a bit, then turned back to him. "Stefan, you did what you had to do to survive. How could I blame you for circumstances beyond your control? Did you enjoy your position?"

"No, that's why I left with Lady Rose's blessing, which is a very rare situation. Usually, if you defy the Council and ask to leave, you're released from duty in a pile of ash. Although I am still obligated to her should something extreme happen and she needs my services." Stefan sat quietly, waiting for Brandy to say something.

Brandy returned to her seat. "Tell me how you met Tristian."

"It's a long story. Hannah and Tristian are waiting on us inside."

"I don't want any more surprises, so give me the short version." Brandy insisted.

"Okay. I was assigned to locate the Vampire Council's stolen Labrys. After a long search, I discovered it within a band of rogue creatures, but there was an innocent involved. After contact with Lady Rose, I discovered that innocent, Angie, was the kidnapped mate of a powerful demon overlord, Bruce. After contact with the overlord, Lady Rose instructed me to stand down and wait for the rescue team headed in my direction. Tristian, Angie's brother, led the team. We kicked ass that night. Terminated the entire rogue group. Tristian rescued Angie, sending her back through the dream realm where the kidnapping took place. Her essence returned to her body and awaiting mate. End of story."

"I see. One question, what is a Labrys?" Brandy wanted to know.

"It's a double-headed, jewel-encrusted magic ax wielded only by vampires of true blood."

"Oh." Brandy took a breath, preparing to ask another question, when the door to the house flew open. An unseen force propelled them inside. Stefan suspected Tristian's magic had a hand in it. They nearly tripped over their luggage sitting inside the entryway.

"Brandy, please don't be mad," Hannah said, wringing her hands as her gaze darted from them to the luggage. "Tristian and I would like to get a chance to know Stefan better. You and I have a lot of catching up to do." She paused, sucking in a breath. "Besides, you both will be safer here than at the motel." Her hand flew up to cover her mouth, as if she'd said something she shouldn't, then she waved the same hand in a dismissive fashion. "We'll explain that situation tomorrow morning. If it's okay?"

Tristian lounged beside the luggage, one wide shoulder leaning against the wall, his expression dark.

Relaxing her shoulders a bit, Hannah continued. "Realizing your need for privacy, we've prepared the bedroom suite on the other side of the house for you. It has a king size bed that should be comfortable for both of you, a small sitting room with fireplace, and its own bathroom. Please stay with us for the rest of your visit."

Brandy glanced over at Stefan. He nodded slowly. *Might as well. Nothing left to hide.*

"Okay, we'll give it a try for a couple of days," Brandy agreed. "We'll see how the arrangement works out."

A smirk curved the corner of his mouth as Tristian snapped his fingers and the luggage disappeared.

Hannah smiled happily and motioned them to follow her up the massive wooden staircase. Their room was huge. In the corner of the room, a fire crackled in the little stone hearth, giving it a warm, cozy feel. There was a comfortable-looking steel-blue-and-cream loveseat and matching rocking chair positioned in front of the fireplace. The bedroom carpet was a frosty gray, butting up to steel-blue tile at the entry to the bathroom. The walk-in shower was bigger than the whole bathroom in his cabin. Stefan touched the cool marble walls, noting the several spray nozzles and a bench running lengthwise.

Hannah opened the linen closet, indicating the towels and extra toiletries. "If you need anything else, let me know." With a smile and a wave, she bustled out the door, leaving them to settle in.

Pausing for beat, she turned. "We'll be downstairs for a while longer if you want to talk. Otherwise we'll see you in the morning." She reached back and closed the door softly behind her.

"I'd like to go downstairs for a few minutes and say goodnight to Tristian and Sis," Brandy said, stifling a yawn. "This has been a strange day."

After putting their clothes away, they walked down the right side of the ornately-carved split wooden staircase that opened into the large family room. Stefan ran his hand over the banister and examined intricate carvings on the newel posts. "Wow, there is a lot of Old World craftsmanship in the woodwork of this home."

Tristian and Hannah sat curled up, arms around each other, beside the crackling fire in the room, talking softly, their heads close together. Tristian glanced up as Stefan and Brandy quietly padded into the room, not changing his intimate position with Hannah, yet his expression was relaxed and inviting.

"The carvings are ancient charms my parents used to protect this house. Join us." He motioned to a couple of enormous royal-blue velvet pillows lying on the floor next to them. Stefan sank down on one and Brandy wound herself into his lap, relaxing her body into the curve of his. *I could definitely get used to this. Brandy is so relaxed and affectionate here.*

"I'm glad you decided to join us," Tristian said slowly. "I appreciate your complete honesty this evening and apologize if my behavior made you uncomfortable. As you know, diplomacy has never been one of my strong suits. Though I am learning." Tristian smiled at Stefan. "Unfortunately, where my family is involved, I tend to act first and ask questions later."

"No problem," Stefan said in a relaxed and friendly manner. "Your concern is understandable. It's good to have everything out in the open."

Over the next couple of hours, the conversation revolved around what Stefan and Brandy wanted to do during their visit and how long they were planning to stay.

Tristian asked, "You're a DJ in Montana now?"

"I am the overnight DJ for Big Fish Radio, a

classic rock radio station in Whitefish. I'd worked there for a while before meeting Brandy. During my time at the station, I've covered extra shifts and took very little vacation. When I asked for an extended leave, my boss was willing to let me take a couple of months off. An intern will fill in. They're a great bunch of people."

Tristian raised one eyebrow questioningly. "You worked among humans on a daily basis?"

"Yeah, sort of. The midnight shift is pretty solitary. The human contact is limited to the guy I come in after and the one who relieves me in the morning."

"Oh, so they know what you are?" Tristian asked incredulously.

"No, not exactly. My good friend and coworker, Cody, has an idea, but he never pushed the issue. The rest just think I like my privacy because I don't socialize much. I have made a few good friends and they are very accepting."

"And the situation with Synn?" Tristian asked again.

Tonight was not the time to discuss it, so Stefan merely said, "Later."

Tristian raised a brow, then nodded. "I'll hold you to it."

Brandy yawned and snuggled into Stefan's chest. A few minutes later, she dozed off.

Hannah's lips curved and her expression softened as she watched Brandy, then looked up at Stefan with true compassion. "The situation today has been very hard on her, though she will never admit it."

"I know," Stefan whispered, running his hand gently through Brandy's hair, curling a strand around his finger, then letting it spring free.

"You handled it with grace and dignity."

"Thank you. If you'll excuse me, I'll take her upstairs. Goodnight. It was a pleasure to see you again, Tristian, and meet you, Hannah. See you in the morning." Stefan stood up in one fluid movement with Brandy in his arms and climbed the stairs to their room.

Quietly, he closed the door with his foot. Stefan stood there, savoring the moment, holding her tightly to his chest.

She stirred, blinking open her emerald eyes, brushing her soft warm lips against his jaw, and bit lightly at the side of his neck. "Make love with me tonight. We'll deal with the other issues when necessary. They're archaic at best."

He sensed something inside her change. She seemed more empowered by her decision, knowing it was the right one for her—for them. Brandy had given in to her fiery desire and aching need for him, which had been building for weeks.

His raw nerves jangled. He went hard at the thought of finally running his hands over her luscious curves, feeling her warm naked body under his, taking her completely.

Wrapping her arms around his neck, he lowered her to her feet. She tangled her fingers in his hair, curving her long, lean, sensuous body to his. Need and desire consumed him as her body moved against his.

She traced her full lips with the tip of her tongue and ran her finger along his jawbone, sending jagged shards of lust straight through his loins. He eased her on the edge of the bed and knelt in front of her.

He laid his cold hands on either side of her beautiful face, enjoying its warmth, looking deep into her bright-green eyes, and whispered, "Are you sure? What about…"

She pressed her fingers to his lips. "Shhhh." Then she nodded, murmuring, "I've never been surer of anything in my life." Her lips were warm and sweet on his as he swept her away with the dreamy intimacy of a kiss.

Sliding her blouse off her soft shoulders, his lips followed the smooth curve. His hands slowly explored the soft lines of her waist and hips as his mouth followed.

Heat flashed into her as she moaned, and her eye lids fluttered closed. When he caressed her skin, her heart raced. He felt her desire, and they both wanted more, wanted it all.

"No, don't close them. I want to watch how my touch makes you feel." His gaze still holding hers, with one hand he yanked his shirt over his head and flung it to the floor.

Brandy slid her hands down the side his neck and over his wide shoulders, her fingers lightly exploring the muscles across his back. Finally, she reached down, unfastening his jeans and sliding them onto the floor with her foot. He stepped out of them. Her gaze lingered over his powerful naked body as if she were seeing it for the first time.

He unhooked her pants, letting them pool at her feet. "Step out of those, beautiful," he whispered, then he kicked them out of the way.

Easing her back onto the bed, she gasped as he lowered his body over hers, then rolled to the side and lay beside her. Propped on one elbow, he slid a hand between her thighs, caressing, exploring, easing a finger into her.

She thrust up against him. "Stefan, please...I want...I need you inside me," she urged, reaching for him, guiding him to her, feeling his moist tip at her opening. Yet he held himself back.

She was so tight, there was no way she was ready to accept him. "Not yet. I want to know every part of you. I want to taste all of you." He continued running his hand over her smooth Irish-cream skin.

When he placed his mouth over her breast and curled his finger into that sweet spot deep inside her, a shiver ripped through her. Heart jolted and pulse pounded as she slid off the edge and cried out his name. Then she was pliant, like melted wax at the base of a candle. He continued to caress her, drawing out her pleasure until the last shudders faded away.

Moving his hand to the small of her back, he held her against him and pushed his erection between her legs, and, rubbing it gently against her until she spread her legs wider for him, he slid his hand between her legs and his fingers into the heat, exploring, stroking, and arousing her again. When he slid farther down, wedging his shoulders between her thighs, she opened for him. *Sweet.*

Brandy writhed underneath him, moaning, and thrust her hips up toward his talented mouth. "Stefan, now, please. I can't stand anymore," she pleaded.

"With pleasure." He moved over her and slipped slowly into her tight, pulsing center, finally filling her.

Joined now, he moved with long slow strokes that pleased and pleasured. She arched up against him, wrapping her legs around his waist, pulling him deeper into her as she stretched to accommodate him. She tensed and pulsed around him. She bit her lip to keep from screaming as she soared to a shuddering peak for the second time. The corners of his mouth curved in a satisfied smile.

Riding the wild passion radiating from the soft core of her body, he still held on and held on until her breath came in long surrendering moans, then buried his face in her wonderfully tangled hair, groaning as he shoved deep inside her, allowing release. Finally, he laid his cheek against her warm breast, snaking his tongue out to caress her rosy nipple as he lay spread over her moist, warm body, still enjoying the afterglow.

Peace and contentment washed over them before he rolled on his side and nestled her head in his shoulder. His arms wrapped securely around her, she succumbed to sleep. Beside her, he watched her full lips pucker, then relax into a smile as though pleased with her dreams. He fervently hoped she wouldn't regret this in the morning.

****

As the first bright-orange rays of sunrise entered their room through the panoramic windows, he enjoyed the way she snuggled against him with their legs intertwined, then considered last night. It was the best night of his existence. Brandy had slept tucked in the crook of his arm. She seemed so at peace here. He wasn't sure whether the change of their relationship or the brutally honest exchange last night was responsible, but he was sure this was how life should be.

Brandy opened her eyes and looked deep into his, sharing such unconditional affection that the passionate feelings, still smoldering from last night, stirred, threatening to ignite.

She murmured, "You are so right," responding to his thoughts. Her warm, sweet lips caressed his bare chest and continued up his neck as her body slid closer into his. As the sun's rays warmed their entwined bodies, he slid between her legs again.

Chapter Eighteen
A Demon Slayer's Home Is Not a Vampire's Happy Place

Much later, they reluctantly got out of bed, showered, dressed, and walked down the stairs. Before Brandy brought up the Christmas trip to Ireland, Stefan needed answers.

What danger was Tristian alluding to last night? Why were they safer here than in the motel? How could their coming to Maine change their lives as well as Tristian and Hannah's?

Last night, he'd answered all of Tristian's questions; today, it was his turn.

"Good morning!" Hannah sang out brightly as their footsteps clicked on the landing. "We're in the kitchen. Come join us."

Entering the kitchen, the aroma of coffee, bacon, eggs, sausage, and pancakes filled the air. Human food...how could it smell so good yet taste disgusting? But Stefan hid his reaction. Brandy loved bacon and eggs, and that was what her sister was putting on their plates. Stefan looked at Brandy, slightly shaking his head. He just couldn't pretend to enjoy that this morning.

"Uh...Hannah...Stefan doesn't eat food like this. Sorry." Brandy grimaced.

"Oh, that's okay. I wasn't sure." She picked up the

plate in front of him and handed it to Brandy. Then she turned to Stefan. "Do you mind if I ask what you do eat?"

"I don't mind, but you might." He winked at her. "It really isn't a topic for your breakfast table. How about we save that for after breakfast?"

"Brandy taught you alternatives to human blood, right?" Hannah's lips pursed and her forehead wrinkled in concern as she rubbed the side of her neck. "I never found the practice attractive, but Brandy did. She always liked to explore the wild side."

"Yes." He smiled, hoping to alleviate her fears.

"Okay." Hannah breathed a sigh of relief as her lips formed a slight smile. "So, did you two sleep well? Was the room to your liking?"

"The room is fantastic. I slept like a baby. But Stefan doesn't require much sleep," Brandy said in between bites of egg and bacon. "Pass the plate of pancakes, please." She took a sip of orange juice, stuck her fork in the stack of pancakes, and shoveled two onto her plate.

"It was a wonderful room to watch Brandy sleep in though!" He grinned, glancing at Brandy. "Watching the moon float across the sky and stars fade as the warm orange glow of the sun spread across the horizon was awesome. I may have napped some in between," he admitted.

"What do you mean you 'napped some'?"

"He's a vampire, Hannah. He doesn't require sleep like mortals." Frustration seeped into Tristian's voice. "In fact, he should be sleeping now. If I remember right, he has some kind of enchantment to allow him to walk in daylight."

"Oh, I didn't know." Hannah's face blushed crimson.

Glancing over at Tristian, Stefan fingered the gold serpentine chain around his neck. "Got time for questions? Or would you rather wait till you are finished eating?"

"Now's fine. Go right ahead." Tristian took a sip of his coffee, put it back on the saucer, and picked up his fork, sliding it under a piece of egg.

"Last night Hannah said it would be safer for us to stay here than at the motel. Why?"

Sighing heavily, Tristian shot a strained glance over at Hannah and stabbed his fork into a piece of bacon with more force than necessary. "Because in my profession, as in your prior profession, I make deadly enemies. There are strong protection spells around our home, making it impenetrable by anyone or anything. My parents originally cast them to protect our family. I've tweaked the spells as time went on, adding to the strength." Taking a bite of bacon from his fork, he chewed thoughtfully.

Stefan nodded in understanding.

"The motel isn't safe for you." Tristian shifted uncomfortably in his chair. "You're better off staying here since being associated with us may alter your lives irrevocably. It's possible they may have been already." He popped the last piece of bacon in his mouth and washed it down with a gulp of coffee.

Considering he was not the only one with secrets, Stefan asked, "Why will our lives be altered? What do you mean 'may have been already'? Are we in danger just being around you? I thought that was my claim to fame."

221

"No, not right now…" He paused as if reconsidering. "At least not that I know of. Actually, we live a pretty normal life. Take certain precautions, which are second nature to us. That's why Hannah is so excited to have you and Brandy visit. We are somewhat isolated by our own design. The Coppervales, who are like family, are our only close neighbors. Hannah works from home or flies to Colorado occasionally, but her company has no idea what I am. She kept her maiden name when we married. When we let our guard down or relax, we depend on the safety of this house."

He paused again, shifting in the chair. "Your being in town, unprotected and unaware, makes you a possible target under the cover of darkness. Well, I guess Brandy, actually, since you don't sleep much. Now that I think of it, requiring little sleep is an added benefit to Brandy's safety." He took another swig of coffee, eyeing Stefan warily.

Unable to sit still any longer, Stefan stood and walked to the kitchen window. "Let me get this straight. If we hadn't come to visit, we could still be at risk because Brandy is related to Hannah, who is married to you? You weren't angry that Brandy came back to me but that she came back from Ireland at all." He whirled around to face Tristian.

Tristian considered and poured more coffee in his cup, adding sugar and cream, stirring it slowly. "Exactly. You're a quick study, Stefan."

"I should be. I am, or was, a creature of the underworld. My ties to it were dissolved when I moved to Whitefish and even more so when Brandy entered my life—until recently." Stefan was beginning to get a picture of what was really going on here and didn't like it one bit.

"That's why you married Hannah and didn't tell her parents till well after the fact. Until you felt it was safe for them to know. Huh? They still don't know that you are an enforcer, do they? Have you ever met Hannah's parents?"

"No, it's safer for them. We've not been married long but have been committed for a while. I didn't want to bring her into my life, especially after Bruce nearly lost Angie. Thank you, by the way. You were gone before I had a chance to properly thank you for saving her. But Hannah convinced me that she could handle the lifestyle." His eyes softened momentarily as he peered at Hannah.

"I didn't save Angie. You did. I just happened upon her in my search for the Labrys."

"Be that as it may, I'm indebted to you."

Stefan's lips twitched. *Having a person such as Tristian indebted to me could have great possibilities.*

Hannah nodded solemnly, putting her arm around Tristian as he continued. "What I didn't foresee was her free-spirited sister and now a vampire, who may soon join our little family, all living within my realm of reality." Tristian closed his eyes and shook his head slowly. "I'd still like to know about the incident that caused Brandy to land on our doorstep a couple months ago. You don't have to go into personal details."

Stefan shoved his hands in his jeans pockets and paced. "It's beginning to make sense now. It wasn't me Synn was after. It was Brandy. I was in the way. Is that possible, Tristian?" Stefan hissed between his teeth, clenching and unclenching his hands as he felt the burn of his fangs poking through his gums. "You should have warned us earlier."

"First of all, I had no idea the man that broke Brandy's heart was you, a former Vampire Council's assassin. A vampire I respected and trusted. You need to tell me what happened before I tell you what I suspect." His tone was cool and his demeanor calculated.

"Guys, you are scaring me." Brandy said quietly, chewing on her bottom lip as she looked from one to the other over the rim of her mug. She took a sip, wrinkled her nose, and set the mug on the table.

All the color had drained out of Hannah's face. Her lips were set in a thin line.

"Tristian, let me see if I got this right," Stefan said in a dangerously calm voice. "Synn, the girl from the radio station who caused all the trouble, is a demon or a creature from the underworld. She wanted me away from Brandy so she could get to her and, in turn, at you. Instead, it backfired. Brandy left and ran straight to you, unaware that was the safest place she could go. Yet you still didn't tell her. Synn remained in Montana on the off chance that Brandy would return to me, which she did. However, before Synn's plans could be revised, we came knocking on your door."

Tristian nodded slowly in agreement, avoiding his wife's look of disbelief. "Taking calculated risks is part of my job."

"Not when it includes innocents out of your realm of protection." Stefan huffed, out a breath.

"I didn't know she'd left Ireland."

Brandy sent Stefan a warning look.

He relaxed his stance. "When we were first introduced to Synn at the radio station, Brandy felt there was something odd about the woman, like she wasn't human. Because Brandy didn't touch her, she couldn't confirm it. As it turns out, she was exactly right."

The quick glimmer of surprise on Tristian's face before he schooled it into a blank expression indicated he didn't know as much as he thought he did, and that worried Stefan.

"Did Brandy tell you that her house was vandalized, reeked of sulfur, and there were scorch marks on her floor? Or that the crime scene resembled a hiker's death scene she'd investigated weeks prior? They all lead back to you, don't they? Have I missed anything?" Narrowing his eyes, Stefan stared menacingly at Tristian.

"No, I am afraid not." Tristian shifted his gaze to the floor, then turned to look at Brandy, his jaw clinched. "I wish you'd told me about your house and the investigation."

"How was I to know, Tristian?" Brandy said, her eyes blazing.

"Why the hell didn't you warn Brandy? If I had not been what I am, she would be dead or worse right now," Stefan growled. "You thought I was a danger to Brandy! I kept her safe till someone made the connection between you and her."

"Stefan, please! Getting angry isn't going to help anything now." Brandy's calm voice did nothing to cover the rage in her eyes.

Scooting his chair closer to Brandy, he draped his arm around her, giving a little squeeze. "Tristian…Hannah, I think you'd better spill everything. Right now" He regained control of his

225

temper, his voice more reasonable but determined.

"You're right," Tristian conceded. "First, let me explain how we seem to have gotten to this point. I'm not an irresponsible person. I haven't lived this long by being careless in my profession or personal life. I take all necessary precautions to keep myself, and recently my family, safe." He leaned back in his chair and tented his fingers.

"A few months ago, I received a tip that there was trouble brewing in Montana. Before I could act on it, Brandy was on my doorstep. We didn't know what was going on, but the demon apparently did. That's why she stuck around, knowing there was a good chance Brandy would return."

"You shipped Brandy off to Ireland for her own safety."

Tristian took a deep breath and blew it out, running his fingers through his hair. "Brandy only told us she was in a serious relationship that had gone bad. No mention of a third party of any kind. I took that to mean it was over."

"Making assumptions in your line of work is dangerous."

Ignoring Stefan's innuendo, Tristian continued. "My first mistake. In my defense, if there is one, gryphons don't keep their commitment a secret, nor do they commit to a one-sided relationship. She must have seen something in you that you didn't even see in yourself. You didn't know she had committed to you long before she left, did you?"

Stefan blew out a breath and answered quietly, "No, I didn't understand a lot about Brandy's people until she returned. We're still not committed."

Tristian's eyes darted to Brandy and back to Stefan, then he nodded, "Oh, really? Then you certainly don't understand Brandy, but I'll leave that to her to explain. It's none of our business." He shot a warning glance to Hannah, who glared at him.

"Anyway, I never investigated further, thinking you were out of the equation and she was safe in Ireland. The first we knew Brandy had returned from Ireland was when she called a few nights ago." Tristian shoved to his feet. "I've never faced such a dilemma. I blame myself for not understanding that family relationships take more attention than I realized. I rarely made mistakes till I met Hannah, and that's a long story for another time."

"We've nothing but time at the moment," Stefan said tersely.

Rolling his shoulders, Tristian heaved a frustrated sigh. "Fine. I was born into one of the most powerful magical families that ever existed. Our ancestry goes back thousands of years. I am human, but a warlock."

"I'm aware," Stefan said.

"My family's Book of Shadows is one of three that contain powerful spells cast to seal the portals of Hell over two thousand years ago. The other two contain the additional spells. When woven together, they prevent undesirables from entering the mortal world through any of those portals. Family members hid the Books for safekeeping. Over the centuries, their locations became blurred making maintaining the enchantments difficult. Apparently, this was why some ancient calendars didn't go past the year 2012."

Stefan let out a low whistle and shook his head.

Tristian shrugged. "I guess they figured the odds

227

were against the world surviving if the gates or portals were breached. The end of 2012 came and went without noticeable major breakdown. Many considered the stories passed down from generation to generation to be old wives' tales."

"But they weren't," Hannah interjected as her husband paced the floor.

"What they didn't account for was the escalation of man's inhumanity to man causing rips in the fabric of time. With the spell that kept the undesirables contained weakening , the lower-level dark demons are again able to escape at different intervals through the breaches and cause havoc in our world. The situation will only get worse as their numbers increase." Tristian crossed the floor and took his seat, handing his cup of cold coffee to Hannah. "Could you warm it up?

Stefan's lips twitched as Hannah looked as if she were about to shove that cup where the sun doesn't shine. But to his surprise, she popped it in the microwave for a few seconds.

Listening intently, Stefan glanced over at Brandy occasionally as she was staring in disbelief at Tristian.

"As the spell weakens, it allows the more powerful demons to slip through and try to gain control of our world. Recent attacks blamed on terrorists are not necessarily so. Locating the Books has taken precedence among magical families. In turn, our efforts make the demons more desperate to get their hands on all three Books and destroy them."

"Which we can't let happen," Hannah insisted.

"Obviously." Tristian glanced at Hannah. "What no one knows for sure is how the spell was cast and by whom. Or why it has been allowed to deteriorate without being monitored in recent years. Something must have happened to those that cast the interwoven spells without proper arrangements made for continuation. It's my responsibility to find out and see that things are put right, then the spells renewed, before it's too late."

"That's a tall order for anyone," Stefan said.

"The demons that were in the mortal world when the spells were put in place don't want the spells to expire either. They don't want to share their domain. Most live among us and have become decent allies. My sister, Angelique, as you know, is married to Bruce, the Western Hemisphere's Demon Overlord, who owns the premier hair salon, The Wycked Hair, in Washington, D.C. All the power players in D.C. frequent his salon. It really helps us keep our fingers on the pulse of demonic and magic creature activity. That is how I discovered what happened to you and Brandy in Montana."

"Tristian, I know your sister is married to a high-level demon but always wondered how that happened? Especially since you are a slayer working for a demon?" Stefan raised an eyebrow.

"The same way Brandy took up with a vampire," Tristian growled. "You just can't control some things, but you can bet I sure tried! Failed miserably." He shifted in his chair and took the mug of steaming coffee Hannah handed him. "Thank you."

She leaned over and whispered loudly, "Next time, do it yourself."

After taking a sip, Tristian glanced at Hannah and continued wearily, "The demons have integrated themselves into our society, using their magic to attain wealth and power. You'd be surprised at their identities.

There are large groupings of them in Washington, D.C.; New York; and Los Angeles. As long as they maintain a low profile, mind their own business, and don't create problems, we leave them alone. Once they use their power against mortals for evil or self-gain, we take them out and acquire all their wealth."

"Well, that explains your house and lifestyle," Stefan muttered, glancing around.

"Yes, I am very good at my profession," Tristian said icily.

The silence was deafening as they looked back and forth at each other, considering the ramifications of all that had happened. There was no way he and Brandy could return to Montana right now. Even the promised visit to Ireland could be in question.

Stefan finally broke the silence, saying stiffly, "Okay, so where does this leave us, Tristian? Returning to Montana would be difficult, if not impossible, without putting ourselves or others around us in danger. Why would they want to use Brandy to get to you? Why not go after Hannah still? What would they gain?"

Brandy's eyes glistened with tears threatening to spill down her cheeks. Hannah was in no better shape, except fury burned in her gaze. Tristian looked from Hannah to Brandy and then his eyes met Stefan's. Looking over at Tristian, Stefan was surprised to see a terrible anguish in his eyes. *This situation has taken a toll on him as it has everyone.* Alone, Tristian couldn't expect to protect everyone; worse, he couldn't protect anyone in his current state of mind.

"It's a guess, but possibly they think I know the location of the Books and would use Brandy to force me to either tell them or turn over the Books. If I had them, which I don't. They apparently thought it was easier to get to Brandy than Hannah since she has the protection of this house and me. She doesn't stray too far from here or protection. Our home in Colorado is also protected with strong magic."

"This is a goddamn deadly game of cat and mouse, and no one wins."

"That's about it."

Brandy caught Stefan's eye and slightly jerked her head toward the stairs leading to their bedroom. He nodded in agreement. "Would it be safe to take a trip, say, to Ireland?"

After a long pause, Tristian nodded slowly. "Possibly, at the moment." He rubbed his chin with thumb and fingers. "Actually, Ireland is one of the safer places because the Irish people take for granted that magic exists. Magic creatures in Ireland are very protective of their Emerald Isle. Therefore, the demons would more likely be discovered and destroyed there than in other places in the world."

"Are you looking for the Books and researching what happened to cause all of this to unravel?" Stefan asked.

Tristian's eyes narrowed to dangerous slits as he hissed out a breath. "We are monitoring the situation and continually looking for the Books, but so far, nothing. However, I have learned that certain events triggered some answers, but recently we've hit a dead end. Not to mention my employer expects me available to do my job."

"It's going to be a dead end for all of us if you don't discover something soon," Stefan said, stretching his arms above his head and rolling his head from side to side, trying to get the kinks out of his neck.

"Don't you think I know that, bloodsucker?" Tristian's face flushed beet red as the vein at his temple pulsed. His hands clenched and unclenched at his side as he stood ramrod straight.

Brandy unceremoniously slid from Stefan's lap as he rose. She jumped to her feet and slipped neatly between the two. "I think you both need some space. Let's split up for a bit and consider all that we've learned today. We'll meet in the family room in a couple of hours when tempers have cooled."

Tristian took a step backward as his color returned to normal, though his face was still unreadable. "Yes, seems like a good idea." He wrapped his arms around Hannah, who clearly stiffened at his touch. They walked toward the other end of the house.

"I'd say by Hannah's expression and body language Tristian has a lot of explaining to do." Stefan said with smug satisfaction as he swept a surprised Brandy up in his arms, kissed her soft lips, and carried her up to their room. He lowered her gently to her feet, and he closed the bedroom door.

"Tristian has the reputation of being a badass. Guess that is well earned," Stefan said grimly. Striking a match, he tossed it into the stack of wood in the fireplace. With a whoosh, the flames shot up the dry wood. In no time, a roaring fire gave a warm, comfortable feel to the room. Brandy ambled over, put her arms around his waist, and laid her hot cheek against his cold back. She slid her hands beneath his shirt and delicately caressed her fingers over the contours of his bare chest—a ritual he truly enjoyed.

"Play for me, Stefan. Please. It relaxes me, as it

does you." She kicked her shoes off and sat on the floor in front of the fireplace. "I can't believe what Tristian just told us. How can that be?" She shook her head. "It's got to be some kind of perverse joke."

Stefan reached over and picked up his guitar, strumming his fingers absently across the strings as he considered Tristian's words. "I don't think it's a joke." If the situation was as dire as Tristian said, was it possible for them to find the Books and stop the dark demons while keeping Brandy safe? He'd let those thoughts simmer while he mindlessly strummed his instrument.

Sitting cross-legged on the floor in front of the little stone fireplace, he wrapped his callused fingers around the strings of the guitar and began playing the melancholy tune he'd started in the days following Brandy's departure. He'd never had the heart to finish it, but now his fingers moved over the strings in a light-hearted, upbeat finish to the tune. Brandy reached over and grabbed a pillow from the bed, stuffed it under her head, and stretched out on the floor next to him, her hand resting on his knee.

"I've never heard you play that song before. It's so moody but yet finishes with such hope and joy. Is it new?"

"Yep. I just finished it tonight," Stefan said proudly.

Brandy's eyes twinkled as she gave his knee an affectionate squeeze. "Amid all this doom and gloom, you finish a song upbeat. How?"

"Because I've learned to live in the moment, and right now I am happier than I have ever been. The song came to me the day you left, but I never had the heart to finish it. Tonight, the rest of it kinda wrote itself. It felt right." Leaning over, he kissed her cheek. "Whatever the future may hold for us, I'm going to enjoy what we have right now."

The corners of Brandy's lips twitched. "I'd like to hear more, then we can discuss this mess."

Brandy lay on the floor, eyes closed, her body swaying with the last strains of a song. "Guess I'm ready to discuss our options now," she said on a sigh as he placed the guitar carefully in its case, pulling the purple silk cover over it and closing the lid carefully, latching the case securely.

Peering at her from under his furrowed brows, he asked, "What options do you see?"

"I'm not sure. I don't know how, but I missed that the girl was demon and that she was after me rather than you. I've never made such bad mistakes in judgment before." Brandy shook her head, looking down at the floor.

"Hey, now, wait a minute. You never had a chance to get close to her. How could you have known? Besides, you gave us another chance. Some would say that is the epitome of bad judgment. To top it off, you bring me to meet your demon slayer brother-in-law." He stopped and took a deep breath, "Now, I would say there is an error in judgment somewhere in there." Grinning outrageously at her, he brushed his knuckles gently across her cheek.

"You just gave me examples of what I've done right. We're working it out together, and you really didn't need to tell Tristian we weren't committed."

"Yes, I did. This whole situation is hard enough. I'll not allow you to lie to them. If we work it out, then they'll be the first to know. Until then, we keep it honest."

She took the pillow out from under her head and flung it at him.

"Not my fault that Tristian's ideas are flawed." Her green eyes sparkled again, the earlier fear gone.

Yes, we are on the right track now. Important decisions can't be made under duress.

Stefan discussed with Brandy the options they saw, whether this situation would change their plans for Ireland, and how Tristian's revelations could impact them, possibly for the rest of their lives. After a couple of hours, he tucked his shirt in, Brandy slipped her feet into her shoes, and they padded downstairs.

Already sitting close to the blazing fire in each other's arms, Tristian and Hannah whispered softly. Walking in, Stefan grabbed a floor pillow and sat down, much as they had last night.

"I really didn't mean to involve you two in my world." Tristian began shaking his head slowly, his expression grim. "Things have never been this outrageously out of control. That's one of the reasons I finally took Hannah as my wife. I thought I could provide a good life for us. Turns out…"

Stefan interrupted, "Tristian, we have to play the cards we are dealt in life. I should know. Brandy and I have decided to stay here for a couple of weeks as planned. Then we'll spend Christmas in Ireland with Brandy's parents. In fact, we'd like you and Hannah to accompany us to Ireland. If I have to meet Brandy's family, I see no reason why you should get out of it."

Tristian grunted, stood up, and shook his head. "That's not possible given the circumstances."

With a mischievous glint in her eye, Brandy looked over at Hannah, who nodded as her mouth curled into a wicked grin. "I'm afraid it is. I've already purchased four tickets to Ireland. We'll spend Christmas with Ma and Da."

"Hannah, you are free to take Brandy and Stefan with you, but I won't go."

"Yes, as a matter of fact, you will. I've gone along with your wishes up till now, but with the recent turn of events, I want to see Ma and Da. You promised a celebration of our wedding. Now is as good a time as any. If the world is to end, I want them to meet you." Hannah stood in front of Tristian, hands fisted on her hips, and blew a strand of dark-red hair out of her face, blue eyes flashing a warning as she set her jaw.

Stefan glanced at Tristian and shrugged, hooking his thumbs in his front pockets. *She's got him by the short hairs.* He coughed to keep from laughing. *Better him than me.* "Besides, we'll need you and Hannah to keep relatives busy when Brandy and I hunt. Revealing what I am and how I live is not something the whole family needs to know right away. Her parents will know soon enough, but it would be best if it ended there. It'll be hard enough to be close to warm-bloods twenty-four hours a day, seven days a week."

"What do you mean 'hunt'?" Hannah tensed, those determined blue eyes now turned in Stefan's direction and then accusingly toward Brandy. "You hunt with him? I thought we'd evolved beyond that." She sniffed.

On a half laugh, Brandy said, "Relax, Hannah. It's not what you think. I transform and hunt with him. It's something I've always done, even before Stefan. Not such a bad way to live, and I don't expect you to understand. But you will have to accept our way of life if we're going to stay with you and Tristian."

Obviously yanking her temper back to a simmer, Hannah blew out a breath. "It's not a problem. I just wondered; that's all."

"From our viewpoint, it looks like you two need all the help you can get," Brandy said smugly.

Chapter Nineteen

Fireplace Apparition—Not a Normal Form of Communication

The worst of the conflicts settled, the couples relaxed around the warm fire. Hannah stood up and stretched. Hands on her hips, she leaned to the far left and then to the right. "Anyone want popcorn?" she asked, moving toward the kitchen.

"Sure. Want some help?" Brandy asked, unfolding herself and getting to her feet.

Before they could leave the room, flames suddenly crackled and popped in the fireplace, then a plume of dark-blue smoke curled around the blaze. Everyone in the room gasped except Tristian as a violent scene played out right in the middle of the raging fire.

****

"You wanted to see me, Baltizar?"

"Yes, Synn, I can't believe you've lost the gryphon girl and her vampire boyfriend!" Baltizar raged, shooting exploding orange fireballs in Synn's direction.

"Hey, back off. I'll tell you what you want to know!" Synn screamed, dodging the fireballs and retaliating with shocking-blue lightning bolts.

"Brandy's capture was your responsibility." Baltizar's face distorted with fury but his voice was deadly calm.

"It would've helped if you'd told me that her

238

brother-in-law was not only a demon slayer but a damn warlock from the oldest, most powerful family ever known." Synn deflected a blazing fireball back at Baltizar. The right side of his black robe went up in flames.

Ignoring her lucky shot, he eyed her menacingly. "How did Brandy make you?"

"I'm not sure she did. She and the vampire saw me in the mall after she returned. When I checked on them two days later, her house was empty. The vampire's cabin was locked up with sheets over the furniture, and there was no trace of Stefan or Brandy. I called the radio station disguising my voice and was told Stefan was on a leave of absence."

"She's a talented gryphon, you fool. She knew what you were before you opened your mouth."

"If they knew I was a demon, why didn't they kill me?"

"I don't know," he said, momentarily rubbing his chin. "You have forty-eight hours to find them and bring Brandy to me. Otherwise I'll kill you myself!" Baltizar took careful aim. A massive blazing red-orange glowing fireball shot from his palm and found its mark.

A horrifying scream escaped Synn's throat as her flaming body writhed in pain.

"That's going to leave a scar." He grinned in satisfaction.

The scene faded within the curling dark-blue smoke, and the flames rose, engulfing the logs again.

****

Tristian stood. "Excuse me." Quickly, he strode out of the room just as his phone rang.

Hannah and Brandy remained riveted to their seats.

239

Stefan stood staring into the fire, privy to Tristian's side of the conversation.

"Hello, Bruce. I was expecting your call…Yes, we all saw the images…I don't know. The damn scene just appeared in the fire. Let me ask and I'll get back to you…Yes, Brandy and Stefan are staying with us…They arrived a couple of days ago…I haven't had time to call you. We've had our own family problems to deal with."

There was a long pause as Tristian listened. "I know I should have, but I didn't…What's done is done. Let's move on…Yes, given the situation, I agree that Synn will probably seek you out…She has no alternative; there is no way she can get to them here. That means that Baltizar will kill her unless you intervene…We were planning a couple of outings to keep up the ruse of normalcy, but we'll wait till she is contained. Then we'll leave town for a few weeks. Family business overseas requires our personal attention."

Stefan moved toward the doorway, bringing Tristian into sight.

"I'm well aware," Tristian said tersely, fisting his free hand repeatedly, punching the air and walking toward the door. "Things are different now. As you've told me repeatedly, I have a family to protect."

Another short pause and Tristian blew out a breath. "It's too late for that. We'll do the best we can. How would you feel if someone told you that you shouldn't have married Angelique?" As soon as the words were out of his mouth, it was apparent that was a bad example.

Tristian held the phone from his ear as a roar of

laughter emitted from the phone.

Stefan covered a grin with his hand. These family dynamics fascinated him as long as he wasn't on the receiving end of bad juju.

"Yeah, I know I did exactly that, but it was for different reasons than what we are talking about now."

Another long pause. "I'll call you back as soon as I explain this whole situation and get answers to your questions." Tristian touched the screen, ending the call, and pocketed the phone.

When Tristian strode back into the room, all eyes were on him. "I assume that you heard my conversation."

"Well, we heard mostly your side of the conversation. What the heck is going on?" Hannah wanted to know.

"Was that real?" Stefan asked, pointing to the fireplace.

"Unfortunately, yes."

"Where did it take place?" Stefan asked, raising a dark brow as he crossed his arms across his chest.

Tristian raked his fingers though his hair and sighed. "All in good time. First, I need to know if Synn was the girl from Montana?"

"Yes," Brandy and Stefan answered simultaneously.

"Okay, let me make one more phone call and I will explain everything."

"No, how about you explain everything first and then…" Stefan growled, standing up and stepping directly in Tristian's path.

"Because if I don't get your answer to my boss, things are going to go south in a big way." Tristian moved menacingly toward him.

Stefan remained standing in the arched doorway of the room. Tristian stood there only a moment. His eyes flicked to Hannah, then he pulled the cell phone out of his pocket, touched the screen, and put the phone to his ear.

"Bruce, yes, Synn is the girl from Montana. Now, I really have to go. I'll talk to you later. Tristian opened his mouth as if to retort, paused, closed his mouth in a firm line, and listened to the voice on the other end.

Finally, Tristian interrupted. "I know, but I have my own set of problems demanding my immediate attention. Once those are settled, then we'll discuss the others. If you don't like it, you know where to find me." He angrily ended the call and shoved the phone in his pocket. He took a long breath and let it out slowly, regaining composure and exuding an air of calm control once again as he turned to the others.

"Stefan, sorry if you feel I'm keeping you in the dark. It's going to be a long night, so please try to be patient. The scene you just witnessed is real and took place in Hell within the last few hours. It was a communication sent to me by Bruce out of Washington, D.C. When he saw the scene and heard your names, he immediately forwarded it to me, which is what you just saw."

"Bruce is married to your sister, Angie, right? The one we rescued a while back," Stefan clarified.

"Unfortunately, yes," Tristian grumbled. "Now, mind if I continue?"

"No, go right ahead," Stefan suggested.

Just then the doorbell rang.

"This is not what I need right now." Tristian strode

to the entrance and yanked open the door. Bruce stepped inside, grasping Tristian by the shoulder. "This matter is too important to wait."

"Welcome, Bruce. I'd rather you let me sort my family situation out before you force me to handle ours." Tristian yanked his shoulder out of Bruce's grip and stepped back. Off-balance slightly, he fell backward, his elbow shattering the glass door of the antique china cabinet standing against the wall. The wood groaned under the sudden impact, and crystal stemware tumbled to the floor, sending shards of sparkling crystal skittering across the polished oak floor.

Bruce reached out to steady him as Tristian waved his good arm toward the door, closing it with a bang.

Bruce's eyes glowed a bright orange tinged with red, but he moved out of Tristian's way. The doorbell rang again. Hannah looked puzzled and started for the door. Tristian reached for the door, jerking it open. His eyes rounded as he stared at his sister. Angelique sprinted through the door into the room.

She grabbed Bruce's arm. "What in Hell's fire are you doing here? You said you were going to let Tristian handle his family matters before complicating things further?" Her tiny, lithe body quivered with anger as she flung her long blonde hair back and glanced behind Bruce to survey the damage. With a wave of her arm and words muttered quietly, the crystal shards reformed into stemware and returned to the shelf. The glass in the china cabinet door flew back into place before she turned her attention back to Bruce. "Explain yourself," she demanded, tapping her tiny foot impatiently.

Bruce calmly put his arms out in front of him,

palms out. "Tristian had a clumsy moment as I arrived." Bruce raised an eyebrow, shrugged, and smiled innocently at Angie. "I don't have to explain myself to anyone. However…"

Angelique narrowed her eyes at Bruce. "Is that so?" She looked from her husband to her brother and then to Hannah. "What happened here?"

"Tristian opened the door. I gripped his shoulder to get his attention. He wrenched his shoulder away, lost his balance, and smashed an elbow into the china cabinet," Bruce said matter-of-factly. "I reached out to steady him and…"

"Okay, so why are your eyes still whirling orange in anger? You know the minute you walk in this house your powers are useless. She placed her hands flat on his chest and glared up at Bruce, who was way over a foot taller than her five feet two inches. "You and Tristian have been getting along so well. Now this!"

"Nothing's changed," Bruce said smoothly. "It was just an accident. Nothing more. I promise." He turned to Tristian for confirmation.

Tristian brushed the dust off his clothes and nodded in agreement. "Everything is fine," he said through clinched teeth.

"Hello, Angie," Hannah greeted her sister-in-law while moving closer to examine Tristian's elbow where blood was seeping through this shirt. "It's been a rough night for all concerned."

Angelique turned, noticing for the first time there were others in the room. With a nonchalant wave of her hand, she said, "Too much testosterone in this room, as usual when you get my husband and brother in the same room. Sorry for the intrusion."

Hannah grinned, nodding her head. "Angie, Bruce, this is my sister, Brandy, and her friend, Stefan. They are visiting with us while we make plans for Christmas, maybe in Ireland."

"Oh, I remember Stefan. Assassin to the Vampire Council, right?" Angie said.

Bruce glanced in Stefan's direction again, and recognition shone in his eyes as they blatantly swept over Stefan's scars, visible above his collar. "Well, well, we meet again. Stefan Talltree, isn't it? And rescuer of damsels in distress," he teased. "Seriously, I owe you a debt of gratitude for rescuing my Angie."

Stefan's eyes steeled as his face went blank. "Former assassin. And you're right, last name is Talltree." *Of all the things to keep catching up with me...Good thing I came clean with Brandy.*

Bruce raised an eyebrow. "Ah...yes, I remember Lady Rose mentioned that at Angie's and my wedding. My mistake."

Brandy just shook her head. Stefan knew further explanations would be required before this bit of information would go away.

"Now that everyone's calmed down, what is so important that it couldn't wait till Tristian had solved his family situation and was ready to discuss the mounting demon one?" Angie glanced up at Bruce, her gaze softening.

"Tristian indicated over the phone his family would be leaving for Ireland soon. That has traditionally been a safe place. However, I've recently learned of unexplained deaths in London and Dublin in recent weeks. We've lost a watch demon, a warrior faerie, and a witch along with a couple of unknowns that have lived there for centuries."

Stefan let out a low whistle. "That's bad."

"Demonic activity seems to be increasing worldwide, making Ireland as dangerous as anywhere else, which leads me to believe the dark demons are getting desperate. I thought this was something my security specialist should know immediately."

"Why didn't you say so?" Tristian demanded.

"I tried. You hung up on me. Therefore, I felt an immediate visit was necessary to impress upon you the urgency of the situation. I am still your boss. However, my temper flared. For that I apologize."

"Understood," Tristian said.

"If we went to Ireland, all of us along with my family residing there could be in danger?" Brandy asked, a crease forming across her forehead.

Bruce rocked back on his heels and tented his fingers. "It depends on how you want to look at it. The time has come that everyone related to those of us in power need to be aware of the danger. Hannah and Brandy, your family in Ireland must be told one way or the other. Their relationship to you and Tristian is easily traceable."

Hannah crossed her arms across her chest and stared at Tristian, an "I told you so" expression on her face.

"Your choice—either you explain that Tristian is a demon hunter and what is going on in the world by phone, or you make a holiday out of it, telling them in person. As I see it, it's the only way to keep everyone safe."

Stefan moved toward Bruce, extending his hand. "I have a couple of things I'd like to clarify."

Bruce tilted his head amicably. "Well, at least someone in this family has manners." He grasped Stefan's hand in a strong handshake, squeezing down hard. "Good to see you again."

Stefan returned the favor twice as hard. Bruce grinned and released his hand but said nothing.

"We don't need to cancel our trip to Ireland. If I understand you correctly, there is no greater risk than here," Stefan confirmed.

"Armed with the knowledge of what is going on, that's exactly right. We have additional eyes and ears in the British Isles now. They haven't seen or heard any further signs of underworld activity. Should Synn come to us, we'll be able get a lot more information. By the way, are there any other humans in your family other than Tristian?"

"No," Brandy said. "Hannah and I are the only ones in relationships outside our kind."

"That's putting it mildly." Laughing, Bruce looked from Brandy to Hannah. "You girls really preferred something different, huh?"

"No more than you apparently did," Brandy shot back, her eyes blazing with contempt.

Bruce raised his hands palms out in surrender. "Take it easy—I meant no harm—merely an observation."

"Mine too," Brandy said, smirking.

"I think preying on a family of gifted gryphons will be difficult. Especially when that includes a vamp with assassin skills and a weapons cache, who doesn't sleep much, and a powerful warlock in that group. If you really want to go, be careful and keep in touch. Don't go anywhere alone. There's safety in numbers. You won't have the protection of this house, but that's the only difference. The choice is yours. I believe Tristian will agree with my assessment."

"Yeah, knowing what your enemies are up to is a great advantage. I can weave a protection spell for our accommodations while we travel," Tristian added reluctantly.

"Then anyone who knows either of you will need to be told you are going on…"

Tristian interrupted, "That won't be necessary. Stefan and Brandy are just visiting and have taken leaves of absences from their employment until the first of the year. As far as my connections, I assume you'll take care of those." For the first time since Bruce had arrived, Tristian's voice was civil and his face relaxed as he looked expectantly over at Bruce, who nodded agreeably.

"Hannah, you're not friendly with any of your neighbors or people in the town that might notice you are gone? Appearance is everything. It can't look like you're running."

"Well…actually, there is Jill and her husband, Evan, down the street and Willow's parents, Birch and Freesia. I work from home or while traveling so no problem from my job. I'll let them know we're going to spend Christmas with family overseas."

"That'll work." Tristian nodded in agreement.

"Mind if I ask, is it always this tense when you two are in the same room?" Stefan looked from Tristian to Bruce.

"Only when it's personal, and this isn't bad. No blood has been spilled." Angie smiled. "It used to be a lot worse. Tristian didn't approve of my choice of mates, and when I married Bruce, it was Tristian's worst nightmare. You'd think I did it on purpose just to spite him."

"You didn't?" Bruce asked disappointedly, then grinned.

Angie raised her hand, threw her weight into it, and swung; Bruce ducked, grabbed her hand, and spun her round to face him, lifting her up off the ground and holding her close to his body as she struggled against him, giggling. She turned her face up toward his; their eyes met. There was so much love reflected in them toward each other. Then he brought his lips down on hers affectionately.

Stefan considered a cheeky response but was beat to the punch by Tristian.

He cleared his throat and shifted uncomfortably. "Get a room, guys, or let's get back to business."

She wriggled free of Bruce's hold, looking at Tristian boldly. "Well, it looks like you have plenty. May we borrow one? A room, I mean." Angie grinned wickedly as she dodged Tristian's attempt to cuff her upside the head and leaned back against Bruce as he grabbed Tristian's wrist in warning.

Pulling free, Tristian's eyes narrowed, and Bruce raised his hand in surrender as Angie elbowed him in the ribs.

"Knock it off, you two. Stefan and Brandy are going to think you're heathens when, in fact, you're both professionals just blowing off a little steam out of the public eye." She smiled sweetly, turning her attention back to her brother. "Please continue."

Setting aside their personal differences, they finalized the plans, deciding that Tristian, Hannah,

Brandy, and Stefan would fly to Ireland for Christmas. Bruce and Angie would handle things locally, with daily contact reports via phone or fireplace.

Hannah broke in, yawning wide, "It's late, guys." She shot Tristian a warning glance as she said sweetly, "Angie, why don't you and Bruce stay with us tonight. We can finish this discussion in the morning when we are all fresh."

Tristian nodded amicably. "As you noticed, we've plenty of room, and security is not an issue."

"We'd love to," Angie said with syrupy sweetness, grinning at her brother. "Tobi and Owen can handle anything that may come up tonight, and the salon is closed tomorrow."

"Who?" Brandy tilted her head and cocked a brow quizzically.

"Tobi and Owen manage The Wycked Hair in D.C. for us. They're demons but are also trusted friends and allies. Bruce has known them for—" Angie hesitated "—a very long time," she finished awkwardly, shrugging.

The scowl on Bruce's face smoothed out. The corners of his mouth slightly curved as Angie snuggled closer in his arms.

"You know what?" Brandy, smiling over at Hannah, her eyes sparkling with mischief, said, "It would be nice for all of us to get to know each other. Why don't you two plan to stay here a few days? Go sightseeing with us." Her eyes darted back and forth between Angie and Bruce. "It would set the stage for a family get together as we discussed."

Stefan turned away to hide a grin he couldn't keep from forming. Tristian looked less than pleased yet could do nothing about it. Then a thought occurred to Stefan. "That sounds like a fine idea. There seems to be precious little recreation done together as a family."

"Shut up, Stefan!" Tristian hissed.

Stefan shrugged and stuffed his hands in his jeans pockets as he walked across the room to look out the window. His back turned, he grinned wide.

"That's a wonderful idea," Angie sang. "Bruce, are you going to call Owen and let him know we will be out of town for a few days, or do you want me to call Tobi? They can open the salon and keep things under control till we get back."

"I'll do it," Bruce said with a heavy sigh. "I don't suppose there is any way of talking you out of…"

"Nope! It's been a long time since we've spent time with family. I'm not going to give it up," Angie said. "Besides, a little R&R is just what you need."

"Okay, but I'll need access to a secure communications line." Bruce glanced over at Tristian.

"Got one here you can use."

"Usually if I'm gone, you take over, but…a few days shouldn't matter. I'll just tell Owen in person and get my laptop." Bruce stepped outside the house and walked down the driveway to a point where he could use magic and disappeared.

Hannah looked over at Angie. "Will he be gone long?"

"I doubt it." Angie smiled.

"Good," Hannah said, turning back to Brandy. "Would you come help me get a room ready for Angie and Bruce?"

"Sure." Brandy raised an eyebrow in question.

"Hey, wait for me. You're not leaving me down

here with them!" Angie jerked her thumb in the men's direction and bounded up the stairs to catch up with Brandy and Hannah.

Before the women reached the first landing, the atmosphere snapped, alerting Tristian to magic use, and a few moments later a light knock sounded on the door. Tristian waved his hand and the door opened. Bruce walked through the door and over to the group, laptop in hand.

"Keeps you on your toes, doesn't she?" Stefan remarked to Bruce, watching with appreciation as the three women ascended the stairs.

"You have no idea," Bruce mused, then smiled. "That's what first attracted me to her."

"I'm going to go on up to our room and wait for Brandy. Goodnight, gentlemen."

A few minutes later, Angie leaned over the banister and called down, "Bruce, our room is ready. Wait till you see it. Hurry!"

Bruce nodded to Tristian and took the stairs two at a time to where Angie stood.

Tristian, still brooding, called up after Bruce, "What about Synn?"

"If she comes to us, Tobi and Owen can handle her till we get back. They are extraordinarily good at what they do too." Bruce replied nonchalantly as he joined Angie and they ambled into their room and closed the door.

****

The dawn brought with it a multitude of colors spreading across the bright-blue sky. By late afternoon, the few white, fluffy clouds turned dark and ominous. Sheets of freezing rain pelted the roof of Tristian and

Hannah's home. The storm raged on through the evening. Thunder crashed and lightning crackled as it streaked violently across the night sky. Stefan couldn't help but wonder if Mother Nature was throwing a temper tantrum, or was it something else? Magic perhaps? He leaned against the counter in the kitchen, observing everyone. Bruce and Tristian eyed the sky pensively. Oblivious to their concern, Brandy and Hannah cheerfully discussed the upcoming trip and the shopping that was necessary before leaving.

Over the next several days, Stefan watched as the animosity of Bruce and Angie's arrival gave way to camaraderie and fun while the girls shopped for the trip and the guys talked shop and favorite vacation spots. He was surprised to find out Tristian owned a bungalow and private beach in Hawaii.

Tristian suggested an impromptu day ski trip, which was the highlight of the week as far as Stefan was concerned. Skiing was a favorite pastime before he was turned. However, the dinners out at the only upscale restaurant in Misty Harbor came in a close second. Not for the food, but kicking back and talking with everyone.

Stefan couldn't remember the last time he'd gone to a theater, but he enjoyed the two movies Hannah suggested they see, especially the one about an actual hitman who was an accountant too. It had a great twist he didn't see coming.

At the end of the impromptu family reunion, Stefan was sorry to see Bruce and Angie leave. She could be a hoot, and Bruce—he was dignified most of the time but wasn't above joining in the spirit of fun, especially at someone else's expense. Stefan chuckled and shook his head. A surprise turn of events, given the start of the visit. While the safety concern was ever present, a good time was had by all. The insight he gained would prove quite useful going forward.

Stefan's concern about meeting Brandy's large family in Ireland intensified as she delighted in telling him there would be a huge celebration. "With all of us home for Christmas, you can bet Ma and Da will throw a grand party." She flicked her long hair over her shoulder and danced a jig. "Everyone living in our small coastal village off the Celtic Sea will be there. Shaughnessy's has catered to magickind for as long as I can remember." Brandy batted her long eyelashes at Stefan, smiling coyly.

Too soon for his liking, it was time embark on their Ireland adventure.

Chapter Twenty
The Emerald Isle's Tales Await

The plane's wheels set down at the Cork Airport just as the fog cleared and the rain gave way to a fine mist. Brandy and Stefan cleared security and customs first, followed by Hannah and Tristian. A small woman with misty green eyes, her short red curls bouncing, rushed up and threw her arms around Brandy, hugging her tightly.

"I've missed you so much." She kissed Brandy's cheek, then drew her back, holding her by the shoulders. The woman's gaze swept over Brandy's face, taking a long look into her eyes, then glanced over at Stefan. "This is the young lad we discussed months ago?"

"Aye, Ma, this is Stefan." Brandy smiled wide and reached out for his hand. "Stefan, this is my ma, Mary Shaughnessy."

"Looks like the two of you worked it out. I'm happy for you, darling," Mary said, patting Brandy on the back lovingly, and reached out to include Stefan in the hug. Leaning over, he put one arm around her while the other still held Brandy's hand. Mary's forehead creased with concern for a moment, then, smiling up at him knowingly, she added, "Welcome, Stefan. You be good to our Brandy, or you'll be answering to her da and me!"

"Yes, ma'am, there's no doubt about that," Stefan said cheerfully.

Hannah, followed by a hesitant Tristian, joined the group. Mary turned and reached out for her oldest daughter. "Hannah, it's been too long. I'm so glad to see you." She shifted, giving Tristian an appraising look. "This must be your young man...uh...husband." She wrapped an arm around his waist. "Welcome to our family."

"I missed you too, Ma. Yes, this is Tristian," Hannah said as she patted his shoulder encouragingly and kissed his cheek.

"I hope you don't mind." Mary beamed. "We've planned a *Ceilidh* at the pub in honor of your wedding, Hannah, and Brandy's return with her young man."

"Gee, now there's a surprise." Brandy laughed, shooting Stefan an "I told you so" look.

He merely smiled at her, sending a thought. *I hope we get to hunt before the celebration. Fourteen hours on the plane and a warm reception by your parents have sorely tested my restraint.*

Of course, she responded in kind. *Can't have you feeding off the townspeople.* Her lips twitched at his scowl.

A tall man with a stocky build, sandy-colored hair graying at the temples, and bright-green eyes waited patiently. "Me girl, I'm so glad to see ya." He wrapped his arms around Brandy, lifting her off the ground in a strong bear hug, and swung her around in a circle like she was a rag doll. When he put her back on her feet, he held her by the shoulders and studied her face. "You look a lot happier than the last time we saw you. There's a twinkle in your eye I haven't seen before."

He reached over with one hand and clasped Stefan's shoulder, giving it a little shake as he grinned. "You put that twinkle in me Brandy's eyes?"

"Aww, Da." Brandy beamed and turned. "Stefan, this is my da, Tim Shaughnessy."

Raising a brow, Stefan said, "I hope so, sir."

Tim's smile reached into his eyes and he had an easy manner about him, a born publican. Brandy could never tell exactly what her da was thinking.

"Da and Ma own the Shaughnessy's Pub in our small fishing village. The pub has been passed down from father to son for generations, like the magic concoctions served alongside the pints of ale."

"How far from here to your home?" Stefan asked, his forehead creased.

"Our home and the pub are in Ballycotton in the county of Cork, Ireland." Brandy said proudly, her Irish lilt becoming more prominent.

"Approximately forty-six kilometers, right?" Tristian glanced at Hannah, who nodded.

Tim released Brandy and Stefan, then strode over, hand extended, to Tristian. "You must be Hannah's young man."

Tristian shook Tim's extended hand and smiled, "Yes, I'm Hannah's husband, Tristian."

Tim narrowed his eyes at Tristian. "Aye…you ran off and secretly married me girl. Then waited damn near to a year before you two owned up to it." He shifted his scrutinizing gaze to Hannah, but his lips gave way to a grin again. "Well then, you're here now, aren't ya? You'll be paying the consequences for that behavior." He thumped Tristian on the back, then let out a hardy laugh, eyes dancing. "Me girls both brought home Yanks." Tim shook his head.

Mary sent him a warning glance. He shrugged. "Well, they did."

Tristian grimaced and glanced over to Stefan.

Stefan immediately put both hands up, palms forward, and mouthed, "You're on your own." He turned back to Mary. "Brandy and I will meet you at your home or the pub after we have checked into our hotel and freshened up. Where could we rent a car?"

"Oh no, you'll not be staying in a hotel," Mary and Tim said simultaneously. Mary shook her head and waved a finger in front of their faces. "You'll be staying with us. We've plenty of room."

"Ma, it's probably better if we stay in a hotel. Stefan and I don't…"

"Ma, Tristian and I have reservations too, so…"

Mary interrupted. "Nonsense. Your father and I won't hear of it." She waved a hand in dismissal. "Whatever is making you four uncomfortable, we won't let it matter. Now come on. Get your luggage loaded, and we'll head for home."

The Shaughnessy's large home sat high on a bluff overlooking the Celtic Sea. Most of the windows had a clear view of the sea and all its moods. When they arrived, the sun peeked through the clouds and rainbows bounced off the waves. But as Tristian and Stefan unloaded the luggage, ominous storm clouds moved in. The bright-blue sky gave way to gray as the fog swirled in. The howling wind brought the frothing white-crested waves crashing into the shore menacingly.

Mary hustled everyone into the house as lightning streaked across the dark sky, thunder rumbled, and torrents of rain pounded the ground.

"Girls, your rooms have been remodeled, but they are still at opposite ends of the house, as always." Mary grinned, shaking her head. "Sisters didn't get along very well when they were teenagers. To keep peace in the house, it was best their rooms be a bit of distance from each other. It's nice to see they're closer now than ever they were." Reaching up, she hugged both girls. "Now, scoot, and take your lads with you."

Brandy padded toward the stairs and stopped to finger the evergreen and pinecone garland wrapped around the newel post and twined up the banister. A huge Christmas tree stood in the living room across from the big bay window that looked out to the ocean. In the soft light flooding the room, delicate red lace bows and crystal snowflakes shimmered on the tree. Bright multicolored bobbles hung from branches and popcorn garlands swirled on its limbs.

Several neatly wrapped packages peeked out from under the lower boughs that swept the floor. Christmas had arrived at the Shaughnessy house.

Tim entered the house soaking wet, shaking a few wet snowflakes from his jacket but grinning from ear to ear. "Rain turning to snow now. Very festive. When you're all settled, come on down. We'll have some tea and cakes in front of the fireplace, then persuade Brandy to tell us some tales. She's a talented *shanachie*, don't you know."

Raising one eyebrow, Stefan tilted his head and shot a questioning glance at him. "A what?"

"Oh." Tim laughed and waved his hand. "A *shanachie*. That's Gaelic for storyteller."

"Geez, Da," Brandy moaned. "Stefan and Tristian

don't want to hear faerie tales. The rest of you've heard tell of them all our lives."

"Aye, that's true enough. I'll wager that your lads never heard of our faeries, legends, and magic."

"You've no idea." Brandy sighed, but nodded her head in agreement, she'd learned a long time ago not to argue with her da. He always won. "Okay, but just a couple to make you happy." She kissed her da on the cheek, turned, and slid her arm around Stefan's waist, pulling him toward the stairs and her bedroom. They unpacked and showered, changing into clean jeans and bulky sweaters.

The mist rolled in off the ocean, and snow mixed with rain pattered on the windows as they entered the large living room. Everyone had settled around the fireplace. A well-worn, overstuffed red chair with its back to the fire faced the semi-circle of chairs. Brandy motioned Stefan to the only seat left, directly in front of her. Mugs of steaming tea sat on the tables between the chairs.

Everyone sipped their tea, passing a tin of peanut butter biscuits and listening to the rise and fall of her voice as she recounted the ancient tales of Irish myth, legend, and magic. Toward the end of the impromptu performance, out of the corner of her eye, she noticed Stefan lean over and slip his untouched mug of tea onto the floor.

Brandy cleared her throat and took several sips of tea. "I believe that's enough blarney for tonight." She giggled and glanced out the window. The snow had stopped for now, but clouds floated across the crescent moon, casting shadows on the newly fallen snow. "Stefan and I are going to go for a walk before bed.

Don't wait up for us." Brandy reached for her coat, but Stefan was already putting it around her shoulders.

"Goodnight, everyone. See you in the morning." Stefan grabbed his coat on the way out and closed the door behind them. "You are a truly gifted storyteller," he said proudly. "I enjoyed the Irish folktales."

"Thank you. I've always loved telling the stories." She paused for a beat, savoring the feeling of having her family around her. "Now let's hunt. She turned to him. A beguiling smile curved her lips before she danced off into the woods behind the house. A moment later, the whoosh of air accompanied by the beat of wings and she was airborne, the most wondrous feeling in the world.

****

Brandy slept in Stefan's arms while he watched the lace curtains flutter as the ocean breeze, heavy with brine, wafted through the window, open just a crack. A white mist swirled into the quiet room through the opening. It grew thicker and began to take shape, settling into the antique rocking chair in the far corner of their cozy room. A man with long, flowing hair the color of straw, dressed in jeans and a shimmering multicolored sweater, now sat in the rocking chair, left boot propped over on his right knee, watching Stefan with genuine interest.

Stefan's body stiffened. His fangs pierced his gums as he shifted Brandy to a more secure position, though he sensed no threat. *Too many stories around the fire?*

Undisturbed, the apparition's lips twitched. "You're the *súmair fala* that stole our Brandy's heart. An interesting turn of events this is," he mused, nodding his head toward the window and pointing his

261

finger toward Stefan, then to the outside. As quickly as he'd appeared, he was gone, leaving only a light mist floating across the floor.

Blinking his eyes, Stefan slowly looked around the room. *What the hell was that? I wasn't asleep so it couldn't have been a dream.* Stealthily, he slid out of bed without disturbing Brandy. He yanked on jeans, pulled an ivory cable-knit sweater over his head, and grabbed his boots as he padded silently down the stairs and out of the house. The storm had passed. The twinkling stars spread across the frosty dark sky. For a moment, he stilled, listening as the waves crashed against the shore off in the distance.

Glancing uneasily around the area in front of the house and toward steep cliffs shrouded in a settling mist, he saw nothing. Following the trail leading to the cliffs and ultimately down to the beach, he sprinted across the rocky terrain. He stopped once and glanced over his shoulder to make sure he'd closed the front door. Turning back around, Stefan skidded to a halt, damn near crashing into what he considered a figment of his imagination. "Who are you?" Stefan demanded.

In an amused voice, the apparition said, "I'm Tiarnan, King of the Warrior Faeries, of course."

"Sure you are, and I'm the King of England," Stefan snapped.

Tiarnan chuckled. "To be sure, there was a king of England, but you're not him, and the queen now sits upon that throne."

"Ha…Ha…Now, who are you really, and what do you want with me?"

Patiently, he repeated, "I am Tiarnan, King of Faeries. My *sidhe* is here and about under the hills of green. Haven't you heard the music floating on the evening breeze?"

"Your what?" This was just too much. He shook his head in amazement as they continued walking along the cliffs, winding their way down toward the beach.

"Me *sidhe*, me palace. The faeries live under the hills here and about. You listened to your girl's telling of the tales this evening?" He waved his hand as if to dismiss the situation. "No matter. I'm here because centuries ago a Book of Shadows was entrusted to me wife and me for safe keeping. It be in my possession, but I've no desire to deal with the ill-tempered warlock. Besides, he must hold only one Book. 'Tis you and Brandy who control the destiny of man and magickind. Sorry I am to lay this at your feet, but it's what I know."

He had Stefan's undivided attention now. "You know about the Books of Shadows?"

"Aye, probably more than ye know yourself, but that's a story for another time. I must warn you, the powers of darkness search for the Books as well. It's safe for now in my possession. The legend foretells of three Books of Shadows united to restore the spells binding the portals of Hell. Does the warlock know where the other two are?"

"Not exactly," Stefan replied, unsure whether he could trust Tiarnan. Hell, he wasn't sure he was actually standing in the drizzling rain, which had started up again, having this conversation. But he had to admit Tiarnan definitely seemed to know more than he did. "We've come here on—"

"I know why you're here," Tiarnan interrupted. Impatient now, he paced on the rocky beach in front of

Stefan. "Time is short. Evil lurks in places it never has before. The Irish have a respect for the magical realm, without question. Makes it less likely for evil to reside here unnoticed by mortals or the real faerie folk." Narrowing his eyes, he stared at Stefan, then threw his head back, roaring with laughter. "You're not even sure that I exist. Are you?"

"Well, let's just say I've never had a conversation like this before. Why are you telling me all this?" Stefan shoved his hands in his pockets, pulled them back out, and raked them through his damp hair. "What do you want from me?"

"I've not questioned your existence as a *súmair fala*, now, have I? Some would."

"A what?"

"*Súmair fala...*" he repeated, then paused at Stefan's puzzled expression. "Gaelic for blood-drinker."

"Oh...been a long while since I heard the term. But...warrior faerie...that's a stretch for anyone."

"To the devil with you. Go ask Brandy if I exist. We'll continue this conversation later when you are more knowledgeable, less doubtful."

Suddenly, Stefan stood alone on the beach, the mist clearing, giving way to slivers of silver moonlight dancing along the rocks. Damp from the spray of the crashing waves, Stefan glanced around. No sign of Tiarnan. On the beach, only one set of footprints were visible. Running his fingers through his hair again and rubbing the knots from the back of his neck, he wondered, hadn't they walked the trail together? *Tiarnan was standing right beside me, wasn't he?* Turning on his heel, Stefan tore up the trail to the house, anxious to tell Brandy about the strange conversation he'd had…with…a faerie?

Returning to her parents' home, he quietly opened the door, took off his boots, and climbed the polished oak stairs without a sound. He undressed and slid into bed next to Brandy.

"Hmmmmm, is everything all right? Where you been?" she asked sleepily.

"Yes, everything is fine. I'm just restless, I guess. Go back to sleep. We'll talk in the morning."

"What time is it?" she murmured as she cuddled closer to him and shivered. "You're wet and cold. Where have you been?"

"Half past three," he answered, wrapping the blanket around her. She pushed at the blanket, then closed her eyes again. Soon her even breathing told him she was asleep.

Dawn arrived with the sun shining brightly for the first time since they'd arrived in Ireland. Gray storm clouds hung over the horizon, warning the sunshine would be short lived. With dawn arrived more questions than Stefan had answers. *Was I really up half the night conversing with a faerie who claimed to have one of the missing Books of Shadows? Why doesn't he want to deal with Tristian? Well, that part is understandable.* Stefan smiled, but it was short lived. *Last of all, why does the outcome of this situation hang on what Brandy and I do?* How the hell did a vampire who did his best to stay out of the way wind up front and center of everything recently? What a damn mess this was.

Restless, he jostled Brandy, contentedly sleeping curled up next to him. Her head snuggled into his chest.

He hoped to wake her up. He needed some answers, and now was as fine a time as any.

"Still restless, Stefan?" Brandy mumbled. She stretched and yawned wide, rubbing her eyes with the back of her hands. "Want to talk?" Smiling, she tipped her face up to his and brushed her lips softly across his, then more eagerly. She rolled over on top of him and leaned on her elbows, peering down at him. "What's wrong?"

Wrapping his arms around her, he buried his face in her wonderfully tangled hair. Inhaling deeply her scent of lemons and cotton candy, he found it incredibly alluring. He sighed. No time for foreplay at the moment. "Brandy, tell me about Tiarnan."

"Tiarnan, King of Faeries?" She repeated with a hint of amusement on her face and disbelief in her voice.

"Yep, that's the one."

A knock sounded on the bedroom door. Without waiting for an answer, Tristian burst through the door. "Stefan, I need to…" He stopped and peered at Brandy laying on top of Stefan, his arms around her. The blood rushed to his face. He opened and shut his mouth several times, reminiscent of a codfish, but stood rooted in the doorway.

Stefan turned his head, thought Tristian looked a bit like a guppy, and grinned at him, letting his hands roam over Brandy a bit. "Awkward, isn't it, Tristian? Get out. Whatever it is can wait…and shut the damn door behind you!"

Tristian backed out of the room quicker than he'd burst in, with a soft, "Sorry to interrupt," and quietly shut the door behind him. His quick footsteps grew silent down the hallway.

Brandy rolled over and sat up, wrapping the blankets around her, then crashed back against the headboard in fits of laughter. "Served him right," she managed to sputter in between giggles.

"Yes, I thought so. We'll let him think he interrupted us."

"Well, now, let's see if I can't bring a little truth to that." She leaned over and reached for him.

"Later, Brandy. Tell me about Tiarnan—the short version, *shanachie*," Stefan said, gently trailing kisses down the side of her soft, warm face to the base of her slender neck.

"Oh, yeah, I got sidetracked," she said, running her fingertip along Stefan's strong jawline. In her best storyteller voice, she began, "Legend has it that Tiarnan was foolish as a young man and fell in love with a witch from a very powerful family. They were caught together by her father after he'd forbade her to see Tiarnan."

"Gee, imagine that." He snorted.

"Do you want to hear the story or not?" she shot back.

"Okay, sorry, go ahead." Leaning back on the bed, he reached for Brandy and brought her down with him.

"Her father in anger issued an ultimatum, forcing her to choose their world or Tiarnan's. She chose Tiarnan's and they fled to his faerie palace. Tiarnan's parents accepted Erin, respecting his choice. They wed inside the faerie *sidhe*. Furious, her father cast a terrible spell. She would never see the light of day in the mortal world until witches, faeries, and demons work together for the good of all."

Tena Stetler

Curious, he leaned up on one elbow, facing Brandy. "Does Erin still remain in the faerie *sidhe* with Tiarnan?"

"Aye, she does. Theirs is a love for the ages. It is said that on moonlit nights you can see them walking the cliffs hand in hand, but she must always return to the sidhe before dawn."

"Have you ever seen them or talked to either one? What does he look like?"

"No, I've never seen either of them, but I know others have. The descriptions I've heard are that he dresses in blue jeans, colorful sweaters, and sturdy boots. Kind of a renegade, if you ask me. Why all the questions?" She laughed again and poked a finger into his chest. "Stefan, have you seen or been talking with faeries?"

He knew she was poking fun at him. *What if what Tiarnan said was true? Her description of him fit to a T.* "Yes," Stefan said simply, waiting for her reaction, and she didn't disappoint.

Her eyes flew wide open in surprise. "Yes what?" she sputtered.

"Yes to both," he said calmly, smiling innocently back at her.

"You've seen and talked with Tiarnan, King of Faeries? When? How?" she demanded.

"Last night. He floated through the window crack as mist into our room and took shape in the rocking chair. He didn't want to wake you. He motioned me outside where I met him on the cliffs. He didn't seem to pose a threat, so I figured no harm could come of it."

"No harm could come of it? You could have been killed. It may have been a setup, or he could have been a demon. What were you thinking?" She jumped out of bed and paced across the floor, apparently forgetting that she was naked, which was all right with him. He loved looking at her beautiful body and hoped that Tristian wouldn't interrupt again.

"Brandy, I'm a vampire, remember—trained assassin? Death doesn't come easy to me. Besides, my preternatural senses didn't perceive a threat. Now, do you want to hear the rest, or…"

She interrupted him midsentence, "There's more?" Wheeling around, her eyes narrowed as she watched him in disbelief and bounced back on the bed.

"Yes. I had a hard time believing the whole scenario. Tiarnan got frustrated with me and wished me straight to the devil. He instructed me to ask you if he existed." Stefan blew out a breath as he finished, watching Brandy as she took it all in. "Does he?"

"Does he what?" Totally flustered by this time, she threw her hands up in the air, letting them drop to her sides, and stared wide-eyed at Stefan.

"Does he exist?"

Brandy took a couple of deep breaths, letting them out slowly as she considered. "Well, you're the one having conversations with him now, aren't you?"

"Yes, but I'm not sure that I wasn't hallucinating."

"Did my description fit the person you saw?"

"Yes, exactly."

"Well, there you have it then. You've had your first encounter with an Irish legend, haven't you?" She smiled, seemingly centered again and interested.

"Yes, I guess. I hope he appears next time when you're around and awake."

"If he does, wake me. By the way, what did he

want?"

"He claims to have one of the Books of Shadows. I guess it's entrusted to the faeries for safekeeping."

"A Book of Shadows? Shouldn't we tell Tristian about this right away?" Brandy jolted upright.

"Well, that's part of the problem. Tiarnan said he doesn't want to deal with the warlock, and that's a direct quote."

She regarded Stefan quizzically for a moment, drawing her legs up under her and sitting cross-legged on the bed facing him. "Really? Now what do we do?"

"That's what I'm asking you."

"No, you asked me if I believed in Tiarnan. That answer is yes, as apparently you do too... now."

"Oh, it gets better. The faerie king also said"— using his best Irish imitation, he repeated Tiarnan's words—"it's you and Brandy that will control the destiny of mankind and magickind alike. 'Tis sorry I am to lay this at your feet, but 'tis what I know.'"

Brandy took another deep breath and blew it out. "I guess it's time to call a family meeting and tell all."

"I don't think we're ready to do that...yet. Let's wait until after the celebration?"

"That might be best," she agreed. "Unless..."

Chapter Twenty-One

A Vampire's Relationship Advice to a Demon Slayer

Stefan was sitting in the living room watching the gulls dive into the white-capped ocean waves when Brandy danced into the room in her stocking feet. "Ready for the celebration at the pub tonight?"

She pirouetted through the room, gracefully coming to rest in front of him. Her arms arched behind her in a fluid movement as she bowed down and then dissolved in a fit of giggles. Reaching out, he gathered her into his lap.

She laid her flushed face against his shoulder, looked up, and sighed. "All our friends and family will be there. Isn't that wonderful? It's been so long since I've seen the lot of them and been in the mood to party." She leapt out of his lap.

He raised a brow, puzzled, and watched her again whirl around the room. "Weren't you here a few months back?"

"Yes, but that was different. I had thinking to do and didn't want to see anyone. I kept to myself, spending time with Ma and Da. Ma helped ease my mind. She listened and said little. When she felt I was ready, she gently suggested that, no matter what had happened, I was still very much in love with you and I'd best be returning to America to try to work things out, or I'd probably regret it. Then she handed me a one-way airline ticket for the next day back to Montana. Ma's a very wise woman." She sighed again and wrapped her arms around Stefan's neck.

Suddenly, without warning, she was up, yanking him out of the chair and tugging him down the hall toward their room, "Now, let's get ready. I feel like celebrating! Don't you?"

Her exuberance was infectious. "Sure, why not?"

She spun around, padding quietly into the closet, pulling out a silky bright-green dress and matching shoes, and holding them up for his approval. "What do you think of these?"

He nodded. "Let's see them on you."

She wriggled out of her jeans and sweatshirt and slipped the holiday dress over her head. Striking a pose, she whirled around so the hem of the dress twirled with her. Stefan enjoyed the view as the frock clung sexily to her curves.

"Perfect." He wanted to wrap his arms around her right then and forget the celebration. She was so beautiful and sexy. Knowing she'd have no part of that, he changed into the black jeans and crimson silk shirt she had laid out for him and waited.

Thankful they had hunted last night, so Stefan's thirst was controlled. He felt confident to be among her family tonight.

There was a sharp rap on the door followed by Tristian's annoyed voice. "Stefan, could I see you for a minute?"

That man is becoming a real thorn in my side. Crossing the room, Stefan opened the door and stepped out into the hallway to face Tristian. "What's up?"

"Do you know what these people are planning?" he hissed. "A celebration. A party tonight. And we are expected to join them. We need to tell these people how much danger they are in, not go to their damn party." Tristian paced the hallway in front of Stefan, running his hand through his tousled blond hair.

"Tristian, relax, man. Let Brandy and Hannah's parents enjoy having the girls home. Get to know your in-laws. That's mainly why we're here. There's plenty of time to tell them."

Fuming, Tristian turned to face Stefan. "But this isn't the way I had it planned." Then Tristian stopped, noticing that Stefan had changed his clothes. Groaning, Tristian rolled his eyes. "You're not planning to go along with this. Are you?"

"Yes, I am, and so are you. Where's Hannah?"

"In our room. We…ah…had a slight disagreement. Oh, hell, we had a big fight. She told me to get out and not come back."

Shaking his head, Stefan laid a hand on Tristian's shoulder. "Oh, let me guess, you told her that you weren't going to the party and neither was she."

Nodding, Tristian brought his arms up from his sides palms up and then let them drop. "What was I supposed to do?"

"First off, you're not running the show here. This is Brandy and Hannah's time to enjoy their family and introduce us. You didn't allow Hannah a big wedding, as I believe is the custom in Irish families. Then, on top of that, you wouldn't allow her to tell her parents she was married."

Tristian's thunderous expression changed little, though he acknowledged Stefan's observations with a

273

curt nod.

"Yet they welcomed you into their home and family like a son. Now you refuse to go to the celebration thrown in our honor. It's Christmas time, man." Stefan stared incredulously for a beat. "On top of that, you tell Hannah she can't go either. Do you know what she is capable of in a fit of anger?"

"What do you mean? She's pretty even-tempered most of the time," Tristian claimed proudly. "With a few exceptions," he admitted.

"Oh, come on. You saw my scars. You know exactly what I mean. Sounds like you have finally pushed Hannah to the breaking point. If you want to keep her, you need to make some drastic changes and quickly. That's what I think."

Brandy opened the door and peeked out. "Tristian, what are you doing standing there in just your jeans?" Laughing, she stepped toward him and ran her index finger down his bare chest. "You've a handsome enough chest, nice muscles, but Stefan's, well, now, puts yours to shame. Run along and get changed. We're all to be at the pub in a bit of a while."

Tristian shifted from one foot to the other, glowering at her.

Stefan put his arm around Brandy, pulling her close, and kissed her soundly. He glanced at the warlock, then cleared his throat. "Brandy…Tristian has a slight problem." Stefan couldn't help grinning at the situation, angling his face away so Tristian couldn't see it. "Hannah threw him out of the room for being his usual charming self."

"Well, for heaven's sake, what'd you do?" she asked, hands on her hips, eyes narrowed. "Oh, never mind. I can guess." With a twitch of hip, Brandy flounced down the hallway toward Hannah's room. "I'll be right back," she called over her shoulder.

In a couple of quick strides, Stefan caught up with her. Reaching around her waist, he spun her around. "Do you think intervening is a good idea? Maybe we should let them work it out for themselves, as we've done."

She stood in the middle of the hallway, frowning. Turning, she glanced back at Tristian, then to Stefan. "Hmmm, maybe."

"The upcoming months aren't going to be easy on anyone. They need to rebuild a relationship on mutual respect and common ground. From what I've seen, Tristian calls the shots and expects Hannah to follow. I think that is about to change. For a healthy relationship, it needs to do just that," Stefan said softly.

Brandy's brows shot up in surprise, then her face softened. "Stefan, when did you get so smart?"

Smiling, he took her hand, walking back toward Tristian. "You were strong when I needed you to be. I was there when you needed me. We've learned the hard way what it takes to make a relationship work, and we're better for it. Now Tristian and Hannah have to learn the same thing, or—" he hesitated, considered, then continued "—go their separate ways for a time."

Chewing on her bottom lip, worry creased her forehead, and she nodded, "You're right. But I suspect this whole situation is pushing Tristian to his limit."

"Better they work it out now rather than later when it could cost us all." Returning to where Tristian still stood, looking miserable, Brandy gave him a pat on the arm, then walked into her room, leaving Stefan to deal with him.

"Tristian, from what you've told me, you're way off base. Compromise is the basis of a good solid relationship. You can't always have your way, just as Hannah can't either. You need to reach an agreement that both can live with. Explain the reasons for your actions, then listen to her. Don't just tell her the way it will be. Communicate."

"Keeping everyone safe is my job. If I explained every little action before I took it… it could be fatal," Tristian hissed, crossing his arms across his chest, his gray-blue eyes dark and foreboding.

"And there lies your problem. This is personal, not professional. If you want to keep her, it's time you did. Family is very important to her."

"I am well aware of that. But I'm only thinking of her safety." He paused. "Hell, the safety of everyone here."

"Are you?" Shrugging, Stefan walked back into Brandy's room. "I gotta finish getting ready. Brandy and I are going to enjoy ourselves tonight. I hope to see you and Hannah there."

Chapter Twenty-Two
A Vampire in the Family Celebration

A fresh evergreen wreath with pinecones and red berries hung on the outside door. Stefan enjoyed the pine scent, then yanked open the heavy wooden door. Laughter and music spilled out from the pub and nearly sent them reeling back out the door. Brandy ducked under his arm, and he followed her into the pub. Bright multicolored twinkle lights hung around the room, tied in the corners with large green and red bows. A few patrons were gathered around the tree at the end of the bar, hanging ornaments, stringing popcorn, and singing carols.

The polished dark wood floor gleamed. Worn brown leather booths were arranged around the walls. Tables and chairs were scattered around the pub. It was standing room only. The aroma of mulligan stew wafted through the air, mixed with holiday evergreens and a yeasty scent. Pleasant, he imagined, by human standards.

Across the room, behind the massive oak bar, Tim stood busily pulling pints and talking with customers. Working the other end of the bar was a younger man with dark-red hair and a quick smile. Tim turned to drop coins into the till. He glanced up at the mirrored wall behind the bar. A wide array of vials of mysterious steaming liquids and more familiar bottles of liquor stood neatly arranged on glass shelving. A wide smile spread across Tim's face. At the same time, the young man at the other end of the bar threw up the pass-through and shoved his way through the crowd to them. Grabbing Brandy up in a bear hug, the man said excitedly, "Welcome home, darling." Then he held her back from him a bit. "You look radiant."

"Aw, Gavin, it's great to see you too. Now quit creating a scene and put me down." She hugged him tight, then wriggled a bit, placing a loud smacking kiss on his cheek.

Setting her back on her feet, he turned to Stefan. "You must be the reason for my sister's radiance." He grasped Stefan's hand firmly. "Gavin Shaughnessy is me name. Sorry I didn't get by the house earlier. I was away scouting out entertainment for the celebration. Had to make sure they were good as people claimed." He polished his fingers on his shirt and grinned. "They're great! Wait till you hear 'em."

Brandy narrowed her eyes. "I'll be the judge of that."

Stefan reached out and shook his hand. "Stefan Talltree, and I'd like to think I am the reason." He winked at Brandy. She sent him a saucy smile and nodded.

Gavin's eyes sharpened. "Have a care with her, or you'll be answering to me." He put his other arm around Stefan and, much to his surprise, gave him a quick hug. "Welcome, Stefan. Me sister is a bit of work, she is, so you'll have your hands full."

"Don't I know it." Stefan grinned back at him, pulling Brandy against him. "But she's worth it."

Gavin jumped up on a chair and let loose an ear-splitting whistle. "Can I have everyone's attention?"

It grew quiet. Even the band paused between songs. Stefan shifted uncomfortably from one foot to the other, glancing around the room. The last thing he needed was to be the center of attention. Brandy laughed and tossed her long, curly hair back and grabbed hold of his hand.

Gavin motioned to them with a sweep of his hand. "'Tis a sad day for all you single lads. Me sister Brandy here is no longer available. She has taken up with this here Yank, Stefan. Help me give him a fine Irish welcome." Gavin hopped to the floor and turned to his sister.

A loud cheer erupted from the crowd, and the band struck up a lively tune. Gavin swung Brandy into a quick step dance, their legs flying. The faster the music, the faster their feet flew. As the crowd yelled for more, Stefan leaned back, relaxing against the bar, watching the most important person in his life. What a concept— one he never thought possible after being turned. Yet here he was, watching other young men in the crowd gaze at her eagerly, then glance sideways at him with envy.

"Brandy and her sister used to be the national step dancing champions," Tim said proudly, then asked, glancing over the crowd, "Where's Hannah and Tristian?"

"They had a few things to work out but should be along shortly," Stefan assured him and fervently hoped that would be the case.

Bouncing over, Brandy twirled around once, then fell into Stefan's arms. Looking up at him, she giggled breathlessly. "I'd forgotten just how much fun being here with family and friends could be."

He gathered her in, wrapping one arm around her waist and raising the other to cup her chin in his hand. Tilting her chin up as he kept his eyes on hers, he brought his mouth down over hers, hot, hard, and proprietary. *She's mine.*

Brandy melted against him as he tightened his arm around her, and the rest of the world ceased to exist. Gradually they became aware of their surroundings again as cheers rose from the crowd, and from across the room a voice called, "That's the way, laddie."

Brandy, not missing a beat, grinned at Stefan. "You've got to learn to step dance." Her green eyes bright with mischief and her cheeks flushed with excitement, she sprang back to her feet, dragging him out onto the dance floor. The crowd parted and fanned out, clearing plenty of room.

Once on the floor, Brandy instructed, "The first thing to remember is that at all times during the dance your arms must be straight and held down by your sides, like this." She demonstrated, tugging his arms down to his sides.

"Nice," she cooed encouragingly.

Talking as she demonstrated the steps slowly. After a couple of poorly executed tries, he finally got his feet untangled and slowly followed her lead.

"Great job. Now let's speed it up a bit." She looked over at the band and winked. The band played the tune faster; still he followed her steps quite well.

"Okay, now the hops." Demonstrating the action as she spoke. "Your turn." Grinning, she bowed slightly, extending her arm toward him, enjoying his discomfort just a bit. He glanced to the bar at Tim and Mary, getting only a wink and a nod of encouragement.

"Now let's add the side step. It's a hop or a jump, moving your leading foot to the side, like this."

Beginning to see the rhythm of the dance, he caught on quickly. The band took advantage and played the tune to tempo. Brandy executed the steps first; he followed—a kind of dueling dance. Brandy was much better at it, but in the end, he managed to complete a tune without falling on his face and without further embarrassment. He considered that a great accomplishment.

When it was over, the crowd clapped and shouted words of encouragement for him and praise to Brandy. Her face flushing bright red with excitement, she threw her arms around his neck, rewarding him with a warm kiss, and, between breathing in big gulps of air, said, "You're a natural, you are. What fun."

Grasping her arms, he spun her around once. "Yes, it was. I can't believe that you wrangled me into that, and in front of strangers."

On the upside, he'd never seen Brandy so happy and carefree. As they wound their way through the crowd back to the bar, he spotted Tristian, arm around Hannah, standing against the wall beside the door. By Tristian's smug smile and amused expression, it was apparent he'd seen the spectacle and probably figured it served Stefan right.

Suddenly, a large burly man with bright-red hair reached a hand out of the crowd, catching Brandy by the arm. "Dance with me, darling. We'll show him"— he flicked his thumb toward Stefan—"how it's done."

"Kevin, I really don't…" Brandy began too late as he had already whisked her back onto the dance floor.

Stefan started after them, but Gavin put a hand on his shoulder and guided him back toward the bar. "Brandy can handle him."

Jealousy swelled up inside Stefan, and he didn't care for it one bit. Ruthlessly shoving the feeling aside, he leaned against the bar, hand grasping the edge, knuckles turning white. Gavin returned to his duties pulling pints.

Tim reached over and laid a hand on Stefan's shoulder, leaning on the bar. "Let Kevin have his dance, then go on over and rescue her. They were involved before she left Ireland. Brandy went her own way partly to get away from him, is me thinking. Kevin never got over her." Tim grimaced. "I don't think he was here when Gavin made the announcement that she was taken. Don't be too hard on the lad."

"Sure," Stefan said, grudgingly forcing an understanding smile. Feelings churning inside him were anything but understanding. He wanted to rip the bastard's head off.

Tristian and Hannah finally made their way to the bar. Tim leaned over the bar and kissed Hannah on the cheek. "Well now, it's about time the two of you showed up. You just missed Brandy and Stefan's dance."

"Nope, that we didn't." Hannah's eyes sparkled. "Saw it all, we did." She grinned from ear to ear.

Tristian, shaking his head and trying to keep a smirk off his face, finally asked, "How'd you let her force you into that?"

"She didn't force me into anything," Stefan said indignantly. "She wanted to teach me to step dance, and I agreed to try. I didn't do too bad, and better than you,

I'll wager." Stefan glanced back at Tim for support, who nodded in agreement as he added the last layer to a Guinness and slid the glass down the bar.

"You mean you did that...willingly?" Tristian laughed in amazement.

"Compromise...remember?" Stefan turned back to talk to Tim and followed his dark glare back to the dance floor. Kevin was trying to kiss Brandy. She was having none of it. Stefan was at her side in a blink of an eye. Calmly, Stefan removed Kevin's hands from Brandy, giving him a little shove, slid his arm around her possessively, and started walking back to the bar.

Kevin grabbed Stefan's shoulder and spun him around. Stefan let go of Brandy and caught Kevin's fist midair, twisting his arm around behind his back. Kevin howled in pain, then began cursing. Stefan circled Kevin's chest with his other arm, yanked his free arm, and wound it around his back also. Holding him there, Stefan hissed, "I think the lady is done dancing with you. I believe you've had a bit too much to drink. Do us both a favor; go home and sleep it off."

"You bloody bastard. I'll kill you." Kevin cursed, trying to break free. "She's me girl, and I'll do with her what I want. What's it to you?"

Drawing in a deep breath, Stefan faced away from the crowd, his fangs descending and claws poking through his fingertips as he tried to regain control. His head pounded with rage and jealously. All the emotions he'd held in check for so long spun out of control.

"Stefan...let me have him," Tristian said tersely, shoving himself between the two men. "Stefan, you need some air...get out of here now!"

Stefan shoved Kevin toward Tristian, then turned,

glancing at Brandy, her face white and contorted in fear as Stefan stalked toward the door.

Kevin broke free and grabbed Stefan's arm, whirling him around. Kevin swung his arm up, his hand fisted. Stefan's hand clamped around Kevin's neck. Kevin's fist glanced off Stefan's jaw. Picking him up off his feet, Stefan shoved Kevin against the wall, his face beet red, eyes bulging out, and mouth open, gasping for air. Stefan heard Brandy scream, "Stefan, no...don't. Please."

Kevin's eyes rounded as the pub lights bounced off Stefan's fangs. Stefan reined in his anger and lowered Kevin to his feet. Stefan still held him by his throat as he loosened his grip. "Kevin," Stefan said in a frighteningly calm voice. "Brandy is NOT your girl. She committed to me. I'm here to meet her family and celebrate."

Stefan looked deep into Kevin's eyes, controlling his will and memory, "Now, unless you do not value your life, I strongly suggest that you leave here immediately. Don't come back till you're sober. Then apologize to Tim and Mary for causing a scene and to Brandy for your behavior." Releasing his hold on Kevin's throat, Stefan pushed him down the wall. Kevin groaned as he hit the floor with a thud.

Tristian grabbed for his arm, but Stefan stepped neatly out of Tristian's reach, calling over his shoulder, "I need some fresh air. Take care of things."

Chapter Twenty-Three
Legends and Lessons—A Secret to Tell

Once outside the pub, Stefan raced along the jagged cliffs until his anger subsided. The cool mist dampened his face and the fresh air cleared his head. Slowing to a walk, he followed the rocky trail down to the beach and sat on a rock, listening to the rhythm of the sea and watching the waves crash to the shore. The full moon shone across the sand, washing everything with a silvery sheen.

"Well now, that was quite a show you put on there, boyo. Not that the lad didn't deserve it, but now he knows your secret. 'Tis a shame, it is."

Disgusted, Stefan turned, glaring into the amused face of Tiarnan. "Kevin won't remember anything except what I told him. Put a cork in it. I'm not in the mood."

Tiarnan sat on a large rock at water's edge, flicking stones into the ocean. "Ahh, a bit testy tonight, aren't we?" Standing up, he walked toward Stefan. The amusement gone from his face, he said thoughtfully, "A temper can be a dangerous thing."

"Yes, and according to the legends that Brandy tells, you'd know of such things."

"Aye, that I would," he said slowly, his face creased with deep sadness. "Temper is the reason my Erin no longer walks these cliffs and beaches with me during the day. As a young lass, there was nothing she enjoyed more than walking along the cliffs and beaches here in about, lifting her face to the warm sun."

Stefan studied the man, great sorrow etched on Tiarnan's face.

Sighing deeply, he continued. "She grew into womanhood, and we fell in love. Though she was a powerful witch and I a faerie of royalty. Her father found out about us and forbade her to see me again. My parents were none too happy either. They were wise enough to know if they tried to stop us, we'd only become more determined."

He paused, his face creased and eyes clouded. "One night her father followed her as she snuck out to meet me. He was furious and forced her to choose either her world or mine. To his shock, she chose mine. We fled to the *Sidhe* below the hill of green. 'Tis then her father, in a fit of temper, cast the spell locking her in the *Sidhe*. She would never see the mortal world's light of day until witches, faeries, and demons work together for the good of all. To his thinking, that would be an eternity."

"That is why you are willing to help us."

"Aye," he said, sitting beside Stefan on the rock.

"How did the Book of Shadows come into your possession?" Thinking back to the tale that Brandy told, there wasn't any mention of such a book.

Tiarnan smiled sadly. "Erin's sister, Sorcha, learned of our midnight walks in the mortal world and met us one night with the Book. She hoped there was a reversal for the spell that her father had cast. We spent weeks reading the Book but found nothing. When last we went to return the Book, Sorcha told us that there was dissension in the coven because of her father's actions against Erin. She felt the Book was safer in our possession."

"What happened to Sorcha and the rest of Erin's family? No one ever came back for the Book?"

"No. They scattered to the four winds. We've not heard from any of them in a very long time. Word came to us that Sorcha moved to America, where she married and bore a son they named Tristian. I've never been able to confirm that."

Standing up, Stefan shoved his hands in his pockets and stared at Tiarnan. "You think Hannah's husband is that Tristian?"

"No. More likely a son of that son." Tiarnan turned his eyes to the sky and sighed. "Powerful family of witches, they are."

Following his gaze, Stefan saw a beautiful gryphon, rainbow wings spread, circling in the starlit sky above them. She landed several lengths in front of them. Brandy's body shimmered and blurred as she shifted to human form, her long blazing-red hair blowing in the cool, misty night air.

"I'll leave you to Brandy. Have a care, Stefan. You mean the world to her but so does her family." And with that, he was gone.

****

Brandy caught sight of the two just before Tiarnan disappeared. She rushed across the sandy beach. "Stefan, I was so worried. Yet here you sit conversing with faeries?"

"A faerie, and not by choice," Stefan grumbled, letting his gaze linger over her beautiful body, still naked from transformation. Stepping to her, he slid his hands leisurely over her shoulders and down her arms. "Are you angry?" He pulled her close and took her mouth with his. She stiffened, putting her hand on his chest, and shoved hard.

"I should be angry, but I'm not. More worried. Kevin had that coming for a long time. I only wish you'd not been the one to give it to him." She sighed, letting her hand slide down his chest to rest at his waist. "You're well aware I can take care of myself. You needn't have stepped in."

He held her closer and laid his cheek on the top of her head. "I know, but I couldn't stand by and watch him treat you like that. Not going to happen." He shook his head vehemently. "Kevin won't remember a thing. I made sure of it." He tilted his head, his expression one of inquiry. "Am I still welcome in the pub?"

"Of course." She pulled away to peer into his face. "With the mixture of magic folk that frequents the pub, if a week goes by without an incident, Ma and Da are amazed."

"Then I suggest that we get your clothes and rejoin the festivities, if they are still going on."

"They are. In fact, Da asked me to go find you and bring you back. My clothes are at the house. We'll stop on our way, and I'll change." She shivered in the cool evening breeze.

He shrugged out of his shirt and wrapped it around her shoulders. "Put this on before you catch a chill."

She slipped her arms into the sleeves, shoved them up, and buttoned the shirt. "Thanks."

They strolled back to the house, hand in hand. Brandy quickly changed into her dress. He slipped into another shirt and returned to the pub.

The heavy wooden door to the pub groaned as Stefan tugged it open. Friendly voices and cheerful music greeted them as if nothing had happened. Tim was behind the bar, smiling, and waved them to a pair of stools at the end of the bar next to Tristian and Hannah.

As they made their way to the bar, Stefan received hardy slaps on the back as Brandy got hugs by just about everyone in the place. There was no sign of Kevin O'Riley, which suited Brandy perfectly. Meandering up to the bar, she took a seat next to Hannah and joined the conversation.

Stefan took the stool beside Brandy and next to Tristian. Putting a hand on his shoulder, Stefan glanced between Hannah and him. "Everything okay?"

Brandy leaned in to hear snippets of the conversation, hoping things between her sister and brother-in-law were handled. She didn't want anything to spoil their time in Ireland.

Tristian nodded. "Yeah, never better, actually. Maybe I was being a little overprotective."

"Huh, ya think?" Stefan raised a brow as feigned shock spread over his face.

"Oh, very funny." Tristian shoved at Stefan. "Seriously, Hannah made me realize that she can handle herself. I was so busy protecting her, I wasn't enjoying what we have together. She wants to be an equal partner in our marriage. I'll admit it'll take some getting used to, but I can handle it." He paused, then added, "Thanks for the advice." He lifted his pint to Stefan. "*Slainte.*"

"Anytime. Women are a puzzle, but one I enjoy solving…most times," Stefan said with a wink.

Tristian sidled closer and lowered his voice. "I heard from Bruce. Synn contacted him, but we can discuss that tomorrow. Tonight, we celebrate with our beautiful women." Tristian raised his pint again, this time in a toast to Hannah and Brandy. "*Slainte*." He put the mug to his lips and drank deeply.

"*Slainte*." Stefan joined in the toast but sat his glass on the bar afterward. Brandy reached for it, taking a sip and setting it in front of her. Leaning over, he nuzzled her neck slowly, kissing her softly. Tim looked over uneasily at the contact but said nothing.

The celebration lasted until the wee hours of the morning. On the way home, they took a quick detour to hunt.

Chapter Twenty-Four
On a Need-to-Know Basis and Most Don't Need to Know

Time spent with Brandy curled warmly beside him was quickly becoming Stefan's favorite pastime. Rather than sleep, he reflected on recent events and their life together. He worked out the kinks life hurtled toward him in the comforting silence of the night as she slept.

At a soft knock at the door, Stefan slid out of bed without disturbing Brandy, put his robe on, and opened the door.

Tim stood shifting uncomfortably from one foot to the other. "Stefan, can we talk?"

"Sure, let me put some clothes on, and I'll meet you downstairs."

Tim peered around Stefan, nodding toward Brandy, keeping his voice soft. "Try not to wake her."

"No problem," Stefan said in a reassuring voice. He knew this was going to be a difficult conversation. When he arrived downstairs, Tim was pacing in front of the warm, inviting fireplace. An open bottle of whisky and two glasses sat on the end table nearest the couch.

Stefan walked across the room, shoving his hands deep in his pockets, and sucked in a breath, letting it out slowly. He paused in front of Tim. "You wanted to talk to me?"

"Aye. Lad, we know you and Brandy have been

together a while, committed, I hope." Beads of sweat formed at his temples. "Are you…" He walked toward the table that held the whiskey, running his hand through his hair.

"Let me make it easy. Your suspicions are correct. I'm a vampire. Brandy wanted to tell you numerous times but didn't feel the time was right. She wanted you to get to know me first. I'm not a danger to her, or any of you, if that's what you're worried about."

"Aye, in part, but…" Tim walked over, picked up the glass, and knocked back the whisky, hissing out a breath as the familiar burning sensation worked its way to warm his belly. Then he motioned to the other glass. "Join me?"

"I really don't metabolize human food or drink very well. If forced I can, but would rather not."

"Of course. I wasn't thinking." He trailed off while staring at his glass and turning it around in his hand, sloshing the amber liquid nervously.

"I don't feed on human blood, if that's what's bothering you. I saw the way you looked at me in the pub tonight when I kissed Brandy's neck. That's when I knew you'd figured it out." Watching his face, Stefan wondered what was going on behind those blue eyes clouded with worry.

Tim tensed when Stefan put his hand on his shoulder. "Brandy and I have had our problems, as I'm sure you are aware. But I never would have allowed her back in my life if I couldn't control myself. In fact, it was Brandy that changed my way of life, showed me how to hunt and exist on animal blood."

"Aye, she always was a bit on the wild side and preferred something different."

Curious now, Stefan sat down on the couch, watching him. "If you knew your daughter that well, why are you surprised?"

Tim shook his head, and his eyes met Stefan's. "I'm not. Not really. More concerned. I don't know how to explain this to her mother or the rest of the family. Your incredible strength and speed when Kevin attacked you set everyone in the pub to talking. How do we explain that to them or him?"

"Don't worry about Kevin. He'll remember only what I told him before I released him. As far as the others in the pub, most have probably forgotten already or blamed it on the drink."

"You could be right, but I saw Kevin's face. He saw what I saw." He paused, looking questioningly at Stefan.

"Let's just say I've many talents, as your daughter does. Besides, Kevin had way too much to drink." He paused, considering what to tell Mary. "As far as Mary is concerned, I don't think she will be any more surprised than you. We'll tell her the truth. Your concern, while understandable, isn't necessary. Brandy and I hunt to keep my thirst under control."

"Telling Mary the truth is best," he agreed.

"Brandy can handle that tomorrow morning. The rest of your large family will be on a need-to-know basis and most won't need to know." Stefan stood up and glanced toward the bedroom.

Rubbing the back of his neck, Tim sighed. "Aye, you'd be right about that."

"You've had a long night. Go on back to bed knowing that you and your family have nothing to fear from me," Stefan said gently.

Tim nodded his head. "Aye, the rest can wait until morning. Tonight I needed to confirm my suspicions and get your measure as a man. I still like what I see. 'Tis just a little unnerving to have a vampire serious about me daughter." With a half laugh, he shook his head. "We knew when she left Ireland that she wouldn't commit to her own kind. She was looking for something else, and I guess she found him. No offense."

Smiling, Stefan nodded "None taken." Returning to their bedroom, he took a quick hot shower. It might rouse Brandy, but she wouldn't think much about it as that was their way of compensating for the differences in body temperatures, especially in bed. Then he could slide back into bed and not chill her as he drew her close.

Standing in the shower, eyes closed, the warm water cascading over his tense body, he heard the bathroom door creak open and then close quietly. The shower door slid open. Still, he kept his eyes closed. Her wonderful scent filled the room and warm gentle hands wrapped around him as her body all but slithered against him.

He enjoyed the arousing sensations rippling through his body as her gentle fingers played lightly over his chest muscles, and slid further down his body. Opening his eyes, he turned slowly, and drank in Brandy's glistening wet naked body, letting his hands roam intimately over her.

She smiled seductively up at him. "Restless again tonight?" she murmured.

"That's part of it, I guess," he whispered against her soft neck pulsing with delicious…Then slowly trailing his tongue across her shoulders and down her chest, he tenderly licked the water droplets from her firm, round breasts.

She moaned softly and arched toward him.

Turning off the water, he scooped her up in his arms and carried her to their bed. Outside, the rain was pinging on the window and the fireplace still glowed with the last embers of the fire started earlier in the evening.

Spilling her out onto the bed, she gasped, then giggled as she grabbed his hand, pulling him down beside her.

"Darling, I'm going to take you for a ride you'll not soon forget." She slowly slid one long, shapely, well-toned leg across his body and rose up over him.

He grinned wide in anticipation, folding his hands behind his head. "Then by all means, have your way with me."

She leaned down, her breasts tantalizingly caressing his bare chest as her lips brushed lightly back and forth over his, lingering a little longer each time.

"You like that?" she whispered seductively.

"Uh-huh." He reached up to cup her firm breasts as he gently rubbed his thumbs over her hardening nipples. Unable to wait any longer, Stefan pulled her down to him and filled his mouth with her breast, scraping his teeth carefully against the nipple as he sucked and gently tugged on the soft mound of female flesh. He closed his eyes and imagined again what it would be like to run his tongue over all of her, taste all of her.

She moaned and called out his name as she shifted slowly, surrounding him and taking him into her. He felt the flames of passion building inside her as she tightened around him. Her body began to quiver with liquid fire as she soared higher and higher until her world shattered into a million shimmering stars.

Finally, cupping the back of her neck, he took her mouth, devouring its softness hungrily. Her flavor spun into him as he slid his hands down to her hips. Grasping them firmly, he thrust up into her hard, fast, and deep, then held on.

"Oh God," she cried as waves of pleasure again pulsed through her.

It was all movement, flesh against flesh, man against woman, sheathed in her satiny smooth, steamy heat until the hot flow of passion raged through both like molten lava scorching everything in its path.

She went limp, as he knew she did now after loving. Draping her body across his, she buried her face in his neck and breathed a slow, sensuous kiss there.

He leaned his cheek against the top of her head and savored the immense satisfaction he felt as contentment and peace flowed between them. She shifted, and he reached up, running his fingers through her soft hair, tangled by his own hand in the night, watching her eyes go dreamy and sleep overtake her. He felt her mind as it flowed in a serene blur of soft colors, rolling green hills, and pleasant visions of home, family, and faerie mounds.

The intimacy of their lovemaking intensified as he shared her thoughts while touching her in all the places that he'd learned she enjoyed, wondering if she felt the same since she was able to tune into his feelings and thoughts as well.

She stirred, answering sleepily in his mind,

Hmmmm, yes, that is one of the best parts of making love with you. Of course the physical release isn't bad either, is it? She smiled and snuggled closer. Stefan caught the last sleepy thought drifting through her mind and wondered...

Tristian's quiet knock on the door and intruding thoughts ended the euphoria for the moment.

He knocked more insistently. "Stefan, I know you're awake."

Irate, Stefan growled. "If you know so much, then you know better than to intrude on my time alone with Brandy. Now, go away. I'm not getting up." Pausing, he listened to Tristian's mind. "Yeah, Tristian, I'm aware that Tim knows my secret, and we've come to terms."

Barely awake, Brandy murmured sleepily, "Go on with him, if you want. I'll be along in just a bit of a while."

Testily, Stefan grumbled, "No, I don't want to, and we'll join the others later." He deliberately avoided telling her of last night's conversation and the promise that he'd made. Grinning now, he thought Hannah and Tristian had enough of their own revelations to share, keeping things interesting until they joined the rest of the family later.

Tristian huffed out a breath on the other side of the door. "I wish you'd stay out of my head, but okay, fine. Have it your own way." His heavy footfalls grew quieter.

Chapter Twenty-Five
Best Kept Family Secrets of Gryphons, Vampires, and Warlocks

Brandy slept peacefully for a couple hours. Her eyelids fluttered open, and she gazed sleepily up at him from under her lashes. "Good morning, my love."

"Good morning, sunshine. Did you sleep well?" He leaned over and pulled her close, lightly kissing the tip of her nose.

"I did, thanks, except for Tristian's interruption. Did I hear Da's voice in the middle of the night, or was I dreaming?" Her voice still a bit sleepy and brows knitted in puzzlement, as she tried hard to remember. She reached up and fingered his gold serpentine neck chain as she had numerous times before. Only this time she wondered, "There's no clasp on your lovely chain. It's not long enough to slide over your head either..." Her voice trailed off.

"You did. Tim wanted to talk to me."

"In the middle of the night? Why?" Fully awake now, her expression concerned, she sat up and gave him her complete attention.

"He wanted to confirm his suspicions about me." Stefan could block his thoughts from her at times, which he'd done last night after his conversation with her da, so she could sleep.

"Oh, is that all. I figured he knew after your

altercation with Kevin." Shrugging, she laid her head back down on his chest.

"Brandy, he's concerned and has every right to be. He is also worried about how to tell your mom. We should have told them when we arrived."

"Aye, maybe we should have. I'm pretty sure Ma knows too. She's waiting for us to bring it up."

"And your brother?"

"I believe he knew from the first time he met you. It would never matter to him. He's dated outside our kind and likes what he's found. Da won't be happy when it's three-for-three since our kind's true blood is dwindling quickly."

"What do you mean?"

"Well, shapeshifters for the most part are human first, then whatever they shift into second. Once they decide not to shapeshift anymore, for whatever reason, they live out the rest of their lifespan as human."

"Okay, but I still don't see."

"In our case, we are gryphons—magical creatures first and the human forms we take second. We'll always be magical creatures no matter how long we remain in human form. We are immortal, as you are."

"I see. So it's not just talents that you have; it's actual use of magic."

Pursing her lips, she sighed, shifted, and sat up again. "Sort of, but the ability to feel others' emotions and hear thoughts is rare. That is a talent, not magic."

"I chose the elite of your kind. Is that what you are saying?" he asked with a cheeky grin.

She swiped at Stefan, nearly knocking him out of bed, then laughed. "Yes, I guess you could say that. I've always had trouble reading Da. I think he's okay with you. Disappointed a bit because you aren't a gryphon, but you'll win him over, if you haven't already. How'd your talk go?"

"His initial concern was your safety and your family's. He resigned himself long ago to the fact that you were looking for something, someone else other than your kind. I assured him that there was no danger from me. Even though you and I both know the possibility will always exist."

Frowning, she shook her head. "I don't believe that."

Shrugging, he gave her a serious look. "I will always be a vampire. You'll do well to remember that. I left the rest of the discussion for this morning and returned to our room, where you took unfair advantage of me."

"Aye, that I did and enjoyed every minute of it." She laughed easily, threw her arms around him, and hugged hard. "I didn't hear any complaints from you."

"Never," he agreed. "Now, I think it's time we get up, get dressed, and meet your family for breakfast. It's going to be an interesting day."

"That it will." She slid out of bed and sauntered seductively to the shower. "Care to join me?" she teased over her shoulder.

"You bet."

Sometime later, they dressed and stepped out into the hallway. "I think by now your da is aware his son-in-law is not what he seems either."

Brandy tossed her hair and shot him a saucy smile. "Want to wager on it?"

"No way. That's a sucker bet, and I'm no sucker."

"Speaking of magic and 'not as it seems,' you

never answered me about the chain around your neck."

"It's a long story, but the short version is, the chain is the reason I am able to enjoy the sunshine and not spontaneously combust."

"But you said that was a myth."

"For me it is as long as I wear this chain." He reached up and tugged thoughtfully at the serpentine chain. "It was conjured for me by my grandfather, a shaman in my tribe and the man who raised me. I didn't mean to ignore your questions. It's just that early in our relationship, trust didn't come easy for me, and the truth put me at risk. Now, I'm happy to tell you everything, but right now let's take care of the situation at hand."

"One more thing. Talking about myths and legends, the Vampire's Kiss—is that legend true?"

He sucked in a deep breath out of habit rather than need and blew it out. "Later."

Reaching out, he took her hand. She intertwined her fingers with his and walked into the kitchen. Tim and Mary sat at the head of the large oak table with Gavin, Tristian, and Hannah seated to the left and across from two empty chairs. If a fire had been lit, it was dying, and there was a slight chill in the room. All eyes turned to her and Stefan as they entered the kitchen.

"Good morning," they said in unison as she walked over, kissing her ma and da on the cheek. Mary reached out and hugged Stefan, patting his back affectionately. He gave her a quick hug and sat down next to Brandy.

Everyone continued to look at them expectantly. They were the center of attention once again. He nudged Brandy.

She grinned. "The floor is yours, Stefan."

"Thanks, Brandy." He looked around uncertainly. "Well, guys, it's going to be an interesting ride."

The cool, uncertain atmosphere started to melt with Tim's half laugh as he leaned back, relaxed slightly, and put his arm around Mary.

"Did we miss breakfast?" Stefan asked, looking around the room.

"What do you care? You don't eat breakfast, at least not our kind," Mary said with a glint of amusement in her eye, if a bit unsure, and a wide grin spreading across her face.

"You got me there." He returned her grin and leaned his chair on its back legs, laying his arm across Brandy's shoulders.

Gavin's chair scraped across the wood floor as he got up and walked over to tend to the fire. After adding a couple more logs, he coaxed the embers into a crackling fire that warmed the room.

Stefan turned to Tristian. "Well, did you tell them?"

"Not yet." He stiffened in his chair, glaring.

"There's still more to tell?" Tim sighed with exasperation. "'Tis not enough that me little girl has taken up with a vampire?"

"Da." Brandy let out an exasperated groan.

Gavin's brows shot up, but he smiled and said, "I knew it."

"Oh, yes, the girls have seen to it that our family is well rounded," Tim said with a deep chuckle rumbling in his throat.

Looking from Tim to Tristian, Stefan opened his mouth only to be interrupted by Tristian.

"I'm a warlock who has spent his adult life as an enforcer…assassin, if you will. Until recently. I manage my teams more than physically go out into the field as an enforcer—a lifestyle change necessitated by having a wife and family…A tale for another time."

Eyebrows shot to the hairline and eyes rounded on individuals sitting around the table as if all they'd heard was 'assassin.'

"Relax. I work for the good of man and magickind, which provides me a very comfortable living."

It was Stefan's turn to look shocked. "Comfortable? More like royalty."

Tristian shot him a warning glance.

Stefan shrugged. "Everything out in the open. Remember?"

Tim shook his head while rolling his eyes and leaning over against Mary, "Where did we go wrong with our girls? Vampires, ah…warlocks. What next?"

"Well, now that you mention it…" Stefan grinned wickedly at Tim and winked at Brandy.

Brandy returned his grin, but it faded quickly. The air around them electrified, and her eyes grew wide.

Chapter Twenty-Six
So Be It...All Hell's About to Break Loose

Unexpectedly, the air in the kitchen crackled as if electrified, and the hair on the back of Stefan's neck stood up straight. He glanced over at Brandy, did a double take, and stared. Feathers sprouted all over the top of her head, her body began to blur, and then three figures materialized across the room.

In a blur of motion, Tim jumped up, transforming. The chair he'd occupied crashed to the floor. Gavin, being quicker, leapt to his feet, transformation complete. Using the seat of his chair as a springboard, he soared over the table and its occupants, landing his gryphon paws toe to toe with the larger figure. His razor-sharp talons extended and ripped into the flesh of the largest figure. A howl of anger and pain erupted. He prepared for retaliation, a blue-orange fireball swirled and snapped in the palm of the large figure's hand.

Tristian jumped out of his chair and sprang over the table, grabbed Bruce's arm, and said gruffly, "Stop."

The large figure closed his hand over the fireball and waited.

Immediately, Stefan shoved himself between them, roughly forcing Gavin backward across the room. "Gavin, chill. It's okay. These are friends. Uninvited but friends just the same." Gavin propelled himself forward again, talons still extended. Stefan sidestepped him as did Bruce, the demon overlord. Gavin went sprawling face-first across the floor littered with pieces of his and Tim's clothing. Stefan placed his foot across the back of Gavin's neck, holding him in place, and barked, "Back off right now before you make matters worse. There is no danger here."

Still in gryphon form, Tim stood ready to defend his family but, at Stefan's urging, backed down slowly. Brandy spun around the table in an effort to restrain her da and ma, if necessary. He saw her body tense as heat flushed up her neck, and a trickle of sweat slipped between the plumes on her forehead. Feathers remained on Mary's head, though she never completed the change. Seeing Brandy's appearance slowly return to normal, Stefan relaxed a little.

Her soft voice purred in his head. *Surprise and danger have that effect on gryphons. I've got things under control here.*

The vein in his neck pulsed as Stefan turned his attention to Bruce, whose fine tailored shirt was shredded and splattered with blood. . "Don't you ever enter a home by knocking?" Stefan demanded.

Bruce smirked, extinguishing the ball of power with a snap. "While I like the element of surprise, you're right." He turned to the others. "Pardon my intrusion, but I have urgent news."

Tristian released him. "This encounter could have turned deadly, overlord or not." He tucked the back of his shirt in and returned to stand behind his seat, hands resting on the chair back.

Bruce shrugged, brushing his palms together. His amber eyes swirled orange as his gaze swept over the room and its occupants, settling on Tristian for a moment, then darting to Stefan and back. "Sorry. Right now I'd like a word with my brother-in-law in private."

Angie stood beside Bruce, a restraining arm wrapped partially around his waist and her other arm out in front of Synn, who stood trance-like slightly behind her.

Tristian straightened and walked around the table. "Why is she here?" His hands balled into fists, the muscles in his arms straining. He brought one hand up and pointed a finger accusingly.

Hannah said furiously, "This is not the time or place." She grasped Tristian's arm and shot a warning glance at Angie, who released her hold on Bruce. Hannah reached out to grab Bruce's arm, but he slipped out of her reach, grabbed hold of her shoulders, and spun her around, breaking her hold on Tristian. He took a menacing step toward Bruce, who held up his hand in warning.

"Now, let's all play nice like the good creatures we are," Bruce said in a dangerously calm voice. "Stefan, you were saying?"

All eyes turned to Stefan. *How the hell do I keep winding up in the middle of this shit?*

He eyed the occupants in the room and suggested, "Let's all sit down, and I'll make the introductions." No one moved. Tim's jaw set in a grim line. Gavin stared at the vampire, his distrust palpable. A muscle quivered in his jaw. Mary looked as if she was ready to cry or kill someone alternately, probably him. "Or not," Stefan said with more confidence than he was feeling.

Angie interrupted. "Sorry for the interruption." She looked genuinely dismayed. "I'm Angelique, Tristian's sister." She shrugged and pointed to Bruce, who had released Hannah to Tristian. "Bruce is the Demon Overlord of the Western Hemisphere and my husband." She tried a little smile. Pointing a thumb behind her, she said, "This is Synn. She's a demon too and has promised to help us in exchange for protection from our enemy, Baltizar."

While Stefan was glad to relinquish the floor to Angie, Tim's bright-red face and Mary's shocked expression prompted him to step in. "Angie, I think that's enough for now. Mary and Tim Shaughnessy are Hannah and Brandy's parents"—he waved a hand toward them—"and have just learned that one daughter married a warlock serving as enforcer at the pleasure of the Overlord of the Western Hemisphere . The other is involved with a vampire. I suspect they need a respite from the drama."

Bruce nodded and shifted his gaze to the male that attacked him.

"Gavin is Hannah and Brandy's brother." Stefan nodded in his direction. "He was thrust in the middle of this and tried to protect his family. We were just sitting down to have a family meeting to explain the situation when you three burst into the house unannounced and uninvited. That's a bad habit, Bruce, overlord or not."

Bruce raised one eyebrow. "I already apologized and meant it. I don't normally go where I'm not invited. In this case, I had to make an exception. If our very existence didn't hang in the balance, I would have asked permission to crash your family gathering. But time is of the essence."

Anger flashed in Tristian's eyes, his mouth set in a thin grim line. The vein at his temple bulged out, threatening to burst. He shifted his gaze from Hannah, who had her arm around him, to Bruce. "You've got some balls, coming in here like…"

Stefan grabbed Bruce's arm. "I've some shirts that may fit you, my lord." Ignoring Hannah and Tristian's scathing look, he said, "Let's go to my room and try them on." *That gives Tim and Gavin a chance to leave the kitchen, transform, and get dressed privately.*

"I want them out of the…" Hannah began.

Stefan's scathing look cut her off mid-sentence. "Meanwhile, Tristian can fill the others in on what is going on. Angie can keep an eye on Synn. Can't ya, darling? It's your spell that's controlling her, right?"

Angie's eyes widened in amazement as she stared at Stefan, then she released Bruce's arm. "Sure, no problem."

Smiling companionably, Stefan motioned down the hallway in the direction of their room. "After you." Stefan made a slight bow, only because it would irritate Bruce.

"When you return, you can tell us why you're here." Brandy reached out and hooked an arm through Bruce's other arm.

Bruce snorted. "As you wish." Bruce shook off Stefan's hold with little effort. Bruce wrinkled his brow, stared quizzically for a moment, and then fell into step beside them. Footsteps echoed on the polished oak floor as they disappeared down the hall.

Curious, Stefan leaned over and whispered to Brandy. "Your wings are beautifully rainbow colored while Gavin and Tim's are a light tawny?"

A laugh bubbled up in her throat. "Because I'm female. Silly."

"Oh, I knew that." Stefan shrugged nonchalantly, turning the handle and walking through the bedroom door.

"Sure you did." Bruce choked back a laugh.

Brandy ignored the whole exchange. "It's best if you leave the kitchen for a while. I don't think my parents have ever seen a demon. Learning that you are extended family is a shock, and my father won't be too complimentary at first. Tristian can explain the situation that has brought us here. Angie is so good at smoothing over feelings. We'll leave it to them to put everyone at ease about you." Brandy's eyes sparkled with mischief that was just a little unsettling.

Stefan sent a thought to Brandy, *What are you up to?*

"Nothing," she said aloud, grinning a little too innocently, then replied telepathically, *I think it's cute that Bruce is a bit uncomfortable without Angie by his side. Don't you see it?*

No, I don't see anything cute about a large, powerful demon overlord. Stefan replied. *By the way, if the legends are true, he's ruled for a few hundred years without her by his side.*

Brandy tipped her head to look at Bruce, just a bit perplexed, "What's so important that you burst in unannounced?" She reached into the closet and brought out two shirts. Holding the garments up in the light, she examined them.

Eyeing the clothing, Bruce said slowly, "A lot of things have changed since you left. I wanted to bring everyone up to speed. Called Tristian a couple of times, leaving messages on each occasion. But he failed to return my calls."

"Perhaps he didn't get your messages," she said, holding the shirts out for Bruce to choose.

He shook his head in frustration, reaching for the burgundy and black print shirt. "That one will do."

"Not until we get you cleaned up." Brandy snatched it out of his reach. "Take your shirt off."

"Sure. Right here?" he asked suggestively.

"Aye. Don't flatter yourself. Stefan has more male prowess than you'll ever have." She smiled sweetly, holding a washcloth under the warm running water. "This might hurt a bit." Then she dabbed gently on his chest at the clotting blood and deep wounds.

"So you say. I believe my mate, Angie, would dispute that statement." He sat unflinching. A smirk played around the corners of his mouth.

"And then you woke up." She chortled, bandaging him so the blood wouldn't seep through and stain the shirt. "You're gonna be sore tomorrow. My brother's talons penetrated pretty deep. Gonna leave scars."

He glanced down. "I'll be fine. Had a lot worse." Shrugging into the shirt, he winced a bit, buttoning the front and tucking the shirttail in his black tailored trousers. He stretched his arms out, checking the sleeve length. "Huh, we're about the same size." He nodded appreciatively toward Stefan. "Thanks for the shirt."

"No problem. Tristian did get your messages. He told me last night that you'd called and Synn had come over to our side. He intended to call you this morning after we'd brought the family into the loop. Then you three popped in. Can she be trusted?"

"Right now Angie has her under a spell, so we know she won't do anything stupid or hear anything she shouldn't. Although when we were in D.C., she was quite compliant and extremely cooperative without magic. The deal is I give her sanctuary and protection. In turn, she will tell us what she knows."

"Yes, but can we trust her?" Stefan repeated. "I have to be frank here. There's too much riding on all of this to have someone we can't trust among us." Uncertainty crept into his voice. He quickly willed it away and continued in a confident tone. "How long was she with Baltizar?"

"She's young but very talented. Baltizar recruited her not long ago. Synn climbed the ranks quickly because of her abilities." Bruce paused a moment, rubbing his chin thoughtfully. "She didn't know what she was getting into. Synn's already told us where another of the Book of Shadows is located, so that leaves only one to find." He straightened his shoulders confidently, then winced slightly again.

No, now we know where they all are. It's time to make our move. Stefan's lips twitched to keep from grinning. "How do we know Baltizar confided the true location to her? Does she know what his plans are or how he's going to retrieve the Book? Or has he?"

"I've not pushed her on that yet but will soon. Baltizar injured her pretty badly. It will be quite a while before her wounds heal. As far as the Book's location, she claims it's common knowledge among his followers who are vying for the chance to retrieve the Book."

"Can't Angie speed that along? She's a healer of some sort, right?" Stefan asked.

Bruce narrowed his eyes as he sucked in a quick breath. "What makes you think that?" He quickly regained his cool, calculating demeanor. "Did Tristan tell you?"

"Nope. I've quite a few talents of my own," Stefan said nonchalantly.

"I've heard. Glad to have you on our side."

The voices died down to a dull roar as Brandy and the men walked back into the kitchen. Silence descended, and everyone's gaze shifted to Bruce.

"Sit down. Make yourself comfortable." Stefan motioned to the chair he'd vacated earlier.

"Thanks, I'll stand." Bruce stood behind Angie, hands resting on the back of her chair.

"Well, what'd we miss?" Brandy inquired, looking intently at her father.

"Nothing you didn't already know," he said ruefully. "This family has quite literally gone to Hell in a handbasket." Tim glared at Bruce, shook his head, then rubbed the back of his neck, rolling his shoulders. His expression softened, as he peered at Brandy. "You've got your work cut out for you, lass, I'll say that." His forehead creased with concern as his gaze swept the individuals in the room.

He patted Mary's hand and fell silent, returning his gaze to Stefan expectantly.

"Aye, we do," Brandy agreed with a long sigh.

Tim shifted in his chair to glance at Tristian. "One thing I'd like to know. If dark demons have been here for centuries without much problem, how come new ones are escaping the underworld to cause havoc now?"

Tristian cleared his throat and shifted uncomfortably in his seat. "I'm certainly no expert, but I'm learning. I wound up in this position only because it's my family's obligation to keep the demons in the underworld and the portals to Hell sealed. Angie and I are all that's left of our family. Our parents were killed before they could pass on any information regarding this situation."

Angie nodded solemnly.

"Anyway, back to your question. It's my understanding the spells weaken every time there is a massacre, a war, or human darkness allowing a momentary rift warping the time space continuum. The dark demons wait for such opportunities and slip through one or two at a time. How we stop it, I've yet to figure out. All I know is that we need all three Books of Shadows used to cast the original spells. I hope they hold the answer."

Tim shuddered. "Our only hope of survival is pinned to the success of—" his eyes met and lingered on each one of them "—this group? God help us." He shook his head slowly.

"We appreciate the vote of confidence," Bruce interjected. "We have good people and creatures. This battle has been ongoing for years. It's time we put a stop to it permanently." He glanced at Tristian, who nodded in agreement.

Stefan considered telling everyone about the Book the faeries held. Still, he had a few questions for Tiarnan so decided against bringing it up. Turning his attention back to Bruce, Stefan said, "Since you burst in to bring us up to speed with the recent events, let's hear it."

Bruce scanned the room and its occupants carefully. He stepped forward and straightened, his hands tucked behind his back. "Well, Synn—" he jerked his head toward the pixie-like demon "—has decided it's in her best interest to join our little band of demons." Amused at the reference, he grinned momentarily at Tristian and Hannah, then sobered at Tristian's steely stare.

Unruffled, Bruce continued. "She has knowledge of Baltizar's plans and information regarding another Book of Shadows.

"What kind of information?" Tim interrupted.

"Its location. Apparently, it's hidden somewhere at Ayers Rock in the Australian outback. Provided Baltizar's minions haven't found the Book yet. If the legends of Ayers Rock are true, it's guarded by dangerous magic. For Synn's cooperation, we'll provide her sanctuary and protection from Baltizar."

Gavin's eyes glinted with male interest as he watched Synn. Brandy followed Gavin's gaze, picked up a paper cup, and threw it across the kitchen table, striking Gavin right between the eyes. "Don't even think about it, fool."

"Wh—what?" Gavin said innocently, raising his hands palms up and shrugging.

Bruce nodded curtly and continued. "Owen and Toni report all remains quiet in D.C. Business is brisk, but no one is talking except the usual political banter." He rolled his shoulders and dropped his arms to his sides.

Stefan noticed that for the first time since they met Bruce's eyes weren't tinged with anger-triggered orange. Well…maybe a couple of times during the family trip in Maine they weren't either. Now there were dark circles under the tired-looking eyes. Guess there wasn't much downtime when you were responsible for keeping the Western Hemisphere's magical creature population in check. *Not an enviable position.*

He nudged Brandy into the seat next to Angie and brought a couple chairs from the other room. Stefan offered Bruce one, who eased into it. Stefan flipped a chair around so it backed the table and straddled it, crossing his arms across the back and leaning forward.

"Bruce, if you don't mind, let me fill everyone in on what I've learned. This is how I see the situation, and I am open to any suggestions. None of this is set in stone. Research into the local legends is necessary before we go tramping around Ayers Rock. We should have a plan to get the Book and get out before even heading that way." He grimaced. "Tristian, you and Bruce are best suited to that adventure."

"True," Tristian agreed. "But someone familiar with D.C., its operations and undercurrents, needs to remain behind."

Grudgingly, Stefan agreed. "Okay, I'll go to Australia with Bruce. Tristian, how about you and Hannah accompany Angie and Synn to D.C. and then continue on to Maine?"

Angie shot Stefan a dirty look. "I can take care of myself and anyone else that gets in my way."

"I'm well aware of that. Thought a little extra protection wouldn't hurt. Besides, I don't think…"

"Angie, he's right." Tristian nodded in agreement. "It's best if Hannah and I go with you and Synn to D.C., stay a day or so, and then continue on to Maine. That way we stand a better chance, making sure we aren't followed. I don't want to lead anyone to the Book of Shadows."

Angie reached for Hannah's arm, a wide smile spread across her face. "Oh, we could have a girl's

315

night out—facials, pedicures, nails, the works. Toni would love it."

Tristian groaned and rolled his eyes. "Great."

"Owen will keep you company, Tristian. You'll be fine," Angie said with a wink and toss of her long blonde hair.

"The joining of the Books of Shadows should be done in Ireland rather than back home?" Tristian wondered aloud.

"I still have some research to do, but local legends lean that way. You don't know of anything that would suggest it should be done elsewhere, do you?" Stefan asked.

"No, my family didn't leave much information regarding this situation. Apparently, they planned on being around when the need arose."

Hopefully, Tiarnan will contact us soon. Stefan shifted in his chair, realizing his thirst was not going to wait much longer. *I need to hunt.* At Brandy's touch, her knowing eyes met his, indicating she was aware.

Tim watched the silent exchange between them intently. He cleared his throat. "How about we meet at the pub in a bit. Bet we all could use a pint. We'll open the pub early, and Gavin can whip up something for us to eat. We can get acquainted in a friendly atmosphere and understand the situation better before opening the doors to the public."

"Great idea," Bruce said. "Thank you." He wrapped an arm around Angie, and the muscles in his neck relaxed. She snuggled into him and patted his knee reassuringly.

"If you need our help in the future, and God, I hope you don't—" Tim turned his gaze to the heavens "—I want to understand fully what it is we'd be jumping into." He looked tentatively over at Tristian and Bruce. "You two can fill us in on anything we've missed. Right?"

"You bet we can," Tristian said.

"Good. I believe Brandy and Stefan have a previous engagement and will join us later. The first Guinness is on the house, if you care to sample the local fare. Otherwise I have plenty of other potions that sate the magic folks here and about."

"Yes, we do, and we're late." Taking the opening that Tim provided, Stefan grasped Brandy's arm and strode purposefully toward the back door, stopping to wave. "See you guys at the pub later." He held the door open for Brandy as they walked out. He'd just about closed the door when something occurred to him, and he poked his head back inside the door. "Gavin, don't even think about it."

Gavin narrowed his eyes and blew out a breath. "I don't know what you are talking about."

Brandy looked questioningly at Stefan. "You saw it too?"

"Of course. I don't think you are the only one in your family that likes the wild side."

Chapter Twenty-Seven
Faerie Legends Abound

Grinning, Stefan raced toward the bushes and dense trees that would cover their activities. Brandy tossed her long red hair and sprinted after him, her heart pumping and breath coming in gasps as she attempted to catch up. Finally, she slowed and stopped long enough to remove her clothes and stash them behind a tree. Her body shimmered and blurred, transforming to gryphon.

She gracefully spread her wings and, with a whoosh of air, took to the sky to hunt. She loved the feel of the wind in her face and the freedom of flight.

After getting their fill, vampire and gryphon walked along the trail, stopping where Brandy's clothes lay neatly folded. She returned to her human form just as Tiarnan appeared above them on the rocky cliffs.

"Crap," Brandy squealed and ducked behind Stefan.

Tiarnan grinned appreciatively as a laugh rumbled in his throat. "Hello Stefan." He leaned over to make eye contact with Brandy. "Good evening to you too."

"You, turn around right this minute," she ordered, hastening to pull on her pants and button her shirt behind the protection of Stefan's body.

"Aye." A smirk slid over his face as he turned his back toward them. "'Tis a beautiful young woman

318

you've become."

Huffing out a breath, she came to stand beside Stefan. "You've no right to sneak up on people that way." She straightened her shirt and tucked it into her jeans.

Tiarnan threw back his head and roared with laughter. "I walk these cliffs at dusk most every night with Erin. 'Tis you that are out of place, Miss Shaughnessy."

"Where is your lady?" Brandy turned in a full circle, searching the cliffs for Erin.

"She'll be right along. The sun wasn't quite down when I started out. I wanted to catch you two alone."

"Well, you've managed that, haven't you?" Brandy said testily.

"Aye, that I have."

A shadow slipped quietly behind Tiarnan. He turned slightly and put his arm behind his back, drawing out a beautiful woman a few inches shorter than him with auburn hair flowing to her waist and misty blue eyes. Dressed in jeans and a pastel-colored knit sweater that hugged her curves, she smiled at them.

"This is my blushing bride, Erin."

Her laugh tinkled like crystal bells. "'Tis many years have passed since I was a blushing bride," Erin said affectionately, wrapping her arm around his waist.

"Seems like only yesterday." He leaned down and kissed her cheek.

"Why are you looking for us?"

"I understand you have located all three of the Books and will be traveling to retrieve them soon. They must be brought back here and merged on holy ground."

"I thought that might be the case. Why not just discuss this with Tristian?" Stefan said.

"I told you, I'll not deal with the warlock. His family may have a part in the original spells, but he is not the one. 'Tis you and Brandy that will fulfill the prophecy. It may be the warlock and his sister will help in the end, but now, it's up to you two."

"Perhaps the best thing to do is to leave the Book of Shadows in your capable hands until we have the other two on Irish soil. Sound like a plan?"

"Aye, that works as long as one of you remains here."

"Brandy will be staying in Ireland while Bruce and I travel to find the last Book of Shadows and bring it here."

"I am? Since when do you decide for me what I will and won't do, Stefan Talltree?" Brandy fisted her hands on her hips and stared defiantly at him.

Reaching for her hand, he gently straightened out her fingers, intertwining them with his. "If your family's participation in this is necessary, they will trust you more than any of the rest of us. If anything goes wrong here while I'm gone, I know you can handle it. Make sense?"

Her defiant stance relaxed, and her gaze softened. "I guess, but I think you're just trying to get around me."

"Darling, I've always been able to do that." He grinned, giving her a wink.

"Tiarnan, you'll keep an eye on Brandy while I'm away, won't you?"

"That I will, lad. Aye, that I will."

Stefan turned toward town. "We're headed to the

pub. Care to walk with…"

"Stefan, they're gone." Brandy said, touching his shoulder lightly. Only the mist crawled along the ground as Brandy and Stefan walked toward the pub in the lightly falling rain.

The pub's wooden door groaned as he yanked it open. The wreath bounced against the plank as he held it for Brandy. Song and laughter flowed out into the night. Brandy smiled as she passed through the doorway, inhaling the yeasty scent of beer mixed with the aroma of Gavin's salmon steaks and pan boxty. At a corner table beside the Christmas tree at the end of the bar, the family leaned back against their chairs, sipping pints. Dirty plates were stacked in the center of the table.

"You missed a grand dinner," Tristian commented, stretching both arms into the air as they approached the table. "Gavin is quite the chef."

Synn shoved through the kitchen doors, scooped up the dirty dishes off the table, and returned to the kitchen. Stefan glanced from Bruce to Angie, jerking his head toward the door as it swung shut behind Synn. "What's up with her?"

"She volunteered to help serve and clean up. Not doing too bad, really," Bruce said easily. "Though her limp is becoming more pronounced."

"Did she?" Stefan walked to the kitchen and pushed open one door quietly. Brandy followed and peeked around his arm. Gavin had his arm around Synn. Her smiling face tilted up toward him, she listened intently.

"Gavin!" Brandy pushed under Stefan's arm and stomped into the room. "What do you think you're doing?"

Gavin straightened, dropping his arm to his side. A dinner plate slipped out of Synn's hand and crashed to the floor. He turned toward Brandy and Stefan. "Ah, just showing Synn how to stack the dishes in the dishwasher." He grinned sheepishly.

"Sure you were." Brandy grabbed Synn by the arm, hauled her out of the kitchen over to the table, and shoved her against Bruce. Between clinched teeth she hissed, "Keep her away from my brother."

Relaxing against the back of his chair, arms folded behind his head, Bruce tried to keep a grin from forming on his lips. "You might want to talk to your brother before you lay all the blame at Synn's feet." He nudged the demon toward a chair and motioned her to sit. She complied, glaring at Brandy. Bruce cuffed Synn upside the head and growled something in her ear. She averted her eyes to the floor, her mouth set in a thin line. Angie frowned at Bruce.

Stefan leaned against the wall, out of the way. Gavin swung through the double kitchen doors on the heels of his sister, wiping his hands on the towel tucked in his waistband.

He grabbed Brandy by the shoulder and spun her around. "Knock it off. I am a grown man and can do as I please. Don't need you coming in here and making a bloody scene when Synn was just helping. Things were fine before you and Stefan arrived," Gavin said, keeping his tone calm so as not to draw any more attention to the situation.

"That's because no one else noticed the gleam in your eye when you first saw Synn. She's a demon," Brandy hissed quietly.

"He's a vampire," Gavin said, jerking his chin toward Stefan, then looking across the table at Tristian. "Do I need to list what you and Hannah have brought into our family?" Gavin reached out gently for Synn and tugged her out of the chair. With his hand at the small of her back, he guided her back to the kitchen, allowing for her slow, uneven gait. She glanced nervously back at the table. Bruce raised his eyebrow and shot a stern glance in warning to Gavin but allowed Synn to go with him.

Brandy glanced over to where her da was wiping the bar off with a lot more effort than was necessary. Then he roughly slid a glass under the tap to build a pint and shook his head.

Stefan took Brandy's elbow and steered her toward the door. "Let's take a walk."

"No." She tried to yank her arm free.

He tightened his grip and smiled, whispering, "Um, yes, you are, either willingly or I'll sling you over my shoulder and walk out with you. Your choice."

"You wouldn't dare."

"Try me."

She sent him a withering glance but hurried toward the door.

Once outside, they stopped. Brandy's gaze still blazed as she crossed her arms over her chest.

Stefan turned to face her. "Think about this for a minute. What better way to make Synn feel a part of the group and get her to open up even more than Gavin befriending her? You said he has a taste for the different. Just like you and your sister. He can also keep an eye on her. Keep her busy while we discuss strategies and make decisions we don't want her to know about."

"I don't care, Stefan. He's my little brother. I don't want him hurt. She's a demon. What if he falls for her?"

"I'm a vampire. So what? Don't look now, but he's all grown up. He didn't think much of your attitude a few minutes ago. I suspect in your long absence he's sampled a wide variety of dishes, so to speak, without harm. You didn't ask anyone's permission to bring home a vampire, now, did you?"

"That's different."

He cocked his head, narrowing his eyes. "How?"

"It just is!" She turned and tried to flounce away.

"Oh, no you don't. We'll finish this here." He reached out and caught her around the waist, pulling her to him. "While you were embarrassing your brother and Synn, I listened to the minds of the others. They all knew what was going on, weighed the pros and cons of Gavin's interest in Synn, and decided to watch the situation without interference. Bruce is going to have a little chat with Gavin in private after we split up for the night. Apparently, Angie, Bruce, and Synn are staying with Gavin for a while until we get things settled."

Her anger spent, she leaned against Stefan and sighed. "I don't like it, but it does make sense."

"Now, let's go back to the pub and enjoy the rest of the evening. Tomorrow we'll discuss the logistics of retrieving the Books located outside Ireland and decide how this is all going to go down."

Inside the pub, now open for business, cheerful voices greeted Brandy and Stefan from a variety of tables around the room. Someone sat at the old piano playing Christmas carols while several patrons, including Tristian and Hannah, joined in the caroling. The aroma of bayberry, pine, gingerbread, and sugar biscuits mixed with the yeasty scent of ale.

"Since when do bars serve Christmas cookie…biscuits? Or what smells like them?" Stefan looked at Brandy, then glanced around. The answer to his question came as Gavin pushed through the doors to the kitchen, a huge platter of biscuits in each hand, followed by Synn, who had two more. They slid the platters onto the bar and cleared a table in the center of the room.

Brandy tossed her head back and laughed. "It's a Shaughnessy tradition to serve our great-great-grandmother's Christmas biscuits in the pub on Saturday nights during December. Only, I think Gavin has improved on the original recipe. The locals all clamor for them even on the nights they are not served. But if Gavin has time, he whips up a batch or two."

"It's quite a family you have," Stefan said above the noise in the pub.

****

It was the wee hours of the morning when Brandy and Stefan finally returned to their room. Stefan pulled her into a warm shower with him. Afterward Brandy fell fast asleep, her face snuggled against his chest.

Thoughts of the impending trip, strategies and pitfalls it entailed, battered Stefan's mind. With the morning's hazy light, the aroma of fresh-brewed coffee, eggs, bacon, sausage, and hash browns wafted into the room. Brandy began to stir, her head on his chest and her body curled warm against him.

She sniffed. "Mmmm, someone is cooking breakfast." Yawning wide, rubbing her eyes with the back of her hands, she murmured sleepily, "Smells wonderful." Inhaling deeply, she released her breath with a sigh.

Stefan wrinkled his nose in distaste. "I'm sorry, I didn't realize you missed such things."

"Don't be. Our life is just different, and I like it as well." She gently patted his chest. "Let's get up, and you can watch me eat."

"Oh, you are so good to me!" He chuckled.

Stopping in the middle of pulling her new rose-colored sweater over her head, her voice muffled, she said, "You don't like the smell of breakfast, do you?"

Stefan shook his head. "Not really. Some things still smell delicious but taste awful. Not the case with breakfast items."

"Sorry. The mist appears light and will probably burn off quickly. You could go for a walk instead." Her head popped out of the sweater. A smile played around her lips and lit up her eyes.

"That's okay, I'll suffer through it. Besides, I enjoy the company of your family."

They hurried down the hallway and into the kitchen. "Good morning, everyone," Stefan said, pulling out a chair for Brandy and slipping into the one beside her.

Bruce slid an insulated, sealed mug across the table to Stefan. It had a capped straw rising out of it. He winked, and his thoughts flowed through Stefan's mind, *Warmed to a balmy 98.6. Enjoy.*

Stefan uncapped the straw, sucked in a breath, and replaced the cap. "Bruce, could I see you in the living room, please?"

Bruce scraped his chair back and stood lazily.

"Sure. Is there a problem?" He followed Stefan nonchalantly.

Once in the other room, Stefan hissed, "What do you think you're doing? I don't drink that stuff anymore. You've got balls sitting that on the table in front of Brandy's family, especially after your stunt yesterday."

"That's why it's sealed. I don't know firsthand, but by all reports, existing as you do, while very noble, weakens vampire abilities. If we are teaming up, I want your many talents at their peak. We're guaranteed an encounter with your kind if I know Baltizar, and I do. You can bet they will have fed on humans."

"Where'd you get it?"

"Out of Gavin's freezer. His ex-girlfriend left a few pints of O positive behind. The date on them is still good."

"Gavin?"

"Yep, that's right," he stated smugly, slowly shaking his head. "Staying with him has been an eye-opening experience even for me. Synn is going to have her hands full. If it's female, he's sampled it. If it's extreme or exhilarating, he's tried it. You get the picture."

Holding up a hand, Stefan frowned. "All right, just stop. I get it." He paced across the room, shoved his hands in his front jeans pockets, and pulled them back out. His mouth watered. "How do you know he's not just embellishing his conquests to impress you?"

"Oh, come on. Do you think I let all of you come over here without checking on the family before you even set foot out of your house? He's true to his tales."

"Brandy doesn't know this side of her brother. Do

Tim and Mary know?"

"Probably not. Gavin is very discreet. He also has quite a file on you. Before Brandy, you were one vicious son of a bitch. Thanks for saving my mate." He laughed and blew out a breath. "Odds of winning this war are going up by the minute. Now, don't let the perfectly good drink, warmed to perfection, go to waste."

Bouncing into the room, Brandy grinned. "Hey, enough male bonding. Your food is getting cold."

"You don't have to tell me twice." Bruce strolled back into the kitchen.

"Come on," she tugged Stefan toward the doorway. "Whatever Gavin and Bruce fixed up for you is getting cold too."

"It's blood, human blood, O positive to be exact," Stefan said flatly.

"What?" She gasped, her heart thundering in her chest. Her palms were sweaty as he took her hands in his. "Why?"

"Because your brother and Bruce think my lifestyle has weakened me and my ability to fight. They want me better prepared for battle. Especially Bruce since I'll have his back in Australia."

"Is that true?"

"Could be. I've never tested it and haven't really noticed. My talents seem as strong as ever, but I've not tested them against other vampires in a while."

"Will you have to now?"

"It's possible, at least Bruce thinks so. There is no way to know what we'll have to defeat in order to get our hands on the Book."

"Where'd the blood come from?" she asked

tentatively.

He snorted. "Your little brother had it in his freezer. Apparently, an ex-girlfriend of his left it there. The dates are still good, so it must have been a recent one."

She turned ashen as the blood drained out of her face. Opening and closing her mouth a couple of times, she attempted to speak, but nothing came out. He waited, not sure what would be the best course of action under the circumstances.

The color returned slowly to her face. "I knew he was dating out of his species, but I didn't have any idea how far."

"There are lots of things you don't know about Gavin. However, right now, the issue is drinking human blood. I know how you feel, and I am still fine with that."

"No." She shook her head slowly. "The circumstances have changed considerably. If it will make you stronger, no human lives lost, and legally obtained, I think you should drink it. You mean too much to me to risk sending you off in less than excellent condition. Though my parents may not feel the same."

"They don't have to know. Apparently, your parents didn't know about Gavin's girlfriend, or they are great actors. Gavin has the blood at his house, and we'll just stop by there."

"Okay, but what about now?"

"It's handled." Returning to the kitchen, Brandy and Stefan eased into their seats. Fresh, hot scrambled eggs, bacon, and a glass of orange juice sat in front of Brandy.

"Drink up, Stefan. It'll set you right." Bruce laughed, then added, "The vamp worries too much and upsets his system." Bruce winked at Brandy. He scanned the others at the table. "Since Stefan doesn't eat breakfast, Gavin whipped up a health drink for him. Probably wouldn't compete with this delicious spread."

"I'm sure we don't want to know," Mary added while she finished shoveling eggs onto everyone's plates.

Stefan enjoyed his drink, listening to the others' strategies and thoughts on departure schedules.

Chapter Twenty-Eight
The Land Down Under Is Calling

Bruce and Stefan sat in first class, awaiting takeoff from Dublin's airport. "It would have been faster to port to Australia," Bruce mused, "rather than wasting nearly twenty-five hours on this plane if there are no delays."

"I realize that you're not used to using public transportation. But by the time your private jet would have arrived in Ireland, we would be well on our way to Australia." Stefan leaned his seat back and stretched out his long legs, thankful for first class leg room.

"I said port. I'm not complaining about the airlines," Bruce said flatly. "I'm accustomed to living a certain way. But that doesn't mean I can't adjust to whatever is necessary. Considering the options available to us, you were right. This is the best." He reached down and pulled out his laptop.

"I'm glad you agree. Porting would have gotten us there immediately, but risky?"

"Yes," Bruce said absently, staring at his computer screen, tapping the keys. "We need to be at our physical peak for this mission. Porting between would subject us to weakness upon arrival, and possibly leave a trail through the portal for demons to follow, making us vulnerable to attack during that time. Not worth the risk."

"You could port us both?" Stefan asked.

"Yes," Bruce said, his eyes still trained on his computer screen as he typed. He stopped and looked over at Stefan. "Are you unable to use magic?"

"Not really sure. It's been a very long time since I even tried." Stefan leaned back against the sleek blue leather seat, resting his head against the seat and closing his eyes. "My talents lie elsewhere."

Stefan knew Bruce didn't like leaving Angie behind with Synn in Ireland any more than he did leaving Brandy. The women would remain with Brandy for a few days. Then Angie would travel with Tristian and Hannah stateside. Angie would stay in D.C. to check on the salon and bring Tobi and Owen up to speed. Tristian and Hannah would head to Maine to unearth Tristian's family's Book of Shadows. Meanwhile, Synn was in Gavin's capable hands until all three Books of Shadows were on Irish soil. Angie would return to Ireland on the salon's private jet, provided all went well and Tristian was able to retrieve the Book without complications.

Since Angie was a healer, it was best to have her centrally located, ready to port anywhere in the world in case of emergency.

Bruce looked up from his computer. "Stefan, you did book more than one flight and to different destinations under a variety of names just in case we are being watched?"

"Of course. Didn't want to broadcast our intentions or whereabouts," Stefan sniped. "I haven't survived this long without being careful and covert."

"Relax, Stefan. Just making sure all the bases are covered. I'm not happy about leaving Angie unprotected and on her own in this situation any more than you are Brandy. Let's get our job done and get back to them. Okay?"

"Agreed," Stefan said firmly.

After hours in flight, the airport came into view.

"Something feels off." Bruce's forehead creased and his eyes narrowed, watching out the window as the plane came to rest on the tarmac. "Let's just hang back and disembark last."

"Yeah, I think you're right. We may have a welcoming party." Stefan swung the duffle bags down from the overhead compartment.

"Ya think?" He caught his bag midair, throwing it over his shoulder, and grimaced. "You ready?"

"Yep." Stefan led the way, sprinting down the stairs from the plane in a blur, and vaulted the railing halfway down, cutting back under the plane and across the tarmac. Behind them the stairs exploded, sending red-hot metal shards through the air. Passengers ran screaming. The metal sliced cleanly through clothing, bloodying the flesh of those pushing and shoving toward the safety of the terminal and trampling others felled by the blast.

Blue smoke curled around the side of the plane as bright-orange flames shot skyward. The searing heat from the fire rolled across the runway in waves. Rescue crews rushed to the scene, spraying white fire-retardant foam across the area in an attempt to contain the blaze before it reached the plane's fuel tank. Ambulances with their lights flashing converged on the scene. Doors flew open as paramedics rushed to victims strewn across the tarmac.

Thrown clear of the fire by the concussion of the

blast, Stefan, followed by Bruce, streaked away from the terminal and toward the empty hangars at the end of the runway.

"What the bloody hell—that was some kind of welcome," Stefan said, racing toward the buildings.

"Good thing we didn't port," Bruce said, sprinting beside Stefan. "We'd have been attacked while in between, unable to use magic, basically defenseless." He glanced back over his shoulder at the chaos bathed in red, blue, and yellow flashing lights.

Stefan glanced at Bruce. "Now what?" A sleek black limo sped toward them, tires squealing, the back end fish-tailing as the rear passenger doors flew open. "Get in," a silver-haired man commanded in a gravelly voice from the open driver's window.

They hesitated only a second as Bruce jumped into the moving vehicle, yanking Stefan in behind him. Then the door slammed shut.

The privacy window slid down to reveal a mouth full of razor-sharp teeth grinning at them. "I thought you might need some assistance after talking to Angie night before last."

"Owen, who's running the salon?" Bruce growled.

"What, no 'thank you,' 'glad to see you'? Nothing?" Owen raised a brow and shot Bruce a challenging look that smoothed into amusement. "Tobi has it under control, as usual."

The stocky man with large amber eyes and wavy silver hair that fell to his shoulders gave Stefan an assessing glance. The lines etched on his face and calm demeanor gave the impression that he was quite a bit older and had served Bruce for a long time.

Bruce waved a hand in the man's direction.

"Stefan, you remember my salon manager, Owen?"

Stefan nodded, remembering the man from Bruce's wedding. He hadn't noticed at the wedding the several deep, raised scars running across Owen's neck, disappearing under his black sleeveless T-shirt only to reappear on his muscular shoulder. A couple of fingers bent at odd angles, as if broken and healed improperly. The scarring from his elbow to wrist indicated he'd seen his share of battles. Yet he was still here to tell the tale.

"We are really glad to see you! Great timing," Stefan said, struggling to sit upright. He thumbed toward Bruce. "A bit bossy."

"Tell me about it."

"Enough. I'm still your boss, and I'm sitting right here. Still, I needed you in D.C." Bruce's jaw muscles flexed.

Unaffected by Bruce's behavior, Owen suggested, "Needed me worst here, don't you think? Besides, you can take that up with Angie."

"Agreed. But since when…"

Owen stomped down on the accelerator. Bruce's words cut off as their bodies slammed back against the seat and the vehicle surged forward. The scenery outside the limo blurred in bright multicolored shards of light.

"The nearest large town to Ayers Rock is Alice Springs. Is that where you want to spend the night?" Owen inquired patiently, showing none of the stress of the situation.

"That'll work," Bruce said. "I'll talk with Angie when we return."

Owen handed a bright silver bag through the

privacy window. "Better turn the cell phones off and put them in this bag. It's shielded."

"Right," Bruce said. "Whatever was waiting for us at the airport can triangulate our position from our cells." He took the phone Stefan handed him and put both in the bag, sealing it, then slid it under the seat.

"I brought a couple of burner phones in my duffle bag. They won't be so easy to trace." Stefan yanked the bag from the floor, pulled out the phones, and handed one to Bruce.

"Good thinking," Bruce said, taking the phone and pocketing it. "Owen, any idea who arranged our welcoming party?"

"Not really. Word in D.C. is that large numbers of Baltizar's minions are already here. That's why Angie thought I should pick you up at the airport. There's no indication that they know exactly where in Ayers Rock the Book is located. My guess is the enemy split up, some to deter you while the others locate the Book and escape," he said thoughtfully.

Bruce leaned back against the soft leather seat, his brow furrowed. "It's a good thing Angie's on top of things. I'll let her slide this time."

Owen snorted. "Great idea."

Stefan leaned back quietly, mulling over the recent events. Interesting creature, Bruce. Dark, dangerously dark, was part of his nature, but Stefan was beginning to understand how he'd triumphed to take the overlord position. There was overwhelming good inside that demon too. Vicious when necessary but fair and understanding when warranted.

Stefan shifted his thoughts back to the problem at hand. Their survival depended on accurate, current intel, and Owen appeared to be fully informed. Rather than press him further, Stefan waited to see what he volunteered. They seemed to have a comfortable working relationship, which only reminded Stefan how inexperienced he was in the concept of teamwork.

The rest of the trip to Alice Springs was uneventful. The speed at which they traveled didn't lend itself to checking to see if anyone followed. A quick glance at the dashboard with all its dials, gauges, gadgets, and monitors told Stefan this was no ordinary limo.

They listened to updates on a police scanner. The radio warned everyone to avoid the airport and surrounding area. All flights in or out of the airport were cancelled until further notice. Film of the attack was all over the news. Stefan watched a video from the local news channel on a monitor perched between them. Though no terrorist faction had claimed responsibility, reports assumed a terrorist cell was to blame. "Bruce, can we get a copy of that video?"

"My thoughts exactly," he muttered, hunkered over his laptop checking e-mail and websites over the secure, scrambled connection inside the limo.

"Hungry?" Owen asked as he stopped the limo in front of The Milky Way Café in Alice Springs. "This place has great food, and it provides the magic of the night sky in the Southern Hemisphere. There are telescopes inside. Tobi and I are regulars when we are in town."

"When have you been to Australia?" Bruce asked, puzzled.

"Even we're allowed vacations. This is one of the many places we visit. Tobi has relatives here, and we

337

like the people. That's another reason that Angie sent me to meet you. I know the area."

"Angie seems to have your back even when she's thousands of miles away," Stefan mused, looking over at Bruce.

"Yeah, I know. She's a keeper." His face remained blank, but a faraway look came into those orange eyes. They mellowed and turned a warm amber, then flashed back to orange. "Let's eat."

"Stefan, your dinner is in the mini-fridge. Just plug the cup in the power outlet for a couple of minutes, and it'll warm your meal to perfection. Bring the mug in with us. The people here won't care. Just keep it sealed when you're not drinking."

"Interesting place. Owen, you can play tourist guide for me any day. Do you have a place in mind where we'll be staying while we're here?"

"As a matter of fact, I took the liberty of reserving interconnecting suites at the Last Desert Sails. Tobi and I've stayed there numerous times, so no red flags upon our return. The manager is a friend. He'll see to our security while we're there. It's not far and close to Ayers Rock. Figured we might as well be comfortable since we don't know how long we'll be here."

Smiling wide, Bruce slapped Owen's shoulder. "Good job, old boy."

"Thanks. I appreciate that." Owen appeared to savor the moment.

True to his word, they arrived at the resort in short order. Owen checked in and handed out the room assignments.

Stepping into the elevator, a thin middle-aged man dressed in trousers and a black sweater joined them.

You could see yourself in the shine of his black shoes.

"My name is Trin. I manage this hotel." He waved a key card past the floor panel and pressed the penthouse button that appeared. "Your suites take up the entire floor and are invisible to the outside world as long as you are here."

The door opened. They stepped out into a hallway carpeted in frosty gray. There were three mahogany doors, one at each end and one in the middle of the hallway. The elevator door disappeared into the wall.

"When you need to leave"—he pressed a hand to the wall and the elevator door appeared—"you have only to do as I have demonstrated. Step into the elevator, wave your key card over the panel, and push the button marked lobby. It will go directly there."

Bruce nodded.

"When you want to return to your floor, do the same, and the penthouse button will appear on the panel. We request that you enter and return this way so there is no interruption to the magic grid protecting your areas." His eyes focused directly on Bruce and Owen and then glanced at Stefan. "I also request that you not feed on our other guests."

Stefan nodded solemnly. "Of course."

Bruce cast a masking spell to disguise the magic signature of the grid, with the permission of Trin.

Bruce and Owen took the suites at either end. Ready for a shower and a bit of relaxation, Stefan pushed the door open to the center suite. That tight ball in his stomach loosened up just a bit as he sat on the sofa, rolling his shoulders and stretching his legs out. He kicked off his boots and reached for the cell phone. Glancing at the clock, he tried to calculate the time in

Ireland. *Was it—oh, hell*. He touched Brandy's number onto the screen, needing to hear her voice. She answered on the first ring.

"Stefan, thank God. Are you and Bruce safe? What happened? It's all over the news. An explosion at the airport? Where are you?"

Her voice washed over him uninterrupted, smoothing that edgy feeling he'd had since arriving. "It's so good to hear your voice. I've missed you. Need to make this short. We're fine and safe at the moment. Owen joined us. I'll tell you about that later."

"Oh, I was so worried. Take care of yourself. I miss you too. See you soon." She hung up before the call could be traced.

Restless, Stefan paced through the suite, then knocked on the adjoining door. Bruce opened the door, cell phone in hand.

"Talked to Angie? Everything all right?"

"Yep," he said, rubbing the back of his neck while he turned to set the phone on an end table, and walked across the light-blue carpeting. Settling on the sofa, he looked up at Stefan, motioning to the overstuffed chair across from him. "I think we need to add a couple of search alternatives to our original plan."

Stefan nodded grimly. "Any idea where to look first?"

"Maybe. Before we left, Angie got word from Den'ta, one of our employees who hacked into Baltizar's secure internet communications. They were encrypted; that slowed him down a bit, but in the end, he was able to decipher the messages and cover his tracks. He also diverted a couple of messages containing coordinates of their search area."

"Isn't that illegal? I mean hacking secure sites."

Bruce's laugh rumbled up from his chest. "Only if you get caught, and Den'ta never gets caught. Remember, it's D.C., where illegal is subject to interpretation."

Bruce's disposable phone rang. He glanced at the screen and took the call. Stefan started toward his room, giving Bruce privacy, then heard Angie's distraught voice through the phone.

"Bruce, The Wycked Hair has been destroyed by an explosion that rocked the entire block. Flames shot into the air as far as I could see. No one was inside. We held the morning staff meeting at the corner coffee shop. Good thing…"

"I'll be right there," Bruce interrupted, ending the call.

"No, you won't." A slight ripple in the air was all there was before Stefan's shoulder crashed squarely into Bruce's solar plexus, knocking the wind out of him, throwing him temporarily off-balance. He toppled over the back of the sofa and sprawled across the floor.

Surprise on his side, Stefan vaulted over the couch, landing on Bruce's back and shoulders, restraining Bruce's hands above his head. "Do you think this might be a trap? Think about it, Bruce," Stefan growled, trying to keep him controlled long enough to think this situation through.

Bruce's arms turned red-hot and seared Stefan's hands. "Shit."

Bruce scrambled to his feet, cursing at Stefan, all the while his forehead creased in concentration. Stefan thought he was searching his mind for a location in D.C. to lock in for porting. He wasn't going if Stefan had anything to say about it. Owen appeared immediately.

"What's going on?"

"Long story short, we gotta keep Bruce from porting to D.C. I'll fill you in later with the details."

Owen shook his head grudgingly but murmured a few words, pinning Bruce to the wall. "That'll hold him for only a few seconds. You better talk fast, or there'll be hell to pay for both of us."

"Got ya. Bruce, can't you see the explosion at Wycked Hair is a trap to get you to port between so they can attack while you are defenseless? No one was hurt because they were down the street to see it explode. Nice effect, don't you think? Baltizar wouldn't make a mistake like that if he meant to hurt or kill someone."

"What! Wycked Hair exploded?" Fear swept over Owen's face as he grabbed Stefan's arm, swinging him around to face him. "Tobi?"

"Relax. She's fine. They were all down the street drinking coffee. Angie just called and told Bruce. He hung up, intending to leave immediately. That's when I tackled him before he could port, where I imagine there is a demon welcoming party."

Bruce's eyes narrowed, his muscles twitching as whatever Owen had used to pin him to the wall released. He stepped toward them, straightening his jacket. He waved a hand at Stefan. "Didn't give me a chance to gather my thoughts. I haven't remained overlord by acting impulsively."

"Well, you just did. And you're welcome." Stefan took several steps backward.

Bruce paused for a beat. "Thank you. But don't

you think I know when I'm being set up? I wasn't going anywhere. The words slipped out of my mouth as a reflex. For your information, I always think through a plan before taking action. Now, if you don't mind, I need to call Angie back and get the details."

"Sure." Stefan turned on his heel and sauntered through the adjoining door. "I'll be in my room when you're ready to discuss our next move." He closed the door.

Stefan spent the rest of the night reading up on the local legends surrounding Ayers Rock and reviewing the crude map of caves, waterholes, and ancient paintings that Owen had drawn.

After reviewing the salon's situation with Angie and Toni, Bruce relayed the information to Owen and Stefan. They devised a plan and left it to Angie's discretion to implement it. Bruce and Owen joined Stefan reviewing the maps and discussing several scenarios and plans of attack.

Chapter Twenty-Nine
Unexpected Reunion and the Battle Rages

The next morning Stefan was ready before dawn, coordinates programmed into the GPS and maps packed as a backup. Food and supplies were in the insulated backpack. The other items, including a first aid kit, were stashed in a separate pack.

At a light rap on the door, Stefan called out, "It's open."

Bruce and Owen strode into the room. "Let's get going." Bruce turned back toward the door. "We're burning daylight.

"Do we have a plan?" Stefan asked.

"Yeah, we'll go with your idea of splitting up while you stay in our minds. If either of us finds anything or runs into a problem, you'll know it and signal the others of the situation." Bruce passed under the door frame.

"We should be able to cover a lot more ground that way," Stefan pointed out as he started to gather their gear.

"That's true, but…"

"Bruce, you got a problem?"

"It bothers me to have someone else in my head, but I agree your idea makes the most sense. Still, don't like the odds. I'll take the Mutitjulu Water Hole at the base of the Uluru." He jabbed his finger to the area on the map spread across the table.

Owen grinned pleasantly, everyone aware that Bruce would rather be giving the orders than taking them. "Since I know the area and have been on the Uluru before, I'll explore the caves on the Eastern side of the rock."

"Well, I guess that leaves me the path to the top of the rock," Stefan said, taking another look at the map before folding it up and putting it in the backpack.

"It's a steep eight-hundred-meter climb. Sure you're up to it, vamp?" The corners of Bruce's lips turned up slightly.

"Yeah, I think I can handle it," he shot back.

"There is a chain handhold edging the entire path, so you can lean on that should you feel weak," Bruce teased, slapping Stefan on the back.

"I'll remember that. One more question. Have you always been a control freak?" Stefan grinned at Bruce.

He did a double take at Stefan and returned the grin. "Only when it's necessary."

"It's not necessary here—old man." Stefan straightened, grasping him by the shoulder.

Bruce glared at his shoulder and back at Stefan. "Understood."

Owen looked from one to the other and shook his head. "Kids, it's time to go."

The earlier tension turned to cautious camaraderie. Grabbing up the rest of the gear, they walked down the hallway to the elevators. Bruce put his hand on the wall, and the door slid open.

Outside the hotel, the sun peeked over the horizon. The sky was clear blue with no hint of the sporadic and violent storms that suddenly inundated the area this time of year. *Itjanu,* as the local aboriginal people referred to it.

Luke, the guide provided by Trin, waited patiently in the car as they threw their gear in the trunk and climbed into the vehicle.

The driver turned onto Lasseter Highway. "Uluru is just a few miles up the highway, mates. Won't take but a few minutes."

Dropping them off at the closest point motorized vehicles were allowed, Luke asked, "Do you want me to play guide for you?"

"We're okay on our own. Just wait in the car."

He nodded knowingly, slunk down in the seat, and pulled his cap over his eyes. "Have it your way. I'll take a nap." Luke hesitated for a moment, then added, "If that's okay with you, mate?"

"That's fine," Bruce said absently as he surveyed the surrounding area.

Owen pointed out the different areas they'd agreed to.

"When you get to the top, keep in mind the wind can really whip up and blow you right off the rock," Owen warned. "Hey, Stefan, you listening to me?"

"What? Oh, yeah, watch the wind."

"Climbing the Uluru is generally closed to the public when high winds are recorded at the top. Stay alert, would you?" Owen shook his head and stared at Stefan intently.

"I got it, okay? Any idea where the Book may be hidden?"

"Tristian and I discussed that at great length. Magic is probably protecting it. The likely places will be in the caves or at the waterhole where magic could disguise the Book, perhaps making it appear part of the landscape. That's where you are at a disadvantage. Owen and I can sense magic; you'll walk right by it." Bruce snickered.

"Oh, so that's why I got the harsh walk up the rock. You guys don't think it's there and don't want to hike up the trail," Stefan said a bit testily. "I said it's been a long time since I've used magic, not that I couldn't."

"Gee, he's not as slow as he looks," Bruce teased, sliding a glance over at Owen. "I stand corrected."

"Fast enough to have saved your mate when you had no idea where she was. Just saying," Stefan shot back.

"Touché. I am indebted to you."

"Thought so." Stefan swaggered a few steps.

Owen rolled his eyes and ducked as Stefan turned and threw one of the backpacks in their direction. It smacked Bruce in the chest, making him take a couple of steps backward.

"Hey, you're the self-described nature boy." A laugh rumbled low in Bruce's throat.

Stefan ignored him. "Let's separate and get going. Once we are out of each other's sight, try sending your thoughts to me."

Hey, Stef, you there? Bruce queried Stefan a few minutes later.

I hear you, Stefan confirmed from the top of the rock. Vampire speed wasn't taken into account when Bruce gave the assignments. Stefan snickered.

Okay, Stef, can you see out across the lake? Something is moving, transforming, between the rock and water.

Yes, are you causing it? Stefan's words wafted

through Bruce's mind.

Demon abilities are amazing, aren't they? But no, it's not me. I'll explain later. You'd better come round here. Now! Owen is already on his way. Stay a few lengths behind me once you're here. No quick movement. Distraction can be deadly. Got it?

Yeah, I get it. Be there momentarily. Stefan's words reverberated louder than necessary in Bruce's mind.

Behind Bruce, a snake slithered onto land, blurring, and changed into what appeared more goddess like in her tight flame-red gown and flowing raven hair, than demon.

She leveled her gaze at Bruce and raised a brow. "Long way from home?" She glided closer, stopping in front, and leaned slightly to the side of Bruce so she had an unobstructed view of Stefan and Owen.

"Brought friends as well. How nice. You should have let me know you were coming. I could have welcomed you properly to my territory," she mused. "You know protocol requires such things." She snorted quietly and waved her hand, smiling weakly as if to dismiss the thought. "Oh, I forgot. You never grasped the concept such things might apply to you."

"Nice to see you too, Lilith, my queen. How have you been?" Bruce bowed slightly, his hand making a long sweeping arc in front of him. His gaze slid from hers to the ground as a sign of respect.

"Well. Very well. Thank you."

Bruce reached for her hand and brought it to his lips. "I'm sorry if I have violated protocol and common courtesy. My friends are Stefan Talltree and my trusted adviser, Owen Brannon, whom you already know.

Since I didn't know how to locate you, I couldn't send a request that you would have refused. I'd have come anyway, landing myself in more trouble than a mere unannounced appearance."

"Still the arrogant, stubborn bastard I, ah, remember." She trailed off with a look that could vaporize molten lava at thirty paces.

"That's me."

Her eyes narrowed as they swept the shoreline. "Where's that little witch of yours? Don't tell me she let you come Down Under without her." Lilith moved closer and laid a delicate hand on his shoulder, letting it slide sinuously down his arm. "Remember when the whole world was our playground?

"That, my lady, is ancient history. Angie's whereabouts are none of your concern." His voice was viciously polite as he casually brushed her hand aside. "But thanks for asking."

"Oh, but it is. Hello, Owen. You're looking ruggedly handsome, as usual."

"Thank you, my queen. Your beauty transcends your age." Owen too lowered his eyes to the ground, then turned his head away as a smirk slid across his lips.

"Your time and service to the Lord of the Western Hemisphere has caused you to forget your manners." Without warning, she sent a blue electric arc from her palm directly at Owen. He sidestepped it, slamming into Stefan, as some sort of invisible force field bounced it back in her direction.

"Try that again, and we'll show you bad manners," Bruce growled menacingly. "Your royal blood is no match for my experience on so many levels, so let's not go there."

"Touché." Unruffled, Lilith shifted her gaze to Stefan in a slow thorough appraisal. "Who's this handsome young stud?" She paused, tapping her finger against her chin thoughtfully. Her eyebrows rose slightly and her eyes rounded before her expression became unreadable. "Keeping company with vampires these days, Bruce? Now that surprises me. They are a bit unpredictable, as I recall, but so sensual."

"The company I keep is also none of your business. What should concern you is the sudden increase in the demonic population in your territory. Not my unannounced arrival and traveling companions."

Bruce's words of wisdom imparted prior to this trip came flooding through Stefan's mind. *It is a delicate balance, fear and respect, obedience and free will. No vampire, demon, or witch respects compassion if interpreted as weakness. If you find the balance, you'll command loyalty and respect. If not, challenge and death await you. That is the world we live in and the one you now occupy. You'd be wise to learn to play the game. Not unlike the vampire creed.*

At the time, Stefan thought he was referring to physical confrontations. But the scene playing out now was a psychological battle of major proportions but no less deadly. Bruce seemed very well armed in this situation, more than Stefan ever thought possible after seeing him and Tristian go at it.

Lilith's long silence hung ominously in the electrified air around them.

Bruce shifted and tilted his head as his eyes whirled orange and foreboding. "Should I take your silence as an indication that you're entertaining the idea of joining forces with Baltizar? In such a case, I would be forced to destroy you where you stand."

"Threats do not endear you to me. No, I don't intend to assist Baltizar in his quest for freedom. I have heard that you are here seeking the Book of Shadows hidden within the Uluru. You would know of such things only through your witch's family." She watched him with mild interest, then she snapped her fingers. "Or have you offered sanctuary to Baltizar's disgraced demon?"

"On a fishing expedition? You'll not get anything from me until I'm sure where your loyalty lies."

"Come now, Bruce. We're selfish creatures. I'll not endanger what I have built for myself. Like you, I'm not willing to share with Baltizar or anyone else."

"You'll help us?"

"Oh, I didn't say that. If you're unsuccessful in locating the Books, Baltizar gains his freedom, destroying you and mankind and imprisoning magickind in the process. The rest of us would be at his mercy. Should he learn that I had assisted you, I would suffer a fate worse than death. So no, I won't help, but I'll not deter you either. You are welcome in my territory."

"Fair enough."

As she turned to walk away, the earth beneath their feet erupted like festering boils, ejecting gray-skinned demon creatures with purple scars, snarling through their sharp, pointed teeth, turning their black, lifeless eyes on Stefan and his group.

At Lilith's direction, the trio scrambled up the sheer rock wall to the protection of a cave. Standing at the cave entrance, Bruce raised his gaze to the heavens, extending his arms to the sky and causing fire to rain down, incinerating everything in its path.

With a wave of Lilith's hand, the lake froze. Lightning bolts slashed the evening sky, crashing into the frozen lake, propelling shards of the lake's frozen holy water skyward. Directed by Bruce's hand, the shards impaled the dark demons who'd taken flight. Screams of pain reverberated off the steep rock walls as the demons exploded, their black ash falling into the lake.

Stefan leaned from the mouth of the cave, launching his wrist arrows soaked in the holy water, destroying those remaining above ground. Owen wove a spell creating a barrier above the parched earth, preventing further penetration by the underworld.

Too late, Stefan screamed a warning, flattening his body against the cave wall. The stench of burning flesh and sulfur permeated the air as an impaled demon flamed into the mouth of the cave and exploded.

The hot black ash seared the left side of Owen's face, Bruce's right forearm, and incinerated Lilith's gown. The battle was over almost before it began. Dark demons were no match for the combined powers of Bruce, Lilith, and Owen or the weaponry wielded by Stefan.

"That's quite a show you put on," Stefan said, nodding toward the others slumped against the sides of the cave, the battle and use of magic having taken its toll on their bodies.

Bruce eyed Stefan warily. "What the hell do you carry in that coat? Was that in your backpack?"

Stefan shrugged and opened the front of his full-length black leather duster, now scarred by the hot ash.

He revealed a large assortment of weapons tucked inside the pockets and strapped to his forearms and thighs. "Oh, just a few things left over from a former profession. I brought them along just in case."

"How'd you get those on the plane?"

"A bit of vampire persuasion," Stefan said with a smug expression. "Now—the sooner we get back to this scavenger hunt, the sooner we find that damn Book and get the hell out of here. I don't like leaving the women alone."

"I'll leave you men to your task," Lilith said. "I believe a bath and new attire are required."

"Beautiful as always," Bruce said smoothly.

Hours later as dusk fell, the group was no closer to finding the Book. Bruce leaned against the rock wall and sipped from a bottle of water. "Time to head back to the hotel and get some rest. We can start the search again at day break with a fresh perspective." He rubbed his eyes with his thumb and index finger. "I think we're all beat."

Owen nodded in agreement and started back toward the car.

"That will give the demons more time to find the Book. You two head back to the hotel. I can continue searching a while longer," Stefan said doggedly. "Vampire endurance, you know."

"And what happens if you run into the entourage of demons looking for the Book? Alone? Not a good strategy. We stick together," Bruce said in a tone that allowed no argument. "Where do you suggest we search in the dark, Stefan?"

Bruce leaned his hand on the hard surface and shoved up to an upright position.

Stefan and Owen stared in astonishment as a small square in the rock wall behind Bruce glowed in the dusk, then melted away to reveal a thin crevice. "Great place to start," Stefan said incredulously.

Bruce turned to see what the others were staring at, then hesitantly reached out, touching the area around the fissure. He snapped his fingers and a ball of light floated close to the fracture, illuminating the area. Peering inside, Bruce reached in and brought out a book. After flipping a few pages, he handed the book to Stefan.

"Yep, this is it," Stefan said, tucking the Book inside his duster.

"Well, well, it looks like we beat Baltizar's demons but not by much," Bruce said, putting his hand on Stefan's shoulder, jerking his chin toward a line of bouncing lights off in the distance. Bruce threw up an invisibility spell as the three of them walked to the car, climbed in, and disappeared into the inky night.

Trin met them in the hotel lobby. "I've taken the liberty of leaving dinner in your rooms. Figured you'd be tired after your search. Any luck?"

"Thank you. About what we expected," Stefan said, leaving Trin to draw his own conclusions.

"Anyone feel like joining me for a beer downstairs after we've cleaned up and eaten?" Owen wanted to know.

"I'll pass. But thanks for the invite. I want to talk to Brandy, make sure everything is all right." Stefan went straight to his room. He hadn't been able to shake the feeling that something was terribly wrong. He tapped the phone's screen and touched in Brandy's number. It immediately rolled into voicemail. *That's strange. She usually picks up on the first ring. Maybe she's on another call.* He left a message, then scrolled down to her parents' number and touched the call icon.

Chapter Thirty
A Gryphon's Worst Nightmare

Brandy awoke disoriented. The room swam around her. Far-off voices permeated her consciousness. *What the hell happened?* She tried to focus on her surroundings without drawing attention to herself. Slight air movement wafted behind her. The last thing she remembered was being restless after going to bed, getting up and dressed, then taking a midnight run along the beach. This was something she'd done since childhood to appease her restless spirit and dispel too much adrenaline in her system after an exciting day.

The voices grew nearer, louder, and angrier. "She's been out for twenty-four hours. You gave her too much. The woman is no good to us dead or brain-damaged. Baltizar will destroy us if you screw this up."

Realizing she had only a few seconds before discovery, she shifted into gryphon form, breaking the restraints that held her. There wasn't enough room in what appeared to be the interior of a cave to spread her wings, so she ran toward the fresh air and away from the voices.

As she reached the mouth of the cave, a terrible stench reached her nostrils and a bony, gnarled claw latched onto the end of her folded wing. She gave a whip of her wing and flung the demon against the rock wall as the beat of her powerful wings lifted her into the dark sky. A sudden flash of heat and flame came at her head on. She spiraled down, looking over her shoulder. *What the hell is out there?*

A huge, leathery dragon banked and shot fire from his mouth over twenty feet away. She maneuvered right, but the beating of the massive beast's wings created dangerous downdrafts and backdrafts, throwing her trajectory off, and the flame singed her wing. She howled in pain. Brandy was agile and quicker than the beast. She avoided a direct hit this time, but she had to get out of here. Getting caught up in the drafts would spell certain death.

The dragon was gaining on her, then suddenly the huge beast backtracked, beating his wings in a backward motion as she attempted to get past him. The backdraft pulled her in. She flipped sideways, hoping to escape. A moment later, the massive head swung around. Its jaws snapped open and shut, catching nothing but air. The dragon missed. Then another wing beat, and the mouth was open again within range and clamped down, catching her wing. Searing pain shot through her as the sound of bones crushing reached her ears. Extending sharp talons, she clawed at the dragon. Her beak bit deep into the beast's neck, but it wasn't enough. It wouldn't let go.

Though she'd clawed out its eye and it was bleeding profusely from the neck, the massive beast shook her like a rag doll. Then its jaws opened, sending her spiraling to the ground with such force she was unable to right herself, her left wing mangled and useless, her right wing unable to steady her. She crashed into the ground and lay there in a crumpled heap, unable to move, her mangled wing lying at an odd angle to her body. Her last thought was to remain as a gryphon because she was too vulnerable in human form. She reached out with her mind and felt Stefan's, then her world went black.

****

Unable to reach Brandy by phone, Stefan resorted to contacting her parents. Brandy was missing. He rushed to catch the first available flight back to Ireland. He left a note for Bruce and Owen detailing his departure. Pausing for a moment, he looked at the Book. Should he leave it for Bruce and Owen, or…no time. He shoved it in his duster and ran to catch his plane

Back on Irish soil, he sprinted off the plane. Suddenly, her pain exploded in his head as the scene played out, knocking him to his knees on the tarmac at the Cork Airport. Holding his head in his hands, Stefan rocked back and forth as Tristian and Angie rushed up to him. Stefan's cell phone rang, lying in its hard plastic case on the asphalt where he'd dropped it.

"Stefan, what's happening," Angie cried, laying a hand on his arm while Tristian helped him to his feet. "I hope you don't mind the intrusion," Angie said, using her healing powers to delve into her patient's mind to assist with the healing. "Oh no!" Her hand flew to her mouth as she sucked in her breath sharply at the scene in Stefan's mind.

Tristian scooped up Stefan's cell phone, noted the caller ID, and flipped it open. "Gavin, where are you?"

Quickly, Angie yanked the phone away from Tristian. "Gavin, Stefan has had mind contact with Brandy. She's hurt badly, and the location looks to be near underground caves. Does this sound familiar?"

"Aye, it's Aillwee Cave."

Stefan grabbed his phone out of Angie's hand. "Tell me the fastest route there." He turned to Angie, grabbing her shoulders. "Port us both there right now."

Angie bit her lip, glancing sideways at Tristian, who inclined his head slightly. "You know the dangers, especially now." She tried to wrench out of Stefan's grasp.

"I don't care. Time's running out for Brandy. Let's go. Now! We'll deal with whatever is waiting in the portal between. I've got to get to Brandy or die trying."

"Take your hands off me, or we'll not be going anywhere!"

Stefan loosened his grip, and she jerked free, narrowing her violet eyes at him. She opened her pack, and a large opal stone floated out, hovering between them. Reaching out, she held it in her hand, closing her eyes. The stone glowed bluish white between her fingers as Angie linked minds with Stefan, locking onto Brandy's last location. Then they were gone. Bone chilling cold and darkness swirled around Stefan.

Unceremoniously, they were dumped onto the rocky ground above the entrance to Aillwee Cave near Ballyvaughan. Rolling quickly to his feet, he surveyed the surrounding territory. A low keening and flash of heat alerted them to the dragon overhead while Brandy's weak voice in his mind directed him to a far corner of the currently uninhabited cave.

"I'll deal with the dragon," Angie said quickly as it bore down on them. "Find Brandy. Gavin and Tristian are almost here." She disappeared as Stefan darted into the cave. His crumpled gryphon lay propped against the cold stone wall, her mangled wing drawn up against her side soaked in blood, the other wing wrapped protectively around her body, large eyes closed. The slight rise and fall of her chest told him she was still alive, but barely.

He searched her mind. *Brandy, I'm here. Angie is right behind me. Just hold on.* He glanced around frantically. Then, to his relief, Brandy opened her large emerald eyes and blinked slowly. Kneeling beside her, he caressed her face. She'd lost a lot of blood. The life-sustaining liquid running through his veins would save her only if he marked her as his own.

Waiting for the right time and place had been his excuse for not marking her as his own. Now it might be too late. She meant everything to him. This would have to be the right time and place, and he'd have to do it without her permission. What a cluster.

He wanted it to be her choice, but she had lost consciousness again. With no Angie in sight, he nuzzled into Brandy's neck, inhaling her weak scent, closed his eyes, gripped her soft fur, and sank his fangs in, drawing deeply of what little blood she had left, then injecting the venom, marking her forever his and taking care not to turn her.

He raked a fang across his wrist, crimson liquid welled up from the wound. He tilted Brandy's head back and opened her beak, dripping the liquid into her mouth and rubbing her throat to assist swallowing. *Where the hell was Angie?* Unsure whether or not Brandy had enough strength, he hoped there was enough time to allow this to work.

Stefan? Brandy's voice whispered weakly in his mind.

Shh, my love, just listen. Please take from my wrist until I tell you to stop. Trust me. I'll explain later.

Angie strutted into the cave, bloodied and battered. "You should see the dragon." She grinned weakly at his quirked brow and questioning look. "What are you doing?" she squealed as the scene before her registered.

"Attempting to save her life while you apparently play with the dragon and whatever else is out there."

"Get away. I'll take over from here."

"She hasn't taken enough." Stefan clung tightly to Brandy, though he was feeling a bit lightheaded.

"If she takes any more, I'll need to heal you both and haven't the strength to do that. Now, let her go and move aside," Angie demanded, wedging herself between them.

Reluctantly, he eased back against the cool stone. Angie leaned over Brandy, eyes closed, hands resting palms down on the gryphon's side and wing. A rose glow emanating from her palms sank deeply into Brandy's body. After what seemed like an eternity, Angie leaned back on her heels, wiped the sweat from her forehead, and glanced over at him. "Your actions saved her life. Healing has begun, but she'll need rest before we try to move her." Angie cocked her head and listened. "Stay with her and rest. I'll see if Tristian and Gavin have mopped up the mess I left. Brandy did major damage to the dragon." Angie gave a low whistle. "Remind me never to piss off your gryphon."

Stefan's nostrils flared as sulfur and the metallic scent of blood wafted through the cave. "No, I'll go. You stay with her."

Angie snorted. "As if. You're too weak and will cause them to lose focus protecting you. Stay here."

No sooner had the order left Angie's lips than a tawny gryphon loomed over Tristian at the entrance of the cavern. Dirty, bloody, and reeking of sulfur, Tristian grinned outrageously and then sobered, staring at Brandy. The gryphon moved to Brandy, nuzzling her cheek.

"Gavin, she'll be fine, thanks to Stefan. Just needs some rest." Angie patted the matted feathers at his shoulder. "How'd it go out there?" She glanced back at Tristian.

"One demon melted into the underground, but we annihilated the rest. Your spell on that monstrous green dragon and his injuries disoriented him enough. We took him out right after you left. It'll take a few hours for the demons to increase their numbers enough for another attack."

Angie pumped a fist in the air. "Good job, guys."

"That's two Books on Irish soil now, correct?" Tristian said wearily.

"Well, not quite yet, but soon. Bruce's plane should be landing at the Cork airport shortly. Hannah is picking him up," Angie said.

Stefan cleared his throat. "Actually, they're all on Irish ground." He patted his duster. A weak smile curved his lips. "Tiarnan, King of the Warrior Faeries, has the third one."

"What?" Angie's eyes flew open wide. Tristian's mouth gaped as he jerked his head around to stare at Stefan.

He shrugged. "Yeah, it was entrusted to him and Erin long ago by your great-great-grandmother. I left it in their care while we searched for the others. For some reason, he didn't want to deal with you."

"Why?" Tristian tilted his head to the side, his brows furrowed and forehead creased in puzzlement.

"I really don't know." Stefan relayed the prior conversations with the faerie to the group.

Tristian shrugged. "I guess the important thing is that we have what we need."

"We'll all rendezvous on holy ground, cast the spell before the demons regroup, and we're home free for a few thousand years." Angie fisted her hands on her hips and winked at Tristian.

"What about the surviving dark demons when we seal the portals?" Stefan asked, shrugging out of his duster. He took off his burgundy shirt and wrapped it around an awake and naked Brandy.

"Bruce will convene the Council and work out a plan, then Tristian and his teams will be very busy for a while with those who fail to comply," Angie stated slowly.

Chapter Thirty-One
The Books of Shadows Reunited…Finally

Brandy awoke in her room. Recent events swirled through her head. A bad dream or…? She moved. A dull pain ached in her right side. She was stiff all over but no visible wounds. Raising her hand to her neck, she felt two marks just right of the base of her throat. She looked across the room. Stefan stood at the window watching the sea, his face drawn and dark-purple shadows under his eyes. He turned to her. A half smile played around his lips as he studied her solemnly.

"What's wrong?" She patted the bed beside her. *Come sit with me.* Her sweet voice swam through his mind.

A slight breeze and impression of movement, then he was sitting next to her, brushing a stray strand of hair from her forehead. "You gave us quite a scare."

"Sorry." She reached for his hand. He twined his fingers in hers and brushed a kiss across her forehead, wishing fervently he didn't have to tell her like this. She'd already touched her fingers over the marks at her neck. She knew.

"Brandy, they'll be coming to get us soon for the ceremony, but I need to explain something first. Nothing matters more to me than you. I love you."

"I know," she said quietly. "I love you too."

"Stop interrupting. This is hard enough. When I

found you, I did something that should have been your choice, but you were unable to…" He ran his hands through his hair and cursed under his breath.

"Stefan, I know you marked me as yours to save my life. What I want to know is, would you have done it if I'd not been dying?"

"That choice should have been yours, to belong to me for eternity or not. I took it away from you."

"Stefan, my choice was made long before you took it away. I committed to you before our terrible fight and believed that you would eventually do the same. The only thing that matters is that you learned to trust and love enough to mark me."

"You took one hell of a chance."

"Not really. You were just the last one to see it," she murmured, smiling, and wrapped her arms around him. "Now tell me, is there any truth to the legend of the Vampire's Kiss?"

"I guess we'll just have to test it out, if you're willing." He quirked a brow and grinned. "How'd you know about that?"

She winked and said, "A faerie told me."

"Figures." He raised an eyebrow and grinned.

"Did Angie and Tristian review the Books? Do we know what spells to use and how we fit into this?"

"Yes." He gave her a handwritten page. "You are to speak these words first to start the process. The other two couples will join in with additional incantations. According to Tiarnan, the cooperation between all of us on the quest for the Books satisfied the requirements that man and magickind work together. If the legends are true and we follow the instructions in the Books of Shadows, we should be able to seal the portals and set the world right.

****

The mist floated in through the open window, crawling across the room to settle in the old rocking chair.

"It's time," Stefan said, watching the mist transform into a man in a multicolored sweater and jeans sitting comfortably in the chair, booted foot resting on his knee.

"Is that the only outfit you own?" Stefan asked. His lips twitched as he tried to hide a grin.

With a raised brow, Tiarnan stared at him for a beat. "Good evening to you, Stefan. 'Tis something you'll never know." He turned his attention to Brandy. Good to see you looking so well, Brandy."

"Nice to see you again, Tiarnan." Brandy grinned as Stefan narrowed his eyes at the faerie.

"Erin has the Book and is waiting on the grounds of Mary's Castle for you two. I've come to escort you." A slight smile played around his lips. "Tomorrow's sunrise will be the first Erin and I have been able to share over the cliffs in centuries. She always loved the feel of the warm sun on her skin," he mused.

****

Lightning streaked across the night sky. Thunder rumbled, shaking the ground underfoot, yet the full moon shone down on the druid altars inside the grounds of Mary's Castle, County Cork, Ireland, where the couples gathered.

Stefan stepped forward with his arm supporting Brandy as she began weaving her spell. Bruce stood beside Angelique, Hannah by Tristian, as they joined her, each murmuring different incantations. The three

Books of Shadows lay open on hallowed ground, glowing as they turned a soft, rich liquid gold, flowing into each other, forming one. The wind howled around the stone formations and whipped around the couples as dark clouds formed, floating across the full moon. Darkness enveloped the land. Only the golden glow of the Books remained. Then it was silent. When the storm clouds parted, the moon shone blood-red with a muted ring of rainbow colors encircling it. The chanting ceased, and the Books slowly separated, returning to their ancient leather-bound form.

"The deed is done," declared Tiarnan, "The world is safe. The gates of Hell are bound tightly, the portals destroyed, the fabric of time strengthened, so there is no possibility of escape…for now.

Stefan quirked a brow and turned toward Tiarnan. "For now?" He inquired incredulously.

"Yes, for now. The remainder of the legend has yet to come full circle. We cannot control the behavior of man, so there will always be a need to patrol magickind." Tiarnan glanced in Stefan's direction but spoke to all three couples. "The progeny of your unions will have the required blood lineage and the power to seal the portals and gates of Hell forever."

"Oh, is that all." Smiling, Stefan took Brandy's warm face in his hands, covering it with soft kisses. "I believe it's time for that large, lavish Irish wedding you've always dreamed of," he whispered, letting his hands slide down her body, grasping the small of her back, bringing her to him. She cuddled against him, wrapping her arms around his waist, resting her face on his chest. Stefan laid his cheek on the top of her head and sighed, loving the feel of her against him. *I'll never take this for granted.* "We'll let the rest take care of itself."

The others nodded in agreement. Each couple picked up their Book of Shadows and watched Erin and Tiarnan walk hand in hand toward the cliffs to greet the sunrise together for the first time in centuries. Tiarnan paused, looking over his shoulder to Stefan. "Oh, by the way, the legend of the Vampire's Kiss is true among fated mates. Brandy is able to bear your children."

A stunned silence met the statement.

Bruce cleared his throat as his lips twitched. "Well, it's about time we get back to D.C. to oversee the reconstruction of The Wycked Hair and return to my other duties. Can't leave everything to Owen and Tobi."

Angie nodded and hugged Brandy. "Please let us know when you set a date for the wedding. We wouldn't miss it for the world."

"Of course. I believe it will be sooner than later. Everyone will be notified in plenty of time to make travel arrangements," Brandy said, smiling up at Stefan, who nodded. "I hate to bring this up, but what about Synn?"

"She's paid her debt and proved her loyalty. Synn earned her freedom and has chosen to remain in Ireland," Bruce said.

"But Gavin...I don't want..." Brandy sputtered.

"Gavin is a grown man. If she's what he wants, it's not your place to stand in their way. After all, you'll be married to a vampire." Stefan chuckled, enveloping her in his arms.

Tristian reached his arm around Hannah's waist, tugging her close. "It's time we departed for home too. I'm sure assignments are piling up as we speak." He cut his gaze to Bruce.

"Oh, no, not getting off that easy. Tomorrow is Christmas Eve and the family is planning a huge celebration," Brandy and Hannah chirped together. "Ma and Da would be pleased if you could delay your departures until the day after Christmas," Hannah continued.

"Then there is the wedding to plan, and"—Brandy smiled thoughtfully—"I guess that could be done after we get home."

Hannah waved her hand in a dismissive gesture. "Oh, Ma will have all the plans set. All you have to do is pick a date. Valentine's Day is a thought," she suggested slyly.

"It would give me enough time to work out another vacation with the boss. If I still have a job," Brandy mused.

"Same here," Stefan grimaced.

"It's settled. Valentine's Day it is, and you're all invited, so mark your calendars," Brandy sang out.

Murmurs of agreement and promises to return for the wedding passed through the couples as Brandy smiled brightly. "Erin and Tiarnan, you are expected to attend the Christmas Party and our wedding." The ocean breeze carried her words toward the couple.

On the cliffs, the warrior faerie turned and waved together with Erin in acknowledgement.

As the couples meandered away, a small, dark shadow slowly eased out of the ground, seemingly out of sight, watching them intently, then slithered away.

If you enjoyed
A VAMPIRE'S UNLIKELY ALLIANCE,
following is a preview of Tena Stetler's next book.

An Angel's Unintentional Entanglement

by

Tena Stetler

Demon's Witch Series, Book 4

Chapter One
Intervention

Screams of terror accompanied by mournful howls pierced the crisp night air as Caden Silverwind settled into his chair in front of the crackling campfire. Shadows from the flames danced across the dark tree trunks, curling and twisting in mesmerizing shapes. Caden had heard it all before, but tonight the usual ceremonial chants ended with menacing growls, then sudden eerie silence, rather than the quiet winding down of previous nights.

Maybe he should investigate the unearthly sounds that echoed against the canyon walls. But he just couldn't. The last battle with dark demons had nearly destroyed his body and shattered his soul. Once shimmering marble-gray wings now hung charcoal black with his muscles barely able to bring them forth from his back to brush the air without severe pain and fatigue.

Against the advice of his superiors, he chose an indefinite sabbatical in the Colorado Rockies. Their rugged strength and majestic beauty allowed him the serenity to pick up the pieces, face his own fears, and contemplate the future. If there was one.

Perhaps I should've remained among the warrior angels and used the facilities above to heal physically and repair what is left of my damaged soul. He shook his head, slowly taking in the bounty of nature around him. *No, I made the right decision.* Leaning back in his chair, he relaxed and watched the dancing flames consume the logs until glowing embers were all that remained in the fire ring.

Caden stood and stretched his arms above his head, letting out a jaw-popping yawn as he walked over to the five-gallon bucket of water. He tossed the water on the embers and trod up the steps to his home and fell into bed. Tossing and turning, dreams kept him awake for most of the night.

Sunrise brought an orange glow spreading over the top of Independence Pass, bathing the valley in warm golden shards of sunlight. Caden stood on the ridge, wings spread, brushing the breeze and absorbing the sun's warmth. *Feels better than yesterday. Finally, I'm gaining some strength back.* Carefully, he tucked his wings in and started down the trail. It was time to move on to Maroon Bells and the lake to enjoy summer in the Rocky Mountains.

****

She lay naked, battered, and beaten several yards off the trail. Her long, straight black hair fanned around her head, tangled with twigs and bits of grass. Caden moved silently toward her, stopped, and picked up a Bureau of Indian Affairs ID just a few yards from where she lay. He stuffed it in his pocket while watching the surrounding area for signs of her attackers. Kneeling down at her side, he saw scratches and bruises on her high-sculpted cheekbones, and her full lips had a shading of blue around them. He placed his hand lightly on her chest, felt a weak heartbeat, and sensed a brave soul unwilling to give up. *God, this is the last thing I need.*

Summoning medical help here was futile. The altitude at 12,092 feet combined with rocky terrain made it difficult for most rescue vehicles. They'd be too late to save her. He slid his hands under her body. At his touch, a scene unfolded in his mind of snarling wolves, the valiant fight she waged against a male until she was too weak to defend herself any longer, then blackness. Anger surged through him as he carried her along the rocky path to the fifth wheel trailer he called home.

He settled her gently on the bed, retrieved a sponge, a washcloth, and small tub of warm water from the bathroom, and began gently cleansing the deep gashes inflicted by canine teeth along with several long deep rows of claw marks. Turning her over carefully, he swore, wincing as he wrung out the sponge, exchanging it for the soft washcloth. It appeared she'd been dragged a long distance over rough terrain, leaving small rocks and gravel embedded in her back. She'd lost a large amount of blood, and her backside was a raw, bleeding mess. Without his intervention, she wouldn't survive.

Still healing himself, he wasn't sure if he had the strength to heal her on his own, or at what cost to him, but there was no other choice. He finished cleaning her wounds and shrugged out of his shirt and jeans, slid his warm muscular body next to her frigid one, then wrapped his arms around her, lifting her gently. Finally, he wrapped his wings around both of them. His dark hair fell across his forehead, and a subtle silver light enveloped them as the sun rose high in the sky.

When he awoke, the full moon was drifting across

the star-strewn western sky. As he lay staring out the bedroom window, he considered the situation. Above the jagged mountain peaks, streaks of pink and orange mingled in the dusky-blue sky. Dawn had arrived. Somehow, they'd both survived the night. Her breathing was regular, her body warm and relaxed against him. She was still unconscious.

Slowly, he opened his wings and carefully slid away from her. A bright patchwork quilt lay folded at the bottom of the bed. He drew the quilt over her, stood, stretching his arms above his head, then leaned over and placed his palms flat on the floor, willing his stiff muscles to relax.

After several minutes, he straightened, rolling his shoulders and tucking his wings gingerly into his back while pulling on a pair of jeans. Wearily, he dropped into a chair next to the bed to wait. He picked up her Bureau of Indian Affairs ID from the nightstand, turning it over repeatedly, considering the possibilities. Leaning back in the chair, his body relaxed, but his stomach rumbled loudly. He pushed up out of the chair.

Warm sunlight streamed through the kitchen window as Caden stirred a pot of oatmeal on the three-burner stove. A low moan came from the bedroom and he breathed a sigh of relief. She was coming around, finally. He flipped off the burner, poured the oatmeal into two bowls, grabbed a couple of spoons, and silently ascended the three stairs. He shouldered the curtain aside that separated the bedroom from the bath and living areas of his trailer. Huge chocolate-brown eyes wide with terror watched him enter and move slowly to the side of the bed. Using his powers of persuasion, he created an aura of calm around her.

"Don't be afraid. You're safe here," he murmured. "You've slept a long time. Hungry? I've a warm bowl of oatmeal ready. It'll put you right, I guarantee." Smiling he eased himself down on the foot of the bed and put one bowl on the floor beside him. The other bowl and spoon he extended toward her.

Warily, she watched him, carefully licking her swollen, cracked lips. Slowly, she reached for the small bowl. He slid up the bed, placing it in her hand, his hand supporting hers.

"Can you sit up a bit?" He wanted to slide his hands under her, but watching the fear in her eyes made him reconsider.

She nodded, pushing herself up with a groan, still keeping her eyes on his as she reached for the spoon.

Caden picked up the bowl from the floor and scooped a spoonful into his mouth, savoring the warm oatmeal sprinkled with brown sugar and cinnamon. He swallowed the bite and glanced sideways at his patient. She hadn't touched the food yet. "Eat. I'll get you a glass of water and be right back. Oh, by the way, I'm Caden, and you are?" He gave her a friendly smile and held up one finger, then disappeared around the corner.

When he returned with a bottle of water, she blinked at him as if to clear bleary vision while she studied him. After several minutes, in a hoarse, scratchy voice, she blurted. "I'm Mystic...Mystic Rayne." Her bronze cheeks pinked when she glanced down at her naked body. Grimacing, she yanked up the quilt to cover herself. He caught the bowl of oatmeal as it careened off the bed before it hit the floor and offered it to her. A quiet moan slipped from her lips as she eased back on the bed, then reached for the bowl.

Wincing, he watched the pained expression cross her face. He moved to the closet, took out a well-worn flannel shirt, and gently tossed it to her. Returning to the bed, he picked up his oatmeal bowl. "Be right back, then we can talk. Okay?"

Not waiting for an answer, he popped another spoonful of lukewarm oatmeal in his mouth and left the room. Frowning, he cradled the bowl in his hand and padded down the stairs into the kitchen. He shoved the bowl in the microwave for a minute, then took it out and grabbed another bottle of water from the fridge and returned to the bedroom. He twisted the cap from one bottle and set it on the nightstand next to her.

Sitting on the edge of the bed, his eyes met hers for a brief moment. He took a swig of his water and shifted his gaze out the window, hoping the lack of direct eye contact would make her feel more comfortable.

He listened to the metal spoon scrape the ceramic bowl as she ate. When the sounds stopped, he ventured a look in her direction. She was watching him intently, taking a sip from the water bottle.

"Feel like a little conversation?" he asked gently, shifting his body farther onto the bed. He spooned up another bite, this one hotter than hell. He sucked in a breath.

She shook her head slowly and leaned against the pillows.

"Don't want to talk? I understand, but there are a few questions that need answered to assure our safety in the short term." He gave her his best devastatingly charming smile as he tucked the blanket around her legs, noting the shirt he'd offered her still lay on the bed. "Who did this to you? Will someone come looking for you, possibly to make sure you're dead or finish the job?"

"I don't know," she murmured. A single tear rolled down her cheek. Sighing deeply, she turned her face away from him and stared out the window. After a few minutes, she closed her eyes.

"Okay." He patted her leg, took her empty bowl, and stood. "Get some rest. I'll be back in a little while."

A word about the author...

Tena Stetler is a paranormal romance and cozy mystery author with an over-active imagination. She wrote her first vampire romance as a 'tween, to the chagrin of her mother and the delight of her friends. Her books tell tales of magical kick-ass women and mystical alpha males that dare to love them.

With the Rocky Mountains outside her window, Tena sits at her computer surrounded by a wide array of paranormal creatures telling her their tales. Colorado is her home, shared with her husband of many moons, a brilliant Chow Chow, a spoiled parrot, and a forty-year-old box turtle.

Any evening, you can find her curled up in front of a crackling fire with a good book, a mug of hot chocolate, and a big bowl of popcorn.

http://www.tenastetler.com

Thank you for purchasing
this publication of The Wild Rose Press, Inc.

If you enjoyed the story, we would appreciate your
letting others know by leaving a review.

For other wonderful stories,
please visit our on-line bookstore at
www.thewildrosepress.com.

For questions or more information
contact us at
info@thewildrosepress.com.

The Wild Rose Press, Inc.
www.thewildrosepress.com

Stay current with The Wild Rose Press, Inc.

Like us on Facebook

https://www.facebook.com/TheWildRosePress

And Follow us on Twitter
https://twitter.com/WildRosePress